THY NEIGHBOUR'S WIFE

Andrew and Annie Bishop and their four children are strangers to village life. They have long dreamed of a place like the Old Rectory in Round Ringford—of a village in the heart of England with changeless rituals: church fetes, harvest suppers, bonfire night and pub gossip; conker fights and children buying sweets in the village shop after school. But they don't understand the delicate blend of friendships and family which holds the fabric of such a place together. Their lack of understanding and their restless needs will set in motion a tragic train of events which changes things forever and tests the village to its heart.

THY NEIGHBOUR'S WIFE

Ann Purser

CHIVERS PRESS
BATH

First published 1997
by
Orion
This Large Print edition published by
Chivers Press
by arrangement with
Orion Books Ltd
1998

ISBN 0 7540 1136 4

British Library Cataloguing in Publication Data available

Printed and bound in Great Britain by
REDWOOD BOOKS, Trowbridge, Wiltshire

CHAPTER ONE

Pat Osman sat on a fishing stool, sneezing occasionally from being too close to waving roadside grasses, and reflected that her bottom was so numb anybody could pinch it without fear of reprisal. Turning to sympathise with her little Cairn dog, tied to a stout hazel sapling in the hedge, she overbalanced and tipped into the grass with her legs in the air. Her papers fell and were caught by the breeze, and her pen disappeared into a thick clump of willow herb growing by the ditch. 'Sod it!' she said loudly, pulling herself up and scrambling to her feet. 'My God, Tiggy,' she addressed the hairy brindled face, 'as you are my witness, if our Colin has another bright idea this year, I am not, definitely not, going to be his faithful little helpmeet any longer. He can find another wife, if it comes to that.'

A cackling laugh brought her round to face the road with a guilty, reddening face. She saw a familiar sight approaching. Three women, one leaning heavily on a stick, walked slowly along the road and stopped to look at Pat struggling to her feet. The laughter came from Ellen Biggs, old and infirm, but helped along by her friends Doris Ashbourne and Ivy Beasley.

'Got yer sittin' countin' cars, 'as 'e? Your

Colin?'

Ellen's question was interrupted with a curt, impatient, 'Be quiet, Ellen. It's a pity you can't say something useful or keep quiet.' Ivy Beasley, stern faced and upright as a gatepost, glared at Ellen, who ignored her and began poking at the long grass by the ditch with her stick.

'There y'are,' she said triumphantly. 'See, Ivy. I done somethin' useful. Found yer pen, Pat. Yer'll 'ave ter pick it up yerself, dear. Can't bend over like I used to.' She put a hand out to the dog, who licked it enthusiastically and rolled over on to its back. 'Dear little dog, that,' Ellen said.

'Dogs!' said Ivy, and there was a world of disapproval in her voice.

The third member of the trio took off her straw hat and brushed her damp brow. 'Very warm for May, Pat,' Doris Ashbourne said. 'I expect you're thirsty, sitting there with the cars throwing up dust all over you.' She looked at Ivy Beasley and Ellen, wondering if they were ready to move on. The threat of a disagreement hung in the air. So far, Ivy and Ellen had been in unusual harmony since leaving the Green, where Ivy lived a solitary life in Victoria Villa, a square, redbrick house as stern as herself. Harmony never lasted long between these two women, however, and Doris could see trouble coming. She often thought of her role as pig-in-the-middle between Ivy and Ellen. Doris had

2

retired now, but had kept the village Post Office Stores for many years, and was practised in diplomacy.

Ellen was curious. "Ow many's bin through 'ere so far, then?' she said.

'Too many,' said Pat. She opened her creased and dirtied notebook and found the right page. 'Hundred and forty-four up to now—and look out, Ellen, here comes the hundred and forty-fifth.' The women retreated towards the hedge as a large white van came much too fast over the brow of the hill, out of sight in the dip, and then scorched into view again, smothering them all with fumes and dust as it sped by.

'It's not right,' said Ivy, brushing down her skirt. 'Never used to be all this traffic through the village.'

'Colin says its the new spur to the motorway,' said Pat. 'Now we're a short cut, specially when there's hold-ups on the approach road. It's why I'm here, Miss Beasley, counting cars. Colin's planning a protest.'

'Much good that'll do,' said Ellen. Further comment was prevented for a minute or so by a run of four cars, carefully noted down by Pat. 'Might as well go back and walk down Bates's End. No cars there. Only 'ave to watch out for Ted Bates's old tractor, Doris. 'Is eyes ain't s'good as they used t'be.' And Ellen chuckled at the thought that Ted, too, was suffering from advancing years.

3

The women had turned and were about fifty yards from Pat Osman when they heard her yell. The little dog had slipped her lead, and was trotting after them down the middle of the road. Then they saw why Pat had screamed. A thundering petrol tanker came over the brow of the hill, filling the narrow lane and throwing up dust in a choking cloud. Ivy Beasley grabbed old Ellen and hustled her on to the verge, and Doris hopped, suddenly nimble, after them. For the little dog, it was too late. The huge wheel of the lorry struck the side of its whiskery head and it was flung like a piece of rag into the long grass.

'Tiggy!' screamed Pat Osman. She scarcely touched the ground as she ran down the road to where Ivy Beasley stood looking down.

The other two hadn't moved, rigid with horror, but Ivy reached the limp body before Pat, bent down and carefully picked it up. 'Here,' she said. 'It'll need a decent burial, nice little dog like that. You'd best let me come home with you, and we'll see to it right away.' In a daze of grief, Pat Osman allowed Ivy Beasley to lead her away, her beloved Tiggy held close to her breast.

After the sad pair had vanished round the bend in the road, Doris was the first to speak. 'How horrible,' she said. 'That poor woman. Still, you have to hand it to our Ivy. She always rises to the occasion.'

'Huh,' said Ellen Biggs. 'Pity it 'as to be a

4

tragedy to move Ivy Beasley.' She hobbled over to where Pat had been sitting. 'We'd better take this, Doris,' she said, unhooking the dog lead. 'Could be upsetting for Mrs Osman to come back and find it. Poor little scrap'll not be needin' it no more.'

*   *   *

'I know, Pat, I know,' said Colin Osman. 'If I hadn't suggested counting traffic, Tiggy would be asleep on the rug between us, and . . .' He couldn't finish, and his red-eyed wife hunched herself back in her chair in abject misery.

'Not your fault,' she croaked. It was gloomy in their usually pleasant sitting-room, with curtains drawn and only one small lamp casting a subdued glow over Tiggy's empty basket.

Colin was consumed with guilt. He knew Pat wanted a baby, but he'd discouraged starting a family too soon, and all her maternal instincts had been lavished on the dog. He'd thought of rushing off to buy another puppy straight away, but Miss Beasley had restrained him, saying that mourning must be gone through. She'd been great, quite unlike her normal caustic self, thought Colin. Bloody tanker . . . what was it doing on the narrow lane anyway? The driver had stopped, and seemed upset, but when Colin asked him where he was going, where he'd come from, he hedged, said he'd have to get going else he'd be late arriving and in

5

trouble. Bloody tanker! Colin's anger was rising, and he stood up to fetch himself a gin. Pat refused, but he made her one anyway, and then several more.

As they climbed wearily into bed, Colin put his arms out to Pat in muddled affection. 'This is it, then,' he said, and she began to protest. How could he, after all they'd ... 'No, no,' he said quickly. 'I mean this is the camel's straw— I mean, well, you know what I mean. It's war from now on! They'll see,' he added fiercely, and fell asleep to a befuddled nightmare of lumbering army tanks and rows of tiny coffins side by side in the vet's waiting-room.

CHAPTER TWO

All peaceful again, thought Peggy Turner, standing in spring sunlight at her shop doorway. The howling gale in the night had moaned in the chimneys and whistled round the corner of the shop, scattering empty cigarette packets and sweet wrappers all over the pavement, but now the late spring morning had dawned quietly in Round Ringford, as if an evil spirit had departed.

Peggy shaded her eyes and looked across the village green, with its clump of trees in new leaf and well-worn footpaths, beyond the glinting Ringle river and the old stone bridge, to the solemn outline of the Hall, dark and bulky against the early sun. Not a soul about, she noted. With a flash of black and white, a magpie flew down from the school roof and circled the playground, alighting on the iron railings, lurching drunkenly. One for sorrow. Peggy looked round anxiously, and was relieved to see its mate strutting busily amongst the detritus left by the gale. Two for joy. That's all right, then.

Her smile soon faded as the quiet street began to rumble with the noise of an approaching vehicle, a reminder that calm and tranquillity were fast becoming rare commodities in Ringford. By the time it reached her, she could feel the old stone shop steps vibrating beneath her feet, and the sky darkened with the huge bulk of a slab-sided lorry. 'Anything, Anytime, Anywhere' it boasted in shrieking scarlet letters.

'Going much too fast,' muttered Peggy. She turned away, choked by diesel fumes, and her eye was caught by a group of children emerging from Macmillan Gardens, the council estate bordering the main street. They dodged a couple of cars and ran across to the Green, screaming and tumbling like dogs off the leash. 'Bill!' Peggy called, looking back through the shop and into the kitchen where her husband was knocking mud off his boots on to a piece of newspaper spread out on the floor. He looked up.

'What is it, Peg?' he shouted.

'Isn't that Eddie? Come and look. He must be feeling better, bless him.'

Bill joined his wife and put his arm around her shoulders. 'You love that boy like he was yours,' he said, and squeezed.

'Nonsense,' she protested. 'But I was worried. It seemed such a long bout of earache this time.'

'Looks quite restored to me,' said Bill, pointing across the Green to where six-year-old Eddie Jenkins was shinning up a broad chestnut tree, using lopped branches as footholds and disappearing from sight into the lush foliage. 'After them squirrels,' he added. 'Just what we used to do as boys, Tom and me.'

Bill was a Ringford boy. He had married a local girl, divorced her after many unhappy years, and taken Peggy as his second wife soon after she was widowed. Opinions on this had, of course, been divided, but more locals had come down in favour than otherwise. Bill's first wife, Joyce, had remarried and returned to the village, where she had caused much trouble. This had eventually been subdued, however, and the small community had turned its attention to the burgeoning problem of traffic through its narrow streets.

'It could easily have been our terrier,' said Jean Jenkins, arriving in the shop with today's topic of conversation already on her lips. 'He's always on the loose. The kids let him out, Peggy, and there's not a lot I can do.' She stood

8

in Ringford Post Office and General Stores, leaning her considerable bulk against the old wooden counter, and watched as Peggy Turner cut and wrapped her weekly pound of tasty Cheddar. She might have bin doin' it all her life, thought Jean. Nobody'd know she'd lived in Coventry and only come here a few years ago. Jean looked at Peggy's pleasant, plump figure the other side of the counter, and envied her trim waist and neat ankles. Jean herself had been big for as long as she could remember. Her hair was fair and permed to a frizz, and she saw in the mirror only a round pink face and extra chin. But her husband, Foxy, had fallen for her open smile and ready laughter when they were infants together in the village school, and had loved her dearly ever since. He had been known to say down at the Arms after a few pints that he couldn't abide a woman with nothing to get hold of.

'Pat loved that dog like a child,' Peggy said sadly.

'Can't see why they haven't got none,' said Jean. She and Foxy had started their marriage in the sure knowledge that they'd soon be a family of three, and the others—the twins Gemma and Amy, Mark, Little Eddie—had followed quickly. All lived in an extended council house in Macmillan Gardens, and although space was limited, Jean and Foxy were skilled at keeping the children on an even keel, and there were fewer storms in number

9

sixteen than in other, larger, houses in the village.

'Colin's against it,' said Peggy, fount of all knowledge, but taught by experience to filter and edit with tact and kindness. 'Pat says he wants to wait until they're well established financially. Not that she agrees,' added Peggy.

'Foxy and me hadn't two ha'pennies to rub together when we got wed, but we done all right,' said Jean.

'Ah, well,' said Peggy diplomatically, 'you're a natural mother, Jean. And look how it's paid off. Lovely children, yours. Especially my Eddie. Thank goodness he's looking better . . .' Peggy had had no children herself, and had never missed an opportunity to give the toddling Eddie a cuddle and a kiss when she first came to the village. He wouldn't want it now, of course, but she often slipped him a small chocolate bar when his mother wasn't looking.

Their conversation came to a halt as a huge transporter loaded with shiny new cars ground to a noisy halt outside the shop, the engine left running as the driver jumped down from his cab. He opened the shop door with a vigorous jangle on the springing bell, and came up to the counter.

Jean Jenkins backed away, disapproval all over her flushed face. 'Pollutin' the village, that's what you're doin', leaving that engine runnin'!' she said, and marched out without a

10

word to Peggy, who stood with an embarrassed smile and what she hoped was a humble grocer's expression.

'Can I help you?' she said. The driver was young, tough, and considerably tattooed. His spotty grey T-shirt bore a legend which Peggy would rather not have read, and she fixed her eyes on his irritated face.

'What's the matter with that old bag?' he said.

'Well,' said Peggy uncomfortably, 'she does have a point. We get so much traffic these days, and we're just not used to the fumes and noise. And a dog was run over yesterday,' she added quietly.

'Should be kept on leads, dogs,' said the driver. He looked around the shop, and continued conversationally, 'Bloody great jams for miles on the A43. Don't suppose the fat lady'd think about a bloke stuck in this bloody sun. Anyway, missus, what cold drinks've you got?'

Peggy piled up cans of Coke, a couple of wrapped pork pies, several filled rolls, and a mound of Mars bars, Yorkies and four red apples. 'Should keep me going for a bit,' the driver said, 'and I'll have one of them big boxes of Black Magic for the wife.' He handed over nearly as much money as Peggy expected to take in an entire morning. 'Might see you again, love, if this short cut is a good time-saver.' He left the village with a mighty revving

11

of engines that blotted out all sounds of birdsong, children's voices in the school playground, and even Ivy Beasley calling her cat next door.

'Oh dear,' said Peggy to her empty shop. 'I can do with the custom, but Jean is right. And we really shouldn't laugh at Colin, especially not now. And poor Pat.'

'What did you say, gel?' said Bill, from the kitchen. 'Talking to yourself? Must be serious ...' Peggy broke the bad news brought in by Jean Jenkins, and he was instantly sympathetic. 'Still,' he said, 'don't worry, Peg. This traffic thing'll sort itself out. Ringford can handle it.'

Peggy frowned. She remembered Pat Osman's face as she passed by in her car earlier. 'It's all a bit beyond Ringford's control now,' she said. 'We'll need to do more than bide our time, Bill. I dread to think what might happen ...' She looked so upset that Bill put his arms round her and rubbed her soft face with his rough cheek.

'It's a rotten business,' he said. 'Best keep an eye on our cat, else she'll be next,' and as he felt Peggy shiver he tightened his arms to blot out future terrors.

CHAPTER THREE

'So, Pat, I think the time has come for a bypass committee.' Colin tried not to notice his wife's expression, and looked out of the wide

12

windows of his sitting-room, across his immaculate garden and away through the park with its spreading chestnuts and grazing sheep to the tall chimneys of the Hall in the distance.

Pat groaned. 'Oh Colin, please,' she said, 'please not another committee.'

'Only way to get things done,' said Colin cheerfully. 'Reverend Brooks is game, and Bill Turner at the shop, and Pete Dodwell in Walnut Close. Most of the village, in fact.'

'Most of the village may be in favour of a bypass,' said Pat wisely, 'but it'll be the usual few who are willing to do anything about it. You'll see. Might as well just reconvene the school closure lot, and carry on fighting—only this time Build Us a Bypass instead of Save Our School.'

Ignoring this cynicism on the part of his wife, Colin sat down with a pad of clean paper and began to write. As well as being an active and vocal member of the District Council, Colin Osman was editor of the village newsletter, and saw a perfect opportunity for a rousing feature and a call to arms. He had statistics now to prove that traffic had grown to what he was sure was an unacceptable level, and he needed to talk to someone who'd had a successful campaign elsewhere in the county.

'Remember that chap we talked to on Open Gardens day?' he said. Pat kept her head down, pretending to be absorbed in her book. 'Pat,' persisted Colin, 'you know, he and his wife said

13

to let them know if any houses came up for sale in Ringford.'

Pat did remember, and looked up. 'Bald head and glasses? Wife had dyed hair and a cleavage? Oh yes, I remember them all right.'

'I'm not asking you to be their best friend,' said Colin, losing patience. 'Just remember their name, so I can look him up in the phone book.'

'It was Underwood or Milkwood or Woodworm or something,' said Pat.

'Thanks a lot, my dear,' said Colin, and began to turn the directory pages to the letter U.

*   *   *

'It's the new motorway spur,' said the Reverend Nigel Brooks, repeating what they all knew already. 'Now there's a new junction off the M1, there's a direct line across to the M40, and when the main road can't cope they all take a short cut through the villages.'

'And one of 'em is Round Ringford,' said a tall, heavily built man who leaned up against the raw stone fireplace of the new vicarage in Bates's End. Tom Price was a farmer whose forebears had been in Ringford for generations, and though he could see no harm in the vast lumbering modern farm machinery which shook the foundations of old village houses at most times of the year, he took great

14

exception to the recent invasion of traffic that had nothing to do with the village.

The new vicarage was still bald and intrusive, sited in the Glebe Field beside the mellow golden stone house where the Reverend Nigel Brooks and his wife Sophie had so happily lived until a short while ago. The old vicarage, with its high-ceilinged rooms, vast kitchen and many bedrooms, had been the chief reason for Sophie agreeing to the move to Ringford from Wales. She had felt at home at once, and the kitchen, warmed by an ancient Aga and full of her favourite china and silver, had become the heart of the house. The blow had fallen when the Church Commissioners announced that they were forced by bad investment to raise some cash and would be selling the large old vicarage. They would, of course, build a nice, easy-to-run modern one for the Brookses.

Sophie had burst into tears, and she was not reconciled yet, especially as her beloved old house lay empty and neglected with For Sale notices from three estate agents stuck in the hedge outside. It was not an easy house to sell. Not many families had the money to keep it going, nor did they need the six bedrooms, and more in the attics where whispering maidservants had once retreated at the end of a hard day's work.

'The first thing to do,' said Colin Osman, seated at the end of a highly polished mahogany table, 'is muster our facts and figures. Our tally of cars passing through has confirmed what we all knew anyway—a more or less constant stream of traffic in daylight hours, and some at night as well. I shall collate all this and get it into a presentable form.'

Colin loved words like 'collate', but Tom Price wondered privately what the silly bugger thought he was up to. Surely a word or two from Mr Richard Standing, squire and hereditary owner of Ringford Hall, in the right ear at County Hall would put a stop to it? Tom had great faith in the old tried-and-true methods of local government. 'What we need, boy,' he said, 'is a couple of them signs banning lorries from the road through Ringford.'

'And what about cars?' said Nigel Brooks, running a finger round the inside of his dog collar. It was very warm, with the sun full on the modern windows, and in the small, claustrophobic room Nigel longed for his old, spacious study.

'No, no, Tom,' said Colin. 'It'll take more than a couple of signs. Looks to me like a cast-iron case for a bypass. Anyway, leave it with me, and I'll report back in a couple of weeks.' He stood up briskly, gathered his papers together and put them in his document case. 'Any takers for the old vicarage yet, Nigel?' he said.

'Someone coming this afternoon, apparently,' said Nigel. 'Sophie heard it from Jean Jenkins, who's keeping an eye on the

16

place and holding a key for the agents.'

'Let's hope they buy, then,' said Tom Price. 'Don't like to see good houses lying empty. That cottage of Bates's over the bridge is falling apart. You'd think some of them homeless would want it. Still,' he added, thinking better of it, 'p'raps it's better empty than occupied by some of that lot.'

It's too hot, thought Nigel Brooks, to preach Christian charity to old Tom, and anyway it would be a complete waste of time. 'No doubt Jean will tell us all about it this afternoon,' he said pacifyingly. 'She has an amazingly keen ear.'

*　　*　　*

In the cool front room of Victoria Villa, Doris Ashbourne sat neatly in a stiffly upholstered chair, handbag on her lap, and waited for Ivy Beasley to bring in the tea. Opposite her, comfortably ensconced in the best chair in the room, her feet up on a stool to rest her swollen ankles, lounged Ellen Biggs, who had hobbled up from her lodge house in the Hall avenue to take tea with her friends. This was a regular weekly event, never missed unless for some extremely dire reason, and looked forward to by the three women more than they would like to admit.

'Storm brewing, Doris,' said Ellen. 'Me radio was all crackles this morning, what with all that electric in the air.'

'Needs a new battery, more likely, you old skinflint,' said Ivy, coming in with a tray and putting it down on the oak table that had been her mother's pride and joy. Ivy had lived at home with her parents, completely under her mother's domineering thumb, until first her father and then her mother had gone to rest in the sunny graveyard by the church. Ivy had stepped into her mother's shoes, very stern and unbending shoes, and carried on her reputation as unofficial keeper of village morals, and occasional malicious gossip.

'That's not fair, Ivy,' said Doris, rising in Ellen's defence. 'Ellen hasn't got money to throw about, as you very well know.' She turned to the old woman, and said, 'I've got a spare battery, Ellen. You can have that.'

Ellen looked at them both and grinned. 'She don't bother me, Doris,' she said. 'Always the same with our Ivy. And anyway, it ain't the battery. I put a new one in last week. It's the electric in the air. You'll see, we shall have a storm later. Just 'ope I get 'ome in time. Time you got pouring, Ivy.'

Ivy Beasley pursed her lips, and began to pour tea into delicate china cups. There was an element of competition about these tea parties, and Ivy was the unacknowledged champ. Her cakes were legendary, and now, sitting proudly on a cut-glass cake stand, was the most perfect strawberry and cream sponge. Ellen could not

18

take her eyes off it.

When tea was poured, and the cake carefully cut and handed out with small cake forks, Ivy relaxed and sat down. She sipped her tea with small, birdlike pecks, and then put cup and saucer down on a table at her side. Taking up her cake and skilfully spearing strawberry, cream and sponge in one go, she said, 'Heard anything about this bypass idea of Mr Osman's, Doris?'

Ellen sighed. So this was to be the subject of today's conversation, and very boring Ellen found it. Down in Bates's End, where her lodge house sat peacefully at the entrance to the Hall's chestnut drive, she was untroubled by traffic noise or pollution. Indeed, she sometimes wished there were more passersby. 'Could do with a little life,' she said. 'Sometimes I get fed up with talkin' to meself.'

'I can understand that,' said Ivy sharply.

'Now, now, Ivy,' said Doris. 'But Ellen,' she continued, 'for us living here on the main street the traffic has got beyond a joke.' And to prove her point, conversation was brought to a halt for a minute or so as a container lorry with trailer pulled up with a squeal of brakes, and ground along in low gear as it negotiated a path between cars parked on both sides of the road. Most were outside the Stores, shoppers from the village and surrounding farms, but two were strangers taking a break from long motorway journeys. Their drivers remained sitting in their cars, puffing cigarettes and contemplating the beauty of the village with its golden stone houses and ancient church just visible above the graveyard yews.

Ellen shrugged. 'Whatever Colin Osman does won't make no difference,' she said. 'Them at the Council in Tresham's got more to worry about than a few cars and lorries goin' through Ringford.' She shifted her legs, making them more comfortable. 'And anyway,' she added, 'what I want to know is who's coming to the old vicarage? Saw some cars parked outside there when I come up.'

'Young folk from down South, Jean said.' Doris was happy to change the subject, knowing that Ivy was likely to get very aerated on the subject of traffic. She suffered most, to be fair. Being next to the shop, and getting customers' cars parked outside her house, and then the trouble of big lorries squeezing through, like just now, all brought noise and fumes into Ivy's house. Still, she was never a one for opening windows, so it wasn't as bad as it might be.

'We could do with a nice big family,' Doris said, pressing down with her little fork, mashing the cake crumbs into a paste and popping them into her mouth. 'That was really delicious, Ivy,' she said hopefully.

'Depends on the family,' said Ivy, ignoring Doris's hint. 'If you ask me,' she continued, 'they should never have moved Reverend

20

Brooks out. He knows how to live in a big house. Not many do, these days.' Ivy was not prone to soft spots, but she had had one for the Reverend Nigel Brooks ever since he first showed his handsome head and perfect smile round the church door in Round Ringford.

'Rubbish,' said Ellen Biggs. She too had finished her cake, and looked longingly at the cut-glass stand on the table. 'Needs children, lots of 'em, that house does,' she said. And then she could wait no longer. 'You goin' to offer us a second slice, Ivy?' she said.

'I wasn't,' said Ivy.

'Why not?' said Ellen.

'It'll keep for my supper,' said Ivy.

'Not that cream, not in this weather,' said Ellen desperately.

'Oh, for goodness' sake,' said Doris Ashbourne, 'give her a piece, Ivy, do. And I wouldn't say no myself.'

'Oh well,' said Ivy, 'seems I have no choice,' and she began to cut three more generous slices, which is what she had intended all along.

*   *   *

Inside the old vicarage there was a musty smell, and little of the warm spring air had permeated through closed doors and windows. Jean Jenkins had gone ahead of the estate agents and their client, and opened a few windows, but the old house needed people, people moving

21

about from room to room, running up and down the wide staircase, skittering along the polished flooring of the big landing, and shouting to each other out of opened windows down to where the long garden met the Glebe Field and the boundary of the new vicarage.

A tall, well-proportioned young woman, with long brown legs in crumpled stone-coloured shorts and slender arms covered with a fine dusting of golden hair, stood in the bay window of what used to be Nigel Brooks's study, looking out at neglected lawns and a great shady cedar tree.

'Oh, Andrew darling,' she said, 'come and look. Can't you just see us having tea under that wonderful old tree? Isn't it marvellous?'

Her husband was deep in a discussion about rates and drainage and covenants on what remained of the Glebe Field, but he turned good-naturedly and joined her at the window. He was some three inches shorter than she, but broad shouldered and stockily built. He too was wearing shorts of much the same colour, and his bristly dark hair stood up in the fashionable shaving-brush style that had yet to reach Round Ringford. His eyes were dark brown, and kind.

'See what you mean, Annie,' he said, putting an arm round her waist. 'But let's look around the rest. Can we see upstairs, please?' he added to the agent, who now had a hopeful smile.

'Of course, this way, please, Mr Bishop.' The

agent's step was bouncy.

Lofty bedrooms with large windows and wonderful views were followed by one extraordinary bathroom, with its huge white enamelled bath standing on four lion's-claw legs. The white taps were equally large, and a black rubber ball plug hung from a massive chain. 'Good God!' said Andrew Bishop. 'That's an original, Annie! None of your reproduction rubbish.' He leaned over and made to turn on one of the taps, but the agent stepped forward.

'Water turned off, of course,' he said, 'but it must be a wonderful gush, Mr Bishop.'

Annie and Andrew Bishop went in single file up the attic stairs, led by the agent, who was becoming more optimistic by the minute. His experience told him that things were looking good. Four children, did they say? Well, there'd certainly be room for them, and more.

Downstairs, Jean Jenkins waited in the kitchen. Wish there was a chair or something, she thought, leaning her bulk against the open kitchen door, breathing fresh air from the garden. They were certainly taking their time up there. She walked forward into the hall and listened at the foot of the stairs.

'Of course, Mr Bishop, any time. Give us a ring at the office, and you can all come and have a good old browse around.' The agent's loud voice was cheerful, full of goodwill and anxiety to please. They're all the same, them estate agents, thought Jean, resting her arm on the newel post and gazing along the curving mahogany banisters. Thinks he's got them. You can tell from the sound of his voice. Well, many a slip. That's what Foxy says, and he's mostly right.

The viewing party reappeared at the head of the stairs, and Jean smiled at them. She's really pretty, she said to herself, and he looks nice. Could do worse, I reckon. 'Lovely house, isn't it?' she said in a friendly fashion. 'Reverend and Mrs Brooks were ever so sorry to leave it.' As she spoke, an old, slow-moving black Labrador with a grey muzzle and rheumy eyes wandered through the open front door into the hall. 'That's Ricky, their dog,' said Jean, hastily turning him round and pointing him at his own garden. 'He's not quite got used to living next door yet. Still, he's a nice old dog. Won't do no harm.'

Annie Bishop was across the hall in a flash. 'Ricky!' she called. 'Here, doggie, here!' The old dog turned and came ambling back to receive a warm greeting and a kiss on the top of his head. 'Isn't he a darling, Andrew? He'll be a friend for Tinker.'

As the party drove off, the Bishops in a very clean, dark blue Range Rover, Jean Jenkins locked the big front door of the vicarage and started off down the weedy gravelled drive. 'Well,' she said aloud, 'couldn't be more suitable. A Bishop living in the vicarage . . .'

24

And she laughed a deep, jolly laugh that startled one of the Brooks's cats and sent it flying up the monkey puzzle tree at the foot of the vicarage drive.

CHAPTER FOUR

The storm broke at exactly two o'clock in the morning, with a rending flash of lightning and an immediate crack of thunder. Peggy Turner, already awake with a migraine brought on by the heavy atmosphere, stuck her fingers in her ears and tried in vain to shut out the violent night. Finally, she got out of bed and went to the window. She pulled back the curtain and saw an extraordinary sight.

'Bill!' she said loudly. 'Come and look at this!' The street had turned into a river of rushing brown, muddy water, swirling round the drains, which were already too full to cope, and then on down to the bus shelter, past Ivy Beasley's Victoria Villa and out of sight by Macmillan Gardens. 'It's stair-rods out there, Bill!'

Bill Turner turned reluctantly on his pillow and opened sleepy eyes. 'Come back to bed, gel,' he said, 'it's only a storm. Soon be over.'

'No, no, Bill, please come and look!'

Bill climbed slowly out of bed and joined Peggy at the window, putting his arm around her waist and loving the feel of her warm flesh through her thin nightie. 'Mmm,' he said, 'come on back to bed, Peg.' Then he glanced out of the window and forgot amorous thoughts at the sight of the water.

Another jagged fork of lightning split the sky, and the following clap of thunder shook the old elm boards of the floor beneath Bill's feet. 'We're in the eye of the storm, gel,' he said. 'Come away from the window, just in case.'

At that moment a long zigzag of spitting lightning lit up the village and seemed to reach its crackling finger right down into the heart of the council houses in Macmillan Gardens.

'Good Christ!' said Bill. 'That was a nasty one.' He turned away from the window, dragging Peggy with him. 'You go straight back to bed,' he said, pulling on trousers over his long bare legs. 'Better take a look and see all's well round there.'

'Bill!' said Peggy. 'You're not going out in this! Don't be so ridiculous! There's plenty of people in the Gardens can cope.'

Bill shook his head. 'Couldn't rest until I'm sure they're OK,' he said. 'There's Doris on her own, and all them Jenkinses. I'll just check. Won't be long.'

And there's Joyce, thought Peggy, pulling the bedclothes up round her ears. He'll just have to check on his Joycey, though he won't say so. Peggy turned restlessly in bed, trying to ease not only her headache but a pain in her

26

side. Indigestion again, I expect, she thought. But it had been there on and off for weeks now, gradually getting worse. 'More on than off now,' Peggy muttered, and reached out for aspirin and a glass of water.

*   *   *

As Bill rounded the corner of the Gardens, he saw a shocking sight. In the valley between the roofs of the Jenkinses and his ex-wife Joyce was a large gaping hole. Rain was still pounding down on to the streaming road and the central square of grass was a soggy quagmire. Bill saw Foxy Jenkins looking up at his roof, and squelched over to him.

'Foxy!' he yelled, trying to make himself heard above the noise of the storm. 'Everybody all right?'

Foxy nodded. 'Thank God!' he said. 'But look at that roof! The ceiling's down in the bathroom and our bedroom. Terrible mess. Jean's trying to clear it up. Kids are scared out of their wits.'

Bill saw the front door of Foxy's house open, and a small figure, fair haired and clad only in pyjamas, rush down the garden path, flinging himself at Foxy and burying his head in his father's dripping jacket.

'Eddie!' shouted Foxy. 'What're you doin' out here? Go on back inside to your mum.'

'I'm scared, Dad!' Eddie's voice was

27

muffled, but full of terror.

'Here,' said Bill, picking up the boy as if he were a puppy, 'come on, you can show me the hole in the ceiling. What a night we're having!' He went swiftly into the house, shielding the little warm body with his coat.

Jean Jenkins was in the kitchen, cursing that there was no electricity to put the kettle on and make a cup of tea. 'Nothing we can do tonight,' she said. 'The storm's movin' away now, anyway. Come on, Eddie, back up to bed. It's all over now.' She led him upstairs, and returned after a few minutes. 'Nice of you to come round, Bill,' she said, sitting down heavily in a kitchen chair.

'Peggy got me out of bed to look at the water,' he said. 'Street's just like a river. Just as well the houses stand up a bit proud. Drains can't cope with the volume.' He hesitated, then said, 'Everything all right next door? I see their roof's damaged too.'

'Dunno,' said Jean wearily. She'd had a hard day, cleaning at the Hall, doing her stint at the playgroup, getting tea for her own children. She needed her sleep, and now felt terrible.

'Perhaps I'll just take a look,' Bill said, and walked quietly out, leaving Jean staring blankly at the wall.

*   *   *

Peggy had a kettle boiling by the time Bill

returned. 'Get those wet clothes off at once,' she said, 'and drink this hot tea. I hope it was worth it, going up there at this time of night.'

'Foxy's house has been hit. Great hole in the roof. And part of Joyce's roof next door.'

'Oh yes,' said Peggy coolly. 'And did you ride in on your white charger and rescue her?'

Bill frowned. 'Not worthy of you, Peg,' he said quietly.

Peggy sighed deeply. 'You're right,' she said. 'I don't know why I say these things.'

'I do,' Bill said, 'and you're wrong.'

CHAPTER FIVE

The hole in Jean Jenkins's roof was not the only damage done by the storm. Up at the Hall, Richard Standing, in his forties and still attractive in spite of a small paunch and touches of grey in his straight dark hair, looked in some dismay at a giant beech tree in the park, split down the middle like a stick of kindling under the chopper.

'Richard! How dreadful! Is there anything we can do?' Richard Standing's wife, Susan, approached him from the lavender walk, their last and much loved daughter Poppy prancing up and down at her side. In spite of his distress about the tree, Richard looked at them fondly. How lovely Susan still was, and darling Poppy was growing so like her, long legged and

29

slender.

'Shall have to ask Bill,' Richard said. 'Looks bad to me. We were lucky it struck the tree and not the Hall. Saw Ted Bates this morning by the pub, and he says he's never seen such lightning, not in all his seventy-one years in Ringford.'

'Stupid old man,' said Poppy.

'Darling, that's not very nice,' said Susan. 'Mr Bates is a kind old man. Well, fairly kind. Sometimes.'

'He loves Joey,' said Poppy. With the wisdom of her four years, Poppy had soon realised that her friend Joey, handicapped and in a wheelchair, could wind his grandfather round his small, thin finger.

'Guess what else I saw,' said Richard, who had got up early, unable to settle after the storm. He'd walked down the chestnut avenue, dodging the heavy drops of clear water still dripping from the thick green leaves that formed a cool tunnel from the village to the Hall.

His village—he thought of it in this way, as had his father and grandfather—had a battered look. The last of the daffodils in Ellen Biggs's lodge house garden were beaten down, and deep puddles had caused Richard to weave his way along the road. Ivy Beasley was out with a fearsome bristle broom, angrily pushing water in front of her like a tidal wave into the big drain outside the shop, cursing the cars that

30

were already speeding through the village. She'd wished Richard a clipped good morning, and not even looked up. He had walked on and seen men with ladders outside the Jenkins's house. The Jenkins's terrier had streaked across the wet grass in pursuit of a cat that looked like Ivy Beasley's Burmese, and Richard had reflected that it was a good thing Ivy's attention was elsewhere. That broom could do a deal of damage to a small dog.

Now Poppy was climbing up the stricken tree, trying to reach into the split trunk, covering her pale blue T-shirt with wet green streaks of bark mould.

'Poppy!' yelled Susan. 'Come down at once. Just look at you! And we're going over to Grannie's this morning.' She turned to go, pulling Poppy firmly by the hand, and then remembered Richard's unanswered question. 'What else did you see?' she called over her shoulder as Poppy dragged behind.

'A young couple with loads of kids getting out of a Range Rover and going into the old vicarage.'

'Really?' said Susan, stopping suddenly and letting go, so that Poppy sat with a bump on the wet grass. 'Any Poppy's age? Any we could swap with this young person?'

'All ages,' said Richard. 'Dozens of 'em.'

'Possibles for the village, do you think?'

'Young chap looked nice, and his wife was pleasant.' Actually, she was much better than pleasant, and had quite caught Richard's eye, but after long experience of not letting Susan know about his fancies, he was casually vague. 'Didn't notice too much about them. Didn't like to stare, really. Anyway, we shall find out soon enough. Jean comes tomorrow, doesn't she? She'll update us, bless her.'

'You didn't say "bless her" when she broke that glass on your desk,' said Poppy, standing up grumpily and brushing her wet bottom. 'You said—'

'Yes, I remember what I said, thanks very much, Poppy,' said Richard, 'and if you don't get going with your mother, I shall think of something on the same lines to say to you.'

After they'd disappeared through the stone arch into the kitchen garden, Richard walked on, checking trees in the park, cattle steaming in the returning sun. 'That girl was certainly pleasant,' he said aloud, prodding his stick into a crusty cowpat and regretting it at once. 'Very pleasant indeed.'

*   *   *

In the bungalow behind the shop, where Ted Bates's son Robert had his motor repair workshop, Robert's wife Mandy sat at the breakfast table, helping Joey in his special chair with one hand, restraining two-year-old Margie with the other, and trying unsuccessfully to grab the occcasional piece of toast for herself.

She sighed with relief as Robert came through the back door, big smile at the ready for his family. He sat down, took the spoon and encouraged cereal into his unwilling daughter's mouth with practised ease.

'That was a bad old storm,' he said. 'I saw dad first thing, and he'd been up the Gardens. Foxy's house was hit.'

'Nobody hurt?' said Mandy anxiously. 'Is Jean all right ... and Eddie?'

'They're all fine,' said Robert. 'Eddie was a bit scared, but apparently Bill Turner came round and helped in the middle of the night.'

'Suppose he was worried about his Joyce,' said Mandy wisely.

'She's not his Joyce any more,' said Robert. 'She's Donald's Joyce.'

'Well, you know what I mean,' said Mandy, and changed the subject. 'What else did Dad say?'

'Nothing much. Said he'd be round for Joey about five this evening and said he'd seen some folk at the old vicarage. And of course he was swearing about the traffic. Says one of them was going so fast it caught the wing mirror on the Land Rover the other day.'

'I'm surprised he's still got wing mirrors on that old thing,' said Mandy. 'Still drives as if there's nothing on the roads, like the good old days he's always talking about.'

'Still, he's got a point,' said Robert. 'The street was busy already when I first got out

33

there.'

'Well,' said Mandy, getting up to fetch a flannel from the sink to wipe round Joey's mouth, 'we'd be up a gum tree without cars, wouldn't we?' She lifted Joey up with difficulty. 'Come on, young man, time for school. The bus will soon be here.'

Robert stood up and took the limp little boy from her arms. 'Here,' he said, 'he's too heavy for you. I'll take him for a pee, then he'll be ready for the off.' Joey grinned at his mother over Robert's shoulder, and Mandy's heart contracted. Still hurts, she thought. I suppose it always will.

Joey attended a special school in Tresham, and was taken and brought home by a small green bus. He had friends there. Sometimes they came home to tea, and sometimes he went to their homes. But his greatest friend was Poppy Standing. It was an odd friendship, started when they were very small and Poppy's Irish nanny and Mandy Bates had banded together in the tricky business of village life. Susan and Richard Standing had not been all that keen, and still felt that Poppy would soon grow out of it, but every week Poppy demanded to know which day she would see Joey, and created mayhem if she didn't get her way. Joey in turn would wriggle his small, unsatisfactory body in delight when Poppy arrived, always bringing some new game or something good to eat. Mandy, like the Standings, was sure it would fizzle out one day, but Poppy showed no signs of cooling off.

'Poppy's coming round after school,' Mandy said, 'so what about your dad?'

'Says he'll take them both to see the new calf,' Robert said.

'Blimey,' said Mandy. 'Wonders will never cease.'

This is what Ted's wife Olive thought, too, down at Bates's End Farm. After a lifetime with a grumpy, unresponsive husband, she had watched him thaw and mellow under the obvious need for help in the bungalow. And love, of course, Olive had thought with growing amazement. Ted loved little Joey more than anything else, more than herself, more than Robert. People said there was always a silver lining, and Olive supposed this was it. She would have undone all the hurt and unhappiness for her son and his young wife if she could, but as she couldn't she gave thanks for the transformation in Ted.

'He says Eddie Jenkins wants to see it, too,' said Robert. 'Dad'll have quite a handful with those three.'

*   *   *

When the old man and his three young charges reached the old, low barn where cow and calf were bedded down safely, the children were strangely quiet, at first.

35

'Glad she wasn't out in the storm last night, Mr Bates,' said Eddie, putting out a tentative, grubby hand to the calf. It was black and white, with a white, soft little face and huge, curious eyes, and it struggled to its feet on slender, still wobbly legs. Ted pushed Joey's wheelchair into the straw, and the old cow nuzzled the boy's knees. She was used to him on the farm, always around the yard when the weather was warm. It was a tussle for Joey whether he spent his free time in his dad's workshop, talking about cars and fiddling with oily fingers, or up at the farm, where his grandad taught him all he knew, still stubbornly determined that Joey should have a chance to follow in his footsteps when he grew up.

Poppy pushed past Eddie to get a better view, and caught her jeans on an old iron hook driven into the stone wall. There was a ripping sound, and a jagged tear appeared. Joey looked at her in dismay, but she shrieked with laughter, twisting round and making the rip worse. 'Oh dear,' she said, still giggling. 'Poor old Grannie. She likes me to be smart.'

Eddie Jenkins did not laugh. He knew what reception he'd get if he went home with a tear in his new jeans. 'P'raps we could mend it,' he said, looking at Ted hopefully.

Ted shook his head. 'No chance,' he said. 'Olive's gone to Tresham, and I ain't no good with a needle.'

'Don't be so silly, Eddie,' said Poppy,

standing on the jutting-out ledge at the back of Joey's chair. 'I've got loads of others. Look!' she said. 'No hands!' She balanced precariously, waving her arms in the air.

The cow hustled her calf to the back of the barn, and Ted decided enough was enough. 'Out we go, then,' he said, 'leave 'em in peace.' His palm itched, but Poppy was the squire's daughter and a law unto herself.

*   *   *

It was just as well that Jean Jenkins had nipped down quickly to the old vicarage an hour or so before the Bishops came for their second visit, all six of them. As she opened the front door, she stepped into an inch of muddy water which swirled around the black and white tiled floor of the vicarage hall. 'Oh, my God!' she said, and backed into the porch, wondering what to do. Only one thing for it, she thought, kicking off her sandals. She took a step gingerly into the hall, and paddled her way through to the kitchen. She could see what had happened. There'd been a blockage in the drain outside the back door, leaves and mud collected while the vicarage had stood empty, and the resulting tide of water had rushed through the gap under the door into the kitchen. With no restriction and nobody to see it, the flood had made its way through to the hall, but fortunately had not risen high enough to penetrate into the other

37

rooms.

'This is all I need,' said Jean Jenkins to old black Ricky, as he poked his grizzled head round the door and thought twice about coming in. There was no one else to clear it up, however, so she collected a motheaten mop from the cupboard, a rusty pail from an outhouse, and set to work.

*   *   *

'Goodness!' said Annie Bishop, heading the line of family that trouped up the vicarage drive and on to the gleaming black and white tiles of the hall. Jean Jenkins still had mop in hand, and was carrying the bucket back to the outhouse. 'You shouldn't have bothered to wash the floor just for us, Mrs Jenkins,' said Annie.

As Jean watched the four children, two boys and two girls, tramp up the still-muddy path and into the house, she reflected that Mrs Bishop was right. Trails of footprints crisscrossed the shining floor, and then Ricky thought it was safe to risk entry and added variety with his limping paw marks.

Well, sod that, thought Jean Jenkins, and did not trust herself to answer Mrs Bishop. She vanished into the kitchen, and heard the estate agent greeting them. He's very chirpy indeed this morning, thought Jean. Thinks he's landed his fish, no doubt.

Before Jean had time to escape, Mrs Bishop followed her into the yard and smiled her lovely open smile. 'Thank you so much, Mrs Jenkins,' she said. 'You have been so kind and welcoming. If we do decide to buy the vicarage, is there any chance you could spare a few hours to set the house to rights once or twice a week?'

So they've decided, thought Jean. She had plenty enough to do without adding another cleaning job to her busy week, but she was beguiled by that smile, and said that she'd certainly try to squeeze Mrs Bishop in, if at all possible.

The yard was sheltered and warm, the glowing gold stone of its walls reflecting the heat of the sun. A thick-stemmed clematis climbed the wash-house wall, with pinkish white flowers in profusion, like stars on a clear night. Against the old stable, an iron pump and long, roughly fashioned stone drinking trough, green with age, caught Annie's eye. She tentatively moved the pump handle, and looked enquiringly at Jean.

'Needs priming first, then it works,' said Jean, thinking she was never going to get away, at this rate.

'Wonderful!' said Annie Bishop, and slipped her arm through her husband's as he joined them. 'Isn't that wonderful, Andrew?' she said. 'And Mrs Jenkins could give us a little of her precious time if and when we do come to Ringford.'

Oh, you'll come, thought Jean. I can see you've made the decision, Mrs Bishop, and it's my guess that that's what counts in this family. She heard the children whooping round the bedrooms and upstairs in the attics, and in spite of her tiredness and a touch of irritation in knowing that she'd been ever so nicely manipulated, she smiled.

'That's what this place needs,' Jean said. 'Lots of kids, to stir the air.'

'Wonderful!' said Andrew Bishop, and beamed at his wife.

CHAPTER SIX

Dr Russell came once a week to Round Ringford, conducting his surgery in the front room of Ivy's Victoria Villa. He ministered to old people he had known for most of their lives, and took just as much trouble with transient executives and their families who came and went in the new houses at Walnut Close, scarcely leaving their mark on the village.

'Morning, Mrs Palmer—I mean Turner,' said Ivy Beasley, as she ushered Peggy into the kitchen-cum-waiting-room.

Time she forgot that little insult, thought Peggy irritably. She had given Ivy the benefit of the doubt for a while. Other people had found it difficult to remember the change of name at first, but now nobody except Ivy made the mistake, and Peggy knew it was carefully calculated, like most things Ivy did.

Others in the waiting-room had arrived early, knowing that the doctor would not be there until the dot of half past ten, but hoping to be first in the queue. Joyce Davie, small and neat, had taken a chair by the back door and stared without acknowledgement as Peggy came in. Peggy could have done without the knowing look she exchanged with Ivy Beasley.

Doris Ashbourne sat by the shining black range, a relic from the days when old Mrs Beasley had baked and preserved, and won prizes at the annual show for her excellent produce. The sharp old lady had passed on her skills to her daughter, but Ivy now traitorously allowed the range fire to go out in the spring and did not relight it until autumn. In the winter it glowed and crackled, and wonderful smells of roast beef and rice pudding still filled the house on Sunday mornings.

Jean Jenkins sat next to Doris, overflowing the narrow kitchen chair, and beside her perched Eddie, his small hand clamped to his left ear and an expression of extreme pain on his face.

'Oh dear,' said Peggy, taking a seat by the scrubbed table, 'not earache again, Eddie?'

Eddie nodded mutely. His mother answered for him, saying that either it was another infection, or, more likely, the thought of school restarting next week.

41

'You still getting them headaches?' Jean continued, looking sympathetically at Peggy.

'Well, no,' said Peggy. She was about to say that this was not why she was here, but Doris's face looked expectant, and Ivy Beasley's ears pricked as she stood by the kitchen door, keeping a look-out for the doctor and feigning indifference as to what could be the matter with Peggy Turner. Peggy was saved by the sound of Dr Russell's car purring to a halt outside Victoria Villa, and Ivy disappeared to let him in.

'Morning, Ivy!' said Guy Russell, and he gently squeezed her arm. 'How are we in Round Ringford this morning? Many customers for me?' He was old himself, near retirement, but had lost none of his charm and knew from long experience how to handle Miss Ivy Beasley, who was now pink with pleasure.

She ushered him into her gleaming sitting-room, which smelled strongly and rather unpleasantly of polish, and held the chair for him as he sat down. A vase of flowers from Ivy's garden stood on one corner of the table, and Guy Russell placed his notes and stethoscope in front of him. He turned to Ivy with a smile.

'Right, then, Ivy, let's be having them,' he said.

In the kitchen, silence had fallen. It was possible, if no one spoke or moved, to hear very faintly what was being said in Ivy's front room. Before Ivy could open her mouth to summon

42

the first patient, Doris Ashbourne was on her feet.

'All right, Ivy,' she said, 'I'm on my way.'

The sun had moved round so that a shaft of bright light forced its way through Ivy's net curtains and fell directly on Peggy's face. She turned her head, and felt the stab of pain between her ribs on her right side. This morning she had nearly changed her mind about seeing Guy Russell. For once she had had no twinges when she got out of bed. Bill had brought her a cup of tea and biscuit first thing, and this had done the trick. Just indigestion, she'd thought to herself, nothing that a couple of Rennies won't put right. But then when she sat down to a bowl of wheatflakes she had felt a great wave of nausea, and got up from the kitchen table to conceal it from Bill.

'You next, Mrs Turner,' said Ivy harshly. She flattened herself against the wall as Peggy squeezed past in the narrow passage.

'Good morning, my dear,' said Guy Russell, smiling kindly at Peggy. 'You're looking a bit peaky this morning. How can I help?'

Peggy relaxed. Thank goodness she could talk to Guy. She hated owning up to Bill that she was feeling rotten. He had had years of Joyce's hypochondria, and Peggy dreaded that she would go the same way, and Bill would tire of her, too. It was nonsense, of course. Bill was a kind and sympathetic man, and the intensity

43

of his love for Peggy still took him by surprise. He had noticed her increasing pallor, and the times when she went to bed early, not wanting supper and apologising for being overtired. He had encouraged her this morning to see the doctor, and as he prepared seed beds in the Hall vegetable garden, he wondered and worried.

'It's just this pain in my side,' said Peggy. 'It comes and goes, but when it comes it certainly makes itself felt. And I do seem to feel sick a lot of the time.'

Guy Russell asked her a number of questions, then stood up and patted her shoulder. 'I'm sure it's nothing to worry about my dear,' he said, 'but I'd like to take a closer look at you. Can't do it here, of course!' He looked round at the overstuffed chairs and sofa. 'Better come into Bagley to the Centre, and we'll sort it all out.' He was reassuring, wrote her a prescription for some calming pills, and smilingly escorted her to the door. 'Regards to Bill,' he said cheerfully. But as he returned to Ivy's sitting-room, his expression changed and he frowned.

CHAPTER SEVEN

Jean Jenkins heard nothing at all from the Bishops for weeks. The For Sale sign still stood, a little crooked now, outside the old vicarage, and she and the village forgot about it. In the Standing Arms there were more pressing matters to discuss. Silage and haymaking had kept the farmers busy, and when they'd appeared in the bar around ten o'clock in the evening, cleaned up and thirsty, the talk was of the coming harvest, the tension rising as always as the corn turned slowly to gold and the fine weather held.

Jean and Doreen Price, Olive Bates, Ivy and Doris, Peggy Turner and Sophie Brooks from the vicarage, all plunged into the summer social round with varying degrees of enthusiasm. In Fletching and Waltonby and all the surrounding villages, there were fêtes, garden parties, horticultural shows, dog shows, pig roasts, barbecues, barn dances. Round Ringford had its share, and it never ceased to amaze Foxy Jenkins how smoothly his good-tempered wife managed to fit in all the extra work, how, with no apparent panic or confusion, marquees were erected, refreshments provided, raffles were organised, tombolas spun and the small treasuries of church, charity and village were once more replenished.

Ringford Show, always the highlight of the season, had been bigger than ever, attracting entries from miles away, across the other side of the country. The show dance, held in the evening and always a rowdy do, had been even noisier and more disruptive than ever, largely

45

because in the cornfield next to the showground, three young idiots had decided that handfuls of stubble, the brittle straw set alight, would make very useful missiles in the darkness. The field had gone up in minutes, black smoke obscuring vain attempts to control the fire. Nobody took the blame, though many knew exactly who was responsible.

Ted Bates, whose field it was, had been philosophical. 'Ain't the first time we've burnt stubble in Ringford,' he'd said slyly.

And then, one wet and chilly morning, summer was gone. School uniforms were brought out, hems let down and new blazers bought from Tresham. For Jean Jenkins, the return to school after the summer holidays was always a relief. Much as she loved her family, the long weeks of providing two meals a day for seven hungry mouths had seemed to fill her life. 'Food, food, food,' she'd said to Foxy. 'I don't care if I never see another lamb chop.'

'Now you know how I feel,' said Foxy. 'Bunging all that feed into them chickens day after day. In one end and out the other.'

'At least you just tip it out of a sack, and there's eggs as a reward,' Jean said, and thought privately how wonderful it would be if family food came ready-to-eat. Just heat 'n' serve, choose your flavour and add water. She chuckled. Suppose it does, in a way, if you got the money, she thought. Anyway, couldn't see that goin' down too well with my lot.

Autumn arrived with dark mornings and chilly winds blowing the leaves in a frenzy round the bus shelter, where Warren, Mark, Gemma and Amy waited with a milling group of children for the school bus to Tresham. Foxy, escorting Mark to the bus on his first morning as a senior, had wryly noted the beginning-of-term smartness, the new uniforms and freshly washed hair, clean shirts and socks, the unscuffed shoes. He had reported to Jean that Mark had been smiling from the back seat of the bus, and wondered how long it would be before that early morning gloss wore off.

'Ah well,' said Jean, giving Eddie a hug and sending him squirming off to the village school, 'at least this one's still here. It'll be a while before he flies off to the comprehensive.'

*   *   *

Eddie Jenkins plodded down the Gardens, where the small cherry trees were mops of flames as the leaves turned, and shifted his backpack bulging with souvenirs of the summer holidays to be shown to teacher and traded with his friends. His best mate was a lad of the same age who arrived on the bus from Fletching each morning. Children from several surrounding villages came to Round Ringford school, and Eddie and George Brant didn't meet during the holidays. Not for Eddie and George the outings to the zoo or Motor

Heritage Centre. That was for other families, with money to spare and time on their hands.

George lived in a small semi in Fletching, one of a pair built on the site of four old cottages. His father had left years ago, and his mother went out to work every day at a packing factory near Bagley. During school holidays, he and his brother were minded by a neighbour who charged almost as much as their mother earned, and what was left of her wages went towards satisfying their insatiable appetites. 'What can I have to eat?' was George's continual cry, once his mother was home and desperately trying to catch up on the housework.

The bus full of infants and juniors was already disgorging its load outside Ringford school. The 'beep-beep-beep' as it backed up to the gate of the school galvanised Eddie into a quick trot, and his floppy blond hair, which Jean refused to have crew-cut in spite of constant pleading, fell into his eyes as he ran.

'We went to Skeggie,' said George, as they met up and made their way into the crowded school cloakroom.

'To stay?' said Eddie, enviously.

George hesitated, decided to be honest, and shook his head. 'For a couple of days out,' he said. 'Mum took two days off, and we went on everything. Cost a bomb, she said. It was really great, Eddie.'

'We went out for days, too,' said Eddie,

feeling more cheerful, 'and we saw *Batman II*.' He charged off into the classroom in a passable imitation of a Batman swoop, until a heavy hand on his shoulder brought him into line.

'Now, Eddie Jenkins,' said Sarah Barnett, 'we don't charge about in school like that, do we? Or have you forgotten in those lazy weeks at home?' Sarah Barnett was young, small and fierce, with a cap of dark brown hair and lively green eyes. Stroppy, some parents in the village thought, but all acknowledged that she was good at her job. She'd arrived in Ringford a complete townie, and had had trouble settling down. Falling in love with farmer John Barnett had helped, and now she almost never thought of her former, more sophisticated life. In fact, when she looked back, she thought how many hours she had wasted in so-called leisure time. Filling-in time would be a better description. Now the demands of the farm, hard, but somehow comforting in their ancient roots, quickly drew her in. She was learning, sharing with John the successes and disappointments, the hardships of cold winter mornings and the glory of bleached golden fields in the hot sun.

And then there was her job at the school. It was tailormade for Sarah. She was happiest when in charge, and the village school was her territory, her empire. She had two staff, and was a particular friend of Gabriella Jones, mother of Octavia. Gabriella took the little ones, and was glad to renew her maternal feelings, long since rejected by Octavia, with children who were not much beyond babyhood when they arrived, tentative and shy, in the reception class at Ringford school.

In the big, main classroom, with its ecclesiastical arched windows, and lofty, beamed ceiling, Sarah quietened the children ready for morning assembly. As she began to speak, welcoming the children in a somewhat cautionary tone, her voice was drowned by the roar of a passing container lorry.

She stopped, and Eddie Jenkins screwed his head round to watch it disappear down the main street. He could see only the top half. More than a hundred years ago the windows had been deliberately placed so that children's concentration would not be distracted by what went on outside. 'That were one of them Sealink lorries, miss,' he said enthusiastically.

'Thank you, Eddie,' said Sarah. 'Whatever it was, we can do without them in Ringford. Now, I'll begin again. We have ten weeks ahead of us, and much work to do . . .'

Eddie's attention had already begun to wander, and he strained his ears to hear the great lorry grind its way out of Ringford, imagined it forging its way down to the coast, on to an exciting container ship, and out into foreign lands known to Eddie only from the big globe in the corner of the schoolroom, or from garbled tales told by children returning from skin-scorching holidays abroad.

50

At playtime, when Renata Roberts from Macmillan Gardens left her dreary home and came to do duty in the small playground, Sarah and Gabriella relaxed with cups of coffee and exchanged village gossip.

'It's getting worse,' said Sarah. 'It seems every five minutes I have to stop talking. The children suffer. That's what I object to. Can't get their attention for long enough to build up a good lesson.'

Gabriella stirred in the unappetising film of coffee dust, and drank. She sighed, and nodded at Sarah. 'Greg's getting together with Colin Osman,' she said. 'They're full of optimism, talking of bypasses and God knows what, but I don't see it myself. There's much worse places for traffic than Round Ringford.'

They drank in silence for a few minutes, and then Sarah stood up, walked out into the cloakroom with the two cups and rinsed them under the tap. 'Don't be defeatist, Gabbie!' she called. 'Don't forget our fight over the school. We won then, and we can win again.'

'That's what Greg says,' said Gabriella gloomily, 'but a bypass costs millions of pounds, and there's the difference.'

*   *   *

Jean Jenkins was halfway out of the front door to meet Eddie from school when her telephone rang. 'Blast!' she said, and returned to the hall.

51

'Hello? Who is it?' She didn't recognise the voice at first, and then the penny dropped. Annie Bishop. 'Thought you'd decided against it,' said Jean. She listened for a few minutes, and then cut into the long account of difficulties in the housing market and contracts fallen through. 'Sorry, Mrs Bishop,' she said. 'Got to go. I'm late for the school. But anyway, I'll cert'nly give you a hand. I've got the date.'

'After all this time,' she said to Peggy in the shop. 'That Annie Bishop phoned from London to ask me to help them move in. Quite soon. Sold their house, and rarin' to go. Says they got lots to do to the vicarage but she don't sound too worried. They're not short of a bob or two, I reckon. All the signs, if you know what I mean.'

'No, Jean,' said Peggy, curious. 'What are the signs?' She knew the signs of former wealth, as represented by the Standings at the Hall. Expensive but well-worn clothes, once beautiful damask curtains brought in for the umpteenth cleaning during the week when the cleaning company had a special offer. And then there was their meagre grocery order, only the emergency things they couldn't get cut-price from the Supashop in Tresham on Friday afternoons.

'There's that four-by-four, for a start,' said Jean. 'And then she's got her own little Peugeot and he has a BMW.' Jean disappeared behind the display stands, filling her wire basket with boxes of cereal, tins of baked beans, dog biscuits and packs of margarine. 'What's more,' she continued, 'them kids've got all the latest gimmicks. I remember her saying, things to keep them occupied on the journey, as if London was a million miles from Ringford. And just now she was talking about new carpets and curtains, and extra furniture for the vicarage's big rooms, just as if she was fillin' up a dolls' house. None of your secondhand stuff from Easy-On-Your-Pocket in Bagley for our Mrs Bishop!'

Jean's flow was interrupted by the door opening with a jangle and admitting Ivy Beasley. She marched up to the counter and banged down some small change. 'Box of matches, please,' she said. Peggy took down a packet of six and extracted one, reflecting that at least Ivy had managed a 'please' this week. It surely was not beyond her means to buy six at a time, but Peggy supposed the Beasleys had always eked out their money with care, and Ivy couldn't break the habit.

'You heard about the Bishops, Miss Beasley?' said Jean, oblivious of Ivy's glare.

'What Bishops?' said Ivy.

'New people at the vicarage, movin' in soon.'

'I'm not one to indulge in gossip, Mrs Jenkins,' said Ivy tartly.

Jean shrugged and turned away to look at washing powders.

After a small silence, Ivy cleared her throat.

'Well,' she said, 'who are the Bishops, anyway?'

'Family from London—rich—lots of kids—quite young. She's pretty, and he's not bad. They want me to work for them.' Jean was generous with village news. Even Ivy Beasley was worth telling. In fact, sometimes she could add a detail or two. But not today.

'Then I suppose we shall know all their secrets in due course,' said Ivy, and picking up her box of matches she left the shop with a sniff.

'What's eating old Poison Ivy today?' said Jean, eyebrows raised.

'Could be anything or nothing,' said Peggy. 'But I do know she's getting in one of her states about these lorries going through the village. She was in her front garden yesterday afternoon, tidying up ready for the winter, and I saw this great thing belch out a cloud of diesel fumes right where she was working. Poor old devil rushed off indoors and slammed the door.'

'Poor?' said Jean. 'She'd not be so charitable towards you, Peggy. Here,' she continued, seeing Peggy wince, 'is anything wrong? You get one of them headaches again?'

Peggy shook her head. 'No, no, I'm fine, Jean, just twisted round and hurt my side a bit, that's all. All set, then? Got everything you need?'

Jean collected her purchases and left the shop, met Renata Roberts on the pavement

54

outside, and walked off towards Macmillan Gardens deep in conversation.

Peggy straightened the cereal packets and rearranged the stack of beans, then went through to the kitchen at the back of the shop. She sat down and took a deep breath. Relax, she told herself, relax and it'll go away. And by the time Bill came in for his lunch, the pain had abated and Peggy greeted him with a cheerful kiss on his cool cheek.

CHAPTER EIGHT

Pat Osman cleared the supper dishes and walked through to the living-room to find Colin putting on his waxed cotton jacket. 'Going out?' she said, surprised. He hadn't mentioned any meeting, though she knew his researches had hotted up, and that he'd arranged to see the man who'd campaigned for a bypass in some other village.

'Just need some fresh air,' he said.

'But it's beginning to rain,' Pat said.

'Doesn't matter,' said Colin.

'Do you want me to come with you?'

'No thanks, I've got some thinking to do, and walking is always good for that.'

It was only seven o'clock, but with the sky overcast and drizzle in the air, it seemed later. Colin walked along by the pub, resisted the temptation to go in and have a half, and carried on round the corner and up Bates's End. He passed Bates's Farm, and heard cattle lowing as Ted moved among them. Colin thought of calling in and asking what Ted thought about the traffic problem, but reflected that he'd probably get a dusty answer. And Olive Bates never had much of an opinion without Ted.

Colin left the village behind and walked on up the hill into the woods. Although it was still early September, the verges were dry and dead. Tufts of old man's beard hung on the hedges, and hogweed rattled as Colin brushed against the copper heads, the seeds long ago shaken out by the wind. Only a small stem of willow herb, pale purple against the fading greens and browns, lingered from the hot, dry summer.

Tall nettles had died back, and Colin walked easily through the wood, following the path that led to the great oak stump, a favourite place for resting and looking over the village. The mossy covering was damp, but Colin took off his jacket and spread it out before sitting down. In spite of the fine rain, the air was warm, and only a small breeze stirred the branches above him. He could see the main street of Ringford below him, and as if to reinforce his determination to tackle the traffic problem, a speeding convoy of six cars threaded its way past Macmillan Gardens, the bus stop, the shop and the school. One peeled off and disappeared up the Bagley Road, but the others accelerated past the village hall and rushed off towards Fletching. Commuters, thought Colin. Each car with one man, hurrying home from a day's work in London or Birmingham, and heaven help anything that gets in the way.

The rain was heavier now, and Colin put on his jacket and strode off towards Tom Price's grass field that sloped all the way down to the village. He knew he could get through the gate at the bottom and cross the rickety footbridge over the Ringle river, ending up near his own back garden. He was halfway down the hill when he saw the cows. They were away over in the opposite corner of the field, and as he peered through the gloom he realised that the big cow in the centre of the group was a bull. His pace quickened, and then he told himself there was no danger. Tom had always said the bull was no trouble when with his cows, and he slowed down again. A single bellow sent a nervous shiver through Colin. Were they moving? It was difficult to see in the half-light.

As Colin broke into a slow trot, he heard more bellows. He looked round, and saw that the herd was indeed moving, and moving fast now. He could hear the hoofs thudding on the dry, hard ground, and it sounded like a stampede on the prairie.

'Oh, bugger it,' he said aloud, and began to run. The gate at the bottom of the field looked miles away, and Colin, glancing back anxiously, couldn't imagine why he'd always thought of cows as slow, lumbering creatures. This lot were galloping, kicking up their heels, and bellowing even louder now. As Colin scrambled over the gate and fell in an exhausted heap on the other side, he heard another sound, different from the excited roars of the cows.

Tom Price, sitting on his tractor by the feeders, surrounded by jostling cattle desperate to get at the sweet-smelling hay, waved his arm in greeting to Colin, and the sound that Colin could hear was Tom laughing, loud, hearty laughter.

*   *   *

It was almost dark when he limped back down the street. He'd hurt his ankle, and decided not to risk struggling through the hedge that led to his garden. He went round the long way, and now stood leaning against the bus shelter, resting his aching leg. A large van came steaming through the rain, headlights full on and ignoring the speed limit. A sudden squeal of brakes brought Colin to attention. He saw a dark streak fly across the road from the Green and disappear into Ivy Beasley's front garden. My God, he thought, that was Ivy's cat. If that had gone under the wheels, the poor old girl would have died of grief.

Pat saw him coming up the lighted drive and opened the front door. 'Whatever have you been doing?' she said, noticing the limp. 'I'd no idea thinking was such a dangerous pastime.'

Colin grunted. 'I'm in no mood for caustic wit, Pat,' he said. 'I need a large whisky and soda, and a bowl of very hot water for my ankle.'

'How . . .?' said Pat.

'Cows,' said Colin shortly. 'Bloody cows.' He tried not to notice that his wife's shoulders were heaving as she left the room.

CHAPTER NINE

'Colin Osman's goin' to see the Council today,' said Jean, standing squarely at the sink, washing up after a bread and cheese lunch with Foxy. He still sat at the table, lingering over a cup of tea before getting back to the farm. A small, sturdy man, smaller than Jean and very gingery, he'd been called Foxy since he started at the village school when he was five. A sharp nose and fiery colouring belied his nature, which was mild and accommodating, and the only time Jean stood back and held her tongue was when Foxy drew himself up to his full height and his eyes narrowed. More often than not this was in defence of one or other of his children, but occasionally some less domestic issue invaded his personal life, and he could be formidable.

'Waste o'time,' said Foxy. 'He 'on't get

59

anywhere with that lot. Still, his sort have got to have somethin' on the boil. Makes 'em feel important.'

Jean rinsed the dish cloth under the hot tap, gave it a good squeeze, and turned the washing-up bowl upside down. She untied her apron strings and turned to look at him. 'Somebody's got to try, though, Foxy. It's getting worse every day. Did you hear about old Ivy's cat? Nearly went under a lorry, Colin Osman said. What'll it be next?'

'Mr Osman's all very well,' said Foxy, 'but 'e'll 'ave to be watched.' Foxy did not object to Colin Osman as such, but he had lived all his life in Round Ringford and believed in biding his time. Agitating and rocking the boat could do more harm than good. He sided with the faction in the pub that thought a traffic increase was inevitable in Ringford, and the more fuss the likes of Colin Osman made the more bloody signs and humps and bloody sleeping policemen they'd end up with.

'What'll it be next?' repeated Jean. 'I'll tell you what next!' Her voice was rising in anger, but Foxy Jenkins had shouldered his old khaki bag and was halfway out of the door.

'Back about six, I should think, so long as the rain don't get any worse,' he shouted as he went. 'Look after yerself, Jean.'

'Trust him,' said Jean to the canary sitting in his cage in the window, hunched up and silent, waiting for a ray of sunlight to cheer him up.

60

'Trust Foxy to have the last word.'

*　　　*　　　*

In a large basement kitchen in North London, Annie Bishop sat at her scrubbed pine table and drank coffee with a friend from around the corner. In an hour or so of peace, whilst little Honor slept under her duvet and Bruce had gone off to play with a chum, before Faith and Helen returned from their school in Ashburn Road, Annie spread before her neighbour a map she had drawn of Round Ringford to familiarise the children with their new environment. That was how she put it, and her friend was impressed.

'Looks like you'll be right in the middle of the community in that lovely old vicarage,' she said. 'I expect you'll soon be drawn into good works and charitable causes!' There was a slight edge to her voice, since Annie Bishop was known for her amazing ability to manage home, husband and children with seeming ease, and yet find time to visit the sick and lonely and hand out soup from the centre for homeless people in the old converted church down the road.

'Goodness,' said Annie modestly, 'I'm sure Round Ringford has everything in order. Such a small village, and quite beautiful. I'm getting so excited about it all I wake up in the middle of the night and have to talk to Andrew. He's

61

so sweet—never minds . . .'

Her friend thought privately that Andrew must be a sodding saint, but she smiled and said she was looking forward to buzzing down to Ringford for summer Sunday lunches in the vicarage, so that all their children could keep up their friendships and not lose touch.

'And there's this wonderful char. Mrs Jenkins, would you believe?' said Annie. 'Big and motherly. She's already promised to come and do for me, and I know she'll want to take us under her wing. Jean, I think she's called.'

Annie's friend sighed. 'I can just imagine it all,' she said. 'Like something out of Joanna Trollope. Who's going to have the first affair?' This last was said with deliberate mischief. It was well known that Annie and Andrew were exclusively devoted to each other, and in spite of the best endeavours of Highgate's flightiest young women, the handsome Andrew seemed not to notice. As for Annie, she seemed unaware of her grace and beauty, and dressed as if she'd not bothered to look in a mirror, with no apparent make-up on her peachy skin. But her best friend was not deceived, saw expensive potions on Annie's bathroom shelf. She was sure that Annie's casual appearance was carefully studied. Still, you had to have the raw material, and she generously acknowledged that Annie was very pretty.

Annie frowned. 'Affair?' she said. 'That's for others, not for Andrew and me.' She looked at the old clock on the wall, got up, and in the nicest possible way dismissed her friend.

*   *   *

The sun that peeked into a corner of Annie Bishop's walled garden at the back of her London house now shone broad and smilingly on the neglected half acre at the rear of the old vicarage in Round Ringford. The morning's rain had soaked the grass, turning it green again after the long drought. Nettles had taken over an old rockery against the wall, and the summerhouse looked neglected and forlorn, with broken garden chairs stacked against the dusty windows and a floorboard split and hanging dangerously at the doorway.

Richard Standing, in his capacity as patron of Ringford church, stood shielding his eyes against the wet, sparkling garden, and tried to assess how much work would have to be done to bring it back into order. It had been agreed that all would be at least tidy for the Bishops to move in.

'Extraordinary, isn't it, Bill,' he said to Bill Turner standing by his side, 'how quickly a garden can go wild?'

Bill nodded. He remembered his own neatly cultivated patch at the back of number fourteen in Macmillan Gardens, where he and Joyce had shared so many unhappy years. Only weeks after he moved out to live with Peggy, he had gone back to collect a garden fork, still stuck in the manure heap, and marvelled at the weeds advancing like a conquering army from the field to the house. 'Still,' he said, 'shouldn't take long to set it right. After all, the Bishops will probably want to make their own garden, redesign it, or something.'

A mild stir had been created when a small, dark woman who'd retired from a job with the BBC to a cottage in Fletching, set up as a garden designer. She'd put up a notice on Ringford bus shelter, and the old gardeners of the village had poured scorn. The only design they'd ever imposed on their gardens was one which used every inch of space for the production of vegetables. The missus was allowed a tiny patch for a few flowers, and that was it. But Colin Osman had paid for a design plan, and even old Ted Bates had had to admit the garden was much improved. 'Made the bugger look twice as big as before,' he had said, to guffaws from his pub cronies who chose deliberately to misunderstand him.

Richard Standing and Bill ambled round the lawns and paths, pushing back brambles and overgrown climbers, easy with one another and mostly silent.

'Well,' said Richard finally, 'I reckon you can see what needs doing, Bill. Can I leave it to you to organise? There's a bit in the kitty to help out with expenses, but not much.'

'Don't worry, we'll manage,' said Bill, and

walked with his boss to the front gate.

'I'd like to be kept informed on progress, though,' said Richard Standing. 'Perhaps if the Bishops come down for a day before they move in, I could come and check that everything's to their liking.'

He didn't fool Bill. They had known each other all their lives, and though always respectful, Bill had no illusions about Richard Standing. Although he'd been very steady for the last few years, since Poppy had been born, Bill firmly believed that a leopard doesn't change its spots, and he grinned. 'She's very attractive, isn't she, sir?' he said, and quickly hopped on his bike and headed across the green for home.

*　　　*　　　*

'Peggy?' Bill called, as he opened the back door and stepped into the warm kitchen. The autumn days were definitely chillier, and the old Rayburn's glowing heat was very welcoming. There was no reply, and Bill walked through into the shop. Peggy sat on a stool, elbows on the counter and her head in her hands. She had clearly not heard him.

'Peggy?' he said again. This time she looked up, and there were dark smudges under her eyes. 'You all right, gel?' said Bill, concerned. He walked round and put his arms round her as she sat on the stool.

She turned her head and pressed her cheek against his cold coat. 'Not so bad, thanks,' she said. And then she smiled and kissed him gently. 'Nothing that a nice hot cup of tea won't put right,' she said, and quietly edged out of his arms.

'So how did you get on at the vicarage?' Peggy unbuttoned her overall and stretched her arms above her head, wincing.

'We had a good look round,' said Bill, noticing but not saying anything more. 'Sooner the Bishops move in the better. It doesn't take long for an old place to go to rack and ruin.'

'Is there a date?' said Peggy.

Bill shook his head. 'Mr Richard didn't say, but I reckon he's looking forward to them coming. She's quite a looker, you know.'

'Oh, no,' said Peggy. 'Not that again . . .' The shop bell jangled, and Peggy sighed. 'Pour yourself a cup,' she said. 'I'll be back in a minute,' and she walked through to cope with the massed Jenkinses, arrived to spend their pocket money.

'Be quick, now!' said Jean, holding on to Eddie, and trying to herd the rest into some sort of order. Warren bought a tin of Coke, paid for it, and disappeared quickly, anxious not to be lumbered with overseeing any of his unruly siblings. Gemma and Amy, secretive and enclosed, hovered in whispers over packets of mints and bars of chocolate, and Mark, tubby already and conscious of it, bought a couple of red apples and stumped off, disregarding his mother's 'Wait for me, Mark! I've got the key.'

Eddie stood quietly by his mother for once, smiling at Peggy and waiting his turn. 'You bin cryin', Mrs Turner?' he said suddenly, and Jean looked down at him in surprise.

Peggy, taken aback, shook her head. 'No, no, Eddie, what have I got to cry about? Here, here's something for you. It got broken open when I unpacked the box.' She handed over a giant packet of crisps, torn at the top.

'Cor, thanks,' said Eddie, delving in. And then he leaned over and offered the packet to Peggy. 'Have a crisp,' he said, reassuringly, 'put you right, that will.'

Jean Jenkins smiled proudly, but wondered, as she saw Peggy wince and turn away.

CHAPTER TEN

The man at the council offices had been polite but guarded. 'What exactly did you want to see me about, Mr Osman?' he'd said. Colin wasn't sure how high up in the Department of Planning and Transportation this disembodied voice was, but he'd been passed from one to another extension and now someone called Bob Quigly was proving difficult to approach.

'A matter of great concern to the villagers of Round Ringford,' said Colin, and wondered whether he should call him sir.

'Ah,' said Bob Quigly. 'I suppose it's to do with the increase of traffic?' He'd already had complaints from other villages on the Ringford road, and had his explanations at the ready.

However, Colin meant to be a match for him. 'I would certainly need only ten minutes of your time,' he said, 'but I'd find it so much easier if we could have a one-to-one chat. I can come along at any time to suit you, Mr Quigly. I appreciate you must have a very busy schedule.' Nothing lost by creeping, he said to himself.

'Very well, Mr Osman,' said Bob Quigly reluctantly. 'Let me look at my diary.' He put his hand over the phone and turned to his secretary. 'Some bloke from Ringford determined to come and see me,' he said. 'Anything next Friday morning?'

*   *   *

County Hall in Tresham was a large, rambling Victorian building with its impressive entrance hall ruined by a reception cubby-hole partitioned off and filled with computers and all the detritus of a modern office. Behind the sliding window—bullet-proof, probably, thought Colin—a fierce, uniformed receptionist with a mannish haircut and thick-lensed glasses raised her eyebrows.

'I've an appointment to see Mr Quigly,'

Colin said. 'A bit early, I'm afraid.'

Showing absolutely no reaction to this, the receptionist spoke briefly into a telephone. 'He'll be down,' she said, and pushed a badge saying 'Visitor' across the counter. She slid the window shut and turned her back on Colin, making it clear that she'd done all she had to do and now washed her hands of him.

It was not Bob Quigly, but his secretary, who appeared several minutes later. She smiled coolly at Colin and said, 'This way, please,' leading him through a rabbit warren of passages and stairways, and endless doors, some of which he could have sworn shut quickly in his face as he passed. By the time he was ushered into an open, airy office five floors up above the busy town, his morale was considerably lowered.

'Good morning, Mr Osman!' A tall, thin man stood up from his desk by the window. His good grey suit was neatly pressed, and his tie betrayed his passion for the local rugby football club. With his thinning dark hair and a surprisingly rakish moustache, he was difficult to categorise. Could have been anything from a geography teacher to a turf accountant, thought Colin.

'Very good of you to see me,' Colin said, taking the chair indicated. He opened his notebook, where he had set down a number of carefully thought out and pertinent questions. 'Now if . . .'

'Not so fast,' said Bob Quigly, sitting down in his chair, slightly higher than Colin's and aggressively upholstered in chocolate-brown leather. He leaned back, rested his elbows on the chair arms and put his fingers together, tip to tip. He smiled. 'First of all,' he said, 'I'd like to tell you a bit about how the Council operates.'

'But I know already . . . the school closure . . .' said Colin.

But Bob Quigly was looking out of the window, still smiling a little, preparing to expound. 'How the Council operates,' he repeated. He proceeded in measured tones to outline the procedures, the committees and their composition, the interdependence of professionals and 'what I hardly dare to call amateurs!'—the elected councillors, good people all, and willing to give their time for the good of their county. Mr Quigly was all benevolence, but Colin picked up a clear message that nothing would be extracted from him that he did not wish to give.

The allotted half-hour was ticking away, and Colin realised he had not yet asked a single one of his questions. He cleared his throat, and Bob Quigly stopped mid-sentence.

'Um, I'd like to ask you,' began Colin, 'how many vehicles have to pass through a village in one day for a bypass to be considered.' Desperation had brought him to the nub of the matter. Probably just as well, he thought. All those meticulously planned questions designed to corner Bob Quigly into revealing County Council secrets would have to be ditched. Here he was, right here, with no time for softening up.

'Ah,' said Bob Quigly, 'now that's a ticklish question. It is not quite as simple as that,' and he launched into a 'hypothetical bypass situation' where several thousand vehicles passed through a village on a main road, and where only thirty per cent of the villagers were in favour of a bypass. 'You see,' he said, leaning towards Colin and addressing him as if he were a slow ten-year-old, 'a decision to build a bypass is a complex issue. Many different aspects must be taken into consideration. It is certainly not just a matter of how many vehicles . . .'

'Yes, but how many, Mr Quigly?' said Colin, gripping his notebook until his knuckles whitened in his effort to get an answer to his question.

'Mmm . . . Well, say a minimum of five thousand . . . ish . . .' Bob Quigly leaned back again against the chocolate-brown leather and smiled at Colin. It was a very patronising smile, and Colin bristled.

'Right,' Colin said, 'and now there were one or two other points . . .'

'Sorry old chap,' said Bob Quigly, 'must let you go now. Another meeting in five minutes. You know how it is.' He put out his hand, and

71

Colin reluctantly shook it. 'Any time you want to clarify any of the items in our discussion,' said Bob Quigly, 'give Susan here a buzz, and she'll chivvy me into sending you a note or two. Goodbye, Mr Osman. Nice to have met you.'

Secretary Susan took him to the head of the stairs, where on the wall he read a cautionary notice about not leaning out of the windows. He turned to ask her how many suicides they'd had from Planning and Transportation, but she was gone and he was on his own. He set off uncertainly down the wide stone stairway, and after many wrong turns and a scary ten minutes in the dimly lit basement, he finally emerged, exhausted and having given up hope of ever seeing daylight again, into the entrance hall. He gave his visitor's badge to the uncaring receptionist, and stepped out shakily into the sunlight of Tresham's main street.

*   *   *

The clouds had rolled over from the west, and it was raining steadily on Colin's prize shaggy chrysanthemums by the time he put on his jacket and called to Pat that he was just going for a quick half and would be back in time for supper. He needed to talk about his morning's ordeal with Peter Dodwell and Robert Bates, and maybe get some words of comfort and wisdom from Tom Price, who from long experience was always ready to cut down to size

72

'that lot at County Hall'.

The Osmans' house stood on Standing land, and had once been a granary before Richard Standing had seen its potential. Living down Bates's End, beyond Ellen Biggs's lodge, and nearly opposite Bates's Farm, the Osmans' only personal experience of traffic noise or fumes was Ted Bates's ancient tractor coughing and spluttering in the early morning. Colin stepped out of his immaculate, weed-free driveway into the narrow lane, where a heap of cow muck steamed gently in the rain. He took a side-step to avoid it, and made a mental note to bring before the Parish Council the need for highway hygiene in Round Ringford. As he passed Ellen Biggs's house, he saw the curtain twitch and knew that he had been monitored. On his right stood the looming bulk of the old vicarage, and he remembered with pleasure the rumour that new people would be moving in soon. Needs a family there, he thought. Hope he'll be a good bloke for the village. Colin sometimes felt very lonely in his attempts to improve the community in which he had made his home.

Bridge Cottage also stood empty, and Colin shook his head disapprovingly. Didn't do a property any good to be shut up like that for so long. Must be nearly three years since Mandy and Robert had moved to the bungalow by the motor repair shop. As he passed the cottage gate swinging in the gusts of wind that flung heavy drops of water in his face, he was surprised to see a figure emerge from the back of the house. He was even more surprised when he saw it was Miss Ivy Beasley, clad from head to foot in a voluminous blackish-blue raincoat and wellington boots, a black felt hat rammed down over her ears.

'Miss Beasley!' Colin said. 'What brings you out on such a dreadful evening?'

Ivy stepped out into the lane and clanged the gate shut behind her. 'That's my business, Mr Osman,' she said primly. 'And I don't have to ask you the same question, I'm sure. Off to the Arms, are we? Quite a crowd in there when I came past. You'd think they'd got something better to do. And spend their money on,' she continued, and set off smartly in front of Colin, leaving him stumped for a reply.

He sighed. Not my day, he thought, and turned into the pub door with relief, greeting the warmth and the camaraderie and the smell of hops and malt with even more than his usual enthusiasm.

He had no need to explain where he'd been. Everyone already knew that he had been up the council offices seeing about them bloody cars. 'How'd you get on, then, boy?' said Tom, ordering a pint of Morton's for Colin. Sympathy and understanding surrounded him, and as he leaned up against the bar and got some of Morton's Best inside him, Colin relaxed.

'Hard nut to crack, that Bob Quigly,' he said,

'but I think I got the better of him. All we need to know to go forward.'

'Bob Quigly?' said Tom, throwing his head back and guffawing loudly. 'That little squit! He was a Ringford boy, you know. Same class as me in the village school. Little weed was no good at all, and spent all his time tale-tellin' to teacher. Couldn't you get to see anyone more important than him?'

Looking discomfited, Colin said that he thought Mr Quigly was comparatively senior in the hierarchy at County Hall, and had certainly had an air of considerable authority.

'They've all got that,' said Robert Bates glumly remembering his struggle to get permission to set up his workshop. 'Specialists in making you feel small. Still, doesn't do to let them get you down.'

Colin stood up straight. He was on his third pint, and the thought of anyone getting him down was quite out of the question. 'Stood up to him, Robert,' he said. 'Told him exactly what we in Ringford think of all this extra traffic. Made him more or less promise to do something about it. Yes, indeed, you should have heard me tell him . . .' and then he couldn't remember exactly what he'd been going to say next, and took a deep swig of beer instead.

'Load of rubbish,' said a gravelly voice behind him. Ted Bates, elder statesman in his own eyes, had come to join the discussion.

'Won't make any difference what we say,' he said. 'Cars is everythin' these days. We all 'as to put up with 'em. Where'd Robert 'ere be without cars? I ask you that, Mr Osman,' he added, and looked challengingly at Colin.

Seeing that Colin had drifted off into a daydream, his friend Peter Dodwell from Walnut Close attempted an answer. But it was too long and detailed for Ted, who turned away to talk to Robert about how he'd taken Joey and Poppy, and young Eddie Jenkins, to see the calf, and how Poppy Standing had been trouble as usual.

'Still, that's a good'un, that old cow,' Ted said. 'Never made a mess of it yet. Mother and child doin' well, as they say.' And he cackled proudly, finally bringing to a halt Peter Dodwell's involved dissertation on the need for a detailed breakdown of the endless traffic through the village.

*   *   *

In the front bedroom of the Jenkins house in Macmillan Gardens, Jean climbed into their big bed, plumping up the pillows and settling herself into the sheets like an old mother hen on the nest. 'Anything interestin' to report from the Arms tonight?' she said.

Foxy neatly folded his trousers and put them with the rest of his clothes on a small chair. He pulled on his pyjama jacket and buttoned it carefully, partly because he was a neat and careful man, but also to show Jean that his dexterity was in no way impaired by an evening at the pub.

'Usual thing,' he said. 'Colin Osman on about the cars. Bin to County Hall today and sorted them out. So he said.' Foxy put out the light and felt his way to the bed. 'Move over, gel,' he said.

'No,' said Jean, her voice light and teasing.

'Ah,' said Foxy. 'Well, I reckon that's a good idea, Jeannie my love. Oops! Ah now, steady on . . .'

Outside, the village was quiet at last. In the cool, wet night an owl hooted over Bagley Woods and was answered. The old cow, settled down in clean straw with her new calf, chewed contentedly and waited for dawn. In Victoria Villa Ivy Beasley lay stiffly between her glassy sheets and wondered which would be the best for Sandra and Sam and their little girl: Bridge Cottage or Fred Mills's council house, newly decorated and awaiting a tenant?

CHAPTER ELEVEN

Jean Jenkins was in a good mood over breakfast. 'Today's the day,' she said to Foxy as he sat reading the sports news.

'What, again?' he said, looking at her over the page.

'Foxy!' said Jean, glancing meaningly at Eddie, who stood wrestling with his back-pack, preparing for school.

'She means the Bishops,' Eddie said, his voice muffled as his face became momentarily covered by his scarlet jersey.

'What *are* you doing, Edward Jenkins?' said his mother, sorting him out and giving him a quick cuddle at the same time.

He wriggled free and made for the door. 'Bishops are moving in today,' he said. 'Mum said so to Mrs Turner at the shop.'

'You're worse than them, you ole gossip,' said Foxy, getting up and pretending to chase Eddie out of the door.

'Be careful!' shouted Jean. 'Mind how you cross the road, now!'

Foxy sat down again, and Jean took the chair opposite him. 'Not in much of a hurry to get back to work?' she said.

Foxy shook his head. 'The rush is over; 'sides, I put in a good many hours overtime not paid for. Mr Richard can wait half an hour, I reckon.'

Foxy Jenkins had worked on the estate farm since he was sixteen, and even before that he had begged Mr Richard for jobs in his holidays and at weekends. School was a waste of time for Foxy. He mastered reading and writing with difficulty, and gave up on mathematics when confronted with logarithms. None of it had any bearing on his very happy way of life, and never

78

would have, as he could clearly see. It was all very well for the teachers at Tresham to lecture him on the value of broadening his mind and enriching his experience. As far as Foxy was concerned, enrichment came when he'd shot a rabbit for the pot, helped to deliver an awkward lamb, seen a harvest field successfully cut and baled in spite of the weather, or gazed modestly at a row of first-class certificates on his vegetables at the annual horticultural show. He was a first-class agricultural worker, and he knew it. Richard Standing knew it, too, and would never have queried Foxy's extra half-hour.

'Thought I'd go blackberrying this afternoon, after I've seen the Bishops in safely,' said Jean, looking down at her plump hands and wishing they were slender with long fingers, like that Annie.

'Any good, are they?' said Foxy.

'Only time will tell,' said Jean. 'So far, Mrs Bishop can't be faulted. Too good to be true, as Ivy Beasley would say. But, speak as you find, they seem a really nice family.'

Foxy looked at the clock over the kitchen cupboard. 'I meant the blackberries,' he said, draining his cup. 'The Bishops can wait. Are the blackberries any good? Shrivelled up little buggers, last time I looked.'

'Well, there you're wrong,' said Jean, irritated by Foxy's lack of interest in the new occupants at the vicarage. 'This last bit o' rain

79

has filled 'em out. Should be good for a few pounds of jam. Down the Spring Field there's a patch where nobody don't go.'

'Just watch what you get up to down there,' said Foxy, stretching his arms and getting to his feet. 'Favourite place for a good snog, that was, in our young days.'

'Oh, yes?' said Jean. 'Well, who knows? I might introduce Mr Andrew Bishop to the joys of blackberryin' . . .'

Foxy laughed and gave her a quick peck on the cheek. 'Bit past all that, aren't we?' he said.

'Blimey,' said Jean. 'Who was that up there with me last night, then?' She looked at herself in the small mirror over the sink and patted her frizzy hair. 'Must make an appointment with Mandy,' she said, and smiled approvingly at herself in the rusty glass.

*   *   *

Eddie dashed up the steps into the shop, pushed open the jangling door and looked round for Peggy Turner. 'Mrs Turner!' he shouted, and smiled as Peggy came through from the kitchen.

'Shouldn't you be in school by now?' she said, touching the top of his head with a light hand.

'Yep,' said Eddie. 'Can I have a pencil, please? Lost mine in the garden.'

Peggy took out a pencil with a rubber at one

end.

'Haven't got enough money for that,' said Eddie. 'Ordinary one, please.'

'That's all right, Eddie,' said Peggy. 'Special offer this morning. Only for boys called Eddie Jenkins. How's Mum?'

'OK,' said Eddie. 'Goin' blackberryin' this afternoon. After she's seen to the Bishops.'

'Off you go, then,' said Peggy. 'Mrs Barnett will be cross if you're late.'

Eddie groaned. 'She's always cross with me,' he said. 'Can't do nothin' right,' but he seemed philosophical about this, and shot out of the shop and across the road, whooping as he saw George getting off the school bus.

Blackberrying, thought Peggy. How lovely. She looked out of the shop window at the green. It was a perfect autumn day, clear blue sky with a few unthreatening drifts of white cloud. A light wind chased flurries of leaves under the chestnut tree, and Peggy knew from the way the children jumped and ran in the playground that it was a warm wind, a kindly wind that ruffled the little girls' ponytails and slapped the frayed rope against the flagpole by the gate.

A large removals van crawled along, past the pub and down Bates's End. That'll be the Bishops' stuff, thought Peggy. Lovely day for moving in. Nothing worse than moving house in the rain. Thoughts of her arrival at the shop in Ringford with Frank began to come

81

unbidden into her mind, and she frowned, not wanting to remember those early days when they struggled together with a new life, so soon to be cut short for Frank.

The telephone rang, and with some relief Peggy turned to answer it, her hand in its now accustomed position holding her side. 'Hello, Mary,' she said. 'Yes, tomorrow as usual, thanks. Several new pension books to hand out, so we could be busy.' Then, on impulse, she added, 'Are you doing anything this afternoon, Mary?'

When Bill came home for lunch, Peggy was smiling. 'Taking the afternoon off,' she said. 'Mary's coming in at two, and I'm going blackberrying.'

'Excellent,' said Bill. 'There's some beauties in the Spring Field, masses of 'em.'

'Where's that?' said Peggy, and closed her eyes to picture the route that Bill described, field by field, footpath by footpath. 'Must be miles from anywhere,' she said.

'You'll be quite safe, gel,' said Bill. 'Nobody goes that way except old Ted when he's ploughing. Peaceful place, that.'

He looked at Peggy, her face pink and animated, and wished he had thought of getting Mary York in more often. Routines, he thought. We're all so bound up in routines. Never think of something simple like taking an afternoon off. My lovely gel, she looks better already.

'By the way,' he said. 'Met Michael Roberts down by the pub.'

'Of course,' said Peggy.

'Well, never mind about that,' said Bill. 'As it happens, he was on his way home. Said his Sandra's coming back to the village.'

'Sandra?' said Peggy, interested now. 'And Sam? And the little one?'

'Seems so,' said Bill. 'They're after old Fred's house, and stand a good chance of getting it, Michael says.'

Sandra Roberts had followed the family tradition in getting married in haste, to a pleasant young building worker at the time Walnut Close was going up. They'd made their home with Sam's parents in Tresham, and the baby had now grown into a little girl, spoilt by all and needing more space to expand. Peggy had tried to help the young couple in their early troubled days, and Sandra had shown her gratitude not in words, which would not have been her way, but in sending little notes on lined pages torn from an exercise book, keeping Peggy up to date with little Alison's progress. Every now and then, they would knock on Peggy's door on Sunday afternoons and spend a few minutes exchanging halting conversation. It wasn't much of a friendship, but Sandra never missed.

'That's really good news!' said Peggy, reaching up for a plastic bag. 'Won't it be nice to have them back, Bill?'

'Suppose so,' said Bill. 'She was nice when she was little, that Sandra, in spite of being a Roberts. But I don't want you getting involved in their rows again. You've got enough to cope with here. Go on, then, I can hear Mary in the shop. Get going, and don't let me hear or see you again till teatime.'

Peggy kissed him lightly, and as she went out Bill's smile faded. Time Doc Russell sorted out that pain of hers. He knew quite well she hid it from him a lot of the time. He couldn't imagine what he'd do without Peg now. 'She's everything to me, God knows,' he muttered, and then shook himself out of morbid thoughts and pedalled off back to the estate.

*   *   *

Richard Standing was waiting for him outside the high stone wall of the kitchen garden, holding Poppy by the hand and trying in vain to stop her teasing Susan's Yorkie, an irascible little dog who'd never quite got over having his position usurped by this late addition to the Standing family.

'Ah, Bill,' Richard said, as Bill propped his bicycle against the wall. 'Just popping down to the vicarage to see how they're getting on. Thought I'd take Poppy along to welcome them.'

'Righto, sir,' said Bill, wondering why Mr Richard should bother to tell him that. Guilty

84

conscience, probably. Bill knew perfectly well why Mr Richard was going down to see the Bishops. Wicked old bugger.

'There was one thing,' said Richard Standing. 'I noticed the water trough's leaking down in the dip between Ted's Spring Field and our corner pasture. Could you get it fixed this afternoon if you've got a spare half-hour?'

Bill watched his boss and his prancing daughter make their way around the side of the house and disappear off down the chestnut drive. Well, now he could take Peggy by surprise and help her pick some blackberries. He smiled to himself, remembering that time she'd surprised him, before they were married, when he'd been fishing at Flasher's Pool. Clinched things, that had. Well it was a lovely, warm afternoon, and Spring Field was, as Peg had said, miles from anywhere.

*   *   *

Jean Jenkins took a big basket and two plastic bags off the shelf in the shed, locked up the house, and set off at a smart pace down Macmillan Gardens. There was no one about, except for Joyce Davie, who was working on the central flower beds, a job she had taken over after old Fred Mills had died. In the high summer, the beds had been patriotic, with red salvias, and clumps of blue lobelia and white alyssum, all neatly planted in rows. Old Ellen complained that it was like the Council park in Tresham, but Doris said that as Ellen didn't have to look at them, she needn't find fault. Joyce Davie hadn't cared what anyone thought, and treated the beds as her own garden. Now she pulled out dead plants and forked the earth neatly for the winter.

'Lovely day,' she called to Jean, and straightened up, stretching her back. 'You off shopping?'

'Nope, blackberrying,' said Jean, slowing down.

'Nice,' said Joyce. 'D'you want some company?'

Jean hesitated. She didn't feel at ease with Joyce. A funny woman, she'd always said to Foxy. But there'd been all those long years when Joyce wouldn't even speak over the garden fence, so she nodded. 'If you can be quick,' she said. 'I've got to be back for the children coming out of school.'

Conversation was easier than Jean had expected. Joyce and Donald had been away for a couple of weeks on a coach tour of Scotland, and she happily rattled on to Jean about lochs and mountains, and the length of tweed she'd bought at a roadside weaver's and the whisky bottle that Donald had dropped outside the hotel in Inverness, sending a stream of golden liquid into the gutter.

'He was actually crying,' she said to Jean. 'Tears streaming down his face.'

Jean thought privately that only wimpy Donald would cry over whisky, but she nodded. 'Shame,' she said. 'What a waste.'

Joyce turned to hold Jean's basket while she clambered down from the stile that wobbled under her weight, and then they were in Spring Field. It was an ancient pasture, not ploughed up in living memory, and took its name from a spring that rose in one corner, flowing into a brick cistern built more than a hundred years ago to collect water for stock. It was a holy spring, according to village legend, and renowned in its time for curing diseases of horses, especially their eyes. Jean was thinking of this, wondering if she should try it on Eddie's ears, when she saw a familiar figure walking along the stream towards the blackberry hedge. 'What's he doing here?' she said.

'Who? Where?' said Joyce.

'Bill. Over there, by the stream.'

'Oh God,' said Joyce. 'Don't particularly want to run into him at the moment.' Some days Joyce laid in wait for Bill, accosting him in the Gardens and keeping him talking, reminding him of the past. At other times she would ignore him altogether, as if she couldn't bear the sight of him, and today was one of those days.

'Come on then,' said Jean, 'we'll go over that side by the trees first. Don't suppose he'll be around long. Then we can go on to the good place.' Looks like that's where he's heading,

87

thought Jean to herself, and regretted bringing Joyce. Could've had half a bagful by now. She always was an awkward woman. Reckon Bill's well shot of her.

*　　　*　'　*

The sun was warm on the back of Peggy's neck, as she bent down to pick large, juicy blackberries from a bramble near the ground. Bill was right, she thought. I've never seen such blackberries. She drifted off into a daydream about other times she had been blackberrying with her mother and then Frank. Frank . . . she hardly thought about him these days, and it was some time since she'd changed the flowers on his grave. It's not that I don't miss you, Frank, she thought. Well, maybe it is that. Life goes by so quickly, and there's so much to think about. And then there's this pain in my side, Frank.

She made a conscious effort to forget all of it, the memories of Frank, the problems in the shop, the pain . . .

The hedgerow above her was a rare find. Nowadays the farmers cut and trimmed the field hedges until they looked as neat and tidy as Hampton Court maze. All very well, as Ivy Beasley said loud and often, but where were the blackberries, the crab apples, the hips and haws? Well, thought Peggy, they're all here. It was Ted Bates's hedge, left to grow into a treasure trove of wild plants and fruits. Sloes

88

hung like grapes, their purplish blue skins frosted over with bloom, nearly ripe and ready to be doused in sugar and gin. Must have some of those too, thought Peggy. Just the thing for carol singing on frosty nights.

There had been an early fall of crab apples, still yellow and some of them squashed by Peggy's boots, but those remaining on the tree would soon be ripe enough for the delicate pink jelly that Ivy made every year. Jars of it turned up at bring-and-buy sales, and were quickly snapped up. Nobody uses hips and haws now, thought Peggy, but she remembered picking rosehips with a girlfriend one autumn long ago. The local pharmaceutical company in Coventry would pay, they said, and the two schoolgirls had walked out one golden morning, beyond the suburbs and into surrounding Warwickshire countryside to pick the orange-red berries. They had picked quantities, and had been amazed at how little they weighed. The reward was small, but it hadn't mattered. The day had been magical.

'Peg?' Bill's voice made her start, and she dropped a handful of blackberries, a vicious bramble snagging the skin on her leg.

'Bill! What are you doing here?'

'Come to look for my own true love,' said Bill. He was pleased to see her smile. She looked relaxed and warm, her blue eyes clear and welcoming, her face pink with a light film of moisture on her upper lip. He leaned forward, took her by the shoulders, and gently licked the salty dampness away. Then he kissed her, and was delighted to feel her arms tighten around him. There'd not been much enthusiasm in her responses lately, but this looked like being a bit of all right.

'Ouch!' said Peggy, pulling out a crackling stem of cow parsley from underneath her. She began to giggle, and Bill tickled her cheek with a soft, downy piece of grass seedhead.

'I love you, Peggy Turner,' he said.

'Truth?' said Peggy, holding his head away from her and looking into his eyes, suddenly serious.

'Always will,' he said, and with the warm sun on his back and his beloved wife so close, he left her in no doubt.

Peggy, her pain and Frank forgotten, did not notice the spilt basket of blackberries until much later.

* * *

'Well!' said Joyce Davie.

'Sshh!' said Jean Jenkins. 'They don't know we're here!'

'I should hope not,' said Joyce. Her face was tight and sharp, and Jean wished heartily that she'd never brought her along. What on earth am I going to do now? she thought. Her dilemma was solved by the Jenkins terrier, who had set out to find Jean, following her scent through the fields, and had come upon her just at this moment with a joyous bark.

'Come on,' whispered Jean, suddenly fiercely authoritative. 'This way. There's another hedge in the next field, nearly as good. Come on, Joyce, be quick about it. And don't make no noise. Dog could be on his own, chasing rabbits. They've not stood up, so come on, Joyce, come this way. Quick sharp!'

She practically bundled Joyce Davie back over the stile and set off at a brisk march away from the embarrassing scene behind them. But not really embarrassing, she thought. Why shouldn't they? They were married, after all. And she remembered vividly the wonderful afternoons she'd spent with Foxy in the hay meadows when they were courting. The sweet smell of dry hay was the best turn-on she'd ever come across. And the sun, the sun on their backs and faces. Crumbs, nothing like it ... She sniffed and made a mental note to suggest to Foxy a picnic down here on Sunday, if the weather held. Without the children, if poss ...

CHAPTER TWELVE

The drawing-room of the old vicarage was no longer its calm, spacious, dignified self. Piles of tea-chests and boxes stood in no apparent order on the parquet floor that Jean Jenkins had polished so conscientiously. A pair of garden steps leaned crazily against the elegant marble fireplace, and a battered tricycle blocked the narrow way left by the removals men.

In the midst of all this stood Annie Bishop, smiling broadly, her arm round the narrow shoulders of her eldest child, Faith, whose smooth brown hair remained miraculously in place under the black velvet hairband, and whose smile directed at her mother was at once loving and trusting.

'First of all, Faith,' said Annie, giving her a squeeze, 'the very first thing we shall do in our new house is what we planned. Remember?' She turned and pulled an old sheet off the upright piano, still to find its final resting place. It rocked a little on the uneven floor. 'Now, are you ready?' she said, lifting the lid, and drawing Faith to her side.

There was no piano stool, no chair even, so they stood, and with a mutual nod of the head, they began to play. It was a simple duet, carefully practised for this occasion, and gradually the family assembled at the door to listen. Andrew, holding three-year-old Honor up to see over the furniture, Helen with a doll clutched anxiously in her arms, and Bruce holding Tinker, a bounding mongrel rescued from patrolling London streets.

Annie and Faith reached the end with a flourish, and were rewarded by a round of applause from Andrew and a tactless howl from Tinker, who was quickly removed by Bruce before he found his full voice.

'Lovely, darlings!' said Andrew, and Annie beamed.

'I want my tea,' said Honor. 'I'm hungry.'

'Very soon,' said Annie. 'Nice Mrs Jenkins has left us some cake and sandwiches, and it won't take a minute for the kettle to boil. And then it's out into the garden for all young ones, while Daddy and I get on with sorting out.'

'I want my tea now,' said Honor. 'Now, now, now . . .'

'That's enough,' said Andrew, putting her down in the hall, and patting her bottom lightly. 'Go and see if you can find that nice doggie from next door. He's always around somewhere.'

Honor looked him in the eye, and opened her mouth. '*I want my tea now!*' she yelled, and stamped her small foot.

'Well, you can't have it yet!' shouted Annie Bishop, emerging from the drawing-room. 'Just shut up and wait!' And then she found her smile again, and disappeared into the kitchen to fill the kettle.

*   *   *

There were no curtains yet at the windows of the Bishops' large, high-ceilinged bedroom, and the absolute darkness and silence pressed

93

in on the couple lying side by side in the roughly made-up bed. It was like a desert island in the middle of a sea of open drawers and heaps of clothes, unsorted piles of towels, sheets and pillowcases.

'Andrew,' said Annie, tentatively.

'Yes, my love,' said Andrew, turning towards her and kissing her affectionately on the cheek.

'Is it going to be all right, Andrew?'

'Of course it is,' said Andrew, smoothing back Annie's long, silky hair. 'Going well, so far, isn't it? Bound to be chaos at first. Inevitable.'

Annie sat up and peered at him, just making out the pale oval of his face in the darkness. 'Mrs Jenkins was very kind, wasn't she? The children seem to have taken to her already.'

'Very kind,' said Andrew, yawning. 'Must see she gets well paid for all she did.'

Annie was silent for a minute, but remained sitting up in bed, her head turned to the window. 'How quiet it is,' she said. 'Even in the middle of the night in London it was never really quiet. Tearaways on motorbikes . . . late-night parties . . .'

'Police cars wailing every five minutes . . .' said Andrew.

At this moment Ivy Beasley's cat, out of her own territory and wary, raised her voice in fierce defence of her honour, snarling and spitting at the old farm cat from Bates's End.

He had fathered a succession of long-haired kittens who looked like nursery toys but proved to be untameable, and he pursued his quarry with a single-minded yowling that curdled the blood.

'Oh no,' said Annie, hearing a small, introductory cry from Honor. 'Now we shall never get to sleep. You go, Andrew, she'll settle for you.' But Honor had cried in her sleep, and silence fell once more.

'It was nice of Richard Standing to come over to welcome us, wasn't it?' said Annie. 'And little Poppy will be a nice friend for Honor.'

'Too old,' said Andrew, sighing and smothering another yawn.

'Well, for Bruce, then,' said Annie.

'Mm,' said Andrew. 'Haven't met Mrs S. yet, have we? Wonder what she's like? Might be a nice friend for Annie . . .'

Annie didn't reply. She was thinking of her amiable neighbour in London, wondering if she was missing them already. Certainly Richard Standing was very pleasant, so there was a chance his wife could be at least as friendly. Older, of course . . .

'Quite attractive, wasn't he?' she said. 'Bit past his best, but in good shape?'

''Ish,' said Andrew, stretching out his own strong, well-muscled legs. 'Lie down, Annie, and let's get some sleep. Tomorrow's another day.'

CHAPTER THIRTEEN

Across the road from the old vicarage, Ellen Biggs had stationed herself with unashamed curiosity at her window to watch the Bishops move in. It had been an entertaining day, what with the big furniture van getting stuck in the entrance to the driveway, and then the dog having a set-to with poor old Ricky from next door. And then the children running all over the place, getting in the men's way and trying to carry things that were too heavy for them.

Better than the telly, thought Ellen, as she finally watched the lights going out from uncurtained windows across the way. She could see figures moving about in the main bedroom, and then that too was plunged into darkness. Ellen filled her hot-water bottle and began to get ready for bed. It took her a long time to undress, but she was used to this and reviewed the day as she pulled off her comfortable shoes and roomy knickers. It'll be strange havin' folk in the vicarage again. Still, should be a bit more life goin' on.

The wind had risen, and Ellen could hear it whistling in the chimney and rattling the small diamond panes in her windows. She shivered. That'll bring the leaves off the trees, she thought. All them chestnuts. Soon as it rains that'll be treacherous out there. She climbed into bed and pulled the covers up round her ears. Glad I'm not the Bishops, she thought. No carpets nor curtains in them great barnlike rooms. Her own lodge had been made comfortable and warm after she'd fallen in her icy kitchen and ended up in hospital. Now there were no cold draughts, and she still marvelled at the constant hot water and cosy chairs, no longer dreading the winter months ahead. Thank goodness I ain't movin' house, she thought. Still, they got plenty of money, from what I 'ear, so I don't 'ave to worry about them. She clutched her hot-water bottle to her chest, and began to drift into sleep. All I got to worry about, she thought, is what I'm goin' to give Ivy and Doris for tea t'morrer.

*   *   *

As Ellen had predicted, the next morning saw the village landscape changed overnight. Sycamores, which until yesterday had been thick with gold and red, were now showing bare branches clothed only with dense, parasitic ivy. Peggy, dreaming at her shop window, thought how warm and protective the ivy looked, when in reality it was a nasty, choking creeper. Expect there's a parallel to be drawn there, she thought, but couldn't be bothered to make it. Those ash trees down Bates's End look like scarecrows with bits of rag clinging to their bony arms. Bet it's tricky in the avenue, she reflected, seeing Ellen approach across the Green.

'Soon be a death trap,' said Ellen, struggling up the shop steps and failing to see the beauty of fallen leaves. 'One wet night, and that avenue turns to a slimy mess. Nearly went for a Burton when I come out this morning, and that was on them mossy stones.'

'Oh dear,' said Peggy. 'I'll get Bill to come down and sweep up for you. Can't have you falling again, Ellen.' She looked at the lined old face and thought sadly that one more fall could carry off the indomitable Ellen. She changed the subject. 'Still, the sun's coming out later, they said, so that should cheer us up. Now, what can I get for you? Your turn, is it?'

Ellen nodded. What a blessing Peggy Turner was. She'd had her rough times, and had come through. A good-looking woman, too, thought Ellen. Make a good pair, they do, Peggy and Bill. 'Yep,' she said, 'it's my turn to entertain happy, smiling Ivy Beasley.'

'And Doris,' said Peggy, trying not to laugh.

'Yep, and Doris. Our Doris gets it from both sides, if you know what I mean, dear. Still, she don't moan a lot. Takes all sorts, she says, and she's right. So 'ave you got one o' them coffee and walnut Mr Kipling's?'

Peggy helped Ellen put the boxed cake into her shopping bag.

'Mind if I rest me bum for a few minutes?' Ellen said, perching on the chair by the Post Office cubicle.

'That's what it's there for,' said Peggy,

thinking she could be getting on with ironing Bill's shirts instead of listening to Ellen's gossip. But the customer's always right, she told herself, even when it's old Ellen who doesn't exactly clear us out of stock. Like most other people in Round Ringford, Ellen did a weekly shop at the Supashop in Tresham, struggling up into the bus that picked up regulars round the villages and constituted a weekly social gathering for Ellen. When she'd been ill and unable to do her own shopping, she had sorely missed her weekly outing. And now, when it was all she could do to get from the bus stop to the supermarket, she refused even to contemplate accepting offers of help from Ivy and Doris. 'As long as I can get on me feet,' she said, 'I'll do me own. Couldn't trust you two to spot the bargains.' Ivy's sniff and Doris's worried look had no effect on Ellen, and she continued to be at the bus stop once a week in all weathers.

'You know Bill would always bring your shopping down to the lodge,' said Peggy. She'd got a few faithful customers who had a weekly order which Bill delivered every Friday after work. These were barely enough to keep the shop viable, but as long as they could stay on the right side of the red line and Bill had his job at the Hall, Peggy loved the daily routine, the children rushing in after school, the bringers of news, good and bad, and the feeling of being needed, useful, a proper villager.

Ellen pulled her unsuitable red hat down over her scratty grey hair and looked across at Peggy. 'I'd go mad, dear,' she said. 'Got to get out and about, see a bit o' life.'

Peggy opened small bags of silver and copper, and filled up the till drawers. 'Never seem to be enough pound coins,' she said, sorting them neatly into light, brassy rolls.

Ellen saw her opportunity and took it. 'Huh,' she said, 'pound coins is not in short supply in the old vicarage, I reckon.'

So that's it, thought Peggy. The Bishops are the subject for this morning's gossip. She knew Ellen would not be the only one, the whole village in their different ways having monitored the new arrivals. Mr Ross from Bagley Road had found that his dog needed two constitutionals yesterday, and William Roberts had kicked his football up and down the lane for a good half-hour, having a good stare as he passed the vicarage drive. When the removals men told him to bugger off, he claimed he was waiting for his mum who was helping out in the house, which was, of course, a lie.

'So did they settle in safely, Ellen?' said Peggy, wondering how long this was going to take.

Ellen nodded. 'All quiet by ten o'clock,' she said.

'It'll be nice for you, having people in the vicarage again,' suggested Peggy, but Ellen

100

shook her head.

'Could be,' she said, 'but on the other 'and, could be worse than nobody. We shall see.'

Ellen hobbled down the steps, clutching her bag, but stopped halfway. 'Peggy dear,' she called. 'I've forgotten the Typhoon. Ivy drinks more than a camel. Gi' me a packet, and I'll pay t'morrer.' The tea joined the cake in the old brown bag, and Ellen reached the bottom step safely. Unfortunately, at that moment Eddie Jenkins, tired of kicking wind-blown leaves at his faithful terrier, and not looking where he was going, ran into Ellen. She grabbed the rail by the shop steps, and managed to keep her balance.

Eddie looked at her, appalled at what might have happened. 'You all right, missus?' he said.

'No thanks to you, Eddie Jenkins,' she said. 'Just you look where you're goin', my lad.'

'Sorry,' he said, and stood looking disconsolately at Ellen's retreating back.

'Eddie!' called Peggy, who had seen it all. 'Come here a minute. Mrs Biggs has forgotten her purse. Run and catch up with her, there's a love.' Eddie took the purse, and, anxious to make amends, chased after Ellen. As Peggy watched, she saw Ellen stop, and after a moment's hesitation and some words from Eddie, the old woman handed over her shopping bag, and the incongruous pair, closely followed by the Jenkins terrier, continued over the Green in the direction of

Ellen's lodge.

*   *   *

By the time Ivy and Doris stepped out towards
Bates's End, the sun had come out and warmed
the village into life. 'Lovely afternoon,' said
Doris, adjusting her stride to keep up with Ivy's
quick march.

'Getting colder,' said Ivy. 'Frost tonight, if
you ask me.'

Oh dear, thought Doris, it's going to be one
of those afternoons. 'I hope not,' she said.
'Haven't got my geraniums in yet. Mind you, a
little ground frost doesn't do much harm.'

'Waste of time keeping them,' said Ivy,
glancing sideways at her friend. In fact, Ivy
always brought in her geraniums, keeping them
in the outhouse behind the kitchen until the
early summer. But contrariness was the order
of the day, and she repeated, 'Waste of time,
Doris. Might as well chuck them in the bin and
buy new ones next year.'

'I don't agree,' said Doris bravely. There's a
limit, she thought. 'Mine always have a good
sleep on the spare room windowsill all winter,
and they come up smiling in June.'

'Smiling!' said Ivy. 'You'll be telling me you
kiss them goodnight next. I suppose you're one
of the talking-to-plants brigade. All a lot of
nonsense, Doris, and you know it.'

Doris sighed. Try another tack, she thought.
'Don't you love autumn, Ivy?' she said. 'It's my

102

favourite time of the year. Bonfires, sweeping up leaves, chrysanthemums, the children getting excited about fireworks...' The moment she'd said it, she knew it was a mistake.

'Fireworks!' exploded Ivy. 'Well, Doris, you know what I think about those nasty, dangerous things. And I suppose they'll be asking me to organise the jumble sale to raise money to burn, as usual.'

Doris nodded. 'Nobody else can do it as well as you, Ivy,' she said, hating herself. 'You've got it down to a fine art now. Anyway, you'll come up for the soup and sausages, won't you?'

But Ivy was opening Ellen's small iron gate with a clatter, walking swiftly up the path. 'Well, that'll depend,' she said, and knocked more firmly than was necessary on Ellen's front door.

*   *   *

'That was very nice, thank you,' said Doris, wiping her lips with a small, lace-edged handkerchief. 'And a very good cup of tea, Ellen.'

'Typhoon,' said Ellen. 'Never buy anything else. Another cup, Ivy?'

'No, it'll be too stewed now,' Ivy said gracelessly, 'but I'll relieve you of a slice more of Mr Kipling's best, if you like.'

Doris avoided Ellen's gaze, and the old

woman cut as small a piece as possible, with no walnut, and slid it on to Ivy's plate.

'Thought you didn't like shop bought,' Ellen said, looking balefully at Ivy.

'Doing you a favour,' Ivy replied. 'Goes stale in a couple of days. Not like home made. Home made'll last a couple of weeks in a good tin.'

'No need to last, with an appetite like yours, Ivy,' said Ellen.

'All right, all right,' said Doris, getting to her feet and going over to the window. 'I didn't come here to listen to you two bickering. I'll have to be off now, anyway. Jean Jenkins asked me to sit in with Eddie while the rest go off to the pictures. Not a suitable film for young Eddie, Jean says.'

'Proper parents, they are,' said Ellen. 'Foxy and Jean have brought up them kids in the old way, and they'll reap the benefit.' She was thinking about Eddie, carrying her shopping and making sure she was safe inside the lodge before running off with his dog.

'They do it for love,' said Doris, 'not for rewards.' She'd babysat for Jean and Foxy since the early days, and seen the children flourish like flowers under a warm sun.

Ivy rose and joined Doris at the window. 'Don't talk to me about bringing up kids,' she said. 'In my time, things were very different.'

'You ain't 'ad no kids, so 'ow d'yer know?' said Ellen cruelly.

'I know how my mother and father brought me up,' began Ivy, and Doris groaned to herself. Oh no, not that old story. But they were spared Ivy's reminiscences of the unrelenting Beasleys by the sight of Annie Bishop crossing the road and pushing open Ellen's gate.

'Well, I never,' said Ivy. 'Hasn't taken her long to come asking for a cup of sugar, has it?'

'Don't be silly,' said Doris. 'Do you want me to go to the door, Ellen?'

Annie Bishop didn't wait to be asked in, and in no time at all she was sitting on the sofa accepting a slice of cake from a bemused Ellen Biggs. 'How lovely,' said Annie. 'I do hope I haven't interrupted your tea party, but I just had to come over and say hello.'

'Not to borrow anything?' said Ivy rudely.

Annie Bishop's eyes opened wide. 'Goodness no,' she said. She looked directly at Ivy Beasley and smiled her irresistible smile. 'I don't think I've had the pleasure, Mrs er . . .?'

'No, you haven't,' said Ivy, and turned to Doris. 'Come along,' she said, 'else you'll be late for the Jenkinses,' and without a further word, she took Doris's arm and left.

'But we haven't said thank you to Ellen, or helped her with the washing-up,' protested Doris, as they reached the gate.

'I'm sure Mrs Goody Twoshoes will have Ellen's dishes sparkling clean in no time,' said Ivy acidly. 'Let's hope we don't get no extra visitors next week. Your turn, I think, Doris.'

CHAPTER FOURTEEN

One week later another removal took place with little fuss and a great deal of goodwill from the residents of Macmillan Gardens. Old Fred's house was occupied at last, and with one of the Gardens' own. Sandra Goodison, formerly Roberts, moved back to the village with her husbnd Sam and small daughter, Alison.

It was a miserable, foggy Saturday, but one of Sam's mates from the building company borrowed a van and made a couple of cheerful trips from Tresham with the Goodisons' few pieces of furniture. Having lived with Sam's parents since Alison was born, they had needed nothing much of their own, and the decision to move back to Ringford had meant withdrawing most of their slender building society account. A visit to the furniture warehouse had equipped them with the necessities, and then it was a case of scrounging round to see what they could beg or borrow. Sam was popular with his workmates, and they had come up with a respectable sofa and two armchairs. Mrs Roberts, Sandra's mother, had dipped into her savings from her job at the school, and bought them a washing machine. This was quite a sacrifice, and Sandra knew it, but the Robertses were not given to flowery speeches of gratitude. 'Thanks, Mum,' was all Sandra said when the machine arrived, but for Renata

Roberts that was more than enough from a daughter who had been a constant worry for most of her teenage years.

Alison had been the reason for Sam and Sandra marrying at such an early age, but all the prophets of doom had been confounded, and the young couple were devoted to each other and, of course, to Alison. Even Michael Roberts, not at all pleased about being a grandfather so soon, had been heard to say in the Arms that his little grand-daughter was quite exceptionally pretty and gifted.

By midday, most of their furniture was in place, and boxes of clothes and crockery, one or two pictures, and a large box of Alison's toys, stood waiting to be unpacked.

'Mum said to go up there for dinner,' Sandra said, 'but I said no, we'd have plenty to do here. Can you nip in to Bagley, Sam, and get a takeaway?'

'Why don't we go down to the pub?' said Sam, thinking he and his mate could happily sink a couple of pints right away.

'You go,' said Sandra. 'I'll stay here with Alison. We can get something from the shop. Mrs Turner said to pop in if we had time.'

Her mother's invitation had faced Sandra with a problem that had kept her awake for several nights. Moving back to Ringford was fine. She had been born in the village, and felt at home there. But like most of its young people, at one time she couldn't wait to get out of it. In time, though, on summer mornings in Tresham, with only a tiny back garden and the scrubby local park for Alison to play in, Sandra had thought nostalgically of the broad, clean turf of Ringford Green, the walk through Bagley Woods, the ducks swimming noisily under the old stone bridge down Bates's End.

She was not, however, in the least nostalgic about her parents—well, about her father, who had more than once knocked her from one side of the room to the other—nor about their untidy, unkempt house in Macmillan Gardens. 'If we go back to Ringford,' she had said to Sam, 'they're not livin' in our pockets. You know Mum. Any excuse for a cup of tea.' She did not tell him that she had privately vowed that her house was going to be a real home. Clean, pretty, warm and welcoming, all the things her parents' was not.

'Right, we'll be off, then,' said Sam. 'Then we'll get stuck into the unpacking this afternoon.' He kissed the top of Alison's smooth, dark head, her hair the exact colour of her mother's. 'Cheers, poppet, be good and help Mum. Back soon, then, Sandra.'

Sandra put down her duster and walked out into old Fred's back garden. It would take some fixing, but Sam was keen, and they couldn't do much in the winter anyway. Clear the ground, and cut back some of the overgrown shrubs.

In the cold, misty air, Sandra took a deep breath, and was suddenly overwhelmed with a sense of old Fred's presence. She'd loved to call on him and his sister. Her earliest memory—she must have been about three—was sitting on Fred's lap and looking at an old picture book. She remembered the strange clothes, the long curls of the little girls and soppy faces of the boys. And the smell of Fred, of the garden and greenhouse, a lingering smell of leeks and beer and tobacco.

'Well, then, Fred,' she said aloud, 'here we are again. Let's hope it's goin' to work out.'

*   *   *

Bill was behind the counter of the shop fixing a new neon strip, his back to Sandra as she came in holding Alison's hand.

'Lo, Mr Turner,' Sandra said.

Bill turned round and smiled broadly. 'Now then,' he said, 'how's it going? Need any help?'

Sandra shook her head. 'Nope, thanks,' she said. 'Sam and Jim've done most of the big stuff. We just got to unpack now.'

'I'm hungry,' said Alison.

'Then you've come to the right place,' said Bill, and turned to call Peggy from the kitchen.

Sandra walked round the shelves, looking for baked beans and sausages, keeping Alison's hands off the sweets and biscuits. It was a funny morning, thought Sandra. It's never happened before, but these things keep coming back. It was as clear as anything, that day Peggy and

109

Frank Palmer had taken over the shop, and Octavia Jones had shoplifted a comb and blamed Sandra. The thought that her Alison might go the same way filled Sandra with horror. 'Put that down at once!' she snapped, as her daughter took a pink plastic hair slide from the display carousel.

'She's not doing any harm,' said Peggy, coming in with a welcoming smile. 'Nice to see you, Sandra. Everything going all right?'

'Yep, thanks,' said Sandra. 'Alison and me need something to eat. Sam's gone to the pub, so I'll do some baked beans on toast. Alison could live on that!'

'Nonsense,' said Peggy. 'I've got a shepherd's pie in the Rayburn for Bill and me, and there's plenty for all of us. Come on into the kitchen, and Alison can help me set the table.' Peggy had been feeling sick all morning, and had thought maybe a good meal would do her good. She'd noticed that while she was eating, the nausea and the pain in her side went away. But it was not slow in coming back most days.

Bill looked at Sandra, in good shape now that her teenage podginess had gone. She'd never be a willowy girl like Octavia Jones, but she was well proportioned, with good legs and generous in all the right places. It's that hair, thought Bill, that shiny, blue-black hair, that makes you want to touch. He'd been fond of Sandra and sorry for her when she got into trouble. He remembered when she was five,

110

just started at the village school, and sobbing bitterly over a bloody gash in her leg. She'd been sitting on the pavement outside her house, and Bill had picked her up and taken her in to wash off the blood. Even then, she'd screamed that he was not to tell her dad. Bloody Roberts, thought Bill, and looked at Alison, same age as her mother had been then, same shiny black hair, same dark eyes. Alison'd be all right, though. Sam was a good lad. Bill followed behind into the kitchen, and reached out, stroking Alison's small head. 'Nice to have you back, Sandra,' he said. 'Anything we can do, just ask. Don't forget. We're always here, me and Peg.'

CHAPTER FIFTEEN

'Two new children for the school!' said Sarah to her husband John Barnett, as they sat having breakfast in the farm kitchen on Sunday morning. 'The eldest Bishop is going to private school over near Bagley, and Honor is too little, but the other two are starting tomorrow. They've had a week settling in, and their mother—seems a really nice woman—wants them to get to know the village children as soon as possible.'

'Village children?' said John, his tone caustic. 'Well, there'll be a real village child for the school when Alison Goodison comes along.

They moved in yesterday.'

Sarah took the plates to the sink and rinsed them quickly, leaving them on the drainer to dry. 'Oh yes, I forgot about Alison. Yes, she's starting tomorrow, too. I've met her father— Sam, is it?—but so far her mother hasn't appeared.'

'She's a Roberts,' said John, going over to the sink and putting his arms round Sarah's waist. 'And you know what that means, Mrs Headmistress? Means she has a lot to live down in this village. Give her a chance, eh?'

*   *   *

In Macmillan Gardens the church clock could be heard clearly. It had struck the hour some while ago, the reverberations stirring up the Jenkins household, but not fast enough.

'Hurry up, Mark!' shouted Jean Jenkins from the foot of the stairs. 'You'll be late for bell-ringing!' Mark had joined his brother Warren in the bell-ringing team, and had been slow to learn, but he had doggedly persisted and was now almost master of the service bells rung each Sunday. Jean returned to the kitchen. 'And Eddie, get your shoes on and stop teasing that dog.'

Foxy sat at the table, finishing his tea and reading yesterday's local evening paper. He looked up at Jean, and said, 'There's a bit about Colin Osman here.' She took the paper and began to read.

The bypass issue had gone quiet lately. Colin had desperately reviewed his statistics, trying in vain to increase the totals. The rest of the village grumbled about the traffic, but went about their business and tried not to notice. This was fairly easy for those who did not live in the High Street, but Ivy Beasley and Peggy and Bill, the Joneses and the Cutts at the pub, all breathed in petrol fumes and had their conversations interrupted by the constant flow. 'Just when you think there's a break, an' a bit o' peace, along comes another of the buggers.' Ted Bates's complaint was registered, based as it was on his long-held right to sit on the bench outside the pub, watching the village go by. But he was lucky, said the others, he did not have to suffer night and day, without a break.

'Poor old Colin,' said Jean. 'Looks like he's not havin' much luck.'

The news item was accompanied by a photograph of a miserable-looking Colin Osman standing outside the Council offices. He'd taken a preliminary report to Planning and Transportation, but had been politely shown the door. Nothing like enough traffic to warrant even an investigation for possible bypass plans. 'They've offered traffic calming,' Colin was reported as saying.

'Traffic calming? What the buggery is that?' said Foxy. 'Do we all stand out there with cups o' tea an' tranquillisers, or what?'

'It's them humps in the road, I expect,' said Jean.

'Bloody humps,' said Foxy grumpily. Why couldn't Ringford be let be? Why did everybody want to change it?

'Bloody humps,' said Eddie, coming in with one shoe on and the other dangling by a broken lace from his hand.

'Edward Jenkins!' said Jean. 'You see, Foxy? Just watch what you say with this lot around. Now then, Eddie, let's get you a new lace and then perhaps I can get a bit o' peace in number sixteen, never mind the traffic. Whoever said Sunday was a day of rest didn't have no kids.'

*   *   *

'Don't you think we could miss church, just for once?' said Andrew Bishop mildly. Annie stood in the long drawing-room holding coats and scarves, handing them out and encouraging their wearers to get a move on.

'Goodness, no, Andrew,' she said. 'It'll be lovely for the children. And living so close, there's no excuse! Just listen to those bells . . .'

She turned her lovely face to the open door. 'They're calling us, aren't they, Faith?' she said. 'Come—to—church, come—to—church . . . you can hear it, can't you, Brucie, darling?'

Bruce Bishop was struggling inside an anorak already zipped up before he put it over his head. 'Mummy!' His muffled voice fell on deaf ears as Annie rushed off to find coins for the collection from her purse.

Andrew Bishop quietly helped his small son emerge from the anorak, and buttoned up Honor's little tweed coat with gentle hands. 'There you are, sweetheart,' he said. 'Now, wait for Mummy, and then we'll be off.' Andrew Bishop was a patient man.

The Reverend Nigel Brooks had already processed from the vestry to his seat in the chancel when the heavy oak door creaked open and the Bishops crept in. Annie's apologetic smile took in Ivy, Doris and Ellen in the back pew, Mr Ross, churchwarden, and Peggy Turner sitting with Doreen Price. Anxious as Annie Bishop was to get everyone sitting down quietly, she did not fail to recognise the bulky figure of Richard Standing, sitting at the front with his elegant wife and squirming daughter.

'O, worship the King, all glorious above,' sang the small congregation, as Annie Bishop leafed through hymn books and handed them to the children, all of whom stared curiously round the little church. St Mary's was six centuries old, and had been built alongside a large Cistercian priory. Only grassy mounds and a crumbling well-head remained to show where fifteen hundred monks had prayed and become hopelessly corrupt. The balk ponds were still there, where the brothers had fished for golden carp, pounced on village girls, and then helped them bury the innocent results in the priory fields' deepest ditches.

The church remained, however, small and squat, with four shaky pinnacles on its square tower. Inside, it was whitewashed and light, smelling of wax polish and Brasso. A small band of ladies obeyed the rota pinned up in the porch, cleaned candlesticks and crosses and arranged flowers as they had been taught in their classes in the village hall. They were the backbone of church life in Ringford, and they were there this morning, singing without needing to look at their books, the words ingrained in their hearts. This, naturally, gave them a chance to look round at the Bishops, surreptitiously of course, but with quick glances they took in the row of children, Annie at one end and Andrew at the other, filling the pew in a very satisfactory way.

'That'll be a bit more in the collection,' said Ellen Biggs to Doris in a harsh, perfectly audible whisper.

'Keep her quiet, for goodness' sake,' mouthed Ivy to Doris.

Doris, sitting between her two friends, cast as arbiter as usual, frowned. 'Shut up, Ellen,' she whispered, and then looked at Ivy. 'You too, Ivy,' she said, and took refuge in the last line of the hymn, which she sang loudly, looking straight ahead at the sun shining through the bright colours of the east window.

'The Lord be with you,' intoned Nigel Brooks.

'And with thy spirit,' replied Richard Standing. He'd heard the door, the whispering children, Annie's heels clacking on the stone floor, and wanted to look round, but Susan was sending him mute appeals for help in subduing Poppy, and he resisted the temptation.

'Almighty God, unto whom all hearts be open, all desires known . . .' said Nigel Brooks, leading his congregation.

Ye Gods, thought Richard Standing, not much hope for me, then. He had this compulsive urge to look round at Annie Bishop. It was like a flea bite that just had to be scratched. His small daughter came to his rescue by dropping her book over the back of the pew, so that he had to turn round and accept it apologetically from Peggy Turner behind. There was plenty of time for a good look at the Bishops. He noted Annie's light hair, pleasantly awry with the last-minute rush, and her eyes reflecting the cornflower blue of her jacket. And—oh yes!—that one-sided smile as she caught his eye.

'Richard!' hissed Susan beside him. 'Don't stare!'

The congregation knelt for the Kyrie, and then sang the Gloria lustily to the old tune. Nigel Brooks had tried, like many another newly appointed village parson, to introduce new music, but in a way that he couldn't quite pinpoint, they had reverted to the familiar chants. Gabriella Jones, enthusiastic at the organ, claimed to have nothing to do with it, saying she was sure he had himself made the decision. The backbone ladies just smiled.

The Bishop children trailed up to the altar rail with their parents, and bowed their small heads for the blessing. And then at last they were out in the winter sunshine, grouped together in the church porch, being greeted by Mr Richard in a very friendly fashion.

'You must come for a drink,' he said, and felt Susan's angry finger in his ribs. He ignored it. 'What are you doing this evening, about six?'

It was clear that a drink was all that was on offer, and Andrew Bishop declined with a feeble excuse. 'Lukewarm gin and a soggy crisp,' he said to a pained Annie when they returned to the old vicarage. 'That's all we've missed. And anyway, what I said was quite true. It is the children's teatime, and we don't have umpteen servants to look after them while we gad about for drinks.'

'Gad about?' said Annie. 'Darling . . . If what you say is true, you could hardly describe it as gadding about. I just think it was a neighbourly gesture, and a tiny bit rude of you to refuse. Still, I'm sure there'll be another occasion. Come along, gang! Let's see how lunch is doing.'

Annie had, of course, cooked on an Aga before, but this one was solid fuel, and temperamental. She'd riddled and stoked before they set off for church, and left it on full draught to raise the oven temperature. Now a distant bubbling noise alarmed her, and when she opened the fire door and saw a red hot furnace, she called in panic for Andrew. 'The water's boiling!' she said. 'Do something, Andrew, for goodness' sake!'

Andrew forbore to say that he had advised against leaving the damper open for over an hour, and went patiently upstairs to run off the spitting, steaming water.

The beef was dry and tasteless, but Annie made a large jugful of rich gravy, and with roast potatoes and garlic popped out of its skin, the family sat round the big pine table and ate with a good appetite.

'Isn't this wonderful, children?' Annie said happily. 'Shall we all go for a long walk this afternoon? What do you think, Andrew? Tinker would love to chase rabbits, don't you think, Brucie?' She cleared their plates and put a large, only slightly burnt apple pie on the table. 'Now, who's for pudding?' There were no refusals, and when the dishes were stacked in the machine, and hands and faces washed, Annie repeated her suggestion for a walk.

'Perhaps we could go up by the Hall and across the field,' she said. 'There's a footpath, and Richard Standing said we were welcome to use it any time.' Andrew looked at her sharply, but her expression was pleasant and bland, as always.

CHAPTER SIXTEEN

Cold weather was on the way from the west, said the early forecast, and the sky over Bagley Woods was heavy. A chill wind blew through the bare sycamore in the school playground, stirring its twiggy outline and chasing flights of sparrows as they swooped down to Peggy's birdtable. They squabbled over birdseed and breadcrumbs, perched on the head of a stone frog in the birdbath, dipped their tiny beaks and then retreated rapidly from the flying droplets sent up by a vigorously bathing starling.

Peggy had the radio on, turned down low, in order not to wake Bill. She'd been up very early with the usual nagging ache, and crept down to make a cup of tea. As she stood watching the birds from her kitchen window, Bill appeared, tousled and wrapped in his dressing-gown.

'Why didn't you come back to bed?' he said. He'd heard Peggy go downstairs and decided to feign sleep. She was liable to be very irritable first thing, and he was learning when to keep quiet.

'No reason,' she said lightly. 'I thought I'd iron your work shirt for this morning, and then just carried on. There was quite a pile . . . and I made this cup of tea . . . do you want one?'

Bill shook his head. 'No thanks,' he said, and continued, 'you only had to ask, you know, and I'd have brought you one in bed. By closing

120

time, you'll be done in.'

Peggy's face silenced Bill, and he allowed her to change the subject. They chatted companionably over breakfast, and while Peggy prepared to open up the shop, Bill got his bike out of the shed. 'Time you were off,' shouted Peggy, but he fiddled about, saying he needed to oil the gears, and generally putting off going to work and leaving Peggy on her own.

I'll just see she's all right to start the day, he said under his breath, then I'll go. Mr Richard will understand.

*   *   *

Bill's late, thought Foxy Jenkins, coming down Bates's End on his outsize tractor. He often met him by the bridge at this time of day, could set his watch by him. Sometimes Foxy pulled up for a chat. Both worked for the estate, and anything that couldn't be discussed in the Arms in the evenings, was sorted out on Ringford bridge before the day's work began. But Foxy's concern about Bill was quickly interrupted by the terrier perched beside him, balancing like a circus dog. He set up a shrill barking and throaty growls at the Bishops' dog standing sentinel at the vicarage gates, and Foxy made a grab as the terrier prepared to spring suicidally into the road. It was all Foxy could do to restrain and steer at the same time. He forgot about Bill, and concentrated on the road.

At this inconvenient moment, a container lorry took the wrong turn on the green and approached Foxy at speed. The lane was hardly wide enough for the tractor, and certainly too narrow for the lorry to pass. With great presence of mind, Foxy turned sharply into the side road by the school house, only just avoiding a hideous accident.

'Blimey!' he said, pulling up and wiping his brow. What the bloody hell was that bloke doin' down Bates's End? There he was now, trying to reverse the bloody great thing into the vicarage drive. Supposin' one of them new kids had been playin' outside? Foxy shuddered at the possibilities. Maybe there was something in what Colin Osman was trying to do, but traffic calming wouldn't have stopped that silly bugger takin' a wrong turnin'. Foxy drove in a circle on the green, leaving tyre marks on the turf that would take weeks to vanish, and headed back to the bridge. He gripped the wheel hard, noticing with dismay that his hands were shaking.

*   *   *

Peggy Turner, standing at her open shop door, had seen the lorry turn off and Foxy approaching from the other direction. 'Bill!' she yelled, as if he could do something about it. By the time he'd joined her at the door, Foxy had taken his rapid evasive action and the crisis was past.

'That was close,' said Bill. 'It's getting serious, all this traffic. Osman's right—but what's to be done? He's banging his head against a brick wall up at County Hall.'

Peggy reached up to kiss Bill's cheek, and was surprised when he put his arms round her and hugged her tight. 'Hey!' she said. 'Anybody could see!'

'So?' said Bill. He kissed her very lovingly and held her hands in his. 'Just take it easy this morning, gel,' he said. 'See if you can sit down for a bit in the kitchen when there's no one in the shop.' He wheeled his bicycle out on to the road and set off, turning to wave at Peggy when he reached the turn to the Hall.

Feeling rotten about deceiving her kindly husband, Peggy took out a letter she had hidden behind the kitchen clock. It was an appointment at Tresham hospital for a scan, and although she knew the contents off by heart, she unfolded it once more. Friday, 2.30 p.m., it said. How was she going to get there without telling Bill? And Mary York, her usual helper in the shop, had another job on Friday afternoons.

The bell jangled, and Peggy put the letter back behind the clock. She went into the shop to find Sandra Goodison standing by the counter. 'Hello, Sandra,' she said. 'You're an early bird this morning.'

'Just taken Alison in to school,' she said.

'Her first morning . . .'

Ah, thought Peggy, so that's why those dark eyes look a bit moist. 'Hasn't she been at school in Tresham?' she said.

'Oh yes,' said Sandra, 'but she'd got loads of friends there. All lived in our road. She don't know anybody here yet. Still,' she added, picking up a packet of mints, 'this should cheer her up when she comes out this afternoon.'

'All settled in now?' said Peggy.

'Yep,' said Sandra. 'Sam's gone off to work this morning. I'm hoping to get a job meself once Alison's all right in school. We need the money, Mrs T., I can tell you that!'

Peggy remembered when Sandra had first gone out with Sam. She hadn't yet left school, and opposition from her father had been extreme and, of course, violent. But in spite of a new baby when she had been scarcely an adult herself, Sandra had tackled marriage with a will, more than relieved to have got away from her father. Money had been tight. Sam had insisted on paying a large slice of his building worker's wages to his parents for bed and board, and they'd saved what was left for the day when they would have their own home. Those savings now used up, the bills of the household would begin to arrive, and Sandra was anxious to be prepared.

As Peggy waited for Sandra to browse through the basket of reduced lines, she had an idea. I don't see why it shouldn't work, she

124

thought. Could do us both a bit of good.

'Sandra,' she said, 'I suppose you wouldn't like to fill in here in the shop for the odd morning or afternoon?'

Sandra's reaction was a broad smile. 'Do you think I could do it, Mrs T.?' she said, but added quickly, 'What about Mrs York, though?' Mary York had helped out for as long as Sandra could remember, and Octavia had always chosen Mary's days for shoplifting adventures. 'She's a doddle,' she'd say to Sandra, instructing her on diversionary tactics.

'Mary's got a part-time job at the garden centre now,' said Peggy. 'Can't always help me here. So it would be useful, if you think you might like it?'

Sandra grinned. 'I'd like anything that pays,' she said. 'And anyway, I rather fancy being behind the counter, Mrs T. I'd really like that.'

'Good,' said Peggy. 'Then maybe you could do Friday afternoon? It's half-day for the Post Office, and I've got some shopping to do. It more or less has to be then,' she tailed off.

'OK,' said Sandra, so delighted with the idea that it did not occur to her to wonder why shopping had to be done on a Friday afternoon. 'Would it be all right if Alison came in here after school, just until you get back?'

'Of course,' said Peggy. 'I should be home around four, or maybe sooner. I'm not quite sure how long I'll take.' Not too long, she thought. Hope it'll be quick and simple. She hated hospitals, knew there was likely to be a long wait, and dreaded that all-pervasive smell.

'Well, that's settled, then, Sandra,' she said, and smiled weakly. 'Thanks very much.'

'Did you see that lorry?' said Sandra, cheerful now, and ready for a gossip. It was in her blood, and back here in Ringford with new confidence as a married woman, she happily took up the family tradition. 'Foxy Jenkins nearly bought it, didn't he! It's a disgrace, I reckon. They ought to do something about it. Thank goodness Alison was safe in the playground.' She paid for her purchases, said again that she really looked forward to Friday and would come early so Mrs T. could show her the ropes.

'You can take your time in Tresham,' she said encouragingly. 'Enjoy the afternoon while you got the chance!'

CHAPTER SEVENTEEN

'Morning, Mrs Bishop,' said Jean Jenkins, tying on her apron and looking around the kitchen. The old vicarage was quiet, all the children safely in school, and Annie Bishop stood by the back door, dog lead in hand. 'Tinker bin for a walk?' said Jean, her voice muffled as she bent down, hunting for a duster in the cupboard under the sink.

'Dusters are in the scullery, Jean,' said

Annie. She'd asked in a very nice way if she could use her Christian name, and of course Jean had said yes, feeling at the same time that it wouldn't have made any difference if she'd said no. 'We're just about to set off,' continued Annie. 'I thought I'd wait until you arrived, so I could tell you what's urgent. Then it'll be walkies time ...' she patted the dog's head affectionately, and he wagged his tail violently in reply. 'Mr Bishop left early this morning, Jean. His first day as a commuter!' Her tone was friendly, conversational.

'Yes, well,' said Jean Jenkins. 'I'll be getting on, then. I have to be up at the Hall by eleven, so what would you like me to do?'

Annie bent down and clipped on the dog lead. 'A general dust round, for a start,' she said. 'And then if you could make the children's beds and tidy up the toys. This floor could do with a good scrub, and there's scraps of paper all over the drawing-room floor where Bruce was cutting out tractors for his scrap book. We thought it would help him with his friends at school if he mugged up on farming!' Jean was swallowing hard, and about to reply with a dusty answer, when Annie continued. 'There's a big pile of washing to go into the machine. And the children's clean pyjamas need ironing for tonight.'

Jean took a deep breath, controlled herself with difficulty, and said, 'Just a minute, Mrs Bishop. I said I could give you an hour and a half before I go up to the Hall. That's just enough time to dust around, do the carpets, and maybe wash this floor with a mop. The rest I'm afraid you'll have to do yourself. Or find someone else . . .' she added. She meant there to be a lurking threat in there. There was no one else. Cleaning help was like gold-dust in Ringford.

Annie Bishop did not answer straight away. She put the dog out into the garden, came back in and shut the door. Pulling a chair out from under the table, she sat down, deliberately and slowly. 'Do sit down, Jean,' she said, motioning her to one of the other chairs.

Jean frowned, began to say she'd better get started, but was interrupted by a firmer command to sit down.

'Now,' said Annie. 'I realise that we are very lucky to have help from you, and we appreciate that, but you will have seen that with this big house and four small children I have my hands more than full.' She smiled her disarming smile straight at Jean, who stared back at her, unmoved.

'I've only got one pair of hands, Mrs Bishop,' she said. 'An hour and a half is all I can spare.' She glanced at the clock on the wall. 'And a quarter of an hour of that is gone already.'

'But we must start off understanding one another,' said Annie smoothly. 'I shall put off my walk until this afternoon, and we'll see just what can be achieved in the time available.

Don't think I shall be checking on you! Goodness, I hope I know better than that. But I can help with your first morning, tell you where things are, and so on. All right, Jean? Shall we see how we go together?'

Get stuffed, thought Jean, but against her better judgement she nodded and stood up. 'Right, then,' she said. 'But this house ain't strange to me, you know. I bin cleanin' here since Reverend Collins's days, and him dead and buried more than two years ago. An' if you're not going out with that dog, you can show me where the Hoover is. I hope it's bin emptied ready.' She sniffed and marched out of the kitchen, leaving Annie Bishop to open the cupboard door and carry out the Hoover.

*   *   *

By early afternoon, the heavy cloud and threat of rain had cleared, and although the sun had still not broken through, it was dry and pleasantly fresh. Annie Bishop pulled on her walking boots—expensive ones with heavily ridged soles—and left the house, locking the door behind her. 'Come on, Tinker,' she said, pulling at the dog lead. Tinker, a young collie crossbreed, seemed reluctant to start, and held back, sniffing at a puddle by the corner of the vicarage. 'Oh, no,' said Annie. 'Old Ricky's been round again. I shall have to speak to Nigel and Sophie. Can't have him being a permanent

129

fixture, can we, Tink?' She jerked hard on the lead, and the dog abandoned the sniff, dutifully following behind as Annie Bishop strode off up the narrow, muddy lane towards the Hall avenue.

Ellen Biggs, sitting in a chair that gave her a good view of anyone who might be passing, saw her go by and struggled to her feet. She peered round the curtain and watched the tall, striding figure until she was out of sight.

'Where's she goin', then?' she said aloud. Used to her solitary life, Ellen often spoke out to an empty room. Denying Ivy's accusation that it was the first sign of madness, she claimed her own voice was better than endless silence, and continued to comment aloud on whatever took her fancy. Talking to herself made her feel less lonely. 'And what's more,' she said to Doris, when Ivy had had another go at her, 'you don't catch me disagreein' with meself!'

Unaware of the monitoring eyes, Annie Bishop had taken deep breaths of cold, clean air, expanding her chest and throwing back her head. She had no scarf or hat, not even the woolly pom-pom one that Andrew had given her for Christmas last year, and her long wheaty hair blew across her face in the wind.

'That must be it, Tinker,' she said, stopping by a gap in the hedge and releasing the dog from his lead. 'Mr Standing said it was on the left, nearly at the end of the avenue.' She pushed through the thorns and found herself in the Hall park. A vista of yellowing grass, close grazed by groups of grey fuzzy sheep, stretched out ahead of her, with clumps of fine chestnuts, oaks and beech trees inviting her to explore.

'Oh Lord, the sheep!' she said, as she saw Tinker take off ahead of her, inbred instincts to the fore. The sheep began to run, and Tinker followed, now and then crouching on his stomach, ears down. 'Oh my God!' said Annie, and began to chase. Those silly, thin sticklike legs under their thick winter bodies could so easily break! Oh no, one of them was limping already. What would Richard Standing say? She ran faster, but the sheep and Tinker had no trouble in outstripping her, and finally she pulled up, gasping and bending down to relieve the stitch in her side.

'Mrs Bishop, is it? Annie?' Richard Standing's voice was solicitous.

She straightened up to see him standing in front of her, a courteous smile mixed with concern on his face. 'Goodness!' she said, still panting. 'I'm so sorry! I'd no idea Tinker would do that!'

'He's not hurting them,' said Richard, reflecting that had it been anyone else he'd have had a quick shot at the bloody dog with the gun he carried under his arm. 'Obviously has sheepdog blood. But still, we'd better get him back, keep him on a lead, if you don't mind. Just where there are sheep, you know.

131

Once you're out of the park, it'll be fine.' And what about the pheasants? he asked himself. Happy for that dog to work the hedges, are we?

'Oh no,' insisted Annie, 'I shall keep him under control all the way. I know how important it is on farmland.' Her favourite country columnist in the Sunday paper had been loud in defence of farmers on just this issue. Why hadn't she remembered it? She felt foolish, flustered and untidy. Her face must be like a beetroot. Not a good start, she thought.

Richard Standing was looking at those clear blue eyes, cheeks pink from exertion and the cold wind, and the strands of creamy hair that had whipped across Annie's face, to be pulled back by ungloved fingers and tucked behind her neat little ears.

*   *   *

'I'll walk for a bit with you, if you like,' he said. 'Point you in the right direction when you reach the fields. It's quite easy, really, once you've got some landmarks to fix your position.'

'How kind!' said Annie. 'You do make it sound rather like a military manoeuvre ...'

'Not at all, my dear,' said Richard. 'Nothing like a good walk on a winter afternoon for giving you an appetite for dinner.' He had an idea, more sensible than some he had entertained on seeing Annie in trouble. 'Perhaps you'd like to call in on your way back.

132

Have a cup of tea? Susan is there, and I'm sure she'd be delighted.' Liar, he told himself, but knew that Susan was too well mannered to do anything but welcome a guest. What she would say when they were on their own was another matter, but he considered it worth the risk. 'Poppy, too,' he said expansively, 'she's always pleased to make new friends.'

Annie smiled apologetically. 'It's really very kind of you,' she said, 'but I must meet the children from school. I shall only just get back in time, and it is so important to be there for them when they come out. It is all quite strange for them, you know.' She'd had visions of the children going to school on their own, trotting across the Green in the sunlight, but it wasn't safe. She'd seen that at once. The Green was too muddy, and the road was full of traffic, especially early in the morning.

What a lovely girl, thought Richard. She's got everything: looks, intelligence, and quite clearly a very warm heart. Ah well, there was plenty of time.

'Well, we'll meet again soon, I'm sure,' he said, and extended his hand. 'Good heavens,' he said, 'you're frozen!' He rubbed her icy fingers between his palms in an avuncular way, and said, 'Some good warm gloves for you, Annie Bishop, that's what's needed.' He could think of other, more wonderful ways of warming her up, but put them firmly out of his mind. 'Good day, then,' he said. 'Enjoy your

133

walk,' and he marched off, forbidding himself to look back and already plotting ways of inviting the Bishops to dinner without antagonising Susan.

*   *   *

Andrew sat in his armchair in front of a roaring log fire and sipped his whisky with considerable satisfaction. The trains had been on time, he'd been able to read up some cases without interruption in his first-class seat, and it had taken no longer than he'd expected to drive back from Tresham to Ringford. True, there'd been more cars on the road than he'd thought, but they were all going his way, most of them commuters leaving the station car park at the same time as himself. They'd bombed along at a decent pace, and he was home in time to read Honor a story before she went to sleep.

'What did you do today, darling?' he said, leafing through the evening paper. Annie sat opposite him, busily knitting a small, dark blue garment which would be suitable for handing down to boy or girl. 'Did our Jean come to clean?'

Annie nodded, and stopped knitting. 'Not quite as easy as I thought,' she said. 'She turns out to be quite prickly. But I sorted it out and I'm sure we know where we are now.' She was not, in fact, so sure as all that. Jean had worked in silence, refused a cup of coffee, and left for

134

the Hall without acknowledging Annie's cheery, 'See you on Wednesday, then!'

Well, we're bound to be different from what she's used to, she thought. She'll settle down. Goodness, dear Carrie in London had wept when they'd left! Annie still had—somewhere—the rather awful vase Carrie had given them on her last morning.

'One interesting thing,' Annie continued. 'She mentioned a fireworks party. Seems they have one every year in the village. Should be a chance to join in, shouldn't it?'

Andrew was listening with only half an ear, and said. 'That's my girl. Did Tinker have a walk?'

Undaunted, Annie smiled. 'He certainly did,' she said. 'We were both plastered in mud by the time we came back. But it was wonderful, marvellous. You must come too at the weekend. I'll show the way, and Honor can sit on your shoulders. It's a spectacular view from the top of the hill!'

She had not forgotten her meeting with Richard Standing, that most helpful of neighbours, but did not mention it.

CHAPTER EIGHTEEN

'Grandad,' yelled Joey Bates indistinctly, his mouth full of food. 'When's fireworks?' He'd come home with a painting, blobby and with trails of colour out of control, but recognisably a bonfire and exploding rockets. Fireworks were a passion with him, and he asked for them for his birthday, his sister's birthday, and any anniversary in between. Robert indulged him with golden rain and sparklers in the garden, but the highlight of the year was the big display for the whole village. 'Ask yer dad,' said old Ted. 'He's in charge.'

Robert had masterminded the village firework party on one of Bates's fields for years. He collected up great piles of dead wood from the farm, added any old rubbish from the village gardens, and made a huge mound, augmented by old mattresses and armchairs chucked on at the dead of night by residents too lazy to go to the dump in Bagley.

'It's next Saturday,' said Mandy. 'Peggy's got a poster in the shop. Robert said he was planning to put it in the Long Field this year, Dad, if it's OK with you?'

'S'long as he clears up the mess, 'e can 'ave it where 'e likes,' said Ted, rolling up his shirt sleeve and testing Margie's bath water with his elbow. He loved to help out with the children's bedtime, and Mandy was glad of another pair of hands. 'This is ready, Mandy, and she's done 'er teeth.'

Joey was wriggling with pleasure now. He could hear Robert's feet on the concrete path, and he twisted round in his chair to smile at his father.

'Hello, old son,' said Robert, his hand on Joey's fine, wispy hair.

'Fireworks, Dad?'

'Sure,' said Robert, taking off his greasy overalls and running hot water to wash his black hands. 'Biggest and best in the county. And this year, a secret surprise!'

'What's that?' said Joey.

'Well, it wouldn't be a secret if I told you, would it?' said Robert, and unstrapped his son, hugging him tight as he lifted him out of his chair.

*   *   *

'Evenin', Ted,' said Tom Price, 'same as usual?' Ted nodded, and leaned comfortably on the bar, pulling out his pipe and beginning the ritual of filling and lighting up. 'How's the family?'

The pub gradually filled up, and was a warm haven, smoky and pleasantly noisy when Robert opened the door and looked around for John Barnett. Although John was older by several years, the two had been friends for a long time, fellow members of the rugby club, and each had been the other's best man.

'Hi, mate,' said Robert, pushing his way through the crowd to where John stood, and noting his old father bent over the dominoes in the corner by the roaring log fire. Ted had taken over as unofficial captain of the dominoes school after Fred Mills's death, although Fred's chair still stood in the corner, with its grimy, flattened cushion, unoccupied except by strangers who knew no better. Fred had been an awkward old sod, but he was much missed.

'What'll you have, Robert?' said John. Both men followed the Ringford tradition of calling in to the pub around ten o'clock and staying till closing time. It had taken Mandy, a town girl from Tresham, quite a while to get used to this, and Sarah Barnett still looked stern when John got up from his armchair at exactly the same time every evening, collected his jacket and disappeared into the night. But Ringford men were not easily changed, and this nightly interlude meant a lot to Robert. Working so close to home meant that he and Mandy were constantly in each other's company, and he needed a chance to chat to John about the farm, the garage business, rugby football—anything, really, except women's gossip and domesticity.

'Been wooding today,' said John. 'D'you need any more for the bonfire? There's a pile of rubbish up in the spinney you can have and welcome.'

Robert nodded, and suggested to John that they finish piling it up on Friday night. 'It'll be bigger than ever, this year,' he said proudly. Ever since a horrible accident in the village when a child had been blinded in one eye, everyone had agreed to set off fireworks in a safe, controlled way. The party had grown, with the Women's Institute doing soup and sausages and hot drinks, and the crowd was often greater than the total population of the village. Some people resented this, said they couldn't see why they should raise money for folks from other villages, but they were in the minority, and it was always a very cheerful, successful event.

Robert signalled to Don Cutt behind the bar, and was halfway through ordering when he realised the publican was not listening to him, but was looking over towards the door, and a silence had fallen. Eyes turned unashamedly towards the newcomer. 'It's that new bloke from the vicarage,' said Robert in an undertone.

Andrew Bishop stood inside the door, smiling. He looked round and nodded at one or two faces he recognised from passing in the street, and made for the bar. Conversation slowly resumed, and Andrew turned to his nearest neighbours, Robert and John. 'Chilly evening,' said Andrew, still smiling.

John nodded. 'We've to expect it now, I suppose,' he said.

There was an awkward pause, and Robert cleared his throat. 'Can I get you a drink, Mr Bishop?' he said.

'No, no,' said Andrew, 'allow me.' His offer was refused, and another silence fell between them.

'Settling in, then?' said John Barnett.

Andrew nodded, and with some relief began to talk about the trials of moving house. It had been Annie's idea, coming down to the pub for a quick drink before bedtime. Get to know a few locals, she'd said. We want them to see we're interested in joining in, becoming part of the community. Andrew would much rather have stayed at home with a last whisky and water by the fire, but he loved Annie dearly, and would do most things to please her, even turning out in the cold night air to drink warm beer in a fuggy atmosphere with people he did not know, nor particularly wished to know.

The firework party inevitably came up. 'Saw the poster,' said Andrew. 'Terrific idea. We shall certainly be there. Is there any help needed? We'd be only too pleased . . .'

Robert shook his head, a little too readily perhaps. 'Maybe the women could do with some help, cooking and that,' he said, relenting.

John shot him a look that said a great deal, including a warning that Tom's wife Doreen, Peggy Turner and the others in the WI would not thank him for passing the buck.

'Great!' said Andrew. 'I'll tell Annie to get in touch. With Peggy in the shop, would it be?'

'Peggy,' is it, already? thought Robert, but he was a good-natured chap, and suggested Mrs Bishop could ask any of the women, who'd be glad of a hand, he was sure.

*   *   *

'Well?' said Annie, as Andrew returned, shivering and rubbing his hands in front of the fire. 'How was it?' The big room was warm, cosy, with the long velvet curtains drawn and Tinker stretched out in front of the fire.

'Much as I expected,' said Andrew.

'Which was?' said Annie.

'Hot, crowded, smoky and noisy. Except when I arrived. Then it was like a Western when the baddie walks in. Conversation dried up and they all stood and stared. Good thing I'm not easily discouraged.'

'But you did talk to some of them?'

'Oh, yes, to a couple of young farmers, I think. Pretty heavy going, but at least I got some information about bonfire night. Seems they're pretty well organised. And yes, before you ask, they reckoned the women could use some help on refreshments.'

Annie's smile was wide. 'Oh, well done, Andrew,' she said. 'I shall offer first thing tomorrow. This old Aga will take loads of sausages and stuff. Goodness, how exciting!'

'Mm,' said Andrew, and made for the drinks cupboard.

*   *   *

'What does she mean?' said Ivy Beasley. 'She's

not even a member. And anyway, we don't need help. We've managed perfectly well up to now, without somebody who's only been here a couple of weeks.'

The shop was crowded. That is, there were five women and one child, and Peggy was busy weighing out sweets from a tall, old-fashioned glass jar. Loose sweets came in plastic containers these days, but she still transferred them to the old, unevenly shaped greenish glass jars that had been in the shop for many years before she had arrived. They were beautiful. She'd said so to Frank when they took over. Too good for the tip, which was what he'd suggested. When she shook out the sweets to weigh them she felt the shades of shopkeepers before her. It was a pleasant feeling, and the sweet jars were still there.

The subject for gossip this morning was, of course, Annie Bishop's offer, made immediately on leaving the children in the school playground, to help with food for Saturday night.

'I've been meaning to call on her,' said Doreen Price, President of the Women's Institute, 'to invite her to join. I reckon it's very nice of her to suggest helping, anyway. What d'you think, Peggy?' As was her habit, Peggy nodded noncommittally.

Jean Jenkins, over by the biscuits, squared her shoulders and addressed Ivy. 'Never refuse an offer of help, Miss Beasley,' she said. 'It

142

might never come again.'

'So?' said Ivy.

'So we might need an extra pair of hands when we're gettin' past it,' contributed Ellen Biggs, perched in her customary place on the chair by the Post Office cubicle.

'Speak for yourself, Ellen Biggs,' sniffed Ivy.

'I do,' said Ellen. 'And even you won't last for ever, Ivy.'

'Morning, Doris!' said Peggy, smiling at Doris Ashbourne as she entered the shop, well wrapped up in scarf and gloves against the grey morning. 'We need you to keep the peace.'

Doris was quickly brought up to date, and gave Jean and Doreen her backing. 'And anyway, Ivy,' she said, 'it'd be only neighbourly to accept her offer. She can do some soup, that always goes first.'

Jean laughed. 'Always supposin' the Aga ain't gone out,' she said. 'She's not too clever with that yet.'

At this point, Sandra emerged from the little side room where Peggy kept her freezer cabinet, holding Alison firmly by the hand. 'If you can eat sweets,' she said sharply, 'you can eat school dinners.' She smiled apologetically at Peggy. 'Said she was feeling sick this morning, but it seems to have gone the minute it's too late to go to school.'

'Typical,' said Ivy Beasley. 'In my day . . .'

'Oh, give over, do,' said Ellen Biggs. 'We all know you was the perfect child, Ivy,' and she

143

cackled as Ivy took up her basket and huffily left the shop.

'Right,' said Doreen. 'I'll call in at the vicarage before I go home, see if Mrs Bishop's there. And Ivy can like it or lump it.'

'She ain't got no choice,' said Ellen Biggs, hobbling across from her chair and leaning up against the counter with a triumphant leer. 'It's four against one. But she'll make Mrs Bishop suffer for it, you can bet yer boots!'

CHAPTER NINETEEN

'Off you go, Mrs T.,' said Sandra. 'I can take care of everything, and if there's a real emergency, I can always get hold of Bill at the estate.' Funny, she thought, I've always called him Bill, and her Mrs T. but then, Bill belongs to Ringford. Everybody calls him Bill. And Mrs T. is from outside, although, of course, very nice, and part of the village now.

Peggy left Sandra behind the counter and went upstairs for her coat. She stood at her bedroom window, looking out at the day. The school playground was wet and shining from steady rain, and bright with yellow netball lines and the new hopscotch pitch which few of the children used. Some nostalgic impulse from the education office, Peggy supposed. She thought of her own childhood, when she'd played on the pavement outside her house, chalked out pitches and taken stones from their neat suburban garden. A central-heating oil lorry drew up outside the school gate, and the driver attached its long snaking pipe to the big tank, filling up for the winter ahead. Heavy raindrops made overlapping circles in the playground puddles and the driver splashed through, like a boy in rubber boots. The children were in the classroom, and Peggy could see outlines of moving children through steamed-up windows. All their lives ahead of them, she thought. Well, today might tell her how much she had left.

She opened the bottom drawer of her dressing table to find a headsquare, and as she rummaged through a pile of scarves, she felt something hard against her fingers. She pulled it out, and stood motionless, shocked, looking down at the face of her dead husband smiling up at her. 'Frank!' she said aloud, tension released as tears ran down her face. She traced his features with her fingertips, and sadly kissed the cold glass. She'd put the photograph there on the morning of her marriage to Bill, a last-minute gesture to a new beginning.

A dreadful sense of longing for Frank filled her, and she sat down on the bed, the photograph held close. He was her past. He'd been there when she was young, and they'd been sweethearts since childhood. He'd grown up with her, played hopscotch on the pavement with her, shyly proposed and stood proudly with her at the altar. They'd longed for children, but none had come, and they'd grown apart a little over that. But they had had that cementing bond of a common background, a shared inheritance of suburban life. They knew where they were with each other, and together they'd ventured into pastures new, moving to a village life that was strange and sometimes frightening. They would never have done it alone. Two halves of one whole, we were, she thought.

She stood up, looking at her watch, and saw a pair of corduroy trousers in a heap by the chair. Bill's. She picked them up and was about to put them away when the smell of him, his own particular smell, made her bury her face, wiping away her tears. After a few minutes, she quietly hung them in the cupboard and took out her mac.

The photograph was still on the bed, and she quickly replaced it in the drawer under her scarves. 'We'll see, Frank,' she said. 'I'll be glad when today is over.'

*   *   *

Tresham General Hospital was on the outskirts of town, and Peggy drove down a long approach road that led to the huge car park. Big as it was, she had trouble in finding a space, and it seemed a long walk from her car to the reception office. The wind struck across the dreary car park, stirring rubbish in concrete

146

corners, whipping car aerials and tugging at Peggy's scarf, penetrating her mac and causing her to shiver. She tried not to notice the smell when she pushed through the swing doors and walked into the warm, antiseptic interior.

'Fourth floor, follow the red line,' said the receptionist.

'Um, where are the lifts?' said Peggy, overawed.

The heavily made-up girl was so young, confident, healthy. 'Over there, dear, by the kiosk,' she said, and pointed. Probably thinks I need a zimmer, Peggy thought, and walked as nimbly as possible in the direction of the lifts.

The scanning department was full of pregnant women. 'Am I in the right place?' said Peggy, doubtfully.

This receptionist was brisk, middle-aged, like herself. 'Oh yes,' she said, 'sit down, please. There'll be a bit of a wait.'

Peggy looked round. All the chairs seemed to be taken by young women in various stages of gestation. None of them were alone. They had friends, or mothers, and even the occasional husband, sitting with them, chatting and looking at dog-eared magazines.

In the far corner of the room Peggy spotted an empty chair. She walked over and sat down, feeling curious eyes on her. Peggy could hear them thinking. Too old to be pregnant, surely? Mind you, they did all kinds of funny things with sperm and eggs and foetuses these days.

There was that grandmother in America who'd just produced a baby. Next to her, a big woman was talking animatedly to her younger friend. Both were well advanced, their bumps taking up a lot of space. Peggy opened a magazine, wondered if she'd catch anything from its well-thumbed pages, and looked blindly at an article about water birthing.

'Well, I told him,' said the woman next to her, 'it's my body, and I can do what I like with it!'

'Quite right,' said her milder companion. 'Treat you like cattle, if you don't speak up.'

Several of the women were looking closely at small folders. One of the women, close enough for Peggy to take a squint at the blurred picture, squeaked with delight. 'Oh look,' she said to her embarrassed husband, 'you can see its little head!'

A nurse pushed a wheelchair down the corridor towards them. In it sat an old man, emaciated and colourless, hunched up in a cocoon of cotton blankets. The nurse parked him by the wall, disappeared into what Peggy presumed was the scanning room and then after a few minutes reappeared and walked off, apparently abandoning her patient. He looks dead already, thought Peggy, and wished desperately she was back in the shop. The children would be coming out of school, rushing in for sweets, quarrelling and pushing, irritable after a day's confinement in school.

Confinement, thought Peggy, there's an appropriate word.

'Mrs Turner?' A nurse in a dark uniform stood by the door and looked round.

'Here,' said Peggy, with relief, and followed her into the scanning room.

'Just undress over there, Mrs Turner,' said the nurse kindly, pointing to a small row of cubicles.

Laid out on a high examination table, Peggy felt the cold jelly applied to her abdomen.

'It won't hurt at all,' said the Indian doctor, scholarly in his steel-rimmed glasses. 'We just pass this around on your skin, and it tells us all we need to know.' He sat on a high stool at her side, looking closely at a small television screen. Peggy glanced at it, and then quickly looked away. She had no desire to see her insides. Much better that they should remain a mystery.

'Ah!' said the doctor, and Peggy's heart sank. The scanning head was over the pain site, and he moved it in a small circle, pressing a little harder, causing her to wince. Her heart began to pound in panic. Now? Was it going to be now? 'Well!' he said, with the air of a man making an important discovery.

'Look at that! You're a lucky woman, Mrs Turner. Loads of gallstones, loads of them.' He smiled at her, congratulating her on her luck.

'What's lucky about that?' she said weakly.

He looked at her sharply, crossly, almost.

'Because we can do something about them!' he said, as if to a slow-learning child. As compared with something you can't do anything about, thought Peggy. She began to feel the relief he was obviously expecting. Gallstones. Well, people had them removed all the time. They could even dispel them with drugs or lasers or something, she was sure. Her spirits began to rise.

*   *   *

Bill looked in the Hall greenhouse and saw a dozen jobs he could be doing: tidying up, cleaning the glass ready for catching the maximum winter sun, repotting indoor plants for the house, turning out geranium cuttings that hadn't rooted, but had collapsed in powdery, mildewed heaps in their little pots. Or he could go down to the bottom fields where Foxy was drilling, see how long it was going to take. Or he could just stay here and worry.

If I hadn't been looking for my spare key, I'd never have found the letter. His thoughts were tumbling, and he couldn't concentrate. He picked up a watering-can and then put it down again, forgetting what he was going to do with it. The envelope had been open, the appointment slip showing clearly, and after he'd read it and put it back where it was hidden, he'd sat down dizzily on a kitchen chair to collect himself. Why hadn't she told him? That pain, it must have been worse than he'd thought. He felt shut out. Why hadn't she trusted him enough to tell him? God, what were husbands for? And he'd had plenty of practice with sick wives ... ah, then that could be it, he thought. She didn't want to be like Joyce, everlastingly ailing. 'But Peggy,' he said miserably, speaking aloud without realising it, 'you should have told me. I love you ...'

'Bill?' It was Richard Standing, staring at Bill with a puzzled expression. 'Something I should know?' He smiled encouragingly, wondering why his tough, always capable estate manager should be quite clearly on the verge of tears.

Bill coughed and turned away. 'No, no, sir,' he said. 'Just thinking aloud.' Then suddenly he couldn't bear it alone, and looked back at his boss, a pleasant man for all his faults, and someone he'd known since they were both lads, fishing in the Ringle together.

'It's Peggy,' he said. 'She's gone to the hospital this afternoon. Tried to keep it a secret, but I found out. I daren't say anything to her, of course, but the thought of her going in there all by herself ...' He looked mutely at Richard Standing, who took a step forward and put out his hand.

'Come on, Bill,' he said. 'We need some help.'

In the consoling warmth of Richard's study,

Bill and he sat either side of the big desk, large glasses of whisky in hand.

'Don't usually drink at this time of day, sir,' said Bill, taking a big gulp.

'Needs must,' said Richard. 'When you feel up to it, you'd better tell me the whole story. I had no idea Peggy was ill. Take your time, old lad, we've got all afternoon.'

There wasn't much to tell, but Richard Standing listened quietly while Bill explained haltingly about the mornings when Peggy seemed withdrawn, pale, the rapidly emptying bottles of painkillers, the hand pressed permanently to her right side.

Bill sighed deeply, then got to his feet. 'I'd better be off now,' he said. 'I'd like to be there when she gets home. Sandra's a nice kid, but Peggy'll need me, whatever happens.'

He rode on his bicycle down the chestnut avenue and out into the open Green. Everything was as usual: the kids running along, school bags bobbing on their backs, the mothers in huddles by the bus shelter, gossiping. The Jenkins terrier chased a ball kicked by Eddie along the muddy footpath, and Bill could hear Jean's voice yelling for him to come back at once, or else. He felt indescribably sad. And then he saw Peggy's car coming down by Price's Farm, and he cycled harder, desperate to be back at the shop before she arrived.

'Bill, why aren't you at work?' Peggy

managed a small smile, and then as she looked into his worried face, knew that he had found out. She moved forward into his arms and they stood silently for long seconds. Then he pushed her gently away from him.

'Well?' he said.

'Gallstones,' she said. 'And the doctor said I was lucky . . .'

'Bloody hell!' exploded Bill, and then they embraced again, the unspoken word, the dreaded, unmentionable malignant invader retreating before them.

'So we wait to hear what happens next?' said Bill, smiling reassuringly at her. 'And whatever it is, I want to be the first to know. I couldn't bear it, Peggy, you know, to think you'd shut me out.'

That doctor was right, thought Peggy, though in a way he couldn't have meant. I am lucky, very lucky indeed.

CHAPTER TWENTY

Vigorous knocking at Ivy Beasley's front door broke the customary quiet of Victoria Villa, and brought Ivy upright from her knees. She had been polishing the lino, its pattern of wood-block flooring worn away in patches with constant traffic of boots, shoes and floorcloths.

'All right, all right!' she said loudly. 'I'm coming! No need to knock the house down!'

Annie Bishop stood on Ivy's spotless steps, her wide smile at the ready. 'Good morning, Miss Beasley,' she said.

'Yes?' said Ivy. She knew perfectly well why Mrs Bishop had come calling so early in the morning, but she waited with an unhelpful expression.

'Er, I believe you are in charge of refreshments for the fireworks party?'

Ivy nodded, and closed the door a fraction. She's not getting a toehold in here, she thought, Bishop or no Bishop.

'Well—er, I wonder if I could just come in and have a word? Doreen said I could be of help—make some soup—with croutons, perhaps . . . ?'

'Mrs Price knows perfectly well everything, including soup, is organised,' said Ivy, 'but I can't stop you making it, if you must. Be up at the field by six o'clock sharp. And make sure it's really hot. May not be room on the grid for another pan. And you can forget about the croutons.'

Annie Bishop renewed her smile with an effort. 'Well, I'm only too pleased to help,' she said. 'It's so important to contribute, I've always thought.'

'That's of no account here in Ringford,' said Ivy stiffly. 'We've always just got on with it. No need to think about it. We all know what has to be done, and we do it. Now, I have work to do, Mrs Bishop . . .' She closed the door firmly,

154

leaving Annie Bishop with nothing to do but retreat.

Not quite a defeat, thought Annie. At least she gave me permission to make soup! She walked down Ivy's well-swept path and unhooked Tinker from the gatepost. The sun had come up out of the early mist, and was shining through a perfect mackerel sky, like a lace sunshade spread out across the village. The air was cold and refreshing, and as Annie strode back across the Green towards the old vicarage she took deep breaths, relaxed and began to rehearse her account of the confrontation with Ivy Beasley. She was adamant, she said to an absent Andrew, quite adamant, but I wouldn't give up, and in the end she'd softened up quite a bit. I'm sure she has a kind heart, you know. I'm sure I'll win her over.

Ivy's front door was sticking, would not quite shut. Irritated by Annie Bishop, she jerked it open and kicked away the small stone that had been trapped by the doormat. ' "Contribute!" ' she said. 'Time enough to contribute when she's lived here long enough to know how things are done.' She knelt down to resume her polishing, and realised she'd left her cloth on the hall stand. 'Drat!' she said, and stood up, but she'd not noticed a small patch of polish by her foot, and slid awkwardly across the floor, one leg crooked beneath her. Pain shot through her ankle, and she struggled upright. She could hardly bear the weight on her right leg, and hopped through to the kitchen, balancing herself against the wall. Tiddles, asleep in front of the glowing range, looked up, sensing, as cats do, that something was wrong.

Ivy lowered herself into her chair and rubbed the damaged ankle. Now what? She had always dreaded something like this happening when she was alone. Well, at least there was the telephone. Robert Bates had insisted she had it installed after she'd collapsed with flu one winter. And because she'd helped Olive look after him when he was small and weakly, and had grown to love him like her own child, Ivy had taken his advice. Her telephone bill was the smallest in Ringford, as she never called anyone unless in dire emergencies. Doris rang her from time to time, but Ivy was no telephone gossip, mistrusted it and suspected that all telephone lines were tapped, so she always cut Doris off with some peremptory excuse.

Well, this is an emergency, I suppose, she thought. The pain was rapidly getting worse, and her ankle puffing up at an alarming rate. She hobbled back into the hall and dialled Doris's number. 'That you, Doris?' she said.

'Who else is it likely to be?' said Doris.

'No need for that,' said Ivy. 'I've twisted my ankle. Looks bad. Swollen up, and I can't walk.'

'Go and sit down,' said Doris, immediately sympathetic, 'and put your foot up on a stool. I'll be down in ten minutes. Don't try anything foolish, Ivy.'

The pain was so bad that Ivy was only too pleased to sit down and do nothing. She leaned her head back against the cushion and closed her eyes. Now, of all times! She had so much to do. There were the sausages to sort out and divide up round the ladies. And bread rolls. And jars of mustard and pickle to be got ready, and a hundred other things. All that wretched Mrs Bishop's fault. Drat!

*　　　*　　　*

'You're lookin' more cheerful, Peggy, my dear,' said Ellen Biggs, crashing her way through the shop door like a rally car out of control. Not that she had much speed, but with layers of multicoloured garments against the cold, her swinging shopping bag and her rubber-tipped stick, the narrow doorway scarcely accommodated her. She lurched through, retrieving her balance by leaning heavily against the counter.

'Careful, Ellen!' said Peggy. 'We don't want another casualty this morning.'

'What d'yer mean?' said Ellen. An accident? Her face brightened. 'Who's the casualty, then?'

'Ivy,' said Peggy. 'She slipped in her hall, twisted her ankle. Doris came in for some painkillers. Said it was very swollen, and would need the doctor. She's phoned, apparently.'

'Well I never,' said Ellen. 'Fancy old Ivy takin' a tumble. Not so clever, after all.' A wicked smile crossed her lined old face. ''Ere, Peggy,' she said, 'give us a packet of them biscuits she likes. Doris'll 'ave a key. I'd better go an' offer me sympathies to the invalid.'

Peggy helped the old woman down the steps, and reflected that Ellen's somewhat triumphant sympathies were probably something Ivy Beasley could do without.

* * *

'Don't worry, Doris,' said Doreen Price, her attention divided between the telephone and a pan of milk heating on the stove. 'I'll see that everything's done. And tell Ivy not to stew. Peggy can get Bill to deliver the sausages and stuff. We've done it so often, it'll all go off perfectly smoothly without Ivy. Still, perhaps you'd better not tell her that.' She had an idea. 'Mrs Bishop's anxious to help,' she added. 'She can take on Ivy's share of the cooking, I'm sure. Oh, and maybe it'd be best not to mention that to Ivy, either.'

Price's farm kitchen was warm, and a distillation of all the smells of the farm—dogs, straw, muck, chickens—permanently pervaded it. Strong meat for someone not used to it, but it meant home to Tom Price. He sat comfortably in a shabby old armchair by the Aga, his springer spaniel curled up at his feet, reading the *Farmer's Weekly*.

'There you are, then, Mother,' he said. He'd called her that since their daughter was tiny, and had never changed it, not even now the child was a mother herself. 'Poor old Ivy's bin struck down.'

'You needn't look so pleased about it,' said Doreen. 'It'll mean more work for me, that's for sure.'

'Thought that new Mrs Whatsername was dying to help?'

'Yes, but she's a newcomer. She'll have to be told. Not like having someone who just gets on with it.' Doreen sighed. 'Ah well,' she said, 'at least I don't have to dance attendance on Ivy Beasley. Poor old Doris is up and down like a yo-yo, taking her food and doing her shopping. Got to keep her foot up for several days, Doctor said.'

Tom stood up and stretched his arms over his head, touching the low ceiling and yawning loudly. 'Never bin known,' he said. 'Bonfire night without Ivy Beasley? Whole thing could grind to a halt. Touch and go, Mother!' He laughed heartily, pulled on his well-worn cap, and made for the door.

'Very funny, Tom Price,' said Doreen sniffily. 'It's all right for you men, but there'd soon be a riot if soup and sausages weren't ready on the dot. And shut that door, do, there's a terrible draught.'

*   *   *

159

Annie Bishop put down the telephone receiver and looked at herself in the large, gilt-framed looking-glass that Andrew had argued was out of keeping in a country vicarage. It was perfect, Annie considered, hanging over the lovely fruitwood table her parents had given her as a house-warming present. Surely there was room for elegance, even in Round Ringford? I bet the Hall is elegant, she thought.

Her smiling face looked back at her. So they do need me after all, she told herself. 'They begged me, Andrew,' she rehearsed aloud. 'Seems they thought of me at once. Poor Miss Beasley ... But it's an ill wind, darling, don't you think?'

In his office in the Farringdon Road, Andrew received no telepathic messages. He handed a pile of documents to his secretary, and considered with dismay the heap still to be dealt with before he could leave. He looked out of the window at the grey London sky and crowds of shoppers muffled against the cold wind, and wondered how Annie would feel about a small flat in town, just for the odd night when the journey back to Tresham looked like being late and tedious.

CHAPTER TWENTY-ONE

It was almost dark by four o'clock, when Robert Bates and John Barnett put the finishing touches to the bonfire. The field was tidy, all the fireworks set up safely, and the surprise giant rocket carefully dug in where everyone would be able to see it. The barbecue, where food was not so much cooked as kept hot, was in its usual place by the line of oak trees. There was some shelter here if it rained, and the high hedge protected the refreshment helpers from any cold wind coming from the north.

Ted Bates was stubborn about his hedges. 'T'ain't a hedge if it ain't got no blackberries nor hips and haws,' he said. 'An' where are the dunnocks goin' to nest if I cut the hedges down to nothin'?' After long years of ribbing in the Arms for being soft in the head, Ted and his views were now becoming fashionably acceptable. He'd even had his picture in the *Advertiser* in the autumn, standing by his unruly hedges with all their glorious harvest.

Olive Bates was sceptical. 'It's true in a way,' she said to Robert, 'what your father says. But them hedges get very thin and straggly at the bottom when they're not trimmed.'

Ivy Beasley had come straight to the point. 'If you ask me,' she said, 'it's just an excuse for being idle. Ted Bates was never over-fond of hard work.'

Agreeing to meet up at the field at six o'clock, John returned to Walnut Farm and Robert went back to his garage.

We shall have a really good show tonight, Robert thought. The jumble sale had brought

161

in more money than before, largely due to Peggy Turner's bric-à-brac stall. Susan Standing at the Hall had been clearing out the attics, and more than the usual amount of junk had emerged. It had taken Peggy hours to sort it out, and most of it was worthless, but there were one or two really good pieces of china, and some old embroidered waistcoats which had been snapped up by a dealer from Tresham as soon as the sale began. Even Ivy Beasley had had to admit that Peggy's total was very useful. Ivy, who regarded the jumble sale as her province, was always loath to let anyone else take credit, especially Peggy Turner.

'All ready, then?' said Mandy, as Robert came into the kitchen for a cup of tea.

He nodded. 'Yep,' he said, 'should be better than ever this year. I'll just take this with me. Can't waste any more time, got to finish Mr Richard's car for tomorrow.' He looked across at Joey, who had just been dropped off by the minibus and was struggling to get his arms out of his anorak by himself. 'Soon be time to go, son,' he said, and turned to Mandy. 'Wrap him well, my duck. The wind's like a knife up there.'

By a quarter past six, the field was a mass of milling people. Every child was given a sparkler at the gate, and Peggy, standing behind the bubbling soup and sizzling sausages, half-closed her eyes and thought it looked just like a field full of fairies. Tinkerbells, darting here and there in the winter night.

'Two soups, please,' said Sandra Goodison, breaking the spell, 'and have you got any orange for Alison?'

Peggy poured out two plastic mugs of soup and directed Sandra to the drinks table, manned by Octavia Jones. 'Tea, coffee and squash over there,' she said. 'You can pay me for everything. Just tell Octavia it's paid for.'

Sandra took the mugs of steaming tomato soup over to Sam and Alison, and went back to fetch orange squash. Standing in the queue, she looked at Octavia, dramatically wrapped in black from head to foot, only the stray wisps of hair shining in the light from the Gaz lamp on her trestle table. 'Hi, Octavia,' she said, when it was her turn. Although they'd met and said hello in the street, Sandra and Octavia had been shy of one another. Firm friends during their teens, they had drifted apart completely when Sandra got pregnant, married Sam and went to live in Tresham. Makes me feel old, thought Sandra, looking at Octavia's laughing face as she flirted with a gang of lads from Fletching. All I've been through, having Alison and that, and she's done nothing yet.

'Any tea or coffee?' said Octavia

'Maybe later,' said Sandra. 'I've paid Mrs T. for everything. She said to tell you.'

Octavia looked at Sandra and grinned. 'Trusts us, now, does she?' she said, and for a moment they were back in their shoplifting days, in league against authority.

163

'Another life, that was,' said Sandra firmly, and took the wobbling cup of squash back across the field to her family.

The fireworks started off modestly, with Catherine wheels spinning on posts, some getting stuck, but most sending out wonderful showers of stars. The Reverend Nigel Brooks applauded the display with the rest of the company, but wondered whether a single person present thought of poor St Catherine, agonisingly martyred on a handy cartwheel for her beliefs.

'Hurray,' shouted Joey, and his little sister echoed him. Mandy tucked the tartan rug tighter down the sides of Joey's wheelchair, and pushed his woolly hat down over his ears. 'Hey, Mum!' he said. 'Can't see!'

A succession of small rockets, golden rain and silver clouds produced choruses of oohs and aahs from the crowd, now getting into its collective stride. The soup had nearly all gone, and only half a dozen rolls remained.

'We've got more sausages than rolls,' said Annie Bishop unwisely. She'd been handing out hot dogs with frozen hands for what seemed to her like hours. The other women exchanged jokes and comments she did not understand, and she felt excluded. Several young men had loomed out of the dark and pretended to fight for the pleasure of being served by her rather than Doris Ashbourne. She couldn't help feeling flattered, but was quick to notice the sour expression on the other women's faces. Oh God, this was more difficult than she'd thought.

'There'll be nothing left, Mrs Bishop, you'll see,' said Doris, a little tartly, and then regretted it. I sound just like Ivy, she thought. Poor woman had done nothing wrong, just wanted to help. 'You've done well,' she added. 'Your first time, and it's been a great help.'

Annie smiled gratefully. 'I've loved every minute of it,' she lied, spreading her hands out over the diminishing fire.

Olive Bates began tidying up the pans and plastic bags. 'Robert's got a surprise finish,' she said. 'Specially for young Joey, I reckon. Nuthin' he won't do for that boy.'

'Your little handicapped grandson, Mrs Bates?' said Annie Bishop. There was an immediate silence. No one in Ringford referred to Joey as handicapped. Especially not to his grannie.

'That's right,' said Olive. 'That's our Joey.'

Over in the far corner of the field, on the edge of the crowd, Richard Standing stood with Poppy and Susan, staring fixedly at the huge bonfire. It was a wonderful sight, much more spectacular than the most expensive firework. Huge leaping flames and showers of sparks shed light and warmth over a radius that encompassed most of the crowd. Guy Fawkes in Bill Turner's old army greatcoat had been immolated in the first few minutes, and now

165

the fire was a furnace of old tree trunks and timbers from a barn that had finally collapsed in the Glebe Field.

'Can we go soon?' said Susan Standing. 'I'm absolutely frozen. And so is Poppy. Surely we've done our bit?'

'I'm not cold,' said Poppy. 'Can I go and see Joey? He's over there, with Mrs Bates. I can see him.' She pulled at her father's hand, trying to drag him along.

'Oh, no, Poppy,' said Susan. 'That'll mean staying here for another half-hour making conversation. Come on, darling, let's go home and make a nice hot drink. Richard, say something. Put your foot down, please!'

But Richard Standing had caught sight of a tall slim figure with an all-enveloping sheepskin coat and pale hair wound up inside a blue angora woolly hat. Her face, reflected in the embers of the fire, was glowing, and her wide smile revealed perfect, pearly teeth. 'There's Annie Bishop,' he said. 'Seems to be getting on all right with Doris Ashbourne and co. Pity about poor old Ivy, but things seem to have gone to plan without her. Perhaps we should just go over and say hello?'

His tone was hopeful, but Susan came down on the suggestion with a swift, 'Certainly not. I don't think we have to worry about Annie Bishop. Knows just what she's doing, that one. Needs no help from us.'

'What do you mean?' said Richard.

He was about to challenge Susan on a truly unfair remark, when Robert Bates got up on an old half-barrel and shouted, 'Attention, everyone!'

'More fireworks!' yelled Joey, and his father smiled broadly. Robert's attention was momentarily distracted by a small figure careering up to him, gesticulating that he had something to say. It was Eddie Jenkins, his vulnerable ears heavily muffled by a grey balaclava and woollen scarf.

'Don't forget the rocket, Mr Bates!'

Robert nodded. 'Just about to announce it, Eddie,' he said. 'Run along, now—and don't go too near the bonfire.'

Eddie shot off again and disappeared into the darkness outside the fiery circle of light.

'As a finale,' continued Robert, 'and thank you, Eddie Jenkins, for reminding me, we have one big surprise for you all. A firework to beat all fireworks. But before we start the countdown to lift-off, I'd just like to thank all our helpers, including our newest recruit, Mrs Bishop from the vicarage.' There were raucous cheers from a group of lads over by the refreshment tables. Robert smiled. 'And to send our best wishes for Ivy Beasley's speedy recovery.' Some cheers and this time one or two boos. Robert was stern. 'Without Ivy organising the jumble sale and refreshments, we wouldn't have had nearly such a good evening, and we look forward to Ivy being here herself next year.'

'You try and stop her!' yelled Mark Jenkins from a distant, dark part of the field. Jean looked round sharply, and Foxy set off in the direction of the voice.

'So, until next year,' Robert wound up, 'goodnight everyone, and here we go! Ten, nine, eight . . .'

The counting was taken up by everyone in the field, and nobody except Poppy, who was now at Joey's side, noticed that Joey had stopped counting and was looking up apprehensively at his mother.

'Three, two, one . . . *Lift-off* !' shouted the crowd. In the hush that followed, everyone heard the whoosh as the rocket sped skywards. And then, in the starlit, quiet country night, there was an earsplitting explosion.

Amid the yells of triumph, laughs and cheers, it was once again Poppy who realised that something was seriously wrong with Joey Bates. 'Mrs Bates!' she shouted.

Mandy bent over the wheelchair and let out a scream. 'Joey! Joey! . . . Robert! Come here quickly!'

Suddenly it was all confusion and noise, as Robert heard the alarm in Mandy's voice and tried to reach her. People anxious to help, or merely curious, gathered round the little group, and Richard Standing pushed a way through, saying he was off for the doctor, and not to worry. Poppy was crying and trying to put her arms round the little boy, now stretched back in an unnatural arch, trembling and jerking, his eyes horribly vacant.

'Excuse me! Make way, at once, please!' The peremptory voice was Annie Bishop's, and recognising its authority, a passage was made for her. She bent over Joey. 'It's all right, Mandy,' she said, 'he's having a fit. Probably the big bang. Don't panic. He'll come out of it. But we have to keep him warm and see he doesn't hurt himself.' She turned to the crowd. 'Go away, everyone!' she said. 'There's nothing to be done here, and you're just making it worse for Mandy.' There were mutterings of protest, amongst which 'bloody newcomer' and 'pokin' 'er nose in' were heard. Annie took no notice whatsover, and continued to calm down Mandy and Robert, Olive and Ted, Susan Standing and Poppy, all of whom looked at her anxiously for guidance.

By the time an ambulance backed carefully into the field, Joey had come round. He was confused and crying, worried by the strangeness and not being able to speak properly. Poppy clung to his chair and would not be removed, although Susan had tried everything to prise her away.

'He's going to be fine now,' said Annie Bishop, bending down to the little girl. 'You'll see, he'll be right as rain and ready to play again very soon. Why don't you go home and do a lovely painting for him as a get-well present?' The calm, gentle voice was persuasive, and Poppy allowed herself to be taken away, calling and waving to Joey until she was out of sight.

Robert and Mandy went in the ambulance with Joey; and Olive and Ted, and little Margie, walked slowly towards the field gate.

'It's quite common, Mr Bates,' Annie Bishop said, 'for children like Joey. The loud noise acts as a trigger. Sometimes it can be flashing lights. And it was a very loud bang!'

There were now very few people left on the field, and Annie turned back to collect her soup saucepan from beside the fire. Andrew had taken the children home, leaving Annie to cope, knowing that she was more than capable. What a bit of luck they'd come along tonight, he had thought proudly. Annie to the rescue!

'Very well done!' Another admirer had come across to where Annie stood, winding her scarf tighter against the cold wind.

'Richard!' she said. 'I thought you'd gone off to telephone.'

'I did,' he said, 'but I thought some more help might be needed.'

Annie shook her head. 'I think we managed,' she said quietly.

Richard took her arm and walked with her to the gate. 'You're shaking,' he said. 'Better get you home and warmed up.'

'I'm not cold,' said Annie, and burst into tears.

170

'Hey!' said Richard. 'Come along, this won't do! It's all been too much for you, and you were so strong and good about it all.' But Annie couldn't stop, and he put his arms around her, just for comfort.

'Poor little soul,' she sobbed. 'He's so thin, and that bloody jerking racked his poor little body, and his poor mother and . . . oh, Richard, it's so unfair, isn't it?'

Richard Standing said nothing, but nodded wisely and tightened his arms.

CHAPTER TWENTY-TWO

In spite of torrential rain running like a waterfall down the sloping pavement outside the shop, it had been a busy morning. Not so much busy with trade, but in the exchange of gossip. Peggy had heard so many different versions of Joey's convulsion in the firework field, varying from a dismissive 'nothing more than a startled jumpin' about a bit' from Michael Roberts, in and out in seconds for his packet of fags, to Ellen Biggs's, 'It were a total collapse, my dear. We all thort 'e was a goner, poor little sod.' When Robert Bates stepped wetly and wearily through the door, Peggy was torn between saying nothing to make his obvious fatigue and depression any worse, and the desire to know the truth. In the event, he told her without prompting.

171

'Joey had an epileptic fit,' he said baldly. 'It was the big rocket, they said at the hospital. Could happen again at any time, or maybe never again. They've given him some pills, and he's looking a bit better this morning.' He sat down heavily on the chair by the Post Office cubicle, water dripping off his jacket and making small puddles on the floor. 'God, I blame myself, Mrs T.,' he said.

'How could you possibly know?' said Peggy. She looked at Robert, his face drawn and anxious, his hair uncombed and untidy. It was such a short time ago that he and Mandy had married in the village church, a beautiful, romantic wedding, and settled down with every expectation of a happy life. Well, that was a false hope for most of us, she thought, but we didn't all get the major blow as soon as Mandy and Robert.

'How's Mandy?' said Peggy. 'Does she need any help?'

'No, thanks all the same,' said Robert. 'Me mum's come round, and she's dealing with Margie while Mandy keeps an eye on Joey. We haven't said anything, but I reckon she feels like me, scared to leave him by himself. It's like walking on eggshells, Mrs T.'

Peggy could think of nothing helpful to say, and was just about to suggest a cup of tea if Robert had time, when a small voice came from behind the display units.

'Mum said I could come down and see him,

172

if you want.' Unnoticed and unrecognisable in his brother's huge old anorak, Eddie Jenkins had followed Robert into the shop and stayed out of sight, listening. Now he emerged, and came up to the counter with a tube of Smarties in his hand. 'He can have some of these,' he said in an excess of charitable impulse.

'That's very kind of you, Eddie,' said Robert. He stood up and passed a hand through his spiky hair. 'You might be just the person we need,' he said, and with a wan attempt at a smile he left the shop with Eddie close behind.

*   *   *

'Of course you may have a friend to tea, Helen,' said Annie Bishop. She was baking bread, kneading wholemeal dough on the floury table in the big vicarage kitchen. It was warm, and the smell of yeast intoxicating. All the children were there, except Honor, who was supposed to be having her afternoon nap in the nursery, but was in fact standing on the windowsill peering delightedly through the childproof bars at the Glebe Field rabbits feeding hungrily on the remains of Annie's cabbages.

Sticking and pasting was this afternoon's activity, and Faith, Helen and Bruce were busy with scissors and old magazines, each allocated a page of the giant scrap book to fill up by teatime.

'It's two friends,' said Helen, without looking up from the outline of a slavering bull terrier slowly emerging from her careful scissors.

'That's fine, darling,' said Annie. 'Those nice girls from Walnut Close?'

Helen shook her head. 'Not girls,' she said. 'Two boys. They're my best friends.' Annie did not miss the sly smile on Faith's face, nor the glance exchanged between her eldest daughter and a giggling Bruce.

'Ah,' said Annie, and summoned up chapter four of the latest authority on child upbringing. 'Well, of course that's fine. Which boys are they?'

'Eddie and George,' said Helen.

Bruce groaned elaborately. 'Oh God,' he said, 'not *George*!'

Helen turned on him. 'What's wrong with George?' she said fiercely.

'He's an oik,' said Bruce, with all the superiority of his six privileged years.

Later, when Annie told Andrew the whole story, she toned down her reaction to Bruce's disgusting remark. She didn't mention grabbing their only son by his arm and dragging him out of his seat. Faith told Andrew later that Mummy had shouted louder than she'd ever heard anyone, and banished Bruce upstairs to bed with a series of biffs to the bottom that sent him flying across the hall floor. All Andrew had said was, 'Naughty Bruce. Is George an oik, then?'

To Annie, sitting composedly in the armchair opposite him, her hair shining in the pool of light from the reading lamp on the table by her chair, Andrew said, 'I suppose we have to expect this kind of thing if we send the children to the village school. Nothing too serious in it, I'm sure of that. And Brucie is only five.'

'Nearly six,' said Annie, a very slight frown wrinkling her high, smooth brow. Her occasional bursts of anger and loss of control faded easily from her mind. 'Anyway,' she said, settling herself more comfortably, and hooking her leg across the arm of the chair, 'Faith said they probably wouldn't come. So that'll be that.'

'How's young Joey?' said Andrew, turning to the financial pages of his newspaper.

'Much better,' said Annie. 'I popped in this afternoon with Honor. Thought it would be a nice gesture to take him a comic, but Honor wouldn't part with it! Eddie Jenkins was there, making Joey laugh so he hardly noticed us. They seem to be coping very well, Mandy and Robert, just as if nothing had happened. Such a nice young couple, aren't they?' But Andrew was deep in the share prices and did not reply.

When Helen came home from school next day crying, saying Eddie and George didn't want to come, Annie dried her tears and smiled with relief, suggesting Poppy Standing as a substitute.

*   *   *

Less than a week had passed before Robert, meeting Colin Osman in the Arms, found him planning next year's firework creative framework, as he called it. 'So no more big rockets, Bob,' said Colin.

Why does he say 'Bob'? thought Robert. Nobody else does, nor never have. Makes me think he's talking to someone else. But Robert hadn't the heart to correct him. He'd got other, more important things to think about. And after all, Colin was the only bloke in the village who took on all the difficult jobs without moaning. He certainly meant well. When the second round of pints was set up, Robert smiled amiably and said, 'How's the bypass idea coming on, Colin? Haven't heard much about it lately . . .'

'Nothing to report, unfortunately,' said Colin. 'I've hit a complete stalemate at County Hall. They say they want more evidence of unacceptable levels of traffic, and I can only give them the numbers we collected, which aren't anywhere near the kind of figures they call critical.'

Robert was sympathetic, muttered something consoling, and looked around the bar. The pub was warm and comforting, with its great log fire and twinkling brasses, and Robert began to relax. Foxy Jenkins soon joined them, and the three stood talking of nothing much,

176

instinctively avoiding all mention of Joey and the disastrous rocket. Then just as Robert was buttoning his jacket and preparing to leave, the door opened and Andrew Bishop stepped in.

'Evening!' he said, and came over to the group by the bar. 'Can I get anyone anything?' They all shook their heads, and Robert muttered that he was about to leave. Silence fell. Then Colin Osman put his foot squarely in it.

'Saw your wife today, Mr Bishop,' he said. 'Out in the park. My lounge window looks over it, you know, wonderful view. There she was, pretty as a picture, up on an enormous horse! Brave girl, that. We haven't forgotten how she took over on bonfire night. Still, at least she'd got Mr Richard there today to look after her. I suppose she's done a lot of riding, has she? Has what I believe is called a good seat!' And Colin laughed loudly, pleased with himself that he could chat confidently to all sections of the village community, as he called it.

'Really?' said Andrew Bishop stiffly. 'Yes, she rode quite a lot as a young girl. So kind of Mr Standing to encourage her.'

As he walked away to sit on his own by the fire, landlord Don Cutt leaned over the bar and hissed in Colin's ear, 'Oops-a-daisy! Bit of a clanger there, Colin old son,' and he took away the dirty glasses to rinse them in his sink, chuckling with real delight.

CHAPTER TWENTY-THREE

'Ten weeks!' said Bill. 'Are they serious? Surely they can do the op before that? You'll not manage Christmas in the shop feeling like you do now.'

Peggy had already thought of that. 'They obviously don't consider gallstones particularly urgent,' she said. 'I'll just have to manage.' She thought of the rush leading up to the festive season, mountains of supplies to be brought back from the wholesalers, gifts, toys, the raw materials for village Christmas cooking. Then there would be extra patience needed when the children came in just on closing time, looking round for a present for Grannie, lifting up and inspecting every item in the Christmas corner.

She groaned without realising it, and Bill got up from his chair. He came across to the window where she was sitting and put his arm around her, kissing the top of her head. 'Peggy, my gel,' he said, 'we're going to get more help. You're to ask Sandra if she'd like to do more hours. She's a quick learner, and Sam'll certainly be glad of the money.'

Peggy relaxed in Bill's arms. He was right, of course, but ten weeks . . .

*   *   *

Sandra was delighted, relished the job and greeted customers with a cheerful smile. She knew most of them, anyway, from when she was a child at home in Macmillan Gardens, and was proud of her new status. Peggy frequently marvelled at the difference marriage and motherhood had made to her. No longer the sulky teenager refusing to meet anyone's eyes, rebellious and rude, now she revelled in the daily gossip, helped Ellen Biggs up and down the steps, offered advice on which were the best biscuits, frozen sausages, eating apples. And Peggy had been able to stretch out on the sofa, finding that being horizontal eased the ache. She dozed away the time, sometimes watched rubbish on television, allowed her mind to float.

One grey afternoon, a magazine programme flickering in the corner of the room warm from the spitting log fire, she surfaced from a daydream about hunting for violets along the old railway track. A couple of women were talking about private health care, and Peggy turned up the volume. Bells rang. Surely Frank had organised their future for every eventuality? He was like that, cautious and pessimistic, anticipating every possible disaster that could befall them. She'd laughed at him, certain that nothing very bad would come their way.

She went quickly to the bureau where Frank had kept their papers so neatly. After his death, the solicitor had sorted out everything, arranged Peggy's finances on a secure footing. He'd taken all their documents into his keeping, and assured her that should she need any help, he was always there. Right, Frank, she thought, picking up the phone, let's hope you have the last laugh.

'This is Mrs Turner, from Round Ringford. I'm a client, and would like to speak to Mr Thompson, please. No, he won't know what it's about, but it won't take long to tell him.' Secretaries nowadays, they think they own the business. It was the same with receptionists at the surgery. It was quite a feat if you could get past them to speak to the doctor himself.

'Absolutely, Mrs Turner,' said Mr Thompson, genuinely pleased to hear from Peggy again. 'Frank was a careful man, and the payments have been kept up by direct debit. You would certainly be covered—yes, the operation also. I'm sure of that. My own wife had her gall bladder removed last year. Still recovering, actually.' I don't wish to know that, thought Peggy. 'Virtually no waiting list,' continued Mr Thompson. 'Would you like me to get in touch with Dr Russell?' Scenting a hefty bill from the solicitor that would defeat Frank's good intentions, Peggy said no, she'd do all that herself, now she knew the payments had been kept up.

'Dear old Frank,' she said, replacing the telephone. 'Hope you're listening.'

More cheerful now, she went through to the shop to tell Sandra the good news. Bill had just come in, and was tickling a giggling Alison.

180

Sandra stood close by, and Bill had put a friendly arm around her, giving her a squeeze. 'See? Mummy's ticklish too!' he whispered in Alison's ear. Then they saw Peggy, and became quiet. 'Hello, my gel,' said Bill. 'Feeling better?'

Peggy put her hand to her side, where a sudden jab reminded her that all was far from well. She blinked, confused, not sure what was going on. 'Well, yes,' she said, and told him what she'd discovered.

'Great, Mrs T.!' said Sandra. 'Means you'll be OK for Christmas. It's really good news. And I can hold the fort here while you're in hospital. Don't suppose it'll be for long. They can't get rid of you quick enough these days!' Sandra rattled on with horror stories of people she had known in and out of hospital, and Peggy tried not to listen. She made a fuss of Alison, and for some reason found it difficult to meet Bill's eyes.

CHAPTER TWENTY-FOUR

A cold light, different from previously dingy grey mornings, filtered through the chink in the Bishops' daisy-sprinkled bedroom curtains, and Annie sat up in bed, rubbing her eyes with a premonition of seeing something new.

She eased herself out from under the duvet, careful not to wake Andrew, and tiptoed across the warm carpet to the window. Pulling the curtain aside, she looked out and saw a sight so beautiful that she drew in her breath sharply, stirring Andrew in his sleep. Snow had fallen, and everywhere was changed. There was no longer any division between the long driveway down to the lane and the lawns, flowerbeds, and paths. All had become one wide spread of undefiled crisp, sparkling whiteness. Annie blinked in the early sun, which rose slowly into a pastel sky. She could see the church, its roof and tower thickly iced, exactly like the tiny one she and the children put each year on the Christmas cake. She half expected Father Christmas to sail magically across the sky in front of her.

'Andrew!' She could not contain herself any longer, and had to share the excitement. There were no sounds from the nursery, or from Faith's bedroom up in the attic. Time enough for the children, and goodness, how they would love it! But now it was just for herself and Andrew. She ran across the room and grabbed his hand, pulling him stumb   t of bed. 'Come on, Andrew! You can't imagine the beauty of it. Come quickly, before it goes away!'

It was not going away, of course, not for several days, but Annie was right in a way. As soon as the post van arrived, and the postman struggled up the driveway, leaving deep footprints in the snow, and after old Ricky and Tinker had tussled in delight on what had been the lawn, leaving bare patches of brown and muddy green showing through, the miraculous virginity of it all had gone. Breakfast was abandoned. Before school, a hastily built snowman had appeared under the cedar tree, lurching drunkenly to one side, and reluctantly left for later, when the children came home, with promises of a warm scarf and Andrew's old hat. There was just time to give him a carrot nose and two shiny pieces of coal for eyes.

The lane had been roughly cleared by Foxy Jenkins and Bill Turner, and as Annie turned out into the road with Faith and Helen in wellies and woollies, Honor wrapped in quilted cotton like a tiny Humpty Dumpty with only small twinkling feet showing, and small Bruce encased in his stiff, unyielding Barbour, they whooped and gathered snowballs, and generally behaved like the innocently delighted townies that they were. Richard Standing, driving at a crawl in his Range Rover, came upon them, and carefully slowed to a halt.

'Morning!' he shouted, smiling into Annie's blue eyes as she straightened up from scooping a fistful of snow.

'Hello Richard,' she said. 'Isn't it the most wonderful morning?' She came up to his window and grinned in such a disarming, childlike way that it was all he could do not to leap out, take her in his arms, and kiss her as thoroughly as he knew how. However, he merely touched her hand lightly, as she held on

183

to the door, keeping her balance in the snow.

'Wonderful,' he agreed, 'but not so good for we poor souls who have to get around the estate. And Andrew? Did he get away for the train?' And if he did, he added to himself, I'll be straight round as soon as you've got these children into school, and we can have jolly romps for as long as you like.

'Yes, he did,' said Annie, 'but I'm not sure if he'll make it home tonight. Ah, there's Jean Jenkins on her way. Good old Jean, she never lets me down. Goodbye, then, Richard!'

Good old Jean, indeed, thought Richard. Saved me from suggesting some very unwise antics with lovely Annie. He sighed, but not seriously, quite confident that the time would come. And the chase was always fun, sometimes more fun than the catch. He drove along behind the Bishops, watching Annie's long legs in their scarlet leggings as she ran from one child to another, picking them up out of snow drifts, scolding Bruce when he pushed a handful of snow down Honor's neck and made her cry.

His mobile phone rang, and with one hand on the wheel he answered it. 'Not too bad, darling,' he said, 'but I think Poppy should stay at home today. I don't think we'll get through to Waltonby without the risk of sliding into the ditch. That sharp turn by the cuttings will be lethal. Yes, I'll be back shortly, as soon as I've consulted with Bill. See you soon, Susan.'

The Bishops were in the school playground now, and Richard accelerated, driving along the main street with relative ease. Bill should be with Foxy down by the spinney, checking the water troughs. He looked in his driving mirror, and saw the scarlet legs flash across the road and disappear into the shop. Lovely Annie. Must really get Susan to invite them to dinner. Nothing like a satisfactory base of friendship to take things a little further. Richard began to hum to himself, a cheerful, seasonal song.

*   *   *

'Where do the weeks go, Mrs Turner?' said Annie, pulling a shopping list from her pocket. 'I expect Christmas is your busiest time?'

Peggy nodded. She'd counted up the weeks this morning on her calendar after opening the letter from Three Counties Hospital in Tresham. One week hence she would be in there, recovering from the operation. The surgeon had been optimistic: 'A good chance, eighty-five per cent I would say, of whipping out the offending portion by what is commonly known as keyhole surgery.' And then he'd gone on to explain how, all things being favourable, they should be able to make four small incisions and insert probes and a tiny camera. And presumably a cutting instrument of some sort, though he tactfully hadn't mentioned it.

'Well, yes, it is,' Peggy said. 'And this year it

185

will be even more hectic. I have to go into hospital for a few days, and Sandra will be taking over, more or less. Bill will help out, of course, but it is going to be difficult, I'm afraid.' What am I telling her all this for? she thought. Perfect stranger, couldn't care less about my gallstones. Annie's face was full of concern, and she immediately offered any help that might be needed. 'I could go to the wholesaler for you, perhaps, or have Alison after school if Sandra is in the shop. Anything like that, Mrs Turner, I'd be only too pleased.'

And she means it, too, thought Peggy, smiling in gratitude. Too good to be true, Doreen Price thinks, as do Ivy Beasley, Doris Ashbourne, and most of the other WI members. But, as Ellen frequently said, speak as you find, and Peggy found Annie Bishop nothing but kind, pleasant and very pretty.

'Thank you,' she said. 'It might be very helpful if you could meet Alison once or twice. Sandra is very particular about being at the school gate, not just in case she should be abducted in front of most of Ringford, but because of the dreadful traffic. And I do agree with her. Only yesterday there was a terrible squeal of brakes as one of the Walnut Close children dashed across in front of a car. Locals know when school's out, and drive accordingly, but the lunatics we get through here now treat the village like a racetrack. That'll be six pounds fifty, please.' She helped Annie fill her

186

wicker shopping basket, and watched her cross the road and stop by the bus shelter to talk to Ellen Biggs, who was peering shortsightedly at a poster advertising a long-gone summer car boot sale in Fletching.

Minutes later, Ellen was safely in the shop, perching on the chair, holding forth about other villages that made sure their elderly residents were safe in the shocking snowy weather that could come at any time.

'You know you only have to send a message with Warren Jenkins when he delivers the papers,' said Peggy. 'Bill will bring whatever you want at whatever time you want it. You know that, Ellen. How did you manage in the snow, anyway?'

Ellen had to admit, grumpily, that Foxy Jenkins had been in first thing and cleared her garden path, and then he and Bill had scraped the pavement and put down salt and grit all the way between the lodge and the main street.

'There you are, then,' said Peggy with a smile.

'Too right, my dear,' said Ellen, looking sheepish. 'It's like Ivy says, I just 'ave to 'ave somethin' to grumble about. No, I'm well taken care of in Ringford, I know that really. 'Ere, you got any new Mr Kipling's? It's my turn today, and Ivy and Doris'll be making snide remarks about my cookin' if I dish out the coffee and walnut one more time.'

Peggy found her a very tasty-looking Dutch

apple cake from a new supplier, and helped the shaky old woman down the shop steps. Bill had scraped these, too, and made them perfectly safe for customers like Ellen.

Once on the pavement, Ellen stopped, leaning on her stick. She looked across the Green, now a broad, snowy space, crisscrossed with tracks made by children, dogs and large black crows looking for something to eat. The sky was clear and heavenly blue, and everywhere sparkled in the thin winter sunlight. Ellen looked back up at Peggy, who stood with her hands in her overall pockets, face turned to the sun, drinking in the loveliness of Ringford under snow.

'Nothin' like it, is there, my dear?' Ellen said. 'They can keep them Switzerland places. Ringford could beat anywhere into a cocked 'at today. Cheerio, then. See yer tomorrer.'

*　　　*　　　*

Andrew had spent the afternoon studying the papers for a very tricky divorce case, and saw nothing of the snowy blessings. There was nothing to see, in any case, in the long wide stretch of the Farringdon Road. London had had only a sprinkling, and this had long since disappeared under the constant stream of traffic and the funny warmth of a city street.

He lifted his telephone and summoned his secretary. 'Do you happen to know the forecast for this evening?' he said. She shook her head, but said she would find out. 'Check the trains from Euston, too, please,' said Andrew. The thought of shivering on a draughty platform, waiting for a train that didn't come, filled him with gloom. His mother lived in Kensington, and he knew she kept his old room and single bed permanently at the ready. Perhaps just for this one night, when everything was bound to be dicey on the journey home. Annie would be fine, and Jean and Foxy would always help out if she needed it. The door opened, and he listened to his secretary's litany of warnings from the traffic information bureau. 'Right,' he said. 'thanks very much. Now could you get me this number straight away?' And in no time at all he was speaking to his delighted mother.

CHAPTER TWENTY-FIVE

'I said to Doris that I thought it would be better to cancel it this afternoon.' Ivy's voice was sharp, sharper than usual. Since wrenching her ankle she was wary about falling, and there was no doubt that in spite of the scraping and gritting, there were still very treacherous patches between her house and Ellen's. 'But, oh no, Doris said we couldn't disappoint Ellen, so here we are. And, of course,' she added nastily, 'it would be a shame if Ellen has been slaving away over a hot stove all morning baking for our tea.'

All this was water off a duck's back to Ellen, and she continued to pour boiling water into her large, chipped teapot. 'You wait, Ivy,' she cackled 'till you tasted my latest triumph. 'Ere, Doris, take this tray, an' I'll bring in the cake. Dutch apple cake, my ole mother used to call it. Recipe passed down through our family, Ivy. Always the best, tried and true.'

How could you, Ellen? thought Doris, who had followed her into the shop this morning and been told that Ellen had bought the last of the new Dutch apple cakes and there wouldn't be another delivery until next week. Still, she would never give her away, and could only listen with admiration as Ellen continued to fill in the background of the ancestral recipe.

The cake was good, Ivy had to admit it, and they all had two slices. Ellen was poor, relatively, but she was ridiculously generous. 'I could wrap up the rest for you, Ivy,' she said. 'I've still got the box.'

The silence following this giveaway lasted for several seconds, and Doris crossed her fingers tightly underneath her plate. Ellen's ruddy face went a slightly darker red, and Ivy bit her lip. Through narrowed eyes, she stared at Ellen. 'Dutch apple cake, eh?' she said in a tight voice. 'Family recipe, handed down?' Ellen nodded miserably. 'Well,' said Ivy with a sniff, 'it was certainly worth keeping. Very nice indeed. But I've already got the remains of the weekend's sponge, so you hang on to it, Ellen. It'll do for tomorrow.'

You could just never tell, thought Doris, which way Ivy would jump. The atmosphere cleared, and the women relaxed into a close examination of how every part of the village was affected by snow, much earlier this year than expected.

'Saw that Mrs Bishop playin' snowballs with 'er children. She's not much more'n a child 'erself,' said Ellen, throwing another log on the glowing fire.

'I have to disagree,' said Ivy. 'If you work it out, Ellen, she must be thirty-three if she's a day. Occupation therapist, or whatever you call it, working for three years before marrying that Andrew, and the eldest—Faith, is it? Nice name, that. She'll soon be ten. She's got one of those faces, that's all.'

'Lucky her,' said Doris. 'And Andrew's good looking, too. Very nice family all round. I reckon we're lucky to have them in the vicarage. When you think what we might have got. . .'

The daylight was fading outside Ellen's diamond-paned windows, and Ivy stood up. 'Best be going, Doris,' she said. 'We want to be home before dark.'

'The funny thing is,' said Ellen, as if Ivy had not spoken, 'that they're not more chummy with the Standin's. You'd a thought 'avin the children and that. Still, Mrs S. is a stuck-up so-

191

and-so. Probably thinks the Bishops aren't good enough.'

'Mr Richard thinks Mrs Bishop is good enough,' said Ivy darkly. Ears pricked, and two interested faces looked at her.

'What d'you mean, Ivy?' said Ellen.

'What I say,' said Ivy. 'Nothing more and nothing less. Mr Richard is like an old tomcat when there's a pretty woman about. Always been the same, silly fool. Still, I never seen a happier married pair than the Bishops, so p'raps he'll have to look elsewhere this time.'

'Well I never,' said Doris Ashbourne. 'You can't be right, Ivy. I've not noticed anything.'

'None so blind as those that won't see,' said Ivy. 'Seeing good in everybody is all very well, Doris, but it'll let you down in time.' And with this gloomy prophecy, Ivy led the way to Ellen's front gate and stepped out cautiously for home.

*   *   *

'Here come the girls, Bill,' giggled Sandra, looking out of the shop window and across the Green to where Ivy and Doris were plodding along the slushy road towards the Arms. They had abandoned the pavement, already beginning to ice over as the afternoon temperature fell, reckoning the road the safer bet. Alison was in the sitting-room with Peggy, curled up on the sofa and watching yet another rerun of *Tom and Jerry*.

Bill had come home early, agreeing with Foxy that there was no point trying to get anything more done today. The stock were safe, warm, fed and watered. They had cleared all the paths and driveways so that the Standings could come and go, and Bill had checked the greenhouses and outbuildings for frozen pipes. Now he sat in the kitchen with his shoes off and a mug of hot tea in his hands.

The door between kitchen and shop was open, and Bill watched Sandra as she stood on a stool, reaching up for a packet of sugared cereals to take home for Alison's breakfast. Her skirt was very short, and as she reached up it was even shorter. Blimey, thought Bill, who'd have thought young Sandra Roberts would have turned out so well. As she turned to come down from the stool, she caught his eye and he looked away quickly, embarrassed lest she should think he was staring. Which, of course, he was. He had to admit that Sandra's exposed thighs were a very pretty sight. God, he thought disgustedly to himself, you are pathetic. Just because poor old Peggy was a bit off it at the moment, here he was getting excited over a girl young enough to be his daughter. Just watch it, Bill, he told himself. He saw with some alarm that Sandra was smiling at him, and it was a knowing smile.

The shop door opened, a welcome interruption. Doris and Ivy both stepped in, and Doris came straight to the counter.

'Sandra,' she said, 'have you got any of those bundles of kindling left? No, it's not for me. The bungalow's gas, as you know. But I noticed Ellen was using damp sticks she must have picked up from her garden.'

'No need for that,' said Bill, padding through in his stockinged feet, his kind face concerned. 'I can take her some dry kindling. Fact is, I had it in mind and this snow made me forget. Soon as I've had a wash and change, I'll take it down. Thanks for reminding me, Doris.'

Ivy sniffed. She had always chopped her own sticks in the back yard, but was beginning to feel her age when the mornings were cold and the axe heavy. 'Gatherin' a few sticks won't kill Ellen Biggs,' she said. 'A bit of exercise never hurt nobody. And you needn't look at Bill like that, Sandra Roberts,' she said. 'I don't recall anyone offerin' kindling to me, not even when I had my foot up.'

Peggy had come in and heard this, and began to protest. 'That is not fair, Miss Beasley,' she said. 'We offered to come in and keep your range going, lift coal and wood and anything else you needed. You're very quick to forget.'

'Ah, but when I said I could cope you all believed me,' said Ivy. 'Probably because I ain't achieved sainthood like Ellen Biggs. St Ellen . . . well, if you ask me it's not a kindness in the end. Sitting all day in her chair is not good for her. Better out gathering sticks.'

Doris, who had been standing quietly by the

194

counter, finally exploded. 'What on earth is all this about, Ivy?' she said. 'All I said was that Ellen could do with some dry kindling. That's all. And if you could for once mind your own business it would be a great relief to us all. Now then, Peggy, I'll take a quarter of ham and two tomatoes, and that will do for my supper.'

*   *   *

'It's the snow,' said Bill, as he and Peggy got undressed in their warm bedroom. An electric radiator had banished the room's usual chill, and now they lingered, Peggy folding her clothes neatly, and Bill staring at himself in the little mirror over the chest of drawers.

'What is?' said Peggy. She was not really listening, her mind already on the next morning's journey in to the Three Counties Hospital. Her bag was packed and she meant to have a bath and wash her hair in the morning.

'All that nonsense with Ivy Beasley in the shop,' he said. 'Everybody's edgy, not feeling comfortable. Changes everything, snow does, and puts folk adrift. They don't feel safe. That's all it was. Ivy was irritable and scared of falling, and Doris worried about old Ellen.'

'The only one who wasn't worried about something was Sandra, bless her,' said Peggy. 'I'm stewing about tomorrow . . .'

'And me,' said Bill. Crossing the room, he put his arms around her and firmly consigned

195

the vision of Sandra's thighs to the back of his mind.

'But at least Sandra and Alison are like a breath of fresh air,' said Peggy. 'Thank God they came back to the village . . . hey, Bill! Oh well, why not?' she chuckled. 'Might be our last chance.'

Fortunately Bill did not catch her last words, as he lifted her bodily and put her down on the bed. 'Nobody matters but us,' he said, climbing in beside her and pulling up the bedclothes. 'Now then, my lovely gel, gently does it.'

CHAPTER TWENTY-SIX

Macmillan Gardens was quiet and empty. Michael Roberts had yet to stagger up from the Arms, and cold moonlight cast dark shadows across the common ground between the houses, now a uniform white except for black patches where the children had scraped up snow to build a snowman far bigger and more threatening than the one in the vicarage garden. William Roberts and Warren Jenkins, ostensibly building for the younger ones, had gone to town. The snowman towered over even the tallest of them, and an old balaclava of William's had been pulled down over a sinisterly small head. Instead of a friendly pipe, the grinning mouth made of curving sticks contained rows of blackened stones for teeth, uneven and ugly. Between his large red carrot fingers, Warren had placed a plastic machine gun and William had contributed a realistic replica hand grenade which rested cosily in the snowman's icy pocket.

'I don't like it,' Eddie Jenkins had wailed ungratefully. 'It's horrible. I want a real snowman, like the Bishops'.' He had set off for home, his wellies sinking deep into the snow. 'I'm gonna tell Mum,' he shouted, and as he reached his garden gate he added, 'and Dad . . .'

Now, at night, long after Eddie had gone to bed, the snowman was even more sinister in the empty Gardens. His shadow was long and still, and as Foxy looked out with Jean to admire the moonlit scene, they agreed that tomorrow it should be knocked down and a more friendly character made for the children.

'William Roberts always was a bit odd,' said Jean, tucking her arm through Foxy's as they stood looking out. 'Still, what can you expect with a father and mother like that? Poor little sod, what chance 'as he got?'

'Darren's doin' all right,' said Foxy. 'Got away in time, I suppose. I worry sometimes about Warren bein' such good friends with William, but it don't seem to have done him no harm so far.' He pulled Jean back from the window and drew the curtains. 'Let's keep out the cold,' he said. 'All right to look at, but I wouldn't complain if it'd all gone by morning.

197

Not so good on the farm, or on the roads, come to that.'

As Jean went out to the kitchen to make a last cup of tea, the telephone in their narrow hall began to ring. 'Who on earth?' she said, and paused as Foxy went to answer it.

'Yes, it's Foxy Jenkins,' he said. 'Oh, it's you, Mrs Bishop. Something wrong? Did you want Jean?' But it was clear to Jean that she wasn't wanted, and as Foxy nodded and said yes and no, she filled the kettle and plugged it in. Eventually Foxy replaced the receiver and came into the kitchen, where Jean was pouring boiling water on to teabags. 'Well,' he said, 'that were a funny one.'

'What did our Annie want?' said Jean. 'What couldn't wait till morning?'

'She sounded scared. Said Andrew was in London for the night, and she was alone, except for the kids, of course. There was a noise outside, she said, and she was sure it was a prowler. She daren't open the curtains, and didn't know what to do.'

'And?' said Jean, knowing what was coming next.

'I said I'd go down and have a look around. Felt sorry for her, really. I don't suppose there's anybody about, but it'll set her mind at rest.'

'Too much imagination, that'll be it,' said Jean crossly. She'd been about to suggest an early night, but now it would be later than usual by the time Foxy returned. 'Go on, then,' she

198

said. 'And don't get lured in for coffee nor nothing. Bit of a siren, our Annie, I reckon. And she don't half fancy herself, so watch out, my lad.'

Foxy snorted and couldn't trust himself to answer, so he pulled on an old coat and cap, his big rubber boots, and grabbing a torch from the kitchen shelf, he left, saying he'd be back in two jiffs.

* * *

It had been a specially good night in the Arms for Michael Roberts. He'd won the darts championship again, and his mates had stood him one round after another, until finally Don Cutt had refused to give him any more. 'Time, gentlemen, *please*!' he'd said for the sixth time, and at last was able to lock and bolt the big oak door behind the last stragglers, one of whom was a very drunken Michael Roberts.

'I shall be fine,' he said in a blurred voice to his best mate from Fletching. 'No' far t'go. Soon b'home.' His friends departed, and left him standing, swaying slightly, in the orange light of the pub's security light. Delicate sparkling snowflakes had started to fall, and he reached out for them, smiling foolishly. 'Gotcha,' he said, and brought his closed fist to his mouth. 'Where's th'gone?' he said to himself, looking in astonishment at his damp palm. 'Bes' be home,' he muttered and set off with his head down, unaware that he was heading in entirely the wrong direction.

By the time he reached the stone bridge over the Ringle, he knew he was lost. Nothing looked familiar in the white, unfriendly moonlight. All the landmarks by which he was accustomed to find his way home had disappeared under the thick layers of snow, and he blundered on, hoping in a befuddled way that he would meet someone soon who could put him right.

Ah, he thought, turning into an opening between hedges, this is it. He shuffled more confidently through the snow and came up to what he could see quite clearly was a house. 'Where's m'door?' he said, and fumbled in his pocket for a key. No, no that wasn't his door. Must be in the wrong garden, he thought, and set off round the building to find his own territory. Have to watch out for the dog, he reminded himself, knowing that his Alsatian would happily have a piece of him if he blundered into the kennel at this time of night.

He'd gone right round the house—it seemed a lot bigger than usual—and come back to the driveway, black tracks showing in the moonlight. What was that, then? He peered with fuzzy eyes at two red lights, stationary at the bottom of the drive. As he tried to focus properly, he heard a car door slam and footsteps approaching. Blimey what the hell was goin' on? He was beginning to realise this

200

was not Macmillan Gardens and he was very far from home. He stumbled clumsily round the side of the building, but kept an eye on the drive in case he needed to run. A tall, dark figure appeared, silhouetted against the moon. I know that man, Michael Roberts thought. Who is it, now? Friend or foe? Stand and deliver! He began to chuckle at his own wit, and the man stopped, listening.

'Christ!' Michael Roberts heard the expletive from where he stood, shivering now and feeling decidedly sick. He began to walk forward, desperate for help, but the figure turned sharply and retreated. The car door slammed again, and the red lights disappeared.

At the same moment, Foxy Jenkins approached the vicarage, and saw the recognisable shape of a Range Rover disappearing. Boss is out late, he thought, and then forgot all about it in the disgusting task of rescuing Michael Roberts, cleaning him up, and telling Annie Bishop that all was well, it was just this bugger on the beer again.

*   *   *

'Poor woman,' he said, as he climbed into bed beside Jean. She had her eyes closed and was sulking, pretending to be asleep, but Foxy knew otherwise. 'She was frightened out of her wits. Trouble about them townies, Jean, they ain't used to village ways. Probably the first time she's bin on her own at night in that old barn of a house.' He put out the bedside light, and snuggled into Jean's ample back. 'Bet you'll hear all about it tomorrow,' he said. It was only as he drifted into sleep that he remembered the Range Rover. Probably Jean would hear about that too, he grinned to himself. Or maybe not . . . Foxy began to snore.

CHAPTER TWENTY-SEVEN

Freezing temperatures in the night had crisped the snow and made the main street treacherous. Bill helped Peggy into the car with care. 'Can't have you slipping over now, Peg,' he said. 'I want you back home as soon as possible. It isn't home when you're not here.'

The last time he'd been anywhere near a hospital had been when his mother was dying, and had been taken in for the last few miserable days. Although he was not at all squeamish, dealing with animals on the estate from birth to death and everything in between, the idea of an operating theatre and people in masks and rubber gloves made him feel physically sick. He even avoided medical series on television. Phrases like 'under the knife' and 'opened up on the table' had floated through his troubled dreams, and he had woken early. Unable to go back to sleep, he'd watched the bedside clock inch forward.

Peggy was quiet in the car. She watched the sun rise above the line of poplars on the Bagley Road, and saw a black crow fly up clumsily from feasting on the carcass of a squashed rabbit in the road. She thought of Frank. It had been just such a macabre meal that had caused him to swerve on an icy road and hit a tree, killing him instantly. She shivered. People had been known to die unexpectedly under anaesthetic.

'Cold, Peggy?' said Bill, and turned up the heating. 'I expect you're nervous, my gel. And I'm not such a fool as to say don't worry. But it'll soon be over, and then we'll have you back home, and maybe we can go away for a few days.'

'And what about Christmas?' said Peggy.

'Well, yes, that's tricky,' said Bill. 'Perhaps you could go and stay with the Markses for a break. It'd be warm and comfortable above their book shop, and you could gossip with Heather and let her cook for you.'

'What about the Post Office? And you've to be at work during the day.'

'Sandra's very good,' said Bill with a smile. 'She's turned out a very capable girl. I'm sure we could cope between us.' He slowed down to a crawl. Coming up was a double bend with high banks and hedges, a danger spot at the best of times, but now it was like a bobsleigh run. He sounded his horn twice to warn any oncoming traffic, and concentrated hard, not really listening to Peggy's reply. This was just as well, because the minute she'd said it, Peggy knew it was silly.

'Not sure I can trust you alone for that long with such a pretty girl.' She meant it to sound teasing, but it came out as a rebuke, and she thanked God for the tractor that suddenly appeared in the middle of the road, causing Bill to brake to a halt.

By the time Bill had reversed into a field gateway, and the tractor had rumbled past with a wave from the farmworker, the moment had fortunately passed, and they began to talk about other things.

'Sure you've got everything, Peg?' said Bill. 'Still, I can always come back. I shall be there this evening, after the op.'

The operation was planned for half past two, and Peggy knew that she would still be very sleepy in the evening. 'Don't bother to come in today,' she said. 'I don't suppose I'll be very useful until tomorrow. It'll be a waste of your time.'

Bill raised his eyebrows and looked at her in surprise. 'Of course I shall be there,' he said. 'Can't trust anybody to look after you properly, not like I can. Doesn't matter if you're asleep. I shan't rest if I can't see for myself that you're OK.'

Peggy reached out and put her hand over his, where it rested big and strong on the steering wheel. She could feel his warmth through her knitted glove. 'You are a dear,' she said, and sniffed, feeling tears on the way. 'Sorry,' she muttered, pulling out her handkerchief. 'Can't help feeling a bit low.'

The Three Counties Hospital had been designed to look like a hotel, and as Peggy and Bill entered the reception lobby they were greeted by a glamorous blonde who smiled and summoned a porter to help them with Peggy's suitcase.

'That won't be necessary,' said Bill stiffly. 'I can carry my wife's things, no trouble. She's not staying long.' The receptionist smiled. I suppose everybody says that, thought Bill and had a moment of absolute panic. We could just turn around and go straight home. Surely gallstones can be dissolved by drugs or something? It's not too late. But Peggy was smiling confidently, as if now she'd arrived she knew what to do. As if the worst was over, thought Bill, and he wanted to cry.

The formalities of admittance took a long time. Peggy's room was on the first floor, and a large window looked out over the front gardens of the hospital and away to the snowbound golf course which was part of the grounds. A big mental hospital, a forbidding Victorian building, loomed through the trees in the distance, and the acres surrounding it had slowly been infilled with extensions and day units, and the nine-hole golf course round which mostly retired business ladies and teachers plodded in colourful clothes on fine days and foul. The Three Counties, a private hospital with first-class facilities, was the latest building to be put up on the fringe of this oasis of green in the middle of Tresham, and Peggy's dapper, bearded surgeon specialist had a permanent post here, with consulting room and mature but attractive secretary in attendance.

'Mr Fisher will be up to see you shortly,' said the nurse, one of several who had come in and asked Peggy questions about allergies and drugs. One of them had weighed her.

'Don't suppose I'll be much less when they've taken out a bit of me,' Peggy said wryly. The nurse laughed, but Bill swallowed hard.

A menu sheet had been left for Peggy to choose from a selection of very elegant-sounding dishes. Bill glanced through it, standing to one side, trying not to look superfluous. He wished desperately that he was back in the Hall gardens, getting on quietly with his jobs, looking forward to seeing Peggy at teatime and settling down to watch telly with her in the chair opposite him, smiling at him, making it home. But if she had to be here, then he would stay for as long as he was allowed. At last they were left alone, awaiting the visitation from Mr Fisher, alias God.

'You all right, gel?' said Bill. 'Want to unpack your things?' He had snooped around and found a cupboard and plenty of drawers, and a very swish, roomy bathroom with shower and loo, and everything sparkling white. 'Look,' he said, 'you've got some of those freebies—bath gel and shampoo and that—just like our honeymoon hotel!' He helped her hang up her clothes and put out her toothbrush and flannel, all new, as if for a special occasion. Well, it was, in a way, thought Bill, though not exactly joyous.

Peggy began to undress. 'This feels really silly,' she said apologetically. 'Getting undressed in the middle of the day.' She unfolded her new nightdress, pale pink to match the new dressing-gown.

'Here,' said Bill, coming close to her and taking her face in his hands, 'shall I get undressed too? We could manage a quick one before this Mr Fisher arrives.' Peggy laughed, as Bill had intended, and they kissed.

Like a star actor in an American hospital drama, Mr Gregory Fisher flung open the door and walked rapidly across to Peggy. He was followed at a respectful distance by a pretty nurse carrying a clipboard and pen. Bill retreated hastily and hovered in the bathroom, trying not to look foolish.

'Mrs Turner. Good morning, my dear,' said Mr Gregory Fisher. He was jovial, made one or two small jokes, explained in simple terms what was going to happen to her, and gave off about as much genuine warmth as an electric coal fire with the heat turned off. Peggy wished he would stop smiling. This wasn't a social occasion, for God's sake. This afternoon she would have her stomach bare in front of this man, and he would cut her open in four places and stick probes and cameras and presumably knives into intimate parts of her that not even she had seen. She didn't want him to tell her about his grandchildren. She just wanted him to ask the necessary medical questions and go away and prepare himself, lie down and relax, or something, for the extremely important task he had to perform at half past two.

After what Peggy was sure was the exact amount of time allocated to her, Mr Fisher stood up from the chair by her bed, nodded to the nurse, flashed an all-embracing smile round the room, and left at the same smart pace with which he had arrived. On to the next gall bladder, thought Peggy. Bet he's forgotten what I look like already.

'You'd better go and get some lunch,' said Peggy, but Bill shook his head.

'If you can't eat, then I shan't, either.'

'Oh Bill,' said Peggy, 'there's no point in both of us starving! Go on, go home and see how Sandra's getting on, and make a sandwich or something. There's the remains of that pie in the fridge, or you could take some sausages out of the shop. Go on, there's a love. I shall be quite happy with my book until they come to take me away ...'

As soon as Bill had gone, looking at his

watch and counting up for her the very small number of hours before he would be back again, Peggy sat on top of the flowery counterpane and took up her book. But the words refused to mean anything, and she put it down again, looking round the room. There was a television set, radio, and a copy of today's *Daily Telegraph*, all neatly arranged where she could easily reach them. Blimey, she thought, you don't get this on the National Health. She felt momentarily guilty, thinking of all the poor souls who were waiting for six months or more for their rotting gall bladders to be removed, but the guilt quickly vanished as she remembered Frank's careful husbandry. He had worked hard for every penny, and it was because he had been sensible with their money that she was able to be here.

Allergic to almost everything that prevented anaesthetic sickness, Peggy duly arrived in the operating theatre fully conscious, without the moral support of pre-medication. A tall, statuesque and rather beautiful woman announced herself as the anaesthetist, and as instructions were called to an off-stage assistant, Peggy heard 'pethidine'. She then incurred the beauty's wrath by saying at this late stage that she was allergic to that, too.

*   *   *

Bill turned up at Peggy's door just as she was

throwing up into a kidney-shaped bowl, her head held sympathetically by a bosomy nurse. If anyone had been looking, they would have seen Bill turn green, but he was able to back out unnoticed and lean his head against the cool glass of a corridor window until the nausea passed.

'She'll sleep now,' said the nurse, as Bill tiptoed into the room and looked anxiously at a comatose Peggy.

'Can I stay for a bit?'

'Of course! Just sit down and hold her hand. I'm sure she'd like that.'

Peggy knew he was there, but couldn't force herself awake to say hello. She gave his hand an imperceptible squeeze, and then drifted off into an extraordinary dream in which she shuffled through swirling snow, her feet bare and only rags for clothes, on and on in dreadful silence, until she came face to face with the oak tree, the squashed rabbit, and Frank's car, half-crushed in the ditch.

Bill saw the frown on her sleeping face, and it was all he could do not to take her up in his arms and straight home. Sod it all, he thought, and sat on, watching over his wife. He was a man who could fix things, used to being the one who sorted out village problems, confident in his physical strength. He bent over and put the smallest of butterfly kisses on Peggy's hand. No good to her now, are you, you bugger? He had never felt so helpless.

By the time Bill drove into the village it was dark and empty, except for the orange light outside the pub, and two figures about to disappear into it for the nightly jar or two. Tom and Foxy. Bill suddenly wanted desperately the company of these two good old friends. He pulled into the pub car park and switched off his engine. Peggy wouldn't mind. He still had had no food since breakfast, but didn't feel like eating. Perhaps after a pint of Morton's he would fancy something.

The bar was warm and welcoming, and Tom Price immediately took Bill's arm and pulled him into the small circle of friends. With a pint inside him, and the reassurance of sharing some of his worries with the lads, Bill at last relaxed.

'Fancy a game of darts?' said Foxy, and Bill found he could throw with a steady hand. He won a couple of games, and was treated to another couple of pints. The thought that he should have something solid as a foundation for all this beer occurred to him only briefly.

'Will you be OK in the house on your own tonight?' said Tom. 'You know Doreen always has a bed made up for emergencies.'

Bill shook his head. 'I shall be fine,' he said. 'I need to be there to open up in the morning. Sandra's coming in early, and the post ladies need to sort the letters at the crack of dawn!'

He laughed loudly, and was aware somewhere in the back of his mind that he hadn't said anything particularly funny.

'Time for bed, then,' said Tom, and took Bill's arm. 'I'll see you home, lad. You're a bit upset, naturally. Not too steady on your pins. Here we go. Good night, all.'

There was no moon, and with a steadily rising temperature, rain had begun to fall, turning the snow to slush. 'Oops!' said Bill, sliding about in the gutter. 'No, Tom, I'll be fine now. You go on home. I can see well enough. Not like Michael Roberts! I know the way to go home, just watch me . . .'

Tom looked doubtful, but set off for the farm glancing back now and then to see that Bill was making progress.

*   *   *

The Parents' Association meeting in the school had gone on much longer than usual, the item on dangerous traffic taking up a large part of the evening. All the parents were worried. They wanted to know what Colin Osman was doing about the problem, and put up several suggestions for solving it. Some of these were wild: chairman Peter Dodwell from Walnut Close suggested manning a barricade at each end of the village until the County Council agreed on a bypass. Jean Jenkins said if they proposed daft things like that, nobody would take them seriously, and why didn't they think about sleeping policemen? Other villages had them, and they certainly made you slow down. Head teacher Sarah Barnett, her farmer husband in mind, said she wondered what effect that would have on loads of muck and straw that passed through the village all the year round. 'There's some I know who won't slow down. Just imagine the result!' she said, wrinkling her nose.

Annie Bishop, this being her first meeting, sat quietly at the back. She spoke only when Jean Jenkins asked her a direct question: 'How did you cope in London, Mrs Bishop? Must be traffic problems there . . .'

Annie said that there were special staggered barriers outside the school where her children went, and that all were met and carefully escorted home. She appreciated that here it was different. Children were used to running around the village on their own. She felt their freedom was important. It was one of the reasons she and her family had come to Ringford. She was tactful, modest, and ended by offering any help that she and her husband could give. 'We do, of course, have a wider experience,' she said, 'and Andrew could certainly help on legal issues.'

Peter Dodwell was effusive in acknowledgement, but some village parents shifted uneasily in their seats, feeling already that things were being taken out of their hands.

Sandra Goodison, also at her first meeting but too shy to say anything, was the last to leave. Head teacher Sarah Barnett had wanted a quick word about Alison, who seemed worried about being behind with her reading. 'It's not a bit serious,' she said to Sandra. 'Make sure she knows we're pleased with her, and that she'll catch up in no time. It's just the change of school. Always has some kind of effect. Just don't let her worry.'

Sarah Barnett drove off back to the farm with a wave to Sandra, who crossed the road and walked along towards Macmillan Gardens. It's very dark tonight, Sandra thought, and quickened her pace. By the shop, she saw something move in the footpath that went round to Peggy's back door. She hesitated. It would be madness to investigate. On the other hand, it could be someone looking for a way to break in. Immediately Sandra wondered if she'd locked up the Post Office cubicle properly. There was a lot of money in the safe, ready for paying out pensions tomorrow, and she'd heard tales about thieves taking the safe, lock, stock and barrel, and the whole lot never seen again. She opened the side gate quietly, and took a hesitant step inside.

'Who's that?' said Bill, looking round.

'Oh, it's you, Bill,' said Sandra, with enormous relief. She walked up the path and stood with him in the yard, under the light outside the back door. 'I thought it might be burglars,' she said. 'And anyway, how's Mrs T.? Still a bit groggy, I expect?' The sympathy and concern in Sandra's voice was too much for Bill, and he choked. Sandra put out a hand to touch his arm, and he grabbed it, pulled her close to him and hugged her tight.

'Hey!' she shouted, her voice muffled by his coat against her mouth. She laughed a bit, and pushed herself away from him. 'Kiss it better, shall I, Bill?' she said, and reached up to peck his cheek. 'There, that'd better be all for now.' She wriggled free and turned to go. 'Night night,' she said. 'Sleep tight, see you in the morning.'

It was a familiar bedtime chant, one Bill remembered his mother saying when he was a child. But he wasn't a child now, and he was dimly horrified at his stirring feelings as he'd held Sandra, young and plump as a partridge, in his arms.

CHAPTER TWENTY-EIGHT

In the suddenly mild morning, with the remaining snow melted and running in muddy rivulets down the road drains, Ivy Beasley rounded the corner of Macmillan Gardens and met Eddie Jenkins head on. He gasped and backed away from her, and Ivy steadied herself by holding on to the wet fence bordering Sandra's garden. Instead of running away as fast as his short legs could take him, Eddie stood and looked at Ivy's red face, waiting for the explosion.

'Very sorry, Miss Beasley!' he said desperately. Perhaps she would put the evil eye on him, and then anything could happen. Even so, he did not run. Something about facing up to what you'd done ran through his mind. It was one of his dad's favourite sayings, and had landed him in hot water in school and out. Still, it was nearly always better to get a bollocking straight away than have to wait until whoever it was came knocking at the door to see Dad. So Eddie stayed facing Ivy, waiting for her to give him the extremely rough edge of her tongue.

'One of these days,' said Ivy slowly, 'I'm going to tie your legs together with a knot nobody will be able to undo. Then perhaps you'll learn to go slowly, especially round corners. I've lost count of how many times you've nearly sent me flying. Well, Eddie Jenkins, this is your last chance. Next time, it'll be the magic knot.' She straightened her coat and marched past him with a face like granite.

Phew! thought Eddie. Not half so bad as I expected. Better get out of sight, before she comes back. But Ivy had reached Doris Ashbourne's bungalow and disappeared through the front door.

Although he wasn't to know, Eddie had been let off lightly because Ivy had serious matters on her mind, and could not wait to get to

Doris's to chew them over. Ellen had arrived already, and had bagged the best chair.

'Comfortable, Ellen?' said Ivy icily.

'Yes, ta,' said Ellen, settling herself deep in the velvet cushions. 'You look grim, Ivy. What's eatin' yer today? Lorries parkin' outside yer 'ouse? Or yer cat bin run over?'

This was a cruel taunt. The thought of the constant traffic finally crushing the life out of her beloved little cat was a recurring nightmare for Ivy. She did not reply, however, and went into the kitchen to help Doris bring in the tea tray.

'I can manage,' said Doris.

'Don't do to be too proud to accept help,' said Ivy. 'You never know when you might need it. When I had my sprained ankle—'

'Ain't we never going to hear the end of that minor injury of yorn?' interrupted Ellen irritably. 'Anybody'd think you were the only person in Ringford who'd ever had a sprained ankle.'

As Ivy spluttered to reply, Doris interceded, soothing ruffled feathers. 'It was a very nasty sprain, Ellen,' she said. 'Nothing more painful, as you should know from that time you went a cropper in your kitchen.'

Ellen chose not to remember, and changed tack. 'Why yer lookin' s'mardy, then, Ivy?' she said. 'Saw you bump into Eddie on your way up, but that can't be it.'

'Eddie Jenkins bumped into *me*,' said Ivy

217

indignantly. 'And I don't know what you mean by mardy. A ridiculous word you dredged up from your misspent youth, no doubt.'

Doris poured steaming cups of tea and handed round buttered currant buns with home-made raspberry jam. 'Nursery fare, today?' said Ivy, sinking her good white teeth into the soft dough.

'Shut up, do, Ivy,' said Doris. 'If you can't say anything pleasant, best keep quiet. What on earth's got into you?'

Ivy looked hard at Doris and then at Ellen, and yawned exaggeratedly. 'If, and I say only *if*, I am out of sorts today, it's because I had a terrible night. Didn't sleep a wink.'

'Why ever not?' said Doris.

'Thoughts,' said Ivy. 'Thoughts going round and round. Thoughts on what I saw from my bedroom window.'

'You should've bin an actress, Ivy Beasley,' said Ellen. 'Never known anyone spin out a tale like you.' This was somewhat hypocritical, as Ellen could keep an audience waiting with the best.

'Out with it, then, Ivy,' said Doris. 'Saw something nasty in the woodshed, did you?'

But Ivy said no, it was not in the woodshed but in the Turners' back yard, under the yard light, that she had seen something that kept her awake all night. 'And his wife lying on her sickbed in hospital,' she said solemnly.

Doris and Ellen exchanged glances. 'Well,'

said Ellen, 'I'd better be gettin' home. Thanks for the tea, Doris . . .'

'Just a minute,' said Ivy. 'You've only just come. What're you going for?'

'Because I can't stand the suspense no longer,' said Ellen, pretending to struggle to her feet.

'It was Bill Turner,' said Ivy triumphantly. 'Bill Turner, who's lost one wife, driven another into hospital, and is now letting his fancy roam in yet another direction. And her young enough to be his daughter.' The other two women stared at her, genuinely shocked.

'Not . . .' said Doris.

'You can't mean our Sandra,' said Ellen, blinking rapidly.

Ivy nodded. 'Entwined, they were. And only one shadow for the two of them.' Satisfied at the reaction she had caused, she sat back in her chair and sipped her tea delicately.

'Well, I don't believe you. It must've been somebody else, not Bill Turner at all.'

'D'you think I wouldn't know that shock of untidy hair anywhere?' said Ivy. 'If you ask me . . .' she began.

'We do, we do,' said Ellen. 'Give us the benefit of yer wise words, Ivy. What'yer reckon it means?'

'When the cat's away. That's what it means. And I for one shall make sure the cat is informed as soon as she returns. Then she'll see what her precious Bill's made of, *and* find out what it's like to be the deceived wife, just like our poor Joyce all those years.'

'You'll do no such thing, Ivy,' said Doris, suddenly very stern. 'There's probably some perfectly innocent explanation, and you are not to go stirring up mud where there isn't any. Or you'll answer to me, and that's a fact.'

Ivy was not used to opposition of this sort, and said no more, but as she pulled on her coat and helped Ellen down the front step, she returned once more to the subject. 'Once a Roberts always a Roberts, if you ask me. What can you expect? Bad blood will out, and Sandra has more than a spoonful of her father's in her veins. No good will come of it, you'll see.'

'Just you keep out of it,' said Doris warningly. 'Think back to the damage you did to that poor vicar and his wife. It'll rebound, Ivy, slap in your face. Gossip always does.' And she closed her door behind them with a worried frown.

CHAPTER TWENTY-NINE

Bates's End was flooded. The Ringle had risen up with the melting snow and overflowed, first into the garden of Bridge Cottage, and then on into the water meadows, covering the lane with a couple of inches of swirling, muddy water. Jean Jenkins had been splashed with liquid mud from the usual procession of cars and lorries in the main street, and now she stood at the edge of the flood, uncertain what to do. She felt like turning back, late for work at the Bishops, and tired with the effort of getting five reluctant children off to school. A sharp toot from behind caused her to move to the verge. It was Bill Turner, waving to her from his old white van, indicating that she should get in.

'Morning, Bill,' she said, settling her bulk in the front seat of his van. It creaked, the few remaining springs stretched to their limit. 'How's Peggy?'

'Doing nicely, thanks,' Bill said. 'I rang this morning, and she'd had breakfast and was sitting up reading the paper. It's amazing how quick they recover these days.'

'Yeah, but not really,' said Jean wisely. 'It takes longer than you think to recover properly. My sister over at Bagley was up and down for a couple of years after she'd had it all out. Not really ill, but not really well, either.'

'But this keyhole surgery,' said Bill, 'it's supposed to be magic. Back to work after a couple of weeks. Least, that's what it said on Peggy's bit of paper.'

'Well, I should watch it, Bill,' said Jean, as he drew up again only yards further on. The flood had not reached the old vicarage, the ground rising gently as the lane wound on past Bates's farm. 'Ta very much, thanks,' she said. 'And just don't let Peggy do too much too soon.'

Bill watched her march heavily up the

221

Bishops' squelchy drive and disappear round to the back door. He sat still, not putting the van into gear, allowing the engine to tick over. His thoughts were uncomfortable. Sandra had greeted him in her usual cheery fashion this morning, not referring at first to the previous night. He'd been reluctant to meet her eye, but as he struggled with his boots in the kitchen before leaving for work, she had called out to him from the shop.

'Hey, Bill, you feeling better now?' There'd been banging and crashing as Sandra shifted boxes of cornflake packets, ready to price them and stack the shelves. 'Bit of a headache, I expect!' She had chuckled sympathetically. 'Still, only to be expected. No harm done. Sam laughed when I told him you'd give me a cuddle in the back yard. Pity you ain't got kids of your own,' she'd added quietly, and then had wondered if she'd gone too far. It was common village knowledge that Bill and Joyce had wanted kids, but she'd miscarried and wouldn't try again. Still, that was a long time ago. And he and Mrs T. were too old now to care, Sandra had thought, with youthful insensitivity.

Bill jerked the van into gear, and with the grating noise he'd been unable to diagnose as anything but old age, began to move slowly down the avenue to the Hall. Seemed as if Sandra had taken it all in her stride. If she'd told Sam, then he could relax. No harm done, she'd said. He began to feel a lot better, and accelerated, sending up great sprays of water and leaves from the van wheels.

*   *   *

In the old vicarage kitchen, Jean Jenkins changed her shoes into soft slippers, apologising to Annie Bishop for being late. 'The water's standing really deep,' she exaggerated. 'Took me ages to struggle through.'

Annie, who'd seen her getting out of Bill's van, said nothing. I'm learning, she thought, as she made a cup of strong tea and spooned sugar into it for a not very contrite Jean. In a gradual, subtle sort of way, Jean Jenkins had changed things, now coming and going more or less in her own good time, and cleaning the house in a routine to suit herself. Silver and brass, windows and grubby paintwork, all were cleaned at intervals established by Jean. Annie ceased to monitor what she did each week, realising that an overall cared-for appearance in the house was Jean's aim and her long experience and common sense achieved this without fuss or organisation from Annie.

'WI next week,' Jean said, as she took a handful of dusters and tin of spray polish out of the cupboard. 'Have you decided to come along, Mrs Bishop?'

Annie had been through conflicting thoughts about the Women's Institute. She

223

couldn't believe how easy it had been to become involved, in the Parochial Church Council, the Parents' Association, the choir, with Gabriella Jones, who'd seemed glad of her helpful suggestions. Unaware that all newcomers to Ringford were deluged with requests to join everything, but that the sensible ones bided their time, Annie had plunged in, offering advice and ideas for improvement. But old images of jam and Jerusalem were hard to erase, and Annie had not so far committed herself to joining the WI. 'I'm not sure it's really me,' she said honestly. There was something about Jean that made her feel at ease, able to be herself.

'Why not come along and try it?' said Jean, on her way up the stairs. 'You needn't join straight away, just give it a try. You can come with me, if you like,' she added without thinking.

Annie hesitated, and then said yes, in that case she would like to see what it was like, as Jean suggested.

Jean was discomfited. She had never dreamt that Annie would agree to come with her, and had felt quite safe suggesting it. The likes of Annie Bishop did not chum up with the likes of Jean Jenkins. Much more suitable if she came to WI with Susan Standing, a former president or, say, Pat Osman. Or Peggy Turner. But, no, Peggy was in hospital. Or anyone else but me, thought Jean.

'Shall I pick you up?' said Annie. 'If this flood gets worse we shall all be marooned!'

Feeling decidedly uneasy, Jean agreed, and got on with her work. Thoughts of Eddie, who'd complained of a sore throat and earache when he got up, drove the WI meeting from her mind, and by the time she was ready to go on up to the Hall, she'd almost forgotten it. Annie reminded her, though, asking if she had to bring anything, do anything, on her first visit.

'No, not first time,' said Jean. 'We do have a monthly competition, and you get points an' that, but only if you decide to be a member.' She set off for the Hall, wishing she'd kept her mouth shut.

*   *   *

'Morning, Mrs Standing.' Jean had arrived in the chilly Hall kitchen, always cold because the big range was no longer lit night and day. Susan Standing had heard her, and come swiftly through the swinging green baize door to greet her char.

'There's a frightful mess in the nursery, I'm afraid,' she said. 'Could you give it a bit of extra time today, please?'

'What kind of mess?' said Jean, frowning. Mrs Standing always treated her as the hired help, but Jean resisted any kind of subservience. She knew her place, she frequently asserted as much to Foxy. She also

225

knew her worth. Once before she had handed in her duster, fed up with Susan's arrogance, but Mr Richard had persuaded her to come back. Now there was a truce between them, but occasionally Susan forgot to tread carefully enough.

'Oh, not too bad,' she said hastily. 'Yesterday Poppy had Joey and Margie to tea. Well, to dolls' tea really, and I'm afraid things got a bit out of hand.'

'Oh, well,' said Jean, softening, 'if young Joey enjoyed it, then that was worth a bit o' mess. Leave it to me.'

Susan sighed with relief, and went out of the kitchen. Richard had annoyed her this morning, harping on about having the Bishops to dinner, and she felt irritable and unsettled. There were the usual signs of his growing interest in something female. The cap left off the toothpaste tube, his clothes cupboard swinging unlatched, a drawer left open with a sock dangling over the edge, a dirty whisky glass abandoned carelessly, making a ring on the antique leather of his desk top. Subtle indications, and dismissed with a laugh by Susan's mother in Bagley when she'd listened to confidences about Susan's suspicions. But they were reliable warnings, and Susan noticed them with a sinking heart. Well, she thought, confront the enemy, that's what Pa used to say. So, not for the first time, Susan made a plan.

'Hello, is that Annie?' Susan's voice was

226

warm, friendly. 'How are you? Quite settled in now?' She sat down on a blackened, carved oak chair, its uncomfortable tapestry seat one of the treasures of the Standing inheritance.

'I'm so glad,' she said. 'Well, I was wondering whether you could bear to try out the WI next week? The women would love it, I know. And it can be quite fun, in a way. I'd be very happy to pick you up, and we could slip away early if the speaker is a terminal bore . . .' She couldn't for the life of her remember who the speaker was, but they never seemed to have anything remotely to do with Susan's everyday concerns. 'Oh, I see,' she said in answer to Annie's hesitant reply. 'With Jean Jenkins? Ah, well . . .' she glanced upstairs to see if Jean was within earshot. No sign of her, but she had learned that Jean was always within earshot, whether visible or not, and lowered her voice. 'You could give her some excuse,' she whispered, 'say you'd forgotten I asked you first.' Annie's reply caused her to frown, and with a cool, 'Very well, goodbye, then,' she put down the telephone. Step one had failed. Still, she'd soon think of something else.

CHAPTER THIRTY

Peggy had been home for ten days, and, though tiring easily, was feeling optimistic and cheerful. Sandra had managed with Bill's help, and they'd had no major dramas. The Post Office returns had balanced, and with Annie Bishop meeting Alison from school, there had been no need to call on Mary York any more than usual. Peggy sat in the window seat of her sitting-room, watching the children in the school playground and the Jenkins terrier trotting along on his daily rounds, narrowly missing the wheels of a speeding sports car. It was because she had nothing much else to do that Peggy noticed again how intrusive the traffic had become. She felt a reluctant sympathy with Ivy Beasley, who had taken to shaking her broom menacingly at any truck driver who had the temerity to park outside her front gate.

'Coo-ee!' It was Doreen Price's voice calling her from the shop. 'Are you there, Peggy? Can I come round?' Doreen walked through and thrust a scarlet poinsettia into Peggy's hands. 'From Bagley market,' she said. 'I can never resist them. They mean Christmas to me.'

Sandra poked her head round the door and offered to make tea. 'Nobody in the shop at the moment,' she said.

Doreen sat down opposite Peggy and looked at her searchingly. 'Well, then,' she said. 'And how are you? The truth, mind. You don't have to be brave with me.'

Peggy smiled. Doreen was such a good old friend, trustworthy and dependable. 'I feel much better,' she said, 'but I'm a bit nervous about moving around too quickly. I go for a stroll in the afternoon, round the Green, and that's about it. Bill won't let me near the kitchen, although Mr Fisher said I could be back at work in a fortnight. I know I should be grateful, but honestly, Doreen, if you're used to a busy day . . .'

'Ah,' said Doreen. 'Well, that's why I called. It's WI on Friday, and I wondered if you felt up to coming. I could pick you up in the car and bring you home, and all you need do is sit and listen. It's Frances Pitts speaking about her travels in Peru. Remember she's been before? Kenya, it was, last time. She's a good laugh, is Frances. Farmer's daughter, from the other side of Bagley. What do you think, Peggy? Might relieve the boredom a bit?'

Peggy's immediate reaction was to refuse. 'Not in the evening, thanks, Doreen. I am quite tired by eight o'clock, and have been going up early. Perhaps next month.'

'You could sleep late next morning,' said Doreen stubbornly. She remembered what it was like after she'd had her veins done. It became a habit to laze around and go to bed early. Eventually Tom had made it quite clear she was wanted on the farm, and she slipped back into the old routine with no harmful effects.

Peggy took the tea tray from Sandra and thanked her, noticing with a smile the little saucer of almond biscuits Sandra had arranged

229

in a neat pattern.

'None for me, thanks, Mrs T.,' said Sandra. 'The kids'll be in from school any minute. By the way,' she added, 'hope you don't think I was eavesdropping, but I agree with Mrs Price. It'd do you good to go to WI. Don't suppose you'll be overwhelmed by the excitement of it all!' She disappeared, laughing with the confidence of one who wouldn't be seen dead at a WI meeting.

*   *   *

Spurred on by Bill, Peggy selected a loose dress from her cupboard. Her scars were still sore, and waistbands were painful. Bill rubbed in Nivea every night, his touch as light as a feather. She understood why the sheep never ran from him, and horses nuzzled his palm for lumps of sugar. You could rely on him. He would never hurt her. Peggy thanked God for Bill every time Renata Roberts came into the shop with a black eye and a transparent excuse about falling over a chair.

She peered at herself in the dressing-table mirror. She hadn't bothered with make-up since the operation. Don't need my happy shopkeeper's face at the moment, she had thought. Still, the WI would notice. She put on foundation, powder and lipstick, and brushed her hair until it sparked. That was a little better. She found her pearl earrings and the little four-leaf clover brooch that Ellen Biggs had given her on her wedding day. Yep, definitely an improvement, she thought.

'Hey!' said Bill, as she went into the kitchen, her heels tapping on the tiled floor. 'Are you sure it's the WI meeting you're going to?' He got up and kissed her cheek. 'You look lovely, my gel,' he said, pleased that she'd made the effort. 'Got your gloves? Wind's turned again.'

'What will you do?' she said, hunting for her gloves in the kitchen table drawer.

'Watch the box, I expect,' he said. 'Might go for a pint, but I'll be back before you, long before.'

A car tooted outside, and Peggy opened the back door. The outside light shone on her hair, and she looked vulnerable, framed in the doorway with an aureole of light around her head. 'Bye, then,' she said. 'See you later.' Bill's smile of love was still hovering round his mouth when he went through to watch the local news.

It was not very warm in the village hall. Doris Ashbourne had got there early, and found the electricity meter needed more money. It took only fifty-pence pieces, and she had to go all the way back home, cursing herself for not anticipating. 'Should always carry some in my bag,' she said to Ivy as they met outside Victoria Villa.

Now she put in a couple more coins for good measure and turned round. 'Peggy!' she said.

231

'How nice to see you!' Her warmth was genuine. Ever since Peggy had taken over her shop, she had kept an eye on how things were going, and had been one of the villagers who'd persuaded her to carry on after Frank died. 'Come over here, dear,' she said. 'There's a cushion on this chair. Used to be Molly Taylor's until she died. Nobody's liked to sit on it since, but it's a lot more comfortable than the others.'

Peggy was superstitious, however, and shook her head. 'I'm better on a hard chair,' she lied. 'Gives me more support. Thanks anyway, Doris.'

The hall filled up, and Doreen took the Chair. After the business part of the meeting, telescoped to an acceptable length by a practised Doreen, the speaker was announced, and a youngish woman with short dark hair, round glasses and a friendly, ready smile, stepped up to face the audience.

'Hello, good evening, everybody.' Her accent was pure and unsullied, instantly recognisable Midlands, but with none of the Birmingham twang. Her farming family had lived in the county for generations, and had married into other such families. The women in the hall relaxed in their seats, happily at home with Frances Pitts.

The journey around Peru—'Just the bottom half this time'—seemed to Annie Bishop, sitting attentively next to an embarrassed Jean

232

Jenkins, to have been total disaster from beginning to end. From the aeroplane with a tail fin missing, to a canoe made of reeds with only one inch clearance above the waters of Lake Titicaca, unpleasant surprises lurked round every corner. The intrepid explorers had been mugged, bitten by giant ants, shadowed by jaguars, drenched in the rainforests, snapped at by caymans, and becalmed in so many broken-down boats that it was a wonder Frances had lived to laugh it all off with a jolly, 'Still, I always say sit tight and do what you're told, and you'll be fine!'

At first Annie found herself making mental notes to make an amusing account for Andrew, but then was drawn in with the others, laughing at such dogged determination to remain British and stoical, whatever Peru might have in store. And finally, as Frances had once more left her camera in the bus, this time when dolphins were surfing on their tails in the Pacific Ocean in front of their very eyes, Annie too joined in the chorus of dismay.

Peggy clutched Doris's arm. Could Mr Fisher's stitches withstand so much merriment? 'Oh dear,' she choked, 'why on earth did she go?'

'Likes the excitement,' whispered Doris. 'She doesn't get much round here . . . not many dolphins in Ringford.'

Frances Pitts had been on her feet for an hour, and was still going strong. 'I'll just put the urn on,' said Doris, and got to her feet, tiptoeing out to the kitchen. This was a recognised signal, and Frances began to wind up. Inca burial grounds, beggars throwing stones in the train windows—'They'd nothing else to do, poor souls!'—and the guinea pig, flattened and spreadeagled on her plate, eaten in a few mouthfuls, all had been grist to Frances's mill. 'Nothing much on a guinea pig!' she'd chortled. 'Don't bother hurrying down to the pet shop tomorrow morning!'

Annie Bishop thought of Fluffy, the children's pet. What an extraordinary woman, an extraordinary evening. Still, better than expected. Worth being a member. Perhaps she could encourage them in participation ... a play or two, perhaps some choral singing ...?

Ivy Beasley got to her feet. 'On behalf of us all,' she began the tried and tested formula, 'I'd like to thank Frances Pitts for her—' But before she could finish her sentence, Frances had popped on her Peruvian bowler hat, and gales of laughter broke out again. Ivy's carefully prepared words were lost, and she sat down in a huff, glowering at Peggy Turner, who had led the outburst. I'll soon settle her hash, thought Ivy maliciously.

Tea and cakes were consumed in a hubbub of conversation, and Susan Standing lingered on for once. She took a seat next to Annie Bishop, and the two could be seen talking quietly, smiling at first, and then more

234

seriously. Wonder what's going on there, thought Peggy. She stood up, realised she had forgotten her twinges for at least half an hour, and asked Doreen if she was ready to leave. 'Better be getting back,' she said, 'though it's been a wonderful evening. Bill will be worried if I'm too late.'

Ivy Beasley, collecting cups and saucers, and well within earshot of Peggy, cleared her throat. 'Huh!' she said to no one in particular. 'Shouldn't hurry back, if I were you. Might catch sight of something better not seen, like I did.'

Peggy turned on her. 'Are you talking to me, Miss Beasley?' she snapped.

Ivy Beasley shrugged, piling up plates dangerously high on the tray. 'If the cap fits,' she said. 'Though I should think you'd be the one most interested in goings-on in your own back yard. And her young enough to be his daughter . . .' Before Peggy could reply, Ivy had marched off to the kitchen, her tray rattling alarmingly.

'Take no notice of 'er,' said Ellen Biggs at Peggy's elbow. 'She's goin' senile, I reckon. Talks nonsense a lot o' the time. Now dear, you be off 'ome and get a good rest. Very nice to see you 'ere, but you'll need to take it easy for a bit.' She smiled kindly, but could see from the expression on Peggy's face that it was too late, the damage had been done.

235

CHAPTER THIRTY-ONE

The pavement was slippery with frost when Peggy got out of Doreen's car. A bright moon lit up the village, and a film of silvery white already covered the short winter grass on the Green. 'Going to be a hard one tonight,' Doreen said. 'Still, it looks very Christmassy, doesn't it? Take care now.' She waved to Peggy, and drove off, wondering why Peggy had not answered, hadn't even seemed to register what she'd said.

The passage beside the shop was in darkness, the moonlight not reaching its narrow depths. Halfway up, Peggy stopped and leaned against the wall. She felt weak, and put her head down, hoping the nauseous feeling would go away. It didn't, and she began to cry softly, soundlessly, wiping her face with the back of her glove. Oh Lord, this wouldn't do. I have to be calm and rational, somehow, she thought. If only my head would stop spinning. She slid slowly down on to her haunches, keeping her torso straight so that her scars wouldn't hurt. If I just say here for a few minutes, I can collect myself, think what I'm going to say to Bill. Maybe nothing, tonight. Probably best to leave it till morning. But then Sandra will be in the shop, and there'll be no chance. She began to cry again at the thought of Bill and Sandra, and Miss Beasley watching.

'Peggy?' Bill had come out into the back

yard, alerted by the faint sounds of distress. She saw his bulky figure silhouetted against the light at the end of the passage, and then he was walking towards her. 'Peggy!' He put out a hand, his eyes unaccustomed to the sudden darkness, and found the top of her head. 'My God! Peg, what on earth . . .?' He pulled her to her feet and held her tight. Now she was sobbing in earnest, and he supported her along the passage and into the warm kitchen. Gilbert was immediately aware that something was wrong, and shot out of the catflap.

Bill, frightened, walked over to the telephone. 'I'll call Dr Russell,' he said.

'No, no,' said Peggy, fumbling in her pocket for her handkerchief and sniffing hard. 'It's nothing, really. I just felt a bit faint.'

Bill stood looking down at her, frowning and worried. 'Did Doreen bring you home?' he said, cursing himself for not meeting her and making sure that she got home safely.

'Yes, of course,' said Peggy. 'It's really nothing, Bill. I expect I was frightened. Natural to feel faint after my first outing, I'm sure. A few more steps and I'd've made it.' With a supreme effort, she managed a wan smile. 'A cup of tea would do the trick,' she said, and Bill filled the kettle.

After a few minutes, Peggy gathered strength. 'It was a good meeting,' she said, sipping the hot tea. 'That Pitts girl was so funny about Peru. Made a refreshing change from old

237

Newnham, with his endless slides of the wonders of Florida.'

Bill barely smiled. He looked closely at her, trying to read her expression. Surely she would have been able to stagger those few yards to the back door, faint or not? And it was not like Peggy to weep, not for herself, anyway. No, there was something else. But he discovered nothing more, and they went to bed early, Bill especially tender and kind.

*   *   *

Annie Bishop took her coat off in the vicarage hall and walked through to the drawing-room. Andrew, dozing in front of the fire, looked up. 'Well?' he said. 'How was it?'

Annie smiled. 'Well,' she said, 'I don't know if I can really describe it.'

'Eh? Not that bad, surely?'

'No, not at all, but . . .' It was strange, Annie thought. She knew she could make Andrew laugh with a mocking account of Round Ringford WI, but something held her back. They'd been so welcoming, friendly. And Jean Jenkins had done her best, though obviously embarrassed by having to introduce her.

Andrew bent down and picked up his *Evening Standard* from the floor. The journey home had been slow and tedious, the frosty weather holding up trains. Points, or something. He'd read the *Standard* from cover

238

to cover, even the small ads, and especially the ones advertising studio flats in central London. One room would do. There were several possibles, and he had to work round to mentioning it to Annie, who was sure to disapprove. She was very hot on family solidarity, and had shown her disappointment on the several occasions he'd stayed with his mother. In fact, Annie's reaction had been so vehement that he'd not told her about taking his secretary, on a sudden impulse, of course, to a film on one of those occasions. His mother had had to go out, but had left him a cold supper, which he'd had to wrap in a plastic bag and dispose of the next day. A friendly snack had seemed only civil after the film. His secretary had, after all, quite a long journey out to Esher.

Annie would have been so understanding, tolerant, liberal, when they'd lived in London, but he'd noticed a change in her lately. She seemed to think he was ratting on some unspoken bargain. But then, she didn't have to run for the train, stand until they got to Watford, breathe the fetid air of a crowded railway carriage, and then negotiate the narrow lanes that led to Ringford. Those last few miles through tiny villages seemed endless. Andrew had forgotten how easy it had all seemed at first, when he wanted it to work.

Annie was talking about Peru. Had he missed something? Andrew realised he'd not been listening to the first sentence or two, and made what he hoped were intelligent replies. 'Great fun, darling,' he said. 'So when are you off?' Annie stared at him.

'Off where?' she said.

'To Peru, of course!' he said, laughing lightly. Blast, that had been wrong. Obviously not a projected summer outing to Lima! He yawned, too tired to work it all out. 'Well, glad you enjoyed it,' he said. 'It'll be something to tell the Parkers. Sara rang me at the office today and said they'd be down on Sunday around twelve. Be nice to see them again, won't it? Catch up on Highgate news . . .'

Annie poked the fire, stirring spitting logs. He wasn't listening to a word I said, she thought resentfully. She felt guilty, too, having quite forgotten about the Parkers coming for lunch. 'By the way,' she said, 'Susan Standing nobbled me. Said she's having a Christmas charity do up at the Hall, and wanted my help. I said I'd be glad to.' She looked at him, willing him to respond, but Andrew had lifted his paper, and was studying the financial report.

'Mmm?' he said.

'It's the usual bring and buy,' said Annie lamely, and felt foolish.

*   *   *

Doris Ashbourne wound her woollen scarf twice round her neck, and pulled her hat well

240

down. 'I'll wait for you, Ivy,' she said sternly. Ivy Beasley was the last to leave the village hall, being a keyholder and responsible for locking up.

'No need,' she called, from the kitchen, where she was banging cupboard doors and generally tidying up what was already tidy. She didn't like the sound of Doris's voice, but she couldn't linger for ever, and eventually emerged on to the sparkling pavement. 'Suppose we should have seen Ellen home,' she said. 'She could easily slip over on this frost.'

'Vicar's wife took her,' said Doris shortly. Ivy was not going to wriggle out of this one.

Ivy measured the distance to Victoria Villa with her eye. She knew what Doris was going to say, and if she could just keep her at bay as far as her front gate, all would be well. But Doris, a reasonable and mild woman most of the time, was primed and ready to fire.

'You don't listen, do you, Ivy Beasley?' she said. 'Had to get it out, that dreadful gossip about Bill and Sandra. I saw Peggy's face go white, and for two pins I'd have dressed you down there and then.'

Ivy marched on, as fast as she could without sliding too dangerously. 'Don't know what you're talking about,' she said. They were already opposite the school. Not much further to go, and she'd be home and dry. 'And as for dressing down, Doris, what gives you the right to speak to me like that?' Injured innocence, that would be best.

Doris halted. Ivy marched on, but then faltered. She couldn't just leave Doris standing there. That would mean a real row, and Ivy feared a broken friendship more than she liked to admit. 'Well, all right, then,' she said. 'I didn't even mention their names. Just a hint, to warn the silly woman, that's all.'

Doris snorted. 'You twist things, Ivy,' she said, 'even to yourself. One of these days, your wickedness will come home to roost, and you'll be sorry. Meantime, you'd best do something to put it right, or I shall think twice about taking tea in your company. We've all had enough of it, Ivy, and that's the truth.' She could see Ivy's expression in the moonlight, and there was no trace of remorse. It was no good, Ivy would not make any attempt to undo what she'd done. And Doris couldn't jeopardise the tea parties, for old Ellen's sake. Everthing would go on the same. Ivy Beasley had won again. Doris sighed deeply and said nothing more, not even goodbye at Ivy's gate, and trudged with a beaten air up the slippery path to her bungalow.

*   *   *

'Eddie's been restless,' said Foxy, as Jean took off her coat. 'Says his ear aches, and he does seem a bit hot.'

'Did you take his temperature?'

'No.' Foxy shook his head. 'He wasn't properly awake. I thought it'd do him more good to get back to sleep.'

'Has he gone off, then?'

'Yep. No sound for an hour or so.'

Jean sank down into the armchair. 'Good meeting,' she said. 'I reckon Lady Bishop quite enjoyed it. Laughin' fit to bust at old Frances. Mind you, she was on good form. Peru! She must be mad.' They were quiet for a few minutes, then Jean eased off her boots. 'Better go and have a peep at the little 'un,' she said. 'Make sure he's covered up.'

She stood beside Eddie's bed, listening to his breathing. Seemed quite regular. His forehead was cool now. Perhaps nothing, this time. But she'd have to have another go at Dr Russell about his ears. It was getting too often, poor little soul. She smoothed his silky, straight hair. Wasted on a boy, she thought, bending down to plant a kiss on his soft cheek. Funny to think in a few years' time he'd be shaving, bristly as his father. She tiptoed out of the room, leaving the door ajar.

CHAPTER THIRTY-TWO

Next morning was too late for Peggy to tackle Bill. The moment had passed, and she tried to tell herself that there could not have been anything in it. Ivy Beasley must have been mistaken. Could have been any courting couple, trespassing, maybe, but they wouldn't have been the first to creep round into a deserted back yard for a cuddle.

Gossip is not that easily disregarded, however, and at lunchtime, when Bill came home for a sandwich, Peggy found herself lurking in the kitchen by the door into the shop; or in the passage between the shop and the sitting-room; or just outside the front door, within earshot. She was disgusted with herself, but it made no difference. By mid-afternoon the feeling of compulsion was fading. Bill and Sandra were exactly as before: he avuncular and sometimes teasing; she cheeky and respectful at the same time, knowing just how far to go. Nothing had changed, as far as Peggy could see. And she was sure they would give the game away if there had been anything extra between them.

'I think I'll just go up and get ten minutes' shut-eye,' she said to Sandra. 'Last night's excitements at WI have taken their toll! I feel really sleepy.' Peggy climbed the stairs and went into their bedroom, clicking the latch shut, but then quietly opened the door again, leaving it ajar. Just one last check, she thought. Bill was due home for a quick cup of tea before he went across to Waltonby to fetch a Christmas tree for the Hall. Peggy sat on the edge of the bed and waited.

Bill's voice calling her interrupted a

daydream about Frank and their life together in Coventry, before she knew Ringford and Bill existed. As she was about to shout an answer, she heard Sandra call from the stockroom: 'Mrs T's asleep. Best not wake her, Bill. She looked pale and tired, I thought.' And then there was silence.

Peggy stood up, slipped off her shoes and crept to the head of the stairs. Silence. Her imagination began to work overtime, and she slowly descended the stairs, one at a time, ears pricked. Still silence. Then she heard a muffled giggle, and stood like a statue, only her heart thudding as if it would burst. 'Bill! For God's sake!' Sandra's voice was full of laughter, and Peggy's head began to spin again, only worse this time. She managed to get to the foot of the stairs, along the passage and arrived at the door into the shop to see Sandra standing on a shelf that ran behind the counter at waist height, clinging on with one hand, while Bill stood beneath her, his hands supporting her. Peggy gasped, and crashed to the floor, hitting her head on the side of the counter as she went.

*   *   *

Annie Bishop was standing outside the school gates, warmly wrapped in Andrew's shooting jacket. Andrew had not yet been out on a shoot, but Richard Standing had thrown out a casual invitation, and Annie wanted him to be prepared. The jacket had been in a sale in Cordings in Piccadilly, and though fiendishly expensive, even in the sale, she had been able to persuade Andrew. 'We can share it,' she'd said, and he'd brought it home in its wonderfully exclusive carrier bag. Its large, pouch pockets were full of bits of stale bread which she and the children planned to throw to the ducks under the bridge on their way home. I'm like a hamster, she thought, looking down at the bulging pouches, and smiled.

The children burst out of the school door in their usual prisoners-on-parole act, and the yells and whoops at first disguised the sound of Sandra Goodison shouting to her from the shop doorway.

'Mrs Bishop! Quick, please come!'

'Mummy,' said Helen, pointing, 'you're wanted.'

Annie stared across to the shop, and could see the panic on Sandra's face. She gathered her brood, plus Alison, and shepherded them across the road.

'It's Mrs T,' said Sandra breathlessly. 'She's had a fall, passed out. Bill's got her upstairs, and phoned the doctor, but I shall have to stay here till closing, so could Alison come home with you?' Alison began to pout. She didn't like going to the old vicarage. They were all really nice to her, but she always felt like a foreigner. Most of the time they spoke a language she didn't understand. But Sandra snapped at her,

246

'Do as you're told, Alison. I'll pick you up at half past five.'

Annie was all sympathy and understanding. 'She can stay as long as you like,' she said. 'And is there anything else I can do? Poor Mrs Turner. Just when she was recovering nicely. How did it happen?'

Sandra shook her head. 'Don't know, exactly,' she said. 'I was stacking the mustards and pickles shelf, up high, and Bill was helping me, when we heard the crash as she went down. Hit her head on the counter. Bruise like half a boiled egg coming up on her forehead.' There were tears in Sandra's eyes, and Annie realised she was still shocked.

'Here,' she said, 'why don't I make you a cup of tea, and you sit down for a bit. I'll manage the shop for half an hour, and the children can go and play in Mrs Turner's garden.' Protests that it was too cold and boring followed, so Annie set them up round Peggy's kitchen table with paper and felt tips, and threatened them with retribution if they made a squeak. In a miraculously short time Sandra was sitting by the Rayburn drinking hot, sweet tea, and Annie in Peggy's overall was wrapping a small brown loaf for a delighted Richard Standing, who always seemed to be around the village at school turning-out time.

'Well!' he said, taking the loaf and managing to stroke her hand fleetingly as he did so. 'So you're the new shop assistant!'

247

Annie explained, trying to impress on him the seriousness of Peggy's fall, but his eyes were laughing at her, full of warmth, and she suddenly saw danger. Why hadn't she recognised it before? It had been a stealthy build-up, she could see that now. At first she'd just been flattered, glad that the squire had seemed interested in the whole family, wanting to take them up. The invitations had pleased her more than Andrew, who had made that plain. He was grumpy, reluctant. Lately he had found an excuse for refusing dinner, lunch, and now an early evening drink.

And me? thought Annie. Haven't I been looking round for Richard, every afternoon outside the school, gratified when I see him in the Range Rover cruising slowly along by the pub, always coinciding with us by the bridge, stopping for a chat? It's those Rudolph Valentino eyes, she thought, slotting Richard firmly into a romantic past. So dark and warm, they positively smoulder. 'Thank you, sir,' she said, mocking, flirting. She handed him his change, leaving her hand in his longer than was necessary. Her cool social voice returned. 'Oh, by the way,' she said. 'I'm afraid Andrew is having to stay in town again tonight, so we'll not be able to come in for that drink. Please tell Susan how sorry we are. It's the trains. And poor old Andrew is snowed under with work . . .'

Stupid old Andrew, thought Richard, as he

left the shop with a light, pleasurable feeling growing inside him. Well, the family motto was 'Always Ready', wasn't it? He felt exactly as he did when the hounds closed in on the fox, though there was nothing foxlike about Annie. More like his young mare, restless under his thighs.

'Afternoon, Richard.' Dr Russell drew up in his big car outside the shop and stepped out.

Richard grinned, pleased to see an old friend. 'Hello!' he said. 'Nice to see you. Poor old Peggy's had a fall, I believe. Nothing too serious, I hope.' He climbed into the Range Rover and drove off, humming.

Bill met Dr Russell at the door, and by the time he'd seen Peggy, pronounced her bruised and shocked, but nothing worse, and driven at his usual snail's pace back to Bagley, most of the village knew that she had fallen, that Bill was taking care of her, and that Mrs Bishop had come to the rescue again.

'Just like she did fireworks night,' said Mandy to Robert, when he came in for his tea. 'I know there's some don't like her, but I reckon she's a real asset in this village. Even Jean's coming round to her.'

'Well, that's all right then,' said Robert with a smile. 'If Jean Jenkins gives her the OK, she must be all right.'

*   *   *

'Well, that's it,' said Susan. 'I'm not asking

them any more. All these last-minute cancellations. It's very inconvenient. I'd asked the others especially to meet them at your request. Well, I shall just put them off. There'll be no point in them coming now.'

Richard was mild, and seemed to agree with her, which alerted her suspicions more than ever. Drawers and doors continued to be left open, and this morning Richard had been singing in his bath. A sure sign. Susan changed the subject.

'You haven't forgotten the coffee morning, have you?' she said. 'You did say you'd find some cheap sherry to make it more Christmassy. I could give them a small glass when they arrive. Put them in a spending mood.'

'Of course I hadn't forgotten, my darling,' said Richard, who had. 'I'll shoot into Tresham to the Supashop. They've always got something on offer. Sweet sherry for the ladies, Poppy!' he said loudly, and picked up his wriggling daughter, sitting her on the smooth banister rail that curved up gracefully from the hall.

'Get me down!' Poppy yelled, and kicked out at her father, who indulged her, pretending to be hurt.

'Come on, then, girl,' he said, and lifted her down. 'You can come with me. Help me choose.'

As they put on their coats and left, chatting happily together, Susan's eyes followed them.

He's in a very good mood, she said to herself. Much too good. And she went to telephone her patient mother in Bagley.

*   *   *

Peggy opened her eyes and saw the shaded bedside lamp glowing softly. 'Bill?' she thought she said, but it was only in her head, and Bill, sitting in a chair by the window, keeping vigil, did not hear her. He had dozed off, and as she became accustomed to the half-darkness, Peggy could see his shadowy figure slumped in the chair. He looked enormous in the low-ceilinged room. Funny, she thought fuzzily. Two husbands, one small and neat, the other big and untidy. So her mother was wrong. You don't always go for the same type. Frank and Bill couldn't be more different. Ay, ay, tiddly ay, the farmer wants a wife . . . Was she a good wife to Bill? Wouldn't he have been better with a real countrywoman, somebody born in the village? She began to drift into sleep, but was jerked away by a sudden picture of Sandra, balancing on the shelf on one foot, supported by . . .

'Bill!' This time it was loud, and he started up, frowning and anxious. He came across and leaned over the bed, smoothing her forehead with his big hand.

'Hush,' he said. 'I'm here, don't fret. Just you rest and not bother yourself. Try to sleep.'

251

Peggy was awake now, and very thirsty. As Bill raised her up and held a cool glass of juice to her lips, she leaned against his arm. The bedroom was warm, and she saw that Bill had put a heater by the bed. In the pink light, everything was soft and comforting. She looked round at the sprigged white curtains at the small window, all tinged and rosy, at the white walls, warmed in the light, and everything reflected and repeated in the long mirror in the wardrobe door. Their bedroom, their warm, private territory. She rested her head, now beginning to ache dully, against Bill's shoulder, and wished they could stay like that for ever.

*   *   *

The drinks guests had been cancelled, and with Poppy safely in bed and dinner out of the way, Susan Standing settled down in front of the television and prepared to enjoy the latest thriller episode. 'Throw another log on, Richard,' she said, as he came into the room and hovered in front of her. He did as she asked, sending a shower of orange sparks up the wide chimney. 'Well, sit down,' she added. 'I can't see the screen.'

'I'll join you later,' Richard said, as casually as he could manage. 'Just have to pop out to see Bill and Foxy. Said I'd join them at the Arms for a quick one, just to go over what we're planning for the Forty Acre.' He waited for the fusillade, but it didn't come.

'Don't be longer than necessary, then,' said Susan, her eyes riveted to the screen. 'I'd quite like an early night, ready for tomorrow's ordeal by coffee morning. Oh, do move, Richard! I missed that bit . . .'

Richard tiptoed away, closing the door quietly, anxious that she should not notice that he'd put on a clean shirt and washed his hair.

CHAPTER THIRTY-THREE

The village next morning seemed to have skipped a season. If there hadn't been Christmas wreaths already up on front doors, and coloured lights threaded through the fir tree outside the pub, if Sandra hadn't struggled with the gigantic Father Christmas for the shop window, anxious that nothing should go behind because of Mrs T.'s illness, it could have been the first day of spring. Such a short time ago the village had been blanketed in snow, the roads and pavements icy death traps, and people had moved about like shapeless Eskimos in their woolly wrappings. This morning, however, it was as if all that arctic weather had never been.

The air was mild, the sky blue with wisps of high cloud, and in the school playground the boys in their scarlet jerseys—no anoraks this morning—chased footballs, while the girls linked arms and ran in long, undulating lines, hysterical with laughter as they trapped small infants unawares. Ellen Biggs, hobbling up to the shop, rested by the school railings and smiled at the children's antics. 'It'll be skipping ropes and 'opscotch soon,' she murmured, remembering the games that went with the seasons of her youth.

In the old vicarage garden, a blackbird sang high up on the topmost branch of the cedar tree, planted so long ago by a devout parson on his return from the Holy Land. He was reputed to have been a great royalist, and after Edward VIII had made his abdication speech, the broken-hearted cleric had retired to bed, turned his face to the wall, and not emerged for a week. Annie Bishop thought of this as she pegged out small T-shirts and vests. Clothes smelt so nice if they dried in the open air. Poor, long-dead parson, she thought sentimentally. Such loyalty. You don't get that these days. Still, they don't exactly inspire it. Loyalty was a two-way thing, thought Annie, and stood still, listening to the powerful, liquid notes of the blackbird's song. It was a triumphant, springtime song.

Annie, still pondering on loyalty, wandered down to the low wall between the garden and the Glebe Field, and marvelled at the nose cones of daffodils already poking through the dark, rich leaf mould. Tinker nosed in the rubbish heap and rolled out a protesting, still-hibernating hedgehog. 'Tinker!' she said, absently. 'Leave it alone, there's a good dog.' He didn't need telling. Hedgehog spines are impenetrable and painful, and Tinker moved on to dig under the beech hedge where he thought he'd left his bone.

'I'd have said loyalty was one of my good points,' she said to Tinker, as he deposited a chewed grey bone like a fossil at her feet. 'And now look at me . . .' She forced herself to think back. It was all very well mooning about the garden in a kind of afterglow, she told herself. Better examine this very carefully. She squatted down to have a closer look at the patch of Christmas roses, their petals greenish white, delicately flushed with pink. The morning was full of contradictions: daffodils in December, roses at Christmas . . . Annie Bishop being unfaithful!

An affair . . . was that what it was? Trying desperately to be honest with herself, Annie knew that she'd been a willing quarry in the hunt. Stealthy as Richard's methods were, and she'd certainly taken time to realise what he was up to, Annie was well aware by yesterday afternoon the way things were going. The touch of his hand in the shop, the clear meaning in his warm brown eyes. And then the gentle tapping at the door after the children were in bed, the tentative enquiry whether Andrew had come home after all, and the bottle of wine magicked out of his capacious pocket.

Andrew had not come home, and serve him

right, thought Annie sharply. She'd just settled down in the kitchen with a cup of coffee to watch television, telling herself she was not lonely and miserable, but she was, and when Richard came in, filling her elegant drawing-room with his confidence and thinly veiled excitement, Annie had drawn the pale grey velvet curtains, turned on reading lamps, and put a match to the fire.

'This is much more pleasant than watching the box,' she'd said. 'Did you say Susan might join us?' Richard had looked her straight in the eye and lied without compunction.

'If she can manage it,' he'd said. 'She's a bit pushed with her coffee morning arrangements. Looking forward to seeing you tomorrow, she said.'

Annie had at once seen the lie, and began to feel like the vixen trapped in a culvert. The kill is at hand, she'd thought to herself. Still, only if I want it. He'd handed Annie a glass of red wine, and propped himself against the marble fireplace with a proprietorial air.

'No, we agreed it would be an errand of mercy. Poor Annie abandoned again, alone in the great big vicarage. Definitely in need of rescuing ...' He'd smiled down at her, and she'd been irritated with herself as she felt the colour in her cheeks.

'Not really alone,' she'd protested. 'I have the children.'

'And now me.' Richard had stretched out his

hand, taken her glass and placed it with his own on the mantelpiece. Oh lord, she'd thought, it's all a bit B-movie, this.

His kiss was soft, like a father's kiss on her burning cheek. Then he'd pulled her close, and his mouth on hers was not in the least fatherly.

The air in the garden cooled her, and she gulped in some deep breaths. Well, he was certainly good at it. Better than Andrew? she asked herself brutally. Different, she protested silently. But she knew she couldn't think of much else this morning, the excitement in the rerun almost as good as the real thing. Still, she had to face Susan Standing quite soon, she realised with a sinking heart. It was the coffee morning, and she was committed to a stall. Oh lor . . .

'Mrs Bishop!' It was Jean Jenkins, waving to her from the back door. 'Telephone!' Jean was also due at the coffee morning, but had time for a quick whip round the old vicarage.

Annie hurried indoors, slipping off her muddy shoes in the scullery, and padded through to the hall. She put out her hand for the receiver, then hesitated. 'Um, I think I'll take it in the bedroom,' she said. 'Could you put this back when you hear me pick up the extension?' Risky, but better than a hovering Jean Jenkins.

Richard's voice was warm, husky. 'Morning,' he said, and her heart skipped a beat. 'How are you, Annie?'

257

'Um, all right. A bit tired,' she said, her voice so low that even Jean, vigorously polishing the stairs, could not hear. He chuckled, and she realised he too was keeping his voice down.

'Not surprised, my darling,' he said. 'That was quite an evening. We didn't disturb the bairns, I hope?'

His voice caressed her, and she closed her eyes, imagining him in his study, lounging back in his father's old library chair, his long fingers idly tapping his desk top as he wooed her with words. She could not, naturally, see that he was still in his pyjamas, torn at the back where the material had worn thin, and an old dressing-gown stained with coffee and egg yolk on the lapels. Nor could she see his lank, uncombed hair and the bleary state of his eyes.

Susan had noticed these, of course, when Richard had shuffled out of the kitchen with a cup of tea in his hand, his worn-down slippers slapping on the stone floor, but then she was used to him. She'd also noted that he had once more left yesterday's clothes in a heap on the bedroom floor and a spot of pink Dentufix on the bathroom shelf, evidence of a shaky hand as he'd fixed his dental plate.

Annie was blissfully unaware of all this, and leaned back against the pillows on her bed, the telephone cradled in her hands.

'When can I see you again?' Richard breathed softly.

Annie shook her head. 'Um, I'm not sure.

Andrew will be home tonight, he promised.'

Richard sighed with what Annie took to be disappointment, but was in fact relief. Not sure he could keep up that pace two nights running . . . 'No matter, Annie dear,' he said. 'I'll be in the village this afternoon as usual. See you by the bridge? I might even be persuaded to accept a neighbourly cup of tea. Bye, darling . . .' He put down the phone quickly, and Annie had a mental image of his study door opening, and Susan, followed by a faithful Labrador, coming in with his letters. She was right in one thing. It was Susan, but she was carrying her scratty little Yorkshire terrier, distinctly long in the tooth and snappy with it, and she had no letters, but one sharp message for him.

'If you don't have a bath and get dressed, Richard, right away, I shall take a hosepipe to you. And my ladies are coming at eleven, or had you forgotten again?'

*   *   *

Who coined the phrase, 'bring and buy'? Probably some American, thought Susan, gazing at her lovely black and white tiled hall, and at the pile of borrowed trestle tables. Whoever it was, she wished them dead. Would Bill come as he had promised, to help her set them up? She knew about Peggy, of course, as did everyone. He might not be able to leave her this morning. Damn! She couldn't manged the
259

heavy old wooden tops on her own, and Richard had finally disappeared into the bathroom. They were at least eight feet long, crudely made from thick elm plank, and had been in the village hall since it was built in the 'twenties. The new lightweight Formica-topped tables were used for school dinners, so she'd not even asked to borrow them.

'Richard!'

'You're screeching, my dear,' he said, materialising halfway down the stairs, dressed, possibly washed, combed and smiling. 'Need a hand?'

As he and Susan were lifting trestle tops on to the triangular bases, he saw through the long windows of the hall a delightful sight. Annie Bishop, in her fir-green leggings and a huge, Norwegian patterned jersey, approached the house, holding three-year-old Honor by the hand, and carrying a large wicker basket covered with a scarlet and white gingham cloth. He edged the trestle forward and turned to greet her. As he did so, Susan tipped her table end sideways, knowing perfectly well that Richard's foot was directly underneath. His yell sent echoes round the high-ceilinged hall, and he collapsed on to the tiles, moaning and clutching his foot. 'You stupid bloody woman!' he yelled, and the small smile which Susan could not quite suppress maddened him further.

'Why don't you take Honor up to the

playroom?' said Susan coolly to Annie. 'I don't suppose she's used to such language. Come on, Richard,' she added, 'get up. It was only a glancing blow, but absolutely my fault. I am so sorry.' She didn't look sorry, however, and helped him to his feet with that small smile still hovering. They went off to his study to take off his sock and shoe and examine the damage.

The bring and buy coffee morning was a success. They always were, up at the Hall. The village still felt vestiges of respect and feudal duty towards the Standings, and if Mrs Standing wanted to raise money for charity, then they would help her. And since the charity was Jean Jenkins's special unit for handicapped youngsters, set up in the Hall's own converted stables, then it counted as a local charity, and as such was even more deserving.

Home-made cakes and other goodies were always the first to go, and as Ivy Beasley and Doris Ashbourne were in charge of the stall, sales this morning went like clockwork. Ivy had a knack of selling two expensive chocolate sponges to customers who'd only intended to buy one, and Doris was so quick and efficient with the money that nobody was kept waiting. Annie Bishop's jars of thick-cut marmalade and raspberry jam were popular, and a reluctant Ivy noted as much to Doris. 'Not bad, for a townie,' she said, holding up a golden, translucent jar to the light. 'I'll have this one, Doris. Put it in my basket under the table.

261

Proof of the puddin's in the eating, nothing surer.'

When Sophie Brooks had been asked to help, she had complained to her unfeeling husband. Why should the vicar's wife always have to contribute? But in the end she'd persuaded Peggy to help her on a plant stall. 'We can do hyacinth bulbs with bits of ribbon and Christmas paper,' she'd said, and thanked Bill for his offer of geranium cuttings from the Hall greenhouse. She'd had to manage on her own this morning, of course, and felt quite proud that her table was nearly empty. A small, scented verbena had remained unsold, and Sophie put it to one side, deciding to take it to Peggy as a present.

'She'll want to hear all about the morning,' Nigel had said, 'so why don't you call in on your way home?'

Pat Osman had offered to do the raffle, and had been bullied by Colin to make a proviso that she could set up some bypass promotional material on an adjoining table. 'Are you coming to answer questions?' she'd snapped, and he had ignored her tone and said yes, of course, if Mrs Standing would have him. In the event, Pat had done extremely well with the raffle tickets, and Colin was gratified and surprised by the interest shown and the number of supporters who'd been prepared to sign his new petition.

'If we get a hundred per cent support from the village,' he said delightedly to Pat, 'we're well on the way.' She hadn't the heart to remind him that all the support in the world wouldn't increase the volume of traffic to those magic numbers which triggered Planning and Transportation into action.

Annie had been given children's toys and books to look after, and had done a roaring trade. Some of the books looked brand new, and several toys were still neatly packed in their boxes as if never touched. Luckily, apart from a brief word at the start, she'd been able to avoid Susan's eye, but between customers she thought anxiously of poor Richard. He'd looked so wounded, sitting there on the floor. The thought that he'd also looked quite ridiculous came into her mind and was expelled instantly. She wondered how she could find him and make sure he was all right, without antagonising Susan. Annie had been genuinely shocked at the chilly, almost callous way Susan had reacted to Richard's accident.

When all unsold goods, some dog-eared already from previous outings, had been packed in boxes for the next event, and everyone had gone home, Annie retrieved Honor from Poppy's playroom and looked around uncertainly. She supposed she should say something to Susan, and possibly see Richard, if only fleetingly. Only Jean Jenkins remained, resolutely counting coppers and silver coins, and noting down totals on the backs of envelopes.

'She's in the kitchen,' she said, guessing why Annie was lingering. Jean had not had time to think out what she was going to do with a large white handkerchief, initialled 'R', which she had found under the long sofa in the vicarage drawing-room. Now she looked sternly at Annie, and said, 'I'd steer clear, if I was you. Now she don't have to be polite, she'll be lethal. I'm off as soon as I've done this.'

'I thought I'd just see how Mr Richard was . . .' But Jean's stare was all-seeing, and Annie almost gave up. Then, as she turned away, Honor dragging reluctantly behind her, she heard a shout from Richard's study.

'Anybody there?' The voice was faint and appealing, and Annie was not proof against such a call for help. Dragging a now protesting Honor by the hand, she gently pushed open the door and went in. He was sitting in an old armchair with his foot up on his father's gout stool and cushions behind his head. 'Annie . . . ah, my angel of mercy!' he said. 'You couldn't find me a whisky, could you?' He reached out a hand, and she moved forward to take it.

'Ah, there you are!' said Susan, coming in like a cold shower. 'Everything packed up, then, Annie? Thank you so much for your help. Couldn't have managed without you. And Jean tells me we are going to have a nice profit for the funds.' She turned to Honor. 'Not too bored, I hope?' she said. And then she turned to Richard. 'Now, what can I get you, my darling?' Her voice sweetened, like treacle. 'I've asked Guy Russell to pop in, just to check. I'm sure he'd recommend a medicinal whisky don't you think?' She crossed the room, adjusted his cushions and dropped a loving kiss on the top of his head. She turned to Annie, smiled and said, 'They're all babies, aren't they . . . these men . . .'

CHAPTER THIRTY-FOUR

'A small token of my esteem,' said Sophie. 'Very small, and probably from Bill's greenhouse, so not even rarity value can excuse its insignificance.'

The small verbena cutting did indeed look limp and measly by the time she presented it to Peggy in the shop. 'I shall cherish it!' laughed Peggy, and slid off the stool where she had been perching behind the counter.

Sandra was there too, relaxed and smiling, and in protective mood. 'Ah, Mrs Brooks,' she said. 'Can you persuade Mrs T. to go and sit down in a comfy chair? She's been here half the morning, getting in my way!'

Sandra meant it kindly, but Peggy was in no mood to be usurped. 'Right,' she said briskly. 'Now, you go and make us a coffee, Sandra, and I'll take care of the shop. There's nobody else about, and Sophie can help herself.'

There was something in Peggy's voice that

meant business, and Sandra shrugged, glanced warningly at Sophie Brooks, and went off to do as she was told.

'How are you, Peggy?' Sophie said. 'That's a nice bump you've got there.'

Peggy put her hand up to her head and laughed. 'Well, there's one good thing,' she said. 'I've discovered you can only think about one twinge at a time.'

'No, but seriously,' said Sophie. 'Shouldn't you be taking it easy after that fall? It sounded really nasty, from what I heard.'

'You know as well as I do,' said Peggy, 'that what you hear seldom bears much relation to the truth. I'm trying very hard to remember that at the moment.'

'So you're saying it wasn't a nasty fall?' said Sophie, not quite sure what Peggy meant.

'Not that bad,' said Peggy. 'I slept well, and had a good breakfast, and apart from a sore head I feel fine. In fact, in a way, I feel a lot better than I did before.'

Still mystified, Sophie decided to change the subject. 'Well,' she said, accepting a mug of coffee from Sandra, 'why don't we go into the kitchen and let Sandra take over, and then I can give you a blow-by-blow account of the big event at the Hall. For starters,' she continued, leading the way, 'our Susan was in a foul mood, and Mr Richard had hurt his foot. Annie Bishop was spreading sweetness and light, and Colin Osman did a good PR job for the bypass lobby.'

'There's more?' said Peggy, following obediently.

'Oh, yes,' said Sophie, 'much more!'

In the end, Sophie stayed for a sandwich lunch. Nigel, she said, had gone to London on diocesan business, and she was on her own. Bill came in and looked anxiously at Peggy, his face clearing when he saw colour in her cheeks and heard her laughing at Sophie's description of Ivy Beasley's renowned sales pitch. 'Honestly, Peggy,' she said, 'she made it a kind of moral obligation to buy. And by the time I nipped across to her stall, she'd only got a flat jam sponge left.'

'And . . .?' said Peggy. With the air of someone confessing to a cocaine stash, Sophie brought out a miserable-looking cake from her basket. 'I suppose I can make a trifle with it,' she said.

Peggy put a bowl of fruit on the table, and a large box of chocolates. 'Here,' she said, 'have a choc, Sophie. One of the consolations of being poorly.' She looked across at Bill, rinsing out plates under the hot tap and stacking them in the drainer. 'You can leave those, Bill,' she said. 'I'm quite capable of washing a few dishes. Time you were off to work, isn't it?' She shepherded him out of the kitchen, through the shop and out of the door, waving a cheerful goodbye as he rode off on his bicycle.

'Trying to get rid of him?' said Sophie.

'Something you've got to tell me?'

Peggy hesitated, then shook her head. 'No secrets today,' she said.

*   *   *

Jean Jenkins put her purchases on the kitchen table and flopped down into a chair without bothering to take off her coat. She was exhausted but happy. They'd had a really successful morning, with over three hundred pounds in the kitty. The Hall group was always short of money for new equipment and extra help, and she was very anxious that the powers that be should not decide to close it down and transfer the special needs children to bigger units in Tresham. Jean and her helpers had built up a very good rapport with local people, and the mix of children worked well. The parents had benefited too. Mandy's Joey was now too old for the group, but she had kept up with a young mother of a small girl from Fletching. They had quickly found their sense of isolation diminish as they swapped experiences and problems. Jean loved to watch the children playing together. 'You should see them, Foxy,' she said. 'After a while, you don't notice the difference. 'Course, it's still there, but the kids don't make no bones about it, and neither should we.'

Staff and transport were expensive, however, and Jean was well aware that they continued to be funded only because of the patronage of the Standing family, who had friends in high places. The more money they could raise themselves, and the fewer demands made on the local authority, the better their chance of survival.

'Well, me duck?' said Foxy, coming in the back door and kissing the back of Jean's neck.

'What you doin' home?' she said. She'd packed up sandwiches for him, and told him not to rely on her for the whole day, as she'd no idea when she'd be finished at the Hall, and then she had to go on to Osmans' to do her usual couple of hours.

'I was passing,' he said, which was not wholly true. He had decided on a detour when he'd caught a glimpse of Jean trudging down the Hall avenue, head down against the freshening wind, weighed down like a bag lady with bargains she couldn't resist.

'Don't you get up,' he said. 'I'll make you a quick cup. On me way up to Grumblers Holt to check them pheasant feeders.' She's such a good gel, he thought, as he stirred the teabag and squeezed it with the back of a spoon. Never stops. He remembered when he'd told his mother he and Jean were getting wed. 'Good workers, them Williamsons,' was all she'd said.

'Weather's turnin' again,' he said, as he sat down opposite her and stirred two spoonfuls of sugar into his tea. 'The wind cut across the river

269

pasture as I came up. Really cold.'

'Hope Eddie remembers his scarf,' said Jean. 'Them kids were out to play with no coats this mornin', Eddie included.'

They were silent for a minute or two, a companionable silence. Then Jean remembered something, and sat up straight, fishing around in her coat pocket. She brought out the large white handkerchief with its telltale initial. 'What d'you think of this?' she said, holding it out to Foxy.

He stared at her, and looked suspiciously at the handkerchief. 'Well, you ain't goin' to bring a white rabbit out of it, I hope,' he said, grinning.

'No, no,' said Jean. 'I mean, look at this.' She turned it round so that Foxy could see the 'R'.

He shrugged. 'Looks like the boss's,' he said. 'D'you want me to take it back?'

Jean shook her head. 'Nope,' she said. 'Not until I've thought a bit more about it.'

Foxy lost patience. 'What's the mystery?' he said. 'Come on, me duck. I've got to be goin'. Spit it out, whatever it is.'

'This handkerchief,' she said with emphasis, 'was on the floor of Bishops' drawing-room, under the long sofa. It wasn't there yesterday,' she added, 'because I looked under everything for Bruce's giant marble. And Mr Andrew stayed in London last night . . .'

Foxy looked at her and frowned. 'That don't

sound too good,' he said slowly. 'Come to think of it, I have seen him walking round the farm with her and that dog of hers.'

'And he's always hoverin' outside school at turning-out time. Do you think there's somethin' going on?'

Foxy sighed. 'What do you think, Jean?' he said. 'We know Mr Richard of old. Can't resist anything in a skirt, if it shows willin'. But what about Mrs Bishop? She seems such a nice woman, and content and happy with her family. Why should she want to mess about with a man of his age?'

'Age don't come into it,' said Jean wisely. 'And anyway, there ain't that much difference.'

'Well, I got to be goin',' said Foxy. 'But mind what you do, Jean. Best not to get mixed up in that kind of stuff, specially as he's the boss. Tread careful, me duck.'

Jean finished her tea and stood up, took off her coat and hung it up on a peg in the narrow hall. The handkerchief lay on the table, and she looked at it speculatively. The sensible thing would be to put it quietly in the washing basket at the Hall next time she went. She picked it up, sniffed it, and then tucked it behind some table mats in the bottom drawer of the kitchen cabinet.

*   *   *

Annie had taken Honor to playschool for the

afternoon, and when she returned home, the old vicarage was quiet and cold. The mild morning had caused her to turn off the expensive new central heating system before going out. 'Like heating a hotel,' Andrew had grumbled, when the first fuel bill came in. Now, as she stood at the front door fumbling for her key, she shivered. Definitely a change in the weather. The weathercock on Ted Bates's old barn had veered to the east. Annie went straight through to the kitchen, where the Aga radiated constant warmth and comfort. She sat down at the table, the long pine table which looked so much more at home here than in London. They ate companionable family meals round it, she covered it with newspapers and Jean cleaned her brass and silver on it, the children sat at it, absorbed with painting or drawing, or making Plasticine dogs and cats and fat, sausage-like aeroplanes that could never fly.

Annie rested her head on her hands and felt depressed, in spite of her success on Toys and Books. She thought of last night and tried to relive the thrill of Richard's skilful progress from that first kiss to his farewell caress as midnight struck tunelessly from the church tower. She'd been wearing jeans and an old shirt of Andrew's when he'd arrived so unexpectedly, and had felt grubby and domestic, but Richard had flattered her, said that no one would have believed she'd had four children. He'd laughed about the loose, voluminous shirt. 'Makes things so much easier . . .' he'd purred.

Now, though, the frissons of pleasure were tempered with guilt. So Andrew had not come home. Was that a sign of wilful neglect? Maybe not, but it was becoming a regular thing, she thought defensively. They'd worked it all out so carefully before deciding to move to the country. He could work on the train, make use of the journey time, and any extra inconvenience would be worth it for the long weekends of fresh air and rural bliss. They'd agreed on it. Annie had given up things, too. Now she tried to think what she missed most, and knew if she was honest it was the companionship of likeminded friends. Nobody in Ringford knew what she was talking about half the time. She felt as if she was trying to play a part without knowing her lines.

Still, it won't be like that for ever, she told herself. There was that nice girl from Walnut Close, and Mandy—well, maybe not Mandy— and . . . She ran out of names, realised the impossibility of including Susan on the list, and got up, calling Tinker from his basket. 'Come on, boy,' she said. 'Let's go for a walk before we collect Honor. Introspection's no good for anybody.'

She fixed his lead, and left the house, reflecting now on the coffee morning, and thinking how she would have improved on it,

273

given it style. Maybe I'll have a fundraising musical soirée here, she thought. The drawing-room would be ideal if we moved the furniture around a bit. That would show them how it should be done. And Faith and I could play our duet. She imagined Richard in the audience, his eyes on her as she sat, slim and romantic at the piano . . .

As she and Tinker passed the dustbin, she saw that Jean had put out a pile of old newspapers. The wind had blown a couple of pages on to the path, and she picked them up, noticing that someone had marked crosses on the small ads section. Curious, she looked closer. They were all flats to let, one-bedroom flats and studios, all central London. It could only have been Andrew. For a moment she couldn't think, and then found unexpected tears plopping out on to the creased newsprint. 'Oh, Tink,' she said. 'What's happening to us?'

Tinker pulled at his lead, anxious to be gone, and Annie followed. At the gate, she paused. Her favourite walk took her along the edge of the estate, and then across the park, at one point quite close to the Hall, where an upturned galvanised trough made a halfway resting place. There was a good view of it from Richard's study window. Asking for trouble, Annie told herself, but she smoothed back her windblown hair, blinked away her tears, and set off.

CHAPTER THIRTY-FIVE

The small Bishops and Alison Goodison had swelled the numbers of children in the village school, and had lightened Sarah Barnett's task of casting the Christmas concert this year. She'd decided on *Hansel and Gretel* and had spent long evenings writing the script herself. John had been helpful, taking parts and acting it out with her in the farm kitchen, just to see if it sounded right. Not long married, they were blissfully happy. Their courtship had not been straightforward, but John's mother was now settled in the school house, and Sarah had taken her place on the farm, shaking down into a life divided between agriculture and her own little empire at the school. Deirdre Barnett was secretly hoping that John and Sarah would soon make her a grandmother, but she said nothing, being in awe of her head teacher daughter-in-law, and well aware that she would be told to mind her own business.

'Helen Bishop is an obvious choice for Gretel,' Sarah said. She and John were sitting in the kitchen in comfortable old armchairs that smelt of warm dog and were sprinkled with wiry white hairs from Sarah's little Cairn, Jemima. John had spent his usual hour in the Arms, and was feeling mellow.

'Whatever you say, my love, but don't forget the Bishops haven't been here five minutes. Won't do to antagonise the village families.'

Sarah thought of arguing that this was just the kind of parochialism she was intending to eradicate from her school, in the hope that it would lead to a more open community in the future, but she already felt herself slipping into the village mould, and settled for compromise.

'You're right,' she said. 'Well, we can fix that by having Eddie Jenkins as Hansel. He'll look the part, with his blue eyes and blond hair. Not so sure about learning his lines. Still, I can give him some extra time after school.'

'Who's right for the wicked stepmother?' said John. 'Ivy Beasley?'

'Don't be silly, John,' said Sarah. 'No, I've been thinking of having a boy for the part, a sort of pantomime figure. Eddie's chum George from Fletching would do it. He's quite a clown when he's got an audience.'

John looked across at her, her cheeks pink from the warmth of the kitchen, her smooth cap of brown hair shining in the light. He could still not quite believe it. He, John Barnett, bachelor and one of the lads, settled down and married to the village schoolmistress. Ah, but what a schoolmistress! He could see now that his rugby club chums who were still fancy free were beginning to look a bit—well, raddled was the word—and couldn't disguise their envy when Sarah came with him to special nights, attractive and intelligent, and so clearly in love with him.

'Let me know when you want a hand with
276

scenery and all that,' he said, pulling her gently to her feet. 'And now it's time for bed.' He lifted her like a child in his strong, farmer's arms, and carried her unprotesting up the old creaking staircase.

*   *   *

'Hansel? Really, Eddie? You're not kidding us?' Jean and Foxy Jenkins looked at their youngest son with growing pride. It seemed he was telling the truth. He was to be Hansel, and Mrs Barnett had told him not to worry about learning his lines, she would give him extra help and she was sure his parents would, too.

'Of course we will, me duckie,' said Jean, so delighted that she gave her squirming Eddie a congratulatory kiss on his chubby cheek. 'Soon as you've got your lines, we'll make a start.'

Eddie had got his lines already, but as it was Saturday, and he had plans for meeting George off the bus and the two of them investigating an oil drum that had beached under the Ringle bridge, he mumbled something about 'next week, I 'spect,' and disappeared.

Gabriella Jones, busy with a nativity play for the youngest group, wondered to Octavia if Sarah hadn't left it a bit late to get Hansel and Gretel off the ground. 'Search me,' said Octavia. 'Does she want any help with costume design? I could get really interested in that.'

'I'll ask her,' said Gabriella. 'She seems

confident, says they get bored if you start too soon. Anyway, it's all cast now, and Helen Bishop knows every word of her part already.'

'Naturally,' said Octavia, and Gabriella looked at her sharply. 'Well, you know,' said Octavia, 'nothing's too much trouble for Mrs Goody-goody Bishop. She'd have them all word-perfect in a couple of days. "Such fun, and we do like to support the village." Her mimicry was deadly, and Gabriella laughed.

'It's a treat for us teachers,' she said, 'to have such co-operative parents. If only they were all like that.'

Nobody could criticise Jean Jenkins for being non co-operative. She drilled Eddie until he rebelled and shut himself in his bedroom with his brother's music playing loudly, but by the dress-rehearsal he knew it all. Sarah Barnett was optimistic, delighted with George's caricature of what could only be his own mother's bad temper, and with Octavia's wonderful costumes conjured out of jumble sale bargains and old curtains from the Bishops' attic.

'It'll be a knock-out,' said John, as he stood with Sarah in the cold wind at the bottom of the playground, heaving stage blocks out of the old children's toilets, now disused and useful for storage.

*   *   *

Peggy looked out of the shop window, across

278

the Green and down to the river, where she could see Mr and Mrs Ross, well wrapped-up against the east wind, with their little black and white dog, taking their morning walk along the river path. A very unsuitable dog for the country, she thought. Should be trotting round Hyde Park, keeping its feet clean. She'd noticed that if the path was muddy, Mr Ross picked up the immaculate creature and carried it until they reached a grassy path. Still, they love it dearly, she reflected, and love's what matters.

This morning, Bill had asked her point blank what was troubling her. She'd determined to put all thoughts of Sandra and Bill to the back of her mind until they vanished with time, but she hadn't been able to bite back a sharp remark when he'd suggested Sandra going in to the warehouse to help him choose last-minute Christmas stock. 'We're doing well this year, gel,' he'd said. 'Sandra's really good with the kids. She can get them spending better than we can.' This had naturally rankled, and Peggy had replied that she planned to go with him herself, and didn't want to see herself taking early retirement just yet.

'Now then, gel,' Bill had said. 'Let's just sit down and get this sorted out. What's eating you? Not like you to be so sharp. Have I done something to upset you? Or has Sandra?'

A vigorous jangling of the shop bell had heralded Ivy Beasley's entrance, and the

279

conversation had to be postponed, but Bill, listening from the kitchen, had heard Peggy being very short, almost rude, and had begun to wonder. Then he'd heard Ivy asking where Sandra was.

'Not given her the sack for unsuitable behaviour, have you?' Ivy had asked in a nasty, cunning voice. My God, that was it. Bill got up and walked swiftly into the shop.

'Morning, Ivy,' he said. 'Not casting aspersions, are you?' His voice was polite. He even smiled, a little.

'A joke,' said Ivy sullenly. 'Only a joke. No offence meant.'

'None taken,' said Bill firmly. 'But you should be careful, Ivy, because folk don't always know the difference between a joke and malicious gossip.' He looked at Peggy's astounded face and winked at her. 'Don't you agree, my darlin' gel?' he said.

He held open the shop door, and Ivy scuttled out as soon as Peggy had taken her money. 'Any more to be said?' said Bill, and walked over and took Peggy's hand across the counter, just like in the old days, when he was just a customer who had fallen in love with her. 'Do we need to spell it out, Peg?'

Peggy shook her head, feeling a mixture of guilt and relief that brought her to the edge of tears again, but she'd done enough crying lately, and now determined to concentrate on getting back to normal. And after all, she was feeling so much better that they wouldn't need Sandra's help for much longer.

*   *   *

'You're a bit subdued, Ivy,' said Doris Ashbourne, as she brought a tray of flowery china teacups, saucers and plates into her warm sitting-room. The gas fire was on full, popping merrily, and since Bill had double-glazed the big window for her, there were no draughts. It was very cosy, and Ellen Biggs and Ivy sat comfortably, waiting for Doris to bring in the tea.

'Be thankful for small mercies, dear,' said Ellen. 'When she do say somethin', it's usually nasty.'

Ivy rounded on her. 'If I'm so much trouble,' she said, 'perhaps you'd be better off without me.'

Doris reappeared with a plate of home-made raisin biscuits and small slices of crunchy lemon cake. 'For goodness sake, you two,' she said. 'Haven't we got enough trouble in the world without you causing more?'

'Don't know about the world,' said Ellen, 'but 'ere in Ringford it's all very quiet at the moment. Dull, you might say. Anyway, Ivy, I'm sorry if I 'urt yer feelings. Come on, Doris, let's be pouring.'

Mollified, Ivy passed the cake plate to Ellen, and then settled into the upright chair by the window. 'Not a soul in sight,' she said. 'Wind's too cold. Everybody's staying by the fire. You're right, Ellen, it's dull when there's nobody about.'

'School will be out soon,' said Doris, 'and then there'll be some life. Too much, sometimes, Ivy, don't you agree?'

Ivy took a small, polite bite of the lemon cake and looked at it with her head on one side. 'Caster sugar, Doris?' she said sweetly.

Doris shook her head. 'Run out,' she said, 'so I had to use granulated. Why? Can you tell the difference?'

Ivy didn't answer, having made her point, but Ellen chipped in, 'It's very delicious, Doris. I wouldn't say no to another slice, if you've enough to spare.'

'Ah,' said Ivy, 'there go the children. Infants first, of course. They're not so noisy, but the next lot are little devils. Still, even they are better than constant traffic. Just drifted off to sleep last night when a great lorry thundered through and woke me up. Then I couldn't get back to sleep. It's a disgrace, if you ask me.'

For once, the three were in total accord. Even Ellen, waiting for the Tresham bus, had been sprayed with mud as she stood at the bus stop. 'Don't seem to be nothin' we can do,' she said, 'though that Colin Osman's doin' his best.'

'Christmas will soon be here,' said Doris, thinking it was time to change the subject,

282

brighten things up a bit. 'Shall we share again? You could come to me this year, and welcome.'

Ivy replied quickly. 'No, no, you come to me. I've got the range, and I can manage better in my own house. I presume you'll be wanting me to do the turkey?' Assured by the other two of the excellence of her Christmas dinner, she relaxed. 'You both going to the school concert?' she said. 'I always reckon Christmas starts with that.'

The big classroom in the school acted as stage and concert hall, and was always full and overflowing with parents and friends. But all were welcome, and this year Sarah had refused to reserve seats. 'Not even for the Standings,' she said. 'After all, they don't send precious Poppy here.'

'No, but he is one of the governors,' John had reminded her, 'and you owe your job mainly to the fact that he couldn't take his eyes off your legs at the interview . . .'

Now Ivy and Ellen agreed to meet Doris at the school gates in plenty of time, so that they would have good seats. 'Specially this year,' said Doris, who'd minded Eddie when he was a toddler and Jean had worked. 'Must get a good view of my little lad. Star part, you know, this year,' she told the others proudly.

'Well, cross your fingers, Doris,' said Ivy. 'There's bound to be one of them talent-spotters in the audience, and our Eddie'll be whipped off to Hollywood before you can say knife.'

'That's quite enough of that,' said Doris, and took up the teapot for second cups.

CHAPTER THIRTY-SIX

Excitement and emotions were running high in the school. For a start, the children were not used to being there in the evening, and with uncurtained windows and all the lights full on in every room, it felt unfamiliar just when they needed reassurance. They'd been brought in early by their parents, and now bold ones were standing on chairs, watching the audience arriving outside in little groups, some of whom lingered to gossip in the orange light of the chilly playground.

In the small classroom, doubling as dressing-room and last-minute rehearsal space, Jean Jenkins, Gabriella Jones, Renata Roberts and Sarah Barnett, marshalled the children, quietened them down, dressed them in their costumes, and generally kept order when panic inevitably broke out.

'I can't remember what comes after "Come on, Gretel, let's sleep under the trees," said Eddie, looking desperate.

'You both lie down and the birds cover you with leaves,' said Sarah. 'You don't have to say anything for a bit.'

'Oh yes,' said Eddie, biting his nails

nervously, 'now I remember, thanks.'

Jean crossed the room and gave Eddie's hair an unnecessary comb. 'You'll be all right, me duck,' she said. 'Always all right on the night. Isn't that what they say, Mrs Barnett?' she laughed, but a bit shakily. She too was nervous, anxious on behalf of Eddie.

Sarah saw this, and sent her out to see whether they could start on time. 'Most people should be here by now,' she said.

'Now, quiet everybody. Let's just check that everyone knows what they're doing.'

*   *   *

Andrew Bishop sat in the train outside Watford and fumed. What the hell was the matter this time? They'd juddered to a halt about ten minutes ago in the middle of nowhere, dark, flat winter fields on either side of the train, and since then nothing had happened, no announcements made, and no comforting inspector coming through the train to explain. As always, his fellow passengers had at first continued to read their evening papers, or chat quietly to one another. Then one had stood up and gone through to the end of the carriage, let down the window, and looked out. Then he'd shaken his head sadly, and come back, telling everyone that there was nothing to see. 'Not a bloody thing for miles,' were his exact words.

Andrew looked at his watch. Six o'clock

285

already. He'd had a dreadful day. That idiot woman barrister had lost their case, when it had seemed a foregone conclusion that they would win it. Then he'd been waylaid by a senior partner who wanted his opinion on an articled clerk who was in fact the son of Andrew's father's best friend. So Andrew had had to be as diplomatic as possible without actually saying that the lad was a complete numbskull and should never have been admitted to the firm.

Then the buses had been virtually stationary all the way along the Euston Road, and in the end Andrew had jumped off and run the last half mile, only to see his train pulling out of the platform as he arrived puffing and panting, and yelling to it to wait for him. But British Rail waits for no man, and he'd stumbled back to the coffee stall to pass the twenty minutes before the next Tresham train. This was an Intercity and crowded, with no spare seats and people standing or sitting on their luggage.

'Ladies and gentlemen,' said a booming voice over the carriage speakers. 'We apologise for the delay, but an engine has apparently broken down the other side of Watford Junction.' Groans all round the stuffy carriage. 'It will be some time, unfortunately, before it can be replaced and the line cleared. Our staff will be on hand for any help you need, and we shall be pleased to offer complimentary refreshments for inconvenienced passengers.'

'I don't believe it!' exploded Andrew. The girl sitting next to him shifted away uneasily. 'It's my children's school concert this evening,' he explained hastily. 'They'll never forgive me if I don't make it. Oh God, what is Annie going to say?' He put his head in his hands, and felt a light touch on his sleeve.

'Don't upset yourself,' said the girl. 'They may be quicker than you think. Let me get you a cup of coffee.'

*   *   *

Annie Bishop sat in the second row, just behind Richard and Susan Standing, with her gloves on the next chair, saving it for Andrew. He'd said it would be best if he came straight to the school from the station, just to make sure he was on time. Annie glanced round at the door for the hundredth time. No sign of him. Where could he have got to? Surely he would have left London on time. He knew how important it was to support the children in all their endeavours.

'Isn't Andrew coming?' It was Susan Standing, twisting round to smile sweetly at Annie. She could see from Annie's face that there was trouble. Trouble in store for Andrew, no doubt of that, thought Susan with some satisfaction. If that confident, smooth young solicitor had spent more time thinking about his nubile young wife, there wouldn't be this

287

boring tussle of wits with Richard once again. She sighed as Richard smiled a warm, protective smile.

'Don't worry, Annie,' he said. 'He'll make it. Come crashing in at the last minute full of good excuses, I expect.' He tried to make it sound light hearted, but Annie was not consoled. If he's late, she thought angrily. . . But just as she was devising punishments that Andrew would never forget, the curtains parted and Sarah Barnett stepped forward.

The infants' nativity was the first item, and Gabriella's babies were as tentative and heartwarming as always. Mary was completely tongue-tied and had to be prompted at every line, and Joseph lost his patience with the innkeeper in a rather unbiblical way. Sarah regretted later that she'd agreed to have Tom Price's old donkey on stage. 'Think of the realism', Gabriella had said wickedly. The ramp they constructed was too slippery for the tiny hoofs, and Mary had stage-fright about being lifted on to the broad felt saddle. Nothing terrible happened, but stagehands and audience alike were so much on edge that it was a relief when the curtain fell on the final tableau.

Octavia's painted scenery for Hansel and Gretel drew a gasp of admiration, and with Sarah prompting and encouraging from the wings, her version of the old story worked its charm. Eddie forgot his nerves, and Helen Bishop moved through her scenes with placid

288

self-assurance and obvious hero worship of her stage brother.

Jean had crept into the back row for the beginning, and had clutched Foxy's hand all through. Tears ran unashamedly down her round face as Eddie and Helen held hands and took their bow. Foxy silently handed her his handkerchief, and swallowed hard himself.

Annie Bishop was rigid with anger and disappointment. She applauded with a fixed smile on her face, and accepted the Standings' compliments with scarcely an acknowledgement. How could he? She looked a fool in front of everybody. It should have been such a lovely occasion. They would have been really part of the village, an important part. Just wait till he finally gets home, she told herself as she waited to collect Helen from the cloakroom door. Just wait.

*   *   *

Andrew's train drew into Tresham two and a half hours late. He elbowed others out of his way in the booking hall, sprinted to the car park and flashed his lights as he nosed out ahead of the others on their way home. If he could just get to the school before they all left, then at least Annie would see that he had tried. Perhaps Helen would still be in the costume that she was so proud of. He put his foot on the accelerator and sped along the long straight road that led from Tresham to Waltonby. After

289

that, it was bends all the way, so he needed to make up time where he could.

The clock on the car's instrument panel moved on remorselessly. He got held up at a junction where a cattle-lorry had broken down halfway across the road. His fingers drummed on the steering wheel, and he turned on the radio. Classic FM. Soothing classical pops. Bach's greatest hits, he said to himself, but could not smile.

As he came down the road into Ringford, he could see the lights were still on in the school. Great! There was still a chance of redemption. He ignored the speed limit sign—just this once, he said to himself—and sped along by Price's farm. He could see one or two shadowy figures standing by the school gate. Oh God, please let me be in time. Let them still be there, he prayed.

And then, just as he was within sight of the playground and sighing with relief, he saw the small figure of Eddie Jenkins, his blond hair shining in the pub's security light, step off the pavement in front of him, and knew in one sickening instant that he could not stop.

CHAPTER THIRTY-SEVEN

Ivy Beasley sat at her window, looking over the cold, grey village, her knitting lying idle on her lap. Heavy clouds had gathered over Bagley

Wood soon after breakfast, and now hung low along the valley. Large drops of rain coursed down Ivy's window, like tears.

She stared out and saw nothing, nothing but a car's headlights and a small body thrown up and over the road, a limp sack that seemed to have nothing to do with Eddie Jenkins. The memory made her feel sick with horror, and she forced herself to pick up her knitting, thick grey socks to keep Robert Bates warm in his workshop. She remembered Robert when he was six, a skinny, quick little lad, who used to call in to see her regularly for his glass of milk and a rock cake. He'd grown into such a steady, capable man. And Eddie . . . now there would be no growing into anything. Ivy choked and pushed her knitting violently to the floor.

In her warm kitchen, she put her kettle to boil, not because she wanted anything to drink, but because it was something to do. For once, she welcomed her dead mother's voice. Sorry for yourself, Ivy? it said. What do you think Jean and Foxy are feeling? If you ask me, she continued sharply, there'll be a lot to be done in the village now. A lot to put right.

What do you mean, Mother? said Ivy in her head. But her mother said no more, leaving Ivy to brood.

Loud knocking at her front door jolted her into action, and she found Ellen Biggs standing on her doorstep, out of breath and taking great gulps of cold air. 'Come in, for goodness' sake,'

Ivy said. 'What are you doing up here? I wasn't expecting you, was I?' Time was out of joint, and anything could happen, anything be forgotten.

'Couldn't stay down there on me own,' said Ellen. Her eyes were red and her voice hoarse. 'Keep thinkin' I see 'im goin' past the gate.'

Ivy looked at her, had a sharp rejoinder on the tip of her tongue, but held it back. Instead, she did something which Ellen never forgot, not even in her most irritated moments with Ivy. Ivy stepped forward, put her arms round Ellen's bulky figure, and hugged her. They stood like that, silently, with tears unchecked, for several minutes.

*   *   *

Doris Ashbourne moved around her small, warm bungalow slowly, picking up magazines, books, and putting them down again, unread. She made a cup of tea and left it on the table in the kitchen until it was stone cold. The post dropped through her letter box, and she saw the postwoman go past her window, head down, face grim. If she'd stopped for a minute, I could have a word, thought Doris. She broke up some stale bread into small pieces for the bird-table and left it on the bread board on the windowsill while she went to get her coat. An hour later, she found the crumbs where she'd left them. She opened the door and threw them out on to the ground. That'll do for this morning, she thought.

She made her bed, taking more time than usual. The bedclothes had been in a muddle, as she'd scarcely slept, tossing and turning all night in a waking dream. Over and over again she saw Jean Jenkins flying towards Eddie, Foxy close behind her. And then the dreadful huddle silhouetted against the car lights: Jean and Foxy bent over the motionless child, and Jean screaming, screaming in that terrible voice that split the village.

Doris shook her head, trying unsuccessfully to dispel the memories that crowded in the minute she stood still. Eddie in her sitting-room, nine months old and sitting squarely in the middle of a heap of toys. What was it he called her? Gaga Doss. That was it, it was the nearest he could get to Auntie Doris.

Oh my God, I can't stand this. Doris walked quickly into her bedroom and took her warmest coat from the cupboard. She tied a scarf tightly round her head, pulled on her fur boots, and without a glance to see if she looked neat and tidy, let herself out of the bungalow and set off for Victoria Villa.

*   *   *

'There goes Doris,' said Jean Jenkins. It was the first thing she had said for hours. She was sitting on a hard chair by the window, still in

293

her nightdress and dressing-gown, a cup of coffee untouched in front of her. The pills the doctor had made her swallow were working, and she felt as heavy and leaden as a suet pudding. It was an effort to move her hand across the table to take Foxy's. Thoughts whirled about in her head in an uncontrolled, unfinished way. They'd tried to make her stay in bed, but she knew there were things to be done, children to be got off to school. And she had to make sure Eddie put on his balaclava against the cold wind. That ear was playing up again. She'd have to take him to Dr Russell on Friday. Eddie . . .

'Don't, me duck,' said Foxy, in a dull voice.

She hadn't realised she'd spoken aloud. She stared at Foxy, and then began to scream again. It was the only way to shut out the nightmare.

Foxy got up and came over to her, holding her tight. 'Come on,' he said. 'Let's get you back to bed,' but Jean tore herself away from him.

'The twins!' she shouted, terror in her voice. 'Where are they? Where's Mark—and Warren! What's happened to them?' She rushed out of the room, into the kitchen and back again. 'Foxy!'

He grabbed her flailing arms and pinned them to her sides, slowly lowering her into a chair by the fire. 'Jean,' he said, and he was crying now, 'Jean, please don't, please. Just stop now, and we'll talk.' It was the silence, the bloody silence he couldn't stand. Even Jean screaming was better than silence.

'The others!' sobbed Jean. 'Where are they?'

'At your mother's,' he said. 'Peggy and Bill took them over last night. It was best, Jean. They was in a terrible state, poor kids.'

'I want them back,' said Jean.

''Course you do, me duck,' said Foxy. 'I'll fetch them soon as we're straight.' He wiped his face with the back of his hand, and shovelled more coal on the fire. The house was cold and horribly empty. He knew what Jean meant, and she was right. However bad it was—and it was bad beyond belief—they'd be better facing it together, all together.

*   *   *

'Dear God,' said Nigel Brooks, lightly touching the crucifix on his desk, 'this is the worst thing I've ever had to do. If you could just stand by me this morning . . .' And then he thought how selfish that was, when all his prayers today should be for Foxy and Jean, and the twins . . . and Mark and Warren . . . and Doris, and . . . and the whole village, really. It was a village death. He walked into the kitchen, where Sophie was leaning against the Aga, her hand stroking old Ricky's head, staring at the floor. She looked up at him and frowned.

'Oh, Nigel,' she said, 'should I come with you, would it help?'

He shook his head. 'I don't think so, thanks. Not yet, anyway. They'll probably not want to see me either, but I should go. There'll be things to arrange.'

It was only when he walked out of his new drive and past the old vicarage that he remembered Andrew Bishop, the instrument of death, and realised that he would have to go and see them, too. Poor sod, he would need prayers just as much as the rest of us, thought Nigel. But not this morning.

He walked on over the bridge, where the cold, grey water ran swiftly with the winter rain, and on over the Green towards Macmillan Gardens. As he passed the shop, the giant Father Christmas caught his eye. Christmas! How were they ever going to celebrate that miracle birth when death had laid its pall over the whole village? It would be up to him, he reflected dismally, to salvage something from it all, to offer the healing balm of Christianity to his troubled parish. Somehow, this morning, he couldn't see them buying it.

* * *

Andrew Bishop raised his head with difficulty from the pillow. The surgical collar round his neck pressed into his chin, and as he slid out to sit on the edge of the bed, an echoing pain struck the base of his spine. The room began to spin, and he rushed for the lavatory, knelt on the floor and began to retch. He thought he would never stop. Every time the nausea subsided, he rested his head on his hands, and then after a few seconds the terror returned and he vomited again, although there was now very little in his stomach to throw up.

'Andrew?' It was Annie, standing at the bathroom door, staring down at him without pity. 'Telephone for you,' she said, holding out the portable. 'It's the office. I just told them you were ill. Nothing else.' She seemed to be forcing out the short sentences with considerable effort. Her face was completely blank, like a lovely doll, although without colour. Even her blue eyes had faded, and her skin was a greyish-white, her lips paler.

Andrew rolled round and sat with his back to the bath, his eyes shut. 'Can't speak,' he whispered, and waved her away.

She turned and left the room, and as she went along the landing he heard her say, 'So sorry, but he's too poorly at the moment. We'll get back to you. And thanks, I'll tell him. Bye.'

The old enamelled bath that they'd been so excited about was cold against his back, and he stood up slowly, gingerly. The nausea seemed to have settled for the moment, and he shuffled his way to the landing. What the hell should he do now? There'd be the police, and the doctor calling again, and he'd have to get a message to that barrister today. He could hear the children's voices from the kitchen, and Annie, snapping at Bruce for spilling his drink. It all sounded so normal.

But actually, in fact, when he had the courage to turn and face it, face what happened last night, to him and to Eddie Jenkins, the world had come to an end.

CHAPTER THIRTY-EIGHT

It had been a bad morning in the shop. After the first uncanny lull, there had been a trickle of villagers, all subdued but needing to talk. The Stores was the obvious place to go, and only Bill knew what it cost Peggy to stand behind the counter, listening and consoling, carrying on the daily business of life when all she could think of was that small death.

The shop had been cold and dark when Peggy first came down to a breakfast neither she nor Bill could eat. She had stood by the door, with its jolly poster for the school concert, staring out at the early bus collecting children for Tresham comprehensive. No shouting this morning: all the Ringford gang had climbed in soberly and sat down, while their mates from other villages looked at them in amazement. Peggy had watched the bus draw away, dreading the coming day and wishing she could leave the shop closed until further notice.

Not a soul appeared during that first long
298

hour or so, but then the first grim-faced customer arrived. It was Susan Standing, absently taking a jar of instant coffee from the shelf and putting it in her basket. She drifted round for a minute or so, and then seemed to make for the door. Peggy noticed automatically that she hadn't paid for the coffee, and wrote it down in the account book. But still Susan didn't go, just stood there, looking anxious.

'Was there something else?' Peggy said.

'I was wondering . . .' Susan was unusually hesitant. 'Have you heard how Jean . . .? I feel I'd like to see her, but don't want to intrude. What do you think, Peggy?'

Peggy wanted to say she was not up to thinking, not about Susan Standing's feelings or anything else except the one child in the village who'd been her special love, the one she'd cuddled as a toddler and kidnapped from his mother in the shop, taking him off to play silly games with Gilbert in the kitchen. She could see his rosy face and ready smile, hear his obedient 'Thanks, Mrs Turner!' as she slipped him a Snoopy chocolate bar when Jean wasn't looking. Well, he'd not be coming in any more. Peggy fumbled for the sodden handkerchief in her overall pocket.

'Probably too soon,' she said shortly. 'But goodness, I don't know, Mrs Standing, she might be glad to see someone.' She tried to imagine what it must be like to be Jean, but found it unbearable and closed her mind. For the second time in her life, Peggy decided that there was no God.

'How can there be?' she said aloud. She was hardly aware that Susan Standing had left the shop, and did not notice Bill standing at the kitchen door, watching her with a worried frown. He'd made a surreptitious call to Mr Richard, asking for the day off, which had been agreed without question. Peggy was behaving like an automaton, going through the motions. He feared she'd not be able to keep it up, and wanted to be standing by.

'How can there be what?' he said quietly.

'A God. And if there is, what kind of bloody God is it?' Peggy's voice was rising with anger and she glared at Bill. 'If he's so all-bloody-powerful, why didn't he hold Eddie back? Ten seconds would have done it, until Andrew Bishop had . . .' But Andrew's name choked in her throat, and she shook her head blindly.

Bill walked through the shop and looked out at the empty street, at the now deserted bus shelter where an empty crisp packet blew in endless circles, trapped in a cross-wind from the Green. Further up, he saw the school playground, and the gate swinging open, its hinges squeaking rustily. It was never left open. Only time he could remember.

'I don't know, gel,' he said gently. 'I really don't know, but we've got to get through the day somehow, and there'll be others coming in and wanting to talk about it. Are you feeling up to it, Peg?'

Late last night, after making sure the road was clear of broken glass, he'd met Sarah Barnett getting into her car. She could scarcely speak, but had jerked out, 'No school tomorrow. Nigel and Mr Standing said.' He'd seen John Barnett at the wheel, and helped Sarah into her seat.

'Look after her, John,' he'd said, but there was no need. John was a steady chap. He'd know what to do.

And had he, Bill, done all he could do for Peggy? He'd been so pleased to see her looking animated and really pretty again, excited by the play's success, and chatting with Foxy and Jean, and everyone else in the audience, really her old self. Now he looked at her pale, drawn face and saw all that good undone. She'd been strong last night, of course. Helped him with Jean, and then they'd taken the Jenkins kids over to their grandmother at Bagley, as Nigel Brooks had suggested. It had been her dreadful task to break the news to the old couple, and to see that the children were settled into bed, the twins sharing a big old brass bedstead, and Mark and Warren lying rigid and shocked in twin beds in a cold back room. Peggy had suggested hot drinks, and stayed with them until they fell asleep, restless and moaning as dreams took over from the nightmare reality.

On the way back to Ringford, she'd been quiet and he had found it hard to concentrate

301

on the winding lanes. Both in shock, I suppose, thought Bill. The whole bloody village was in shock. It was only when Peggy had picked up her little cat, Gilbert, to put her out for the night, that she'd held the soft furry body to her cheek and begun to cry.

Now she spoke again, more quietly. 'Sorry, Bill,' she said. 'I'll be all right. We're all in the same boat this morning. Oh Lord, here comes Gabriella Jones, looking like a walking ghost.'

Bill stood aside to let Gabriella into the shop, touched her shoulder lightly in a gesture that meant more than words, and then returned to the kitchen. He could prepare something for lunch, ready for Peggy when she needed it. As he opened the high cupboard door, he noticed the calendar with a pencilled ring around the date. He frowned, couldn't recall anything special happening today, and was about to ask Peggy when he remembered. Oh my God, that was it. Today. The anniversary of Frank's death, killed in a road accident three years ago. My poor, poor Peggy, he thought. And poor Foxy and Jean . . . and every one of us.

CHAPTER THIRTY-NINE

Annie Bishop sat on the edge of the sofa in her drawing-room, looking down at a printed sheet of paper. It was from Nigel Brooks, and had been pushed through the door yesterday morning. A festive orange with a candle stuck in it announced the Christingle service on Sunday. Nigel had written across the top, 'Could do with an extra pair of hands if you're free! Last-minute meeting Sat., 3 p.m. in the vicarage.' Annie read it automatically, not really taking it in.

After a scratch lunch, the children had retreated to the attic playroom, sensing they'd be better out of the way. They had heard their father being sick, and were puzzled by the strange silence between their parents. The unexpected holiday from school disorientated them, and Faith had tried to take over from her mother, shepherding the younger ones upstairs. No help or guidance had come from Annie. She seemed unaware of their presence once lunch was over. The dishes were still on the kitchen table, and she had wandered through to the drawing-room trying in vain to collect her thoughts.

Where *had* he been, arriving only after the concert had finished? She'd heard him muttering to the police something about a delayed train, but no train she'd ever travelled in had been held up for so long. Perhaps there was someone else, someone who was more important than his own children? Annie stood up abruptly, and walked to the window, looking out at the fragile Christmas roses under the cedar tree. So delicate and pure, and . . .

childlike ... Oh God, dear God, what am I going to do?

Annie coloured with shame, knowing that her suspicion of Andrew would never have entered her head a couple of months ago, before she and Richard ... She couldn't bear to think of it, and yet how wonderful it would be if Richard were here right now, to comfort her with his breezy confidence. And Andrew? She found she couldn't look at him. For better, for worse? Well, it couldn't get much worse. Standing by Andrew's side in the lovely old church in her parents' village, she had been so certain, so much in love, that she could not imagine being put to the test. It had been a flowery path ever since. The children, all perfectly healthy and bright, had followed at intended intervals. Andrew's career had prospered—he was known as a high flier—and he had plans for his own practice in the not too distant future.

And what of that future now? Annie shivered with despair at a sudden glimpse of what was ahead of them. How could he have done this to her? Her whole life wrecked in one split second. She turned around and began to pick up newspapers scattered round Andrew's chair. On Jean Jenkins's days she always tidied up, leaving Jean a clear field for cleaning ...

Annie stopped dead, cushion in hand. Jean! She rushed into the hall and reached for the telephone. She must help, offer to do something. And then, like stepping into an icy bath, she realised that no one would want her help now, least of all Jean Jenkins. She replaced the receiver and sat down heavily. She'd better think of an excuse to get out of the Christingle service. But maybe she wouldn't need one. Nigel would be embarrassed by her presence now. I hate you, Andrew Bishop, she said to herself. Her unhappiness was deep, but she shed no tears.

*   *   *

'I've got to go and see him,' said Jean suddenly into the silence that had fallen on Foxy and herself, sitting quietly now in a cocoon of misery.

Their small sitting-room was crowded with all the furniture and trappings of a family. The sofa and chairs were comfortable, but frayed with clambering children's shoes, and the television and video took up most of one corner. There were books and toys on every surface, on the windowsill, the display cabinet which held Jean's collection of glass animals, the scarred coffee table by the wall. No room for cups of coffee on this one: an elaborate construction of interlinked plastic pieces, looking very like a steam engine, took up its entire surface. Eddie had spent days coupling its rods and wheels together, his nose wrinkling with the effort of concentration. He had

305

allowed nobody to touch it.

'But . . .?' Foxy was puzzled. Eddie's battered little body was lying at the undertaker's. It was customary. It's what people do, thought Foxy, isn't it? But Jean hadn't meant Eddie.

'We could both go. Wouldn't take long to walk down there, and Bill reckoned he wouldn't be back with the children until fiveish.' This was the longest sentence Jean had managed so far.

'Go where?' said Foxy, frowning. He thought he knew. But surely Jean couldn't . . .

'Bishops',' said Jean. 'I've got to ask him some questions. Why he didn't stop in time . . . why he didn't see Eddie on the pavement. Was he going too fast!' Her voice was rising now, hysteria very near the surface. 'Why didn't he bloody *STOP*!' She stood up, her shoulders shaking, and rushed out for more kitchen paper to blot up this fresh burst of sorrow.

Foxy followed her, and once again put his arms around her. They stood in the dark kitchen until her tears subsided. 'But I can't go, can I?' she said, her voice muffled by his broad shoulder.

Foxy shook his head. What should they do now? They'd had so many cups of tea and coffee, half-finished and scummy and still on the draining-board in an untidy heap. He could think of nothing to do. What was the point? Everything had been taken care of by the police and the undertakers. The vicar had been, and Jean had seemed to take some comfort from his visit. But now what? They couldn't sit staring at one another any longer. It wasn't natural. Neither of them was accustomed to it.

'Jean,' he said, his voice suddenly firm. 'Get your coat on, we're going out.'

'But we can't ... can't go down there. It wouldn't be right.'

'Not to Bishops',' he said. 'We'll walk. Anything's better than sitting here with all Eddie's things, and ...' He choked, and turned away. Then, pulling himself together with a supreme effort, he took Jean into the hall, got her into her coat and pulled on his own old working jacket.

As he went to the front door, Jean moaned. 'I can't do it, Foxy,' she said. 'I can't go out there.'

He took no notice, but opened the door wide and gently propelled her out into the cold, grey garden. 'There's two of us,' he said. 'We've always managed, you and me. Come on, me duck, chin up.'

It was her village, her beloved Macmillan Gardens, where she and Foxy had lived since their wedding day, but to Jean, walking along clutching Foxy's arm, her head down and eyes on the pavement, it was a threatening landscape. She was scared of every step, of where it would take her. Down there, at the end of the Gardens, was the place.

'No, Foxy, I can't,' she said, but Foxy kept walking, holding tight to her hand.

'We'll go up the hill,' he said. 'See if there's rabbits in the wood.'

Jean looked at him in amazement. Had he lost his wits? 'Foxy!' she said, and stopped dead. 'You are all right, I mean . . .?'

He turned and looked at her. 'I'm as all right as you,' he said. 'But our little lad is dead, and I can't think of a better place to think about it than Bagley Woods. So come on, Jean. Let's go together.'

CHAPTER FORTY

High up in Bagley Woods, winter had taken possession. As Foxy pushed open the broken gate, bare brambles tugged at Jean's coat. Her shoes crunched on dry, dead leaves and a brittle stick snapped under her tread. Up here, a chill wind blew through the bare trees, and Foxy shivered. 'Hang on a minute, me duck,' he said. He stood in front of her and buttoned up her coat, pulling the collar up round her neck, just as he did with the children when they went off to school. She looked at him and for the first time seemed to see him.

'How are we ever going to . . .?' She couldn't say any more, but Foxy nodded. He had understood. They didn't need words.

At first, the woods were quiet, keeping

themselves to themselves, but everywhere there were listening ears, watching eyes. A rabbit suddenly shot out from under their feet and disappeared into the network of burrows that ran under the pitted, muddy surface. With a squawk of alarm, a blackbird flew out from a dense holly bush, causing little flurries and scuttles in the underbrush. Jean and Foxy walked on, their pace slowing after a while to a more relaxed rhythm. It was a well-worn path, often used in good weather, and particularly in spring, when people came for miles to see the bluebells. But now there were no signs of human presence. The path led to a wide oak stump surrounded by a grassy, open glade, with a view down the hill and across Tom Price's fields to the village in the valley below.

'Let's sit down for a minute,' said Foxy. Not caring whether it was damp and cold, Jean perched on the edge of the stump and Foxy sat down next to her, his arms around her shoulders.

*   *   *

On the other side of the wood, Tinker nosed into a rabbit hole and began to push his way in. 'Out!' said Annie Bishop sharply. She grabbed his tail and pulled, and he backed out reluctantly, his nose covered in yellowy-brown clay. Annie had been overcome by the claustrophobic atmosphere of the old vicarage and shouted to Andrew to keep an ear on the children, she was going for a walk. She'd thought of going through the park, in the hope of some comfort from Richard, but decided against it. Things were complicated enough. So she'd taken Tinker and set off on the footpath to the woods.

'Keep out of those rabbit holes,' she said, tapping Tinker on the head. He trotted obediently in front of her for a few yards, and then took off after an imaginary quarry that turned out to be a dead leaf, blowing in the wind. He'd left the path, and now Annie branched off to follow him. She was cold, and didn't want to spend hours chasing the dog. This walk was a waste of time, anyway. Her thoughts were no clearer up here than at home, and she'd forgotten her gloves. She stepped into a hollow full of icy water and swore, turning around to see where Tinker could have gone.

Was that him? No, it wasn't, but the sight of two people sitting on the old stump brought her up short. Damn, she wasn't in the mood for conversation. Their faces were turned away, looking over the valley, but there was no mistaking their slumped backs. It was Jean and Foxy Jenkins. Annie froze, biting her lip. Without thinking of Tinker, she turned around as quietly as possible and crept away. And as she went blindly back through the wood, she finally allowed herself to think of Eddie, little Eddie Jenkins, and hot tears rushed down her pale cheeks.

CHAPTER FORTY-ONE

'Everyone will be going to the funeral, Colin, you needn't worry about intruding,' said Pat Osman. Like most of the village, they'd had no heart for making Christmas preparations. Pat had been hard hit, mourning her little dog all over again, and ashamed to admit it in the face of Jenkinses' loss of a child. But Colin had noticed, and on the way home from work had bought a small Christmas tree, which they were now decorating with tiny silver balls and golden bells. 'No good wallowing,' he'd said, wondering if that didn't sound a bit heartless, but Pat had nodded, helping him set the tree in an old bucket, disguising it with red crêpe paper and a silver bow.

'I was just thinking of Foxy and Jean,' said Colin. 'Might be harder for them, having a crowd. Still, they'll all be locals, people they know. But I'd not say we were locals, not really.' Colin struggled with the lurching silver star, and Pat thought of all that Colin had tried to do for the village.

'Not so sure,' she said. 'I reckon they'd expect you to be there. We're sort of local, aren't we?'

Their few years in Ringford had changed them. Colin realised this when he turned down promotion that meant they had to move to Swindon. There was something womblike about village life. Irritating as the endless round of gossip and speculation undoubtedly was, there was a kind of insulating protectiveness about the small community. Every time Colin drove down the hill into the village, he felt himself relax and sigh with relief as the wooded hills encircled him once more. It was something more than just coming home. He wondered if the Bishops felt the same.

'There's one bloke won't be there,' he said. 'Poor sod.'

'How can you say that?' said Pat fiercely.

'Because I mean it,' said Colin. 'Nobody knows what Andrew Bishop's going through. God knows there's little excuse for knocking down a child, but we don't know the full facts yet. Could be he couldn't avoid him.'

'He was going too fast,' said Pat baldly. 'And I don't want to hear you defending him to anybody.'

They sat by the fire in silence for a few minutes, the debris of tree-decorating around them. Then Pat got up and began to collect up pieces of twig and torn paper, broken bells and tiny shards of silver glass. Have to get a few more next year, she thought. Then her mind went back to the Bishops. She was a fair-minded woman, and several times she'd had the same thought as Colin, though she wouldn't admit it right now. Nobody knew exactly how it had happened. The police would be taking statements, but they left it a few days until people had got over the shock. Not too long, young PC Cowgill had said, in case people forgot, but they liked to be compassionate where possible, he'd added. With his troubled face, he'd looked very compassionate, very upset.

'Course, the Bishops aren't liked,' Pat said. 'Too pushy too soon. The old ducks in the shop were chewing it over, and you could tell they'd have been more sympathetic with her if she hadn't pushed in everywhere, trying to reorganise and tell everybody what to do. And there's that business with Mr Richard. Everybody knows.'

'Mm,' said Colin, ignoring this digression. 'Still, you can't win in this village. They don't like it if you don't offer to help and join in, and they resent it if you do.'

Pat shook her head. 'Not true,' she said. 'There's degrees. You've just got to be a bit careful, that's all.'

Colin stabbed his finger on a pine needle and cursed, sucking the tiny bubble of blood. He had been thinking in these dark days since the accident, of his campaign to make Ringford a safer village. But none of the remedies— humps, zebra crossings, extra warning signs, even a bypass—would have made any difference to the death of Eddie Jenkins. He'd been killed by a resident in a hurry, a driver who knew the road well and should have been aware of the dangers. Colin couldn't help wishing it had been a complete stranger. Then

I'd have got somewhere, he reflected sadly. Something would have been done then. He could see the headlines in his mind. DEATH OF CHILD MAKES COUNCILLORS ACT! But not now, not with things as they are. At least then the Jenkinses could have said Eddie's death had not been wholly in vain. Now, there was nothing but tragic waste. All the blame lay at Andrew Bishop's door, and when Colin thought of the poor bugger having to answer for it, he shivered.

*   *   *

When the season is right, pheasants have to be shot, whatever tragedy lies over the village and its surrounding woods and fields, but for all his philandering and autocratic ways, Richard Standing was not an insensitive man, and he had made sure all shooting was cancelled until after Eddie Jenkins's funeral. Now, in need of fresh air and time to think, he whistled to his dog and set off on the footpath behind the Hall. He hoped the land where generations of Standings had walked and farmed would comfort him.

The biting wind slapped his face as he rounded a corner and stepped out of the shelter of the wood. A large, ploughed field in front of him rose in a gentle curve and then dipped again, away towards the river. His dog barked twice, a reminder that they had to keep moving if any decent business was to be done. Alarmed, a huge flock of lapwings rose up in unison, beating wings showing flashes of black and white as they flew off in a great wheeling arc towards the woods. Peewits, thought Richard, hearing their distinctive cries. That's what we used to call them as boys. Boys. Eddie Jenkins had still had a lot of boyhood left, time for his father to teach him his enormous store of country knowledge. Poor Foxy. Poor devil.

Richard stepped out, keeping to the narrow grassy verge around the edge of the field, avoiding where possible the deep furrows of sticky clay soil. He headed downwind, making for the sheltered spot where one of the Ringle's tributary streams widened out to form a still pool. A couple of years ago, in summer, he had been standing thinking of nothing in particular, gazing into the clear water and seeing small stirring insects in its muddy bottom, when a large, lazy perch had swum into the middle of the pool, near to the surface, and stopped. Richard could have sworn it was looking at him, and had kept perfectly still. Then two more fish, just as weirdly large, had joined the single one, and the three of them moved in graceful curves around the pool, occasionally snapping at an unfortunate pond-skater skimming the surface.

On reflection, Richard realised that the fish must have arrived as small fry in the pool, and stayed, growing large in accord with their surroundings. There was a heron down there, Richard had seen him many times, but because the pool was deep, the sides sheer and a thicket of blackthorn overhung three quarters of the surface, these fish had survived and multiplied. Now there was a shoal, and if Richard, on one of his regular visits, happened to move and catch their eye, they would become a thrashing throng, stirring up the mud and clouding the water in an instant and effective smokescreen.

He stood there now, the spaniel sniffing around, picking up scents of foxes and rabbits. Not a fish to be seen. Richard's mind went back to a hot day in summer when he'd approached the pool and seen a small figure, unmistakably fishing. When he got up close, he'd seen it was Eddie, and the fishing rod and line were the traditional bent twig and a piece of string. It was a real fish hook, though, with a wriggling worm attached. Eddie had jumped up in alarm, and stuttered his excuses. Dad had said it would be all right, so long as he threw the fish back alive. If he caught anything, that was. His dad had laughed at his rod, and said no self-respecting fish would go anywhere near it. Richard had seen that this was true, and let Eddie off lightly, pointing out that it would be more fun to sit quietly and watch the fish moving about like exotic strangers in this lonely pool.

They'd sat there for half an hour or so, talking in whispers, and Eddie had lost his shyness, confiding all kinds of family secrets to an amused Richard. 'Might see you again then, Mr Richard,' Eddie had said, as he left with his modest fishing tackle over his shoulder.

Oh, what a bloody awful thing to have happened! Richard continued along the stream until he came to the old railway track, where although the rails had been taken up, hardpacked clinker made it easier to walk. Pigeons clattered through the overhead branches, and he had to watch out for badgers' tunnels. There was a big set along the track, expanding all the time, with new holes to trap the unwary.

I'd hate to be Andrew Bishop right now. Richard knew it was a despicable thought, but he couldn't help a touch of gratification that trouble had arrived in a big way in the old vicarage, almost inevitably destined to drive Andrew and Annie further apart. He hadn't seen Annie since the accident, he'd thought about her a great deal, although oddly, it wasn't the feel of her warm, young body in his arms, or the thrill of clandestine meetings that occupied his daydreams. It was a kind of anxious, almost paternal worry about her, wondering how she was coping and whether she'd ever be able to smile that wonderful, open, candid smile again. He wanted to be near her, to reassure her that time would take care of it all. It always did, one way or another. This powerful need to talk to her was close to physical pain, and Richard

317

examined it in surprise. He'd had a good many flirtations, affairs even, and it had never been like this before. Oh Annie, he thought, have I fallen in love, at my time of life? A balding, paunchy middle-aged man, with a wife and children, and an estate to run?

The sky had darkened, and slow, heavy raindrops began to strike the dry leaves under his feet with a light, spasmodic tapping. 'Come on, girl!' he called, and his spaniel appeared obediently from a tangle of brambles and bare saplings. What the hell am I going to do about it? Nothing at all, his common sense told him. Turn up at the funeral tomorrow and say and do all the right things, hold Susan's arm and give her his support, and keep his private thoughts to himself.

CHAPTER FORTY-TWO

For a few minutes, as she struggled out of a heavy sleep that was still pill-induced, Jean Jenkins could not remember why today was special. She sat up and looked across to where Foxy should be, but his side of the bed was empty. She shook her head, trying to focus on the day. Then it came back to her, and she had a moment of absolute panic.

'Foxy!' Her voice was high and shrill, and Foxy came running upstairs at the double.

'Now, now, me duck,' he said, putting his

318

arms round her, 'you'll frighten the kids.' He knew just what to say, and Jean quietened down immediately.

'Where are they?' she said.

'Having breakfast,' said Foxy. 'We thought we'd let you sleep in. Here,' he continued, plumping up pillows behind her, 'sit back and I'll bring you a cup of tea.'

Jean obeyed, like a sick child, and looked out of the window at a perfectly clear blue sky and a pair of pigeons wheeling about in the bright air. Nearly Christmas, thought Jean, and it looks like spring out there. Dear God, how am I goin' to get through it? Then her thoughts slid off into a jumble of images and snatches of conversation, and she closed her eyes, leaning back into the comfort of warm pillows. She knew the sedative drugs were protecting her from the unbearable reality, but also, because she was a very sensible, practical woman who had never shirked a problem in her life, she knew that soon she would have to face up to the fact that her beloved youngest child was dead.

A shout of anger from Mark downstairs brought her upright again. She struggled out of bed, pulled on her dressing-gown and slippers and went to the bedroom door. 'Foxy! Don't bother with that tea, I'm coming down.'

As she opened the kitchen door—never normally closed, but this morning shutting in the noise of the children in an endeavour not to wake her—she saw them all sitting at the small table, breakfast in front of them: Mark, plump and angry with his twin sisters, who'd finished the marmalade between them, leaving none for him; Warren, aloof and pale with his eyes fixed on a farming magazine; and Foxy, dear Foxy, trying inexpertly to cut slices of bread from a loaf of woolly white bread.

'Here,' she said, marching over to him, 'let me do that. Have a look in that top cupboard. There's plenty of marmalade in there. And be quiet, Mark, you'll not die for a spoonful of . . .'

The silence was horrible. Then Gemma began to cry, and Amy, who always followed her twin, joined in. Mark snuffled, and Warren's chin began to wobble. Foxy dropped the bread knife and put his hands over his face. Jean looked round in total anguish. She was the one who always put things right, and now she might just as well have lobbed a hand grenade into her own family. She leaned against the dresser and tried her very best not to weep, but it was no good. In a quiet, hopeless, desperate, despairing way she cried without sound, the tears running down her cheeks and on to her clenched hands. For several minutes in the small, hot kitchen, full of frying smells and steam, the Jenkins family were completely united.

Then Warren, wiping his face on his sleeve, stood up and went over to Jean. 'Don't, Mum,' he said. 'We'll all be there. Even Eddie'll be there, won't he?'

Jean looked at his streaked face, his blue eyes so like Eddie's, and knew what she had to do. God knows how, she thought, but somehow it's up to me to get us all to the end of this nightmare. She put both hands on Warren's thin shoulders and kissed him firmly on the cheek. 'Of course he'll be there,' she said. 'Not in that wooden box, but here, inside all of us, with us, all the time.' She took up the bread knife and began cutting fiercely. 'Sit down, Foxy,' she said. 'I'll bet you've had nothin' to eat. Clear a space for your father, Gemma, and stop that noise. It won't help nobody. And Mark, open that window and let in some fresh air. At least it's not raining.' She put bread under the grill, opened a new pot of marmalade, and began to set things right.

*   *   *

Bill Turner stood in the bell chamber and looked out of the narrow slit window across the village. He thought of all the times he'd tolled the bell for people he'd known, some he'd loved, like old Fred Mills, who'd more than reached his allotted span. And then there'd been Frank Palmer, Peg's husband, killed in an instant before his time, and old Reverend Collins, lying at peace in the churchyard he'd walked so many times.

This is the worst one, he said to himself, idly swinging the bell-rope back and forth. What can be said about the death of a child, except that it is a bloody awful tragedy? He felt sorry for Reverend Brooks, having to say something to a congregation that would include Foxy and Jean, Gran and Grandad, Warren and the others. I suppose they get trained for it, he thought, but it couldn't be easy. He looked at his watch. It was time to start, and he grasped the rope firmly. The least he could do was make a good job of it.

*   *   *

'For goodness' sake, Ellen, stop snivelling!' Ivy Beasley and Doris had walked across the Green under a cloudless sky, past the children's play area where Eddie had chased his mates and swung too high on the swings, and on down Bates's End to collect Ellen from her lodge cottage. Now they stood waiting while Ellen hunted for her gloves and sniffed violently, trying to control herself.

'Here,' said Doris, handing Ellen a clean, neatly pressed handkerchief. 'Don't worry, Ellen, it's only natural. No, no, I've got a spare in my pocket. Always carry two to funerals.'

Ellen mopped her eyes and took a pink felt hat from the table.

'You're not wearing that!' said Ivy Beasley, herself dressed soberly in black coat and grey

322

hat.

'Oh yes I am,' said Ellen stubbornly. 'It ain't right to go to a child's funeral in miserable clothes. Don't mean I don't feel just as bad as you, Ivy.'

Ivy shrugged disapprovingly, and made for the door. 'Well, get a move on, do,' she said. 'It certainly ain't right to be late for anybody's funeral.' She marched off down the narrow garden path and the others followed meekly behind.

*   *   *

Extra wooden chairs, old and uncomfortable, had been placed down the sides of the church. Nigel Brooks guessed there would be a full congregation, and he was right. Every place was taken, except for the front three pews reserved for the family. Ivy, Ellen and Doris sat towards the back, and Ivy looked round in amazement at the flowers. 'I want them everywhere,' Jean had said, and the ladies of the WI had not let her down.

'Must have cost a fortune, Doris,' whispered Ellen, as they knelt to greet their Maker.

Peggy Turner sat in a pew right at the back, in a corner, as far away from everything as possible. Bill had said the Jenkinses would quite understand if she could not face it, what with Frank and that, but she had insisted on coming, and now huddled white-faced against the damp plastered wall. Think of Jean, she reminded herself, over and over again. Just think of Jean. And Foxy, and the children. She heard the warning scuffle of feet and subdued voices in the church porch. They had arrived. This is always the worst bit, Peggy thought, seeing the coffin, the faces of the mourners. She shoved her clenched fists hard into the pockets of her coat and bit her lip. Oh, dear God, help me, help us all, she prayed.

Nigel Brooks, in response to his calling, was solid as a rock. He led the little coffin with its bowed and broken followers into the church with the sureness of a benign Pied Piper. '. . . and God will wipe away all tears from their eyes,' he said, in a voice that brooked no disagreement. 'Heavenly Father,' he continued, 'whose Son our Saviour took little children into his arms and blessed them: receive, we pray, your child Eddie in your never-failing love, comfort all who have loved him on earth . . .' Here, an epidemic of sniffs and coughs filled the church. '. . . and bring us all to your everlasting kingdom; through Jesus Christ our Lord.'

Then it was Richard Standing's turn. Foxy had asked him to read, and as he stood at the lectern given by his great-grandfather to the church, his voice faltered over the familiar words of comfort. As he sat down, Susan's hand slipped into his, and he felt such pain in his heart that he could have cried out. There sat

Foxy and Jean, and their little family, grieving with such dignity and composure, drawing strength from their very visible love for each other. He turned and looked at Susan, and she gave him a ghostly smile. He felt sick, and bowed his head.

*　　　*　　　*

In the small cemetery overlooking the Ringle valley, a chilly breeze had sprung up, blowing dry heads of cow parsley against the iron railings. As it freshened it ruffled the light, pale hair of a woman standing uncertainly by the pathetically small open grave, dug with unusual care by Michael Roberts, whose family had had the job for generations. She looked round and across at the church, and stepped nervously forward towards the long row of flowery wreaths lining the cemetery path.

What's she up to? Michael Roberts was lurking discreetly by a laurel bush in the corner, waiting for the funeral party to arrive. His head ached, though for once not because of a heavy night in the Arms. Renata had pleaded with him not to go out, and much to his own surprise he'd agreed. They'd watched television, scarcely speaking to each other all evening, and now his eyes felt itchy and hot. Still, it had seemed to make Renata feel better, and his headache was not so bad as many a hangover he could remember. He admitted to himself with rare honesty that at least he'd not had to take it out on Renata this morning, with the usual bad-tempered slap.

She's got a nerve, that woman, hasn't she? He saw that it was Annie Bishop. With another quick glance towards the church, she bent down and placed something on the edge of the path, then straightened up and hurried out of the open gates, disappearing from Michael Roberts's view. He walked quickly over and looked down. On the sparse winter grass, neatly bunched in leaves of dark green ivy, was a posy of greenish-white Christmas roses, freshly picked and shining out among the exotic tributes of hothouse flowers. Well, I'm buggered, thought Michael Roberts, and retreated to his corner as he saw the first of the undertakers with their sad burden heading towards the grave.

CHAPTER FORTY-THREE

'Where have you been?' said Andrew Bishop listlessly, as Annie came into the kitchen through the back door. He'd heard the funeral bell, and had tried to shut out the sound by turning up the radio, but its insistent tolling had penetrated everything, even when he clapped his hands over his ears in desperation. When it finally ceased, he'd turned off the radio and sat down at the kitchen table, idly turning over the pages of the newspaper but taking in very little. There'd been another IRA bomb in London. Two children had been killed, taking a short cut across a car park to see their grandmother. The bomb had been packed in a lorry, and the explosion was huge.

Two children killed, thought Andrew, and all over the world children are being killed every day. After the first dismay and horror, the impact soon fades and in a week we're all thinking about something else. But the death of this child, this Eddie Jenkins, won't fade, because I killed him, and it will stay with me for the rest of my life.

'You've surely not . . .?' he said.

Annie shook her head. 'No, of course not. I just needed a breath of air. It's very hot in this kitchen, and out there it's like spring.' Her voice was high, unnatural, like someone making conversation with a stranger. She busied herself around the kitchen, sorting out the ironing, folding small vests and pants and pairing up socks into handy balls. Not once did she look at Andrew. He wondered if she would ever look at him again.

Was it entirely his fault? He had gone over in his mind a hundred times those last few terrible minutes in the dark street, and could remember only having his eyes fixed on the school playground, trying to identify his own family among the milling crowd. Surely he must have been slowing up, preparing to stop by the school gate? But he knew he'd flashed past the speed limit, telling himself it would be all right, this once.

'I just don't know,' he said aloud.

'Don't know what?' said Annie, hoisting the basket full of clean clothes on to her hip, ready to take upstairs. Her eyes were on neatly folded T-shirts, straightening them unnecessarily.

'Look at me, Annie!' said Andrew, his voice suddenly loud and harsh.

She looked up, startled, and stared at him.

'What I mean is,' he said, articulating as if to a deaf child, 'what I mean is that I just don't know anything any more, and most of all I don't know what the hell to do next.' He held her eyes, pleading.

'You'll think of something,' said Annie, and disappeared from the kitchen, shutting the door behind her.

*   *   *

The police had arrived to take Andrew's statement yesterday. It looked as if he might be charged with driving without due care and attention and be brought before the magistrate's court. It was a long time since he'd handled a client for a driving offence, but he knew that they'd found nothing wrong with his car. Brakes and steering were all in good order. The breath test had been negative, thank God. He'd only had a shandy on the train, taking into account the drive home. Well, his forethought might save him. It hadn't saved Eddie Jenkins.

Tyre marks. He remembered those were important. He'd skidded, trying to pull up, and no doubt they'd deduced something from that. Would they take into account the circumstances? The delay on the train, his urgent need to get back home? No, he remembered enough to know that this would make no difference. There could be no such excuses for killing a child.

Witnesses. Surely someone had seen Eddie step out in front of him, giving him no time to stop? He could swear Eddie had been looking backwards at his mother following on behind, but who would believe him, if nobody else saw it? Several people said they'd seen him approach, but his car lights had blinded them and they'd looked away. Were his headlights on full? That wouldn't look good, in a built-up area.

Andrew was still sitting at the table when the chldren came rushing into the kitchen, demanding something to eat. Glad of the interruption, he got to his feet and began opening cupboards and tins. He'd have to get back to the office. It would be the only way, fill his mind with something else. He handed round chocolate biscuits, and for a moment felt more cheerful. But then Annie returned, and once more ignored his presence so pointedly that he left the room and took refuge in the loo.

*   *   *

There'd been no school again this afternoon, out of respect to Eddie Jenkins. George, his best friend, had begged Sarah Barnett to take him to the funeral. His mum, he'd said, was working, so she couldn't go. Sarah had been reluctant, but in the end had agreed, faced with George's obvious distress. She could remember no guidance in her teacher training to cope with this one.

'You'd better come back with me and have some squash,' she said, looking worriedly down at George's white face. 'When's your mum get back home?' Sarah had met George off the bus, but had sent a message to his mother that she would deliver him back home herself.

''Bout five,' he said. 'But Auntie May's there. She fills in when we're not at school.'

Sarah drove back to the farm, George silent and subdued at her side. Perhaps it had not been such a good idea after all. Poor little chap, he probably didn't understand much of what had been said. And that dreadful moment when the small coffin had been lowered into the grave. His hand holding hers had tightened convulsively, and she'd pulled him close to her, trying to convey reassurance.

'Would you like to see the horses?' she said, after George had drained his glass of orange and stood looking at her, waiting for instructions.

'Yep,' he said.

'Yes what?' said Sarah, automatically.

'Yep, please,' said George obediently.

He seemed to warm up a bit, stroking the hunter's velvety nose, and Sarah stayed with him, saying nothing, waiting in case he should need to talk.

'Miss,' he said finally, climbing off the barred stable door.

'Yes, George,' said Sarah gently.

'Where's he gone, then?'

Here it was, then, the question to which no one has a satisfactory answer. Sarah decided it was not the time for a philosophical discussion on the afterlife, and took both George's hands in hers.

'To heaven, of course,' she said. 'And God is jolly lucky to have him. Our Eddie.' She couldn't say any more for the choking lump in her throat, but it was enough. George turned away and walked firmly towards her car.

'Better be getting back, now,' he said. 'Thanks for taking me, Miss.'

CHAPTER FORTY-FOUR

Pushing back his bedroom curtains, feeling his soul expand under the early morning sunlight streaming in and blinding him, Nigel Brooks had to admit that it had been the most joyless Christmas he could remember. He was glad, yes, glad, that it was gone and quickly forgotten. All the ritual had had to take place, of course, but none of the village had any enthusiasm for it. Midnight mass had been as crowded as usual, but the farmers had arrived on time, sober, and in company with their wives. 'Unheard of,' Nigel had said to Sophie afterwards.

'Solidarity,' she'd replied. 'They've closed ranks, bearing up Jean and Foxy. It's very touching, I think.'

One of Nigel's most difficult tasks had been a mission to the old vicarage next door. The Bishop children had, of course, continued to play in the garden, and he and Sophie had made a point of saying hello. It would be unthinkable if village feeling about Andrew's guilt caused innocent children to suffer. Still, they seemed as bouncy and self-confident as ever, and he'd seen Richard Standing delivering Poppy for tea with the family a couple of times. It was a different matter with Andrew and Annie. He'd seen Annie, well muffled-up in scarves, setting off on walks around the fields, but so far neither he nor Sophie could remember seeing her in the shop since the accident. And as for Andrew, he'd not set eyes on him once. He heard the car leave early in the morning and come back late at night, and presumed Andrew had returned to work. Finally, Nigel had found an excuse to call when Tinker strayed in, and he'd grabbed him and taken him back.

'Just in case he goes under a . . .' Nigel had swallowed the end of that sentence just in time, and started again. 'And are you all well?' he'd said to an unsmiling Annie at the door. She had confirmed that they were, and not invited him in. Finally, running out of small talk on the doorstep, he'd offered a lame consolation on their difficulties and said that if either of them ever wanted a listening ear, they knew where to come. Since then, he'd seen little of Annie and still nothing of Andrew. I must ask Peggy about it, he thought, going downstairs to wonderful smells of frying bacon. She gets to know most things at the Stores.

At the shop, Peggy's experience was much the same. Once or twice the eldest, Faith, had come in for sweets, but Peggy believed very strongly that you should not quiz children about their parents and had said nothing more than that she hoped they were all fine and had had a good Christmas. Like the vicar, she had been glad to see the back of the unfestive festive season, and decorations had been cleared away long before Twelfth Night. 'Shove these up in the loft for me, Bill,' she'd said, handing him the pile of tinsel and ornaments. 'I'm going to fill the window with gardening stuff. Try to get people looking forward. God knows we've never needed the spring more than we do now.'

Now, several slow weeks later, with spring unmistakably in the air, she looked at Bill's frame silhouetted in the shop doorway, and felt deeply ashamed that it had taken the unthinkable death of Eddie Jenkins to drive out all lurking suspicions of his dalliance with Sandra. She felt sick when she thought of it. How petty and despicable, compared with all we've had to face, she reminded herself, and for some, like the Jenkinses and, she supposed, the Bishops, it's far from over yet.

It was a fine, clear morning, and the air coming into the shop through the open doorway was clean and fresh, the day too new to be contaminated by the continuing progression of lorries and cars through the village. Peggy knew that Colin Osman had collected his new petition together and handed it in, but had once more been fobbed off with excuses of Council meeting agendas and reports and the need to proceed through the correct channels. Lately, though, there had been rumours that the end was in sight for work on the main route dual carriageway. Perhaps that would let him off a campaign that was becoming increasingly a lost cause.

'All quiet at the Hall?' she asked Bill, as he stood stretching in the doorway. He'd been up early and put in a good couple of hours' work before coming back for breakfast.

'Too quiet,' he said, smiling at Peggy.

'Ominous, I reckon, if what we hear is right.'

'Mm, well, less said about that the better,' said Peggy, and was about to contradict herself by elaborating, when Sandra bounced up the steps carrying a white cardboard box.

'Morning, Bill, morning, Mrs T.,' she said. She edged past Bill and put the burden on the counter, winking heavily at Peggy. 'Shall we let him have it now, or make him wait until this afternoon?' Bill looked disappointed, but Peggy laughed.

'Open it up, Sandra,' she said, 'he's like a child on his birthday! Wants to open all his presents at once.'

Peggy had given him a new watch, which claimed indestructibility, and he was wearing it, his cuff pushed back so that he could glance at it every few seconds. Now there was this box from Sandra, obviously the result of collusion between her and Peggy. Peg was right. He had never lost that thrill of waking up knowing that it was his birthday. Although his father had died young, and there never seemed to be enough money in the house, his mother had always managed something special, if only a new jumper to replace the thin, much-darned one he'd been wearing long after it was outgrown.

He opened the box and saw a large, square cake, richly decorated with blue and white icing. 'HAPPY BIRTHDAY, BILL!' he read with a widening grin. He grabbed Sandra at once and gave her a hug. 'Thank you, my dear,' he said, and kissed her firmly on her plump cheek. 'It's wonderful! Much too good to leave until this afternoon. Now then, let's find a suitable bottle, and have a small celebration.'

'Isn't it a bit early?' Peggy protested, but he shook his head, and opened sparkling wine, handing glasses round and proposing a toast to himself and his amazing state of preservation at the advanced age of fifty-six.

Peggy cut the cake and complimented Sandra on her baking. It had been Sandra's idea, but she'd consulted Peggy first in case she should be treading on toes, as she'd put it. Goodness, how near I came to making an absolute fool of myself, thought Peggy. I wonder if I'll ever learn. Bill was refilling glasses and telling a long story about Tom Price and himself as roving boys in the village, when Ellen Biggs struggled up the steps and caught them still eating and drinking. After explanations and none too subtle hints from Ellen, Peggy cut her a generous slice and Bill put a glass in her gnarled old hand.

'Best breakfast I can remember!' said Ellen, licking her lips. 'Wait till I tell old Ivy. Don't give her none, will you?' she added conspiratorially.

'The day I bake for Ivy Beasley you can send for a straitjacket,' said Sandra, and began to clear the plates away. 'As a special treat, Mrs

T.,' she said, 'I'm working for nothin' this morning, and you and Bill are going off to have lunch as far away from Ringford as you can get in that old wreck of his.' She'd been very scathing when Peggy decided to sell her car, making do with the old van, but it had been one of the necessary economies which had enabled Peggy and Bill to give Sandra her job.

'Quite right too,' said Ellen, nodding violently. 'Lovely day out there, and here comes His Nibs, so I should get going if you don't want the latest on Miss Poppy Standing's beauty and brillyance.'

It was some time later, as Peggy sat with Bill in front of a huge fire in Tresham's best hotel, drinking coffee after a very good meal, that an odd thought occurred to her. 'Bill,' she said, and took his hand. 'I've just realised that while we were talking to Sandra and Ellen, chatting away for quite a while, none of us mentioned Eddie. Not once. Isn't that awful?'

Bill planted a kiss in the palm of her hand. 'Not awful at all, my lovely gel,' he said. 'We've not forgotten, never will. But we have to get on with it, life and that. Foxy and Jean would be the first to agree, though it'll take them a lot longer than us, God knows.' They finished their coffee, paid the bill and wandered arm-in-arm into the streets of Tresham, there to find the old van and return home.

*   *   *

337

On this same beautiful, early spring day, Andrew Bishop, now back at work in his London office, and cutting himself off as completely as possible from life in Round Ringford, drew a blind against the brilliant sun and opened a letter marked personal. He found to his relief that he was indeed to be charged with driving without due care and attention, and that there was no question of further litigation from the Jenkinses or anyone else. With luck, the magistrates would accept his version of Eddie stepping out without looking directly under his wheels. Version? No, that was the wrong word. It was the truth. Now that shock and confusion had subsided, a couple of people who'd been driving through in the opposite direction and seen it happen had come forward to support him.

'Thank God for that,' he said to his secretary. She raised well-groomed eyebrows.

'Just that it all looks as if I might be let off lightly,' he continued. But not restored to marital bliss, he added to himself. Annie and he had reached a kind of awful neutrality.

They slept in the same bed but never touched, and although conversation was polite, he felt a million miles away from her. He'd tried to explain the circumstances of his delayed journey home that night, but she would never let him get beyond the first sentence, and he was too frightened of her icy calm to persist. He had the feeling that a forced showdown would be the end. If only he could carry on, give her time, he was sure she would finally thaw, and then he could put it right between them. Could never be the same, of course, but maybe they would build on a new beginning. Maybe. He had never felt so depressed.

'Will you be catching the usual train, Andrew?' said his secretary. She looked at him sympathetically. He looked awful, but then, he'd looked awful for weeks. His work was suffering, and in spite of all her efforts to conceal it from the others, the senior partner had started checking Andrew's cases, so far without comment. He can't go on like this, his secretary thought, looking at Andrew's untidy hair, his grubby shirt collar and crooked tie. Lately he'd taken to staying on after everyone else had gone, catching a late train. That way he could arrive home at the end of the evening, postponing the painful business of facing Annie once more.

On his desk now lay a pile of particulars of small flats. He'd done nothing more about them, feeling that unhappy as he was, he should at least return home at night. There had been too many neighbourly calls from Richard Standing, too many early morning rides across the park, too many occasions when Annie put down the telephone as Andrew approached, her cheeks warm and her eyes shining. For the first time in his life, Andrew Bishop wondered if he was being cuckolded, and then faced the fact that he unquestionably was. Surely Susan Standing must know? What did she think about it? It was all very well for Annie to challenge him with stony eyes to do something about it, but Susan would not be so consumed with guilt as he was, nor need to tread so carefully to keep a fragile marriage intact in the hope of future reconciliation. Probably waiting for the right opportunity to bollock the mighty Richard, thought Andrew. Her sort gave nothing away. It would all be very civilised and calculated.

'By the way, Andrew, did you see this?' His secretary handed him the property pages of the *Standard*. 'Isn't that your old house in Highgate?' She'd seen it and wondered. Surely it would be better than the way Andrew was living now?

He peered at the smudged photograph and his heart lurched. It was indeed their first home, the comfortable, roomy old house where the children had been born and he and Annie had been so happy. 'Price is about the same,' he muttered. And then the seed of an idea began to grow in his mind. It might be the only way, the answer to all their difficulties. Move back, buy their old house, begin again.

'Give them a ring, would you?' he said, handing the paper back to his smiling secretary. 'And ask them to send particulars.' He was clutching at straws, he knew that, but it was better than drowning.

CHAPTER FORTY-FIVE

'All the colours of the rainbow, Ellen,' said Ivy generously, as she and Doris greeted the old woman at her garden gate. Spring was in full swing now, and Ellen's garden was the glorious confusion of colour that she loved. Sunny daffodils, pale lemon primroses, a giant yellow pompom shrub completely out of control, blue grape hyacinths and a flame-coloured japonica quince in full bloom, and tulips everywhere, red, yellow and white, all anyhow and all flourishing.

Ellen looked smug. 'Yep,' she said, 'I've always loved a spring garden. The lodge at its best, I always say. Pays for all that 'ard work.'

Ivy couldn't let her get away with this. 'Oh no, Ellen Biggs,' she said, her magnanimous tone sharpening, 'you don't fool us. All this lot comes up year after year without you lifting a trowel. It's the summer that shows a good gardener, don't you agree, Doris?'

'There's work to be done at all times of the year,' said Doris the peacemaker. 'Are you going to let us in, Ellen? My throat's parched after walking over the Green in the full sun. It's as hot as summer out of the wind.'

'Perhaps yer'd like to take tea in the garden?' said Ellen. This was said deliberately to annoy Ivy. On one occasion only, on a balmy summer's day, Ellen had laid a table on the scrubby grass that passed for a lawn, and

341

waited for Ivy's wrath. She had not waited in vain. But Doris and she had stuck it out, and Ivy had been forced to sit on a rickety chair in full view of passersby, and drink her tea with very bad grace.

'Don't be ridiculous,' said Ivy, now marching firmly up the path and into the lodge. She walked round Ellen's little sitting-room and ran her finger along the top of a damp-stained print of Loch Lomond in winter, and said, 'You been spring-cleaning, Ellen?'

Doris frowned. 'That's enough, Ivy,' she said quietly. 'It's not kind, what with her being crippled with arthritis and that. Just give over, do.'

Ivy sat down with her nose in the air, and folded her hands. 'Sorry I spoke, I'm sure,' she said. In the silence that followed, Ellen hobbled in with a tray of tea things and set it down with a crash on the small table under the window. She returned to the kitchen and collected a fine china cake stand, only slightly chipped from long service at the Hall, on which a feathery chocolate sponge stood proudly, its top decorated with icing and walnuts.

'Ellen!' exclaimed Doris. 'Where did you get that wonderful cake?' It was clearly home made, and there was no question that the maker had been an expert.

Ellen drew herself up, and looked fixedly at Ivy Beasley. 'Well,' she said, as if preparing

342

herself for a long speech. 'Well, it's like this 'ere. Every time it's my turn to do tea, our Ivy 'as a go at me about me refreshments. So I thort I'd give 'er somethin' to think about. In my day,' she added, pausing nostalgically, 'when I was cook at the 'all, I could put on as good a tea as anyone. And this 'ere cake proves it. Not lost me touch, 'ave I, Ivy?'

For once, Ivy Beasley was lost for words. She leaned forward and had a good look at the cake. It was indeed very fine, and there was no possibility of it not tasting as good as it looked, but Ivy was still suspicious. Ellen Biggs was a terrible old liar, known for it.

'If you ask me,' said Ivy, 'it's the taste that matters. So get slicing, Ellen, and let's all give it a try. What say you, Doris?'

Doris was puzzled. She'd seen Ellen at the shop that morning, and she'd bought no chocolate cake ingredients. Ah well, she could have had them by her. 'Looks delicious,' she said. 'Shall I pour, Ellen, while you cut?'

Several quiet minutes later, after cake had been consumed and second slices handed round, Ivy spoke. 'This is a very good cake, and if you really did make it, Ellen, then I can't see why you go buying those sawdust things from the shop. Now you've set a standard, you'll have to keep it up.'

Ellen shook her head. 'Not likely,' she cackled. 'Can't be bothered. Lifetime's cooking turns you off. No, Ivy, it's just a one-off. Just to

343

show I can. Make the most of it.' And she went to refill the pot, laughing with delight at her triumph.

Time to change the subject, thought Doris. She sighed, wishing she didn't always have to be on the watch for when Ivy went too far, or Ellen's feelings were really hurt. And Ellen could be sharp, too. Still, maybe it kept them going, this running battle of theirs.

'Seen anything of Jean?' she said, wiping her hands delicately on her handkerchief. Ivy shook her head, but Ellen nodded.

'Yep,' Ellen said. 'Saw 'er in the shop yesterday. Lost a lot of weight, poor kid, but she were bein' very brave, talkin' about takin' the others to the seaside in the holidays. Said they deserve a treat this year. Don't know 'ow she does it. But then, Foxy and 'er is a very lovin' couple. Always was. Gain strength from it, them two.'

'Not back at work yet, is she?' Doris said.

'At the 'all, yep,' said Ellen. 'Not at the Bishops', though.'

'I should think not!' exploded Ivy. 'If you ask me, she'll never set foot through that door again, not while that lot are there.'

'Never see them these days,' said Doris. 'I suppose he's keeping his head down, but he can't do that for ever. She's around and about in the car with the children, but you don't see her walking in the village like she used to.'

Ivy sniffed. 'Not in the village, no, Doris,' she

said. 'But I've seen her round the fields many times with that scruffy dog of hers, *and* she's not been on her own.'

'Wotcha mean, Ivy?' said Ellen innocently. She knew perfectly well what Ivy meant, but now that it was clear the subject of Richard Standing and Annie Bishop was about to be aired, she didn't want to be the one to tell all she knew first.

Gossip's like a card game, thought Doris philosophically, well aware of Ellen's ruse. Bluff and timing. Weaving and dodging so's you can come up with the best bit at the end. Ah well, might as well put down the first card. 'I suppose you mean the wicked squire,' she said. 'That's pretty common knowledge, now. Half the village has seen them together all over the place. And they're not too careful about who's watching.'

'Smooching on the oak stump in the woods,' said Ivy.

'Kissin' up on the old railway line,' said Ellen happily.

'Him leaving the old vicarage late at night,' said Doris.

''Er 'angin' out her lace undies for everybody to see,' capped Ellen.

'It's a disgrace,' said Ivy Beasley. 'And I for one think it's time Susan Standing did something about it.'

'She will,' said Ellen knowingly. 'Not the first time for 'er, o' course. 'E's 'ad 'is little flings

345

before, and she's always reined 'im in. Just gives 'im enough rope to 'ang 'imself, and then *chop*! 'E'll get it in the neck sooner or later, mark my words.'

The sun had moved round, leaving the little room chilly, reminding the tea-drinkers that it was not yet summer. Ivy shivered and pulled her cardigan round her shoulders. 'You having a fire in the evenings, Ellen?' she said. 'It still chills the bones in here once the sun's gone.'

Doris stood up. 'Can we give you a hand with the washing-up?' she said ritually.

'No, ta,' said Ellen. 'I can still manage a few tea things.' She too stood up and looked out of her window across to the old vicarage.

'Sad,' she said. 'Should've turned out better. And now that Andrew's wanderin' about 'is own garden lookin' like an old tramp, and the word is they don't even speak.'

'Trouble breeds trouble, my mother used to say,' said Ivy, walking to the small, arched front door. 'Like an avalanche,' she added, with a rare poetic turn, 'there's no stopping it, and woe betide them as gets in the way.'

For some time, after her two old friends had gone, Ellen Biggs stood in her cooling garden and thought about the Bishops. She'd resented Annie when she first arrived, pushing and poking in everywhere, but she'd quite liked Andrew, specially after he'd given her a hand with changing a lightbulb she couldn't reach. 'Sad,' she said again, out loud to her rainbow

346

garden. 'Families should stick together, I reckon.' Ellen had never had a family, knew what it was to be lonely, and so was quite certain on this point.

CHAPTER FORTY-SIX

'Can you be loitering without intent somewhere along the Waltonby road around two fifteen? Good! I've something special to show you. See you then, my darling.' Richard put down the telephone in his study and leaned back in his chair. He swivelled round to look out across the park where ancient oaks and beech planted by his ancestors were in full spring leaf. Maytime ... springtime ... a very pretty ringtime, when birds do sing Hey ding a ding a ding! Sweet lovers love the spring ... Richard hummed the old tune to himself and reflected that Annie was a very sweet lover indeed.

He stood up and gazed out at the sheep grazing peacefully on new grass, big woolly ewes with the usual shitty tails, and new lambs still clean and toylike, gambolling about and chasing one another like—well, like lambs. He turned back to the room and his eye was caught by the big portrait of his father over the fireplace. The old boy looked him straight in the eye, and it seemed to Richard that he had a distinctly reproving air this morning.

'Well,' said Richard, addressing his parent. 'Did you never fall in love? Oh, I know you did with Mama, but then she was a famous beauty. Didn't that wear off and didn't you indulge yourself with a few fancies during those boring years when we were growing up? Must have. You were quite good looking in your way. Bit military, maybe. But your eyes twinkled. Yes, I definitely remember that twinkle, especially when old Ellen was young and cooking for us all in the kitchen. Aha, don't look at me like that, Papa! I'll never disgrace the family, though that sort of thing doesn't count for much these days. And anyway, I'm very fond of Susan. Just that the romance has worn off a bit.' He looked into the brown eyes that were so like his own, hoping for some tolerant softening in his father's expression, but seeing none.

He turned away again and resumed his station at the window. There was a stiff breeze, and a bright blue fertiliser sack blew like a sailboat across the grass by the old summerhouse, lodging temporarily in a corner between the timber frame and an overhanging cherry tree. Must speak to Bill about that, Richard thought. Most important to keep those plastic things under control. Dangerous, as well as unsightly.

His thoughts returned to Annie, sweet Annie. Sweet Annie Laurie. Funny how musical he felt this morning! But then, he felt a lot of things these days that he had forgotten were so delicious. And important. After all, he was not in his dotage yet, and his world seemed to have settled down to a boring round of local committees, local politics, estate management. He knew only too well that Bill Turner could easily manage the estate with little help from him, and Susan was totally preoccupied with their growing daughter Poppy.

He sat down again at his desk and began to turn over papers without interest. Nothing here that needed his urgent attention. Perhaps he'd drive into Bagley and find a little something for Annie, surprise her with it this afternoon when they met.

* * *

Bagley was a small market town with a very ancient history. It had been a Roman town on the main route to the west, and periodic archaeological digs turned up a surprising number of artefacts: pieces of mosaic, amphora, shield buckles, touching domestic and personal things like hand mirrors and unguent spoons. There was clear evidence that once the town had been large and flourishing, well protected by earthworks and stone walls.

Richard Standing was honorary president of the Local History Society, and had found himself becoming much more than a name at the top of their writing paper. The history of

349

the area fascinated him, and he had collaborated with Nick Brown, the most successful antique dealer in the town, on producing a book about the various periods of building and commerce in the town. Bagley had not been its Roman name, of course. Balnea, it was, supposedly because of bath houses whose tesselated floors still lay under the large, sixteenth-century church. Too soon, before archaeologists and historians had exhausted the fascinating evidence, other sites had been covered over by supermarkets and housing estates, in spite of vigorous protests from the History Society. But Richard and Nick were at present working on a theory that the outlying villages must have been small farming settlements to supply the town, and planned a series of digs next year. He'd hoped Susan would join him in this growing interest, but Poppy was all she thought about—Poppy's health, Poppy's school, Poppy's friends, Poppy's clothes—and much as he loved his small daughter, Richard sometimes found it hard to smother a yawn.

Wonder if Annie would be interested in a dig? he thought. Still, mustn't forget the need for discretion. Can't flaunt it, as one of his old flames used to say. Which one was that, now? He ran through names he could remember. Must have been young Josie Barnett. He chuckled to himself. She'd been a jolly little number! Married an American in the end, rich as Croesus and twice her age.

Richard parked his car in the centre of Bagley and walked along the crowded main street to Nick's antique shop in the square. It was market day, and the gaily striped stall awnings fluttered and slapped in the brisk wind. He didn't notice Susan's mother buying her weekly plaice fillet at the fish stall, but she saw him, and her salty blue eyes narrowed. Handing over the correct money, she tagged along behind, watching where he went.

'Morning, Nick! Grand morning!' Richard grasped the tall, swarthy man's hand and shook it firmly. Nick Brown's dark, curly hair was thinning now, but he still wore it rather long and rakishly, giving him a faintly Dickensian, unreliable air, which of course ideally suited his profession.

'Morning, Richard. You're in a good mood! Just come in for a chat, or can I interest you in something old and delightful?' Nick never dropped his dealer mode. It was like a second skin, and as long as there was a potential customer in the shop he never gave up his pursuit of a sale. Like fishing, he often thought, playing them along with persuasive words, reeling them in at the right moment. Still, Richard Standing was too much of an old hand, and he could see there was no intention to buy this morning. At least, that's what he thought, until Richard leaned over the jewellery case and peered at a Victorian brooch, an

351

enamelled four-pence coin in a chased silver setting. It was pretty, not too ostentatious, and very Annie, thought Richard.

'How much is that, Nick?' he said.

'To you,' said Nick, 'forty pounds.'

'Rubbish,' said Richard. 'Bet you gave no more than a tenner.'

Nick grinned. 'Thirty-five, then,' he said.

'Find me a nice box for it, and I'll give you thirty,' said Richard.

'I shall never be rich,' said Nick, and went away to look for a box, while Richard walked to the window to examine the brooch in daylight. Then he wandered around the shop, picking up pieces of fine porcelain, peering inside the elegant tea caddies that were Nick's special interest. As he looked in an ornate, gilt-framed mirror, he could see behind him the busy market square, milling with colourful shoppers. One of them looked very familiar. Wasn't that . . .? He turned round quickly, and was sure that the retreating elderly figure on the pavement outside Nick's shop was that of Susan's mother.

*　　　*　　　*

Annie had left the car in a concealed turning by a spinney on the Waltonby road. It was so warm, wonderfully warm for May, that she had decided on shorts and a white, baggy shirt with the sleeves rolled up above her firm forearms.

She never really lost her summer tan, and her long legs were smooth and brown. White canvas shoes completed the effect of careless elegance that she always managed, seemingly without trying, though only Andrew knew how much thought she gave to it, how many magazines were carefully perused each season for the right look.

She walked along the verge, slowly, stopping to collect single sprays of red ragged robin, purple dead nettle, yellow vetch. One stalk of each wouldn't do any harm, surely, though she'd firmly forbidden the children to pick at random. There was always a rough blue pottery jug on the kitchen table, filled with wildflowers that Annie had looked up in a book. She repeated the old country names to the children, encouraging them to remember. She considered it very important.

A skylark hung on the air above her, its trilling song filling the sunny sky, but when she looked up, shading her eyes against the brightness, she could see nothing. I wonder why they do that, she thought. Maybe just for the hell of it, to see how high they can go. It must be wonderful up there, out of sight, away from it all. She frowned, and shook her head, spots before her eyes from the sun. No, there's always a good practical reason in nature. None of your romantic nonsense in a skylark's life. I'll look it up, or ask Richard. He knows an awful lot about the country. Quite a lot about romantic nonsense, too. She smiled, and turned round as a short toot on a car horn signalled his arrival. Annie did not wait for him to jump out and open the door for her, as he usually did, but pulled it open herself and hopped in, stretching her long, bare legs in the roomy interior.

Richard leaned over and kissed her cool cheek. 'How's my darling?' he said.

'Fine,' said Annie. 'Better get going, in case someone comes along.'

Not far along the Waltonby road was a turning to the left, and Richard took it, driving slowly along lanes with lush grass verges and high hedges full of pink budded honeysuckle. 'Where're we going?' said Annie.

'Ah,' said Richard, 'it's a secret known only to me. And the Bateses, of course.'

'The Bateses?'

'Old Ted Bates's brother,' said Richard. 'He farms down here. You'll see why I brought you in a minute, if you can be patient, young Annie!'

They drove in that silence which is always tense between lovers, until the hedges stopped and post and rail fencing took over. Across a wide paddock Annie could see horses, several mares grouped against a stone-walled barn.

'Richard, stop!' she said suddenly. 'Look over there!'

'We can get closer than this,' he said, continuing slowly along the narrow lane. 'I

354

know just the spot.'

At a discreet distance from the mares, Richard stopped the car, and got out, closing the door quietly. 'Come on, then,' he said. 'It's quite safe.'

Annie slipped out of the car and joined him at the rail. 'Oh, Richard, how absolutely wonderful!'

Now she could see clearly. Each mare had a foal, some smaller than others and all spindly-legged and quite new. A tiny chestnut nuzzled his mother, and one dark bay mare stood protectively in front of her light-coloured new arrival. All the mothers looked apprehensively across to where Richard and Annie stood shoulder to shoulder at the fence. They sized up these strange visitors, ready to shepherd their young away to a distant corner of the field. 'Just stand quite still,' said Richard quietly, and after a while the biggest of the foals, chestnut with a white blaze and four delicate white socks, began to walk slowly towards them. 'Curiosity,' whispered Richard. 'Always gets the better of them'.

The mare followed her rash infant, and to Annie's delight the entire group gradually moved over to where they stood. She put out her hand, but the chestnut foal started back, sheltering against his mother. They continued to linger and stare, pushing each other out of the way, until a sudden barking from the farm dog set up an alarm signal, and they all cantered away, manes and tails tossing in the wind.

Annie turned to Richard. 'Oh, how wonderful, how beautiful!' There were tears in her eyes, and it was all Richard could do to prevent himself taking her in his arms there and then. But old Bates could easily be spying from a dozen different vantage points, so he just took her arm and led her back to the car.

'Come on,' he said. 'Let's go somewhere more private.'

*   *   *

'Such a lovely afternoon,' said Peggy, looking round her empty shop. 'Can you manage for an hour or so, Sandra, while I go for a breath of fresh air? That stockroom is so stuffy and dark, and it's taken me ages to sort out Bill's trip to the wholesaler.'

With Sandra's assurances ringing in her ears, Peggy stepped out firmly along the Waltonby road. She knew where she was going, a favourite spot for Bill and herself when they were still meeting secretly away from village eyes. Miss Ivy Beasley's eyes, to be exact! she thought, remembering it now with a kind of affection she certainly did not feel at the time. When she came to the field gate, she turned off and saw Mr Richard's car parked there. Inspecting the wheat, probably, she thought. Still, he never minds me walking round the estate. It was just this one cornfield, swaying like a blue-green sea in the wind, and then she'd be in the spinney. She might be lucky today, see a muntjac or maybe a fallow deer. There had been one magical afternoon with Bill, when a doe had stepped into the dappled sunlight to drink from a stream. Was that the time they'd quarrelled in the tree hide he'd built for Susan Standing during her bird-watching phase? No, not that time. There'd been no quarrel to mar that gentle scene.

There it was, still there, the timber shelter high up in the angle of three big branches. Probably not used now, Peggy thought, looking up at it with amused nostalgia. Susan was a great one for enthusiasms, none of which lasted long.

Peggy stiffened. Was that a voice? Oh my God, it was. What's more it was two voices, and one of them was Mr Richard's. Peggy did not immediately recognise the other, laughing now in a squeal of delight. One thing she knew. That laugh was not Susan Standing's, definitely not.

CHAPTER FORTY-SEVEN

Andrew Bishop paused at the flower kiosk at Euston station, hesitated, and then picked up a couple of bunches of sweet-smelling freesias. She could only throw them in his face. Even that would be better than being constantly ignored. He hurried on to the platform, got on his train and settled down in a corner seat by the window. He'd been careful to finish all his work by five o'clock and now here he was on the usual commuter train, the one he'd always caught when they first moved to Ringford, anxious then to get home as quickly as possible.

Home. Somehow he'd never thought of the old vicarage as their real home. Home was that muddled old house in Highgate, with its twisting stairways, and odd little rooms tucked into unexpected corners. He'd felt the continuity of family life there, and remembered finding old wallpaper in Faith's room, busy with faded little houses and people, another world that had delighted the eyes of a previous generation of children. In the vicarage, all he felt was the child of a critical, chiding religion, of standards upheld at all costs, and the inevitable unhappiness of those who'd not been able to conform. Or was it just the child of his unloving wife? He sighed and tried to concentrate on the evening paper. Nothing interested him, so he pulled out once more the particulars of the Highgate house. He'd have to put it very carefully and tactfully. He had a hollow feeling that this was his last chance.

At Tresham station there was the usual rush of men running to be first in the car park. Pathetic, thought Andrew, walking obstinately slowly. Like a bunch of schoolboys trying to be first into the dining-room. He sat in his car and waited until the BMWs and the Mercedes and the Peugeot GTIs had roared away, and then he put his own scruffy, mud-spattered car into gear and drove slowly through the suburbs and along the lanes to Ringford. Suppose the car is a good indicator, he thought. Mine used to be as shiny and smart as those others. Now you'd never know it was a BMW under all that grime. Still, who cares? I certainly don't. He found it difficult to think of anything he did care about, except Annie. Even the children seemed to get on perfectly well without him, ignoring him most of the time, taking a leaf from their mother.

Annie was in the kitchen, and did not turn round when he came in. 'Hello, darling,' he said, keeping his voice light. It cost him quite a lot now, knowing that if there was any response at all it would be negative.

'Oh, it's you,' said Annie, running water into a saucepan of peeled potatoes and banging them down on the Aga. 'Supper's not ready yet. It'll be another half-hour. Bruce wants you to go up and say good night.' She said this as if it was beyond her to understand why anyone should want to say good night to Andrew.

'Right,' said Andrew. 'Um, I've got something to show you later.' She showed no interest whatsoever. 'Still,' he added, 'it'll keep. I'll just pop upstairs, then . . . um . . . see Bruce, and . . .' He left the room, feeling that for all the impact he'd made he might just as

359

well be the Invisible Man.

Bruce was not in bed. He was in his pyjamas, crouched over a garage he'd made from a cardboard box and glue. Some of the glue had spread over the box and Bruce was trying to scrape it off. 'Sticks to the cars, Daddy,' he said, without looking up.

Andrew squatted down beside his son and put his arms around him. 'I'll get it off for you,' he said. 'Needs a man's hand to do that job. We'll tackle it tomorrow. Bedtime now, old son.' He lifted up Bruce and took him over to his bed. The small boy snuggled down under his quilt and looked up at his father.

'Vicar came to school today,' he said. Andrew sat on the edge of the bed and waited. 'He said Jesus said we got to love each other,' said Bruce. Andrew nodded, feeling a shiver of fear. 'Do you love Mummy?' Well, that was easy enough to answer.

'Yes, of course. Very much.'

The little boy smiled quickly, but then his face was serious once more. 'I don't think she loves you,' he said, and turned over, burying his face in the pillow.

Andrew put out a hand and ruffled the boy's hair, then hurried out of the room before Bruce could see his tears.

*   *   *

The big drawing-room was cool, always cool,

even on the hottest day, and Annie had filled a jug full of flowers that scented the air. Andrew sat in his usual chair, tight with tension. Surely she'd be coming in soon. There'd not been much washing-up, and although she'd refused his help, it couldn't take her much longer.

'Ah, there you are. Would you like a brandy?' Andrew did not know how to begin a conversation with Annie. It was ridiculous, like living with an unfriendly stranger. She shook her head and sat down, picking up the television remote control.

'Do you mind not putting that on for a moment,' Andrew said. That sounded a bit bossy, and he tried again. 'Could we just talk for a second? I've got something to show you . . .' He took the particulars out of his briefcase and stood up, walked across to where she sat and put them on her lap.

'Quite a coincidence!' he said, with false jollity. 'It just occurred to me . . . well . . . things have not been too good lately.' Why doesn't she say something? he thought desperately, and struggled on. 'And then quite by chance my secretary pointed out this ad in the paper.' She was looking at it now, but her face gave away nothing.

'So I wondered,' said Andrew, feeling his meagre confidence ebbing rapidly, 'whether it might be a good idea for us to think about moving back.'

The silence was endless. Then Annie threw

361

the particulars on to the floor at his feet. 'Don't be ridiculous, Andrew,' she said, and left the room.

Andrew found the freesias next morning, still in their cellophane wrapping, in the bin under the sink. He decided not to go to the office, and rang first his senior partner and then Dr Russell. They both told him he needed a good rest, and not to think of going back to work until he was really well again.

CHAPTER FORTY-EIGHT

Morning sunlight streamed in through the long windows of the Hall, and in the lofty entrance Susan Standing stooped to pick up the post. The usual assortment of bills, bank statements and charity appeals, she thought, but then pulled out a crested, official-looking letter with a London postmark. It was addressed to Richard, but ... well ... might as well take a look, she thought, and went off to the kitchen.

Poppy sat at the big table painting a colourful picture of ships at sea. 'That's nice, darling,' said Susan absently, as she prised open the envelope. Fortunately, it was one of the self-sticking kind, which with care she would be able to reseal without detection. 'Well!' She read through it with a growing smile. Now that could be the answer, or at least part of the answer. 'Heaven sent,' she added, and smiled broadly at Poppy.

'What is?' said Poppy, over-filling her brush with paint and dripping it on the wooden table.

'Oh, just something that will please Daddy no end,' said Susan. 'Take his mind off his worries,' she added wryly.

'Dad's not worried,' Poppy said flatly, swishing bright blue paint across her cloudless sky. 'He's happy. He told Bill, yesterday.'

Bully for you, Richard, Susan thought. 'What did Bill say?' she added, curious.

'Oh, I don't know,' said Poppy impatiently. 'Can I have Joey up to play?'

Susan decided to leave it there. 'Not this morning, darling,' she said. 'We're going over to Grannie's, so you'd better smarten up a bit. You know she hates you looking scruffy.'

'I don't want to smarten up. I hate smart clothes,' said Poppy resentfully. She took her paint-water jar to the sink and tipped it out with a splash. 'Bill said Dad looked smart,' she said absently. 'And Dad said it was the sign of a happy man.' She fetched her paint brushes and washed them slowly and thoroughly under the tap.

'For goodness' sake, Poppy, get a move on!' said Susan sharply. 'I'm leaving in five minutes!'

*   *   *

Richard Standing's general air of good

humour, and one or two obviously new and expensive outfits, had naturally not escaped village notice, and the subject had been aired more than once in the Stores. This morning, with the good weather lasting and the village opening out like a gigantic flower, the shop was full. Peggy, in her clean pink overall and looking healthy and cheerful, worked at her old speed, dealing efficiently with customers without making them feel hurried, but keeping nobody waiting too long.

It was quite an art, one she'd taken a while to learn, judging how long people wanted to stay in the shop. If she dealt with them too quickly, when they'd come in for a bit of socialising and idle gossip, they felt cheated and went away dissatisfied. On the other hand, some folks were in a genuine hurry and needed to get away to meet children, or make a telephone call, or leap back into a giant tractor left with its engine running outside the shop.

This morning, everyone seemed to want to linger. Ellen was perched on the chair by the Post Office cubicle, and Doris Ashbourne stood in a shaft of sunlight coming through the big window, warming herself like an old cat. Joyce Davie, back from a holiday in Tenerife with her Donald, and dying to show off, waited for an opening to make Peggy jealous. When had Bill ever saved enough for such a holiday? Pat Osman sifted untidily through the frozen food packets, looking for pancakes in cheese sauce to cheer up Colin. He was getting nowhere with the Council, and talked about giving up. Still, he'd starting planning a separate dog show for the autumn, not linked to the annual fête, but an event on its own, expanded and, as he said, casting a wider net. That should take his mind off bypasses.

Jean Jenkins stood squarely at the counter, her basket full. She'd found it difficult at first, dreading meeting people in the shop and having to talk. When she was sure the shop was empty she would make a fleeting visit, at ease with Peggy, but dreading the door opening on another customer. Now she'd got over all that, and found her old friends tactful and kind.

Not until Jean had paid for her shopping and left, did Ellen feel able to introduce a subject that was sure to get round to the Bishops. 'Never seen our squire s'clean and tidy,' she said with a grin. ''E were always a shabby-lookin' man, even when young. There were some as said Susan could've done a lot better for 'erself at the time.'

'Oh, I don't know,' said Peggy. 'Mr Richard's got a lot of charm, even when he looks as if his hair's not seen a comb for weeks. But still, I agree, Ellen. There's a definite improvement these days.' She stopped, not wanting to encourage the inevitable. Although she loved a bit of good gossip as well as anyone, she did try to prevent the shop from becoming a hotbed.

'Not like poor Andrew,' continued Ellen,

with no such scruples. 'Don't see much of 'im, which, considerin' I live opposite, is strange. But when I do, 'e's let 'imself go to pot. Off work again, I reckon. Nice-lookin' chap, too, 'e was. Sad, i'n'it?'

Doris moved up to the counter, her purchases complete. 'I think you're right, Ellen,' she said. 'It is sad, very sad, to see him in such a bad way. Goodness knows it's none of our business.' All present nodded virtuously. 'But unless something is done soon, we shall have some very nasty upsets here in Ringford.'

A small silence fell, with no one feeling confident enough to make predictions. The brisk arrival of Ivy Beasley got things going again, though her contribution was short and to the point. 'Mr Bishop is a job for his wife, and her attention is elsewhere,' she said. 'Now, this is all I want, Mrs Turner,' she added, dumping a packet of clothes pegs on the counter.

'It's not your turn, Ivy,' said Ellen, annoyed.

'Got to get the bus,' said Ivy, handing over the exact money. She glanced round at Ellen's basket of groceries. 'You'd better leave those in my porch and I'll bring them down later,' she said. The bus drew up outside the shelter, and she left at speed.

'Well, ain't that just like Ivy?' said Ellen, heaving herself up from the chair. 'Just when we could do with her invalu'ble advice, she goes all mimsy on us. 'Ere, Doris,' she added, 'you can carry me basket for me if you're goin' my way.'

CHAPTER FORTY-NINE

The telephone continued to ring for several minutes, echoing round the old vicarage, insistently demanding Andrew's attention. Where on earth's Annie now? he thought. Lately he'd taken to ignoring the telephone, along with any other approach from the outside world. He'd got old Dr Russell to give him a sick note, and was glad he'd not had to tell his secretary that the Highgate house idea had been a non-starter. Now this creeping lethargy had got such a hold on him that he'd begun to think himself really ill.

Surely it'll stop in a minute. Andrew hauled himself up wearily from his chair and made for the hall. It stopped just as he reached the telephone table, so he sighed with relief and turned away. Then it began again. Cursing under his breath, this time he lifted the receiver straight away and said crossly, 'Yes?'

'Is that you, Andrew?' A cool, authoritative woman's voice. 'It's Susan Standing here.'

'Ah, yes,' said Andrew apprehensively. Hell hath no fury, he thought, and waited.

'I don't think we need waste time with pleasantries,' said Susan. Andrew said nothing. 'Are you there? You could just say yes, or something, just so that I know I'm not talking to myself.'

'I'm listening,' said Andrew, beginning to bristle, to feel the old juices stirring.

'Very well,' said Susan. 'Now, listen carefully. Something has to be done, and I hope I don't have to spell out what I mean?'

'No,' said Andrew.

'Then we must meet and discuss it. I suggest my mother's house in Bagley. There's no possibility of our being disturbed or observed. She is quite happy about this, and suggests this afternoon, say two thirty.'

'Hey, wait a minute,' said Andrew, his solicitor's caution beginning to surface. 'What exactly are we going to discuss that we are not already perfectly well aware of?'

'Strategy,' said Susan. 'Mother's is the last house on the left as you leave Bagley. Lions on the gateposts. You can't miss it, but I'll look out for you. Goodbye.' And she was gone.

Oh my God, thought Andrew. That means I'll have to get dressed. I don't know if there's any petrol in the car. Perhaps I'll ring back and say the doctor's forbidden me to leave the house. What can she possibly be up to, anyway?

'Who was that?' Annie had come quietly down the stairs and stood looking at him curiously.

'Where were you?' he said, thinking irritably that all this could have been prevented if Annie had answered the phone.

'In the attic,' she said shortly. 'I heard the phone, and hoped you could find enough energy to answer it.' She walked through to the kitchen and called back to him. 'Can you meet

368

the children this afternoon? I have to be out.'

'Where?' said Andrew.

'Oh, here and there,' said Annie carelessly. She had ceased thinking up convincing excuses.

Andrew tightened his dressing-gown cord and began to climb the stairs. 'No, sorry,' he said loudly. 'Have to go out myself. Boring, but there it is. You'll have to make other arrangements.'

As he began to get dressed, taking up the old, grubby clothes he had worn yesterday, he felt unaccountably . . . well, not exactly cheerful . . . but the cloud hovering permanently around his head was not quite so black.

*   *   *

Susan's next telephone call was to Ivy Beasley. 'Good morning, Miss Beasley,' she said. 'I wonder if you could spare me a few moments? I have a rather difficult job on hand, and wondered whether you would help me? Perhaps I could pop in one morning?'

Ivy replaced her telephone and frowned. Now what was all this about? thought Ivy. She couldn't help feeling flattered that Mrs Standing should ask for her help, but then that had happened before, and it usually meant standing behind some rickety table in the pouring rain, selling drooping plants and flowers at a charity do organised by one of her posh friends. Well, this time, she'd say no, however much Susan turned on the charm. Getting too old, said Ivy to herself, resuming her dusting in the front room. She wiped the glass on her mother's photograph, and blew away the film of dust on the frame.

Lazy! said her mother's voice. Goes somewhere else, you know, Ivy. That dust doesn't vanish into space.

Neither have you, Mother, said Ivy acidly.

Bad tempered, are we? Just because Mrs Standing asks a favour? In my day we did everything we could to help up at the Hall. They always treated us right, and we were grateful. And anyway, she continued, her voice following Ivy into the kitchen, Mrs Standing said 'a rather difficult job'. That isn't going to be another plant stall, is it, Ivy? You can do those standing on your head.

Perhaps that's what she wants, said Ivy with a grim smile. Charity fête in Australia, all travelling expenses paid. Difficult thing is, I'd be upside down, Mother.

Oh well, said her mother huffily, if you're going to be silly, Ivy Dorothy, there's no more to be said.

*   *   *

The widowed Lady Maidford, standing at the big window of her Georgian house, set back from the Waltonby road on the outskirts of Bagley, watched her daughter approach, and

370

worried. Susan had always confided in her, and she'd listened with a sinking heart as once more the sorry tale of Richard's infidelity unfolded. She'd thought after Poppy was born that there would be no more of it. Richard had been so besotted with his new daughter, and Susan had basked in his newfound love for herself and their enchanting baby. But now, it seemed, the novelty had worn off, and Richard was up to his old tricks.

If it had been just that, Lady Maidford told herself, she would not have been so worried. Susan knew exactly how to deal with the flirtations, the brief affairs. She'd handled them skilfully, and the even tenor of life at the Hall was scarcely disturbed. This time, however, Susan was much more deeply concerned, and her unhappiness was plain for her mother to see.

'I think he may have fallen in love, Mother,' she'd said, her face turned away so that her mother should not see her expression.

My poor Susan, thought her mother. It's beginning to be too much. 'Buck up, darling,' she said. 'Probably just a passing fancy, like the rest.'

'Maybe,' said Susan, 'but this one isn't passing.'

'You've never been beaten before,' said her mother, a small challenge in her voice.

Susan sniffed and squared her shoulders. 'Of course not,' she said, 'but this time is different,

I'm afraid. It's all very mixed up with that dreadful Jenkins accident. But I haven't admitted defeat yet. That's why Andrew Bishop is on his way, I hope.' She gave her mother a wintry smile, and followed her into the kitchen.

*   *   *

Lions, thought Andrew, cruising slowly along the road, looking to his left. Ah, there they are. Quite small, discreet lions, as one would expect. He turned into the drive. The house was an architectural gem, with all its proportions harmonious and not one ostentatious pinnacle to be seen. It was at one time set in its own small park, with a looping carriageway and all the necessary offices tucked around the back. The parkland had long since been sold off for municipal leisure, but with judicious tree-planting Lady Maidford had managed to keep her privacy and maintain a pleasant, rural way of life. At the same time, she was handy for the town, with its chemist and doctor's surgery, library and church, and all the resources that an ageing woman living on her own might require.

Andrew parked his muddy car at the side of the house and walked to the front door.

'Is that him?' said Lady Maidford incredulously, peering from behind the curtain. 'Looks like a tramp, Susan. No wonder his wife fancies Richard . . .' Susan shot her a steely look, and she shrugged apologetically. 'I'll vanish, now, darling,' she said. 'Good luck.'

Susan walked to the door and opened it. Andrew stood on the steps, trying in vain to smooth down his untidy, far from clean hair.

'There you are, then,' said Susan. 'Please come in'.

CHAPTER FIFTY

Under Susan's clear-eyed scrutiny, Andrew Bishop began to feel very uncomfortable. He sat in a large armchair in a room full of light and the scent of roses, and wondered if his filthy jeans would leave a mark when he stood up. His shoes, too, were caked in mud from the garden where there'd been a leaky gutter for weeks. 'I'll fix it tomorrow,' he had said repeatedly to Annie.

After a silence that was beginning to be very pregnant indeed, Susan cleared her throat and spoke. 'Just look at you!' she said. Her cool, calm exterior belied confusion within. Where to start? She hardly knew this scruffy young man, yet remembered that when they'd first met she had liked his face, had thought him kind and straightforward, a person much easier to talk to than his apparently flawless wife. In the end, she relied on instinct and said the first thing that came into her head. 'My mother thought you were a tramp, and I must say I agree with her. What on earth has happened to you, Andrew?'

What a bloody nerve! Andrew sat up straighter in his chair. 'It cannot have escaped your notice,' he said stiffly, in his best legal voice, 'that I was involved in a horrible, very tragic accident. And on top of that,' he said, warming to the heart of the matter which brought him here, 'your husband has seduced my wife just when I most needed her support.'

The cards were down on the table, and Susan looked at them unflinchingly. She suppressed an angry retort on the lines that there were two parties to a seduction, and in her view Annie was far from an innocent country maid. With considerable effort, she took a conciliatory line.

'Look, Andrew,' she said, sitting down on the sofa opposite, not more than four feet away from him. 'There's absolutely no point in our being enemies. We both want the same thing. You want your wife, I want my husband. To get them back we have to work together. Do you agree with that, so far?'

Andrew frowned. 'I'm really not very well . . .' he muttered.

'Nonsense!' said Susan. It was a risk, but she felt now was the time to be brutal. After all, if Jean and Foxy Jenkins could find some way to get on with their lives, surely Andrew Bishop could have the courage to do the same?

'Nonsense,' she repeated, and continued, not giving him time to interrupt. 'You've had the most dreadful shock. No one would deny that. But shock fades, and time moves on. If you don't mind my saying so, Andrew...' She looked at his angry face and hoped this was going to work. If not, all was probably lost. 'To be frank, you're wallowing, as my father used to say. Retreating and wallowing. Couldn't be a worse combination.'

'Perhaps you'd kindly explain exactly what you and your father mean by that?' said Andrew icily.

'Well, my father's dead,' said Susan, with a ghost of a smile, 'but I can speak for both of us. As I said, just look at you. You're dirty, untidy and your hair needs cutting. Your fingernails are filthy, and your shoes are leaving clods of mud on my mother's carpet. There's a tear in your jacket, and those jeans would stand up by themselves. Not to put too fine a point on it, Andrew, you smell.'

Andrew began to stand up. 'That's enough,' he said. 'I don't have to stay here to be—'

Susan interrupted him sharply. 'Oh, but yes, you do,' she said. 'You have nothing else to do, nowhere else to go, except to a house that has ceased to be your home, and a woman who has ceased to be your wife. As for your children, you clearly don't give a fig for them, otherwise you wouldn't have wallowed so deep and for so long.'

He sank back into the big chair and covered his face with grubby hands. Susan continued.

'Instead of facing up to it all, you've retreated into a non-illness. You haven't been seen in the village for weeks, and people are talking. Our families' affairs are the talk of the village.'

'That's not my fault,' said Andrew, from behind his hands.

'Are you sure? Weren't you spending more and more time in London, staying overnight whenever there was the least threat of bad weather? Reluctant to join Annie's enthusiasm for village life? You know as well as I do,' Susan added, 'that this affair between Richard and your wife had begun long before poor Eddie's accident.'

Andrew silently nodded. He put his hands in his lap and looked straight at Susan. 'I tried to get her to move back to London,' he said limply. 'She wouldn't even entertain it.'

'Of course not!' said Susan. 'Who would want to face all that upheaval with you as you are now? At least in Ringford she has my husband to give her a bit of excitement. He can be good at that, you know.'

Something in her voice made Andrew look at her properly for the first time. He saw a slender, attractive woman in early middle age, with the wholesome air of someone who always used expensive soap, scent only sparingly, the faintest trace of make-up. A woman who, for

376

some God-knows-what reason, loved that boisterous idiot who'd taken Annie from him. He looked at her hands, lying quietly in her lap, and was moved by the thin, small fingers. Good God, he thought, she's really suffering. This must be difficult for her, too. What am I thinking of? I of all people should know that there are two sides to every problem. He made to stretch out a hand to her, feeling a surge of manly protectiveness, and then saw the dirty, bitten fingernails and withdrew it hastily.

Susan saw the gesture and knew that she had won. 'Well,' she said, 'if you agree, Andrew, I think we should have a cup of coffee, strong coffee, and get down to some serious plans.' She smiled tentatively at him, and this time he smiled back, quite firmly, and slowly nodded his head.

'But first,' he said, 'I wonder if I might just wash my hands?'

CHAPTER FIFTY-ONE

Ivy Beasley stood at her front door and watched Susan Standing's retreating back. She acknowledged the conspiratorial wave of the hand as Susan opened her car door, then turned slowly back into her hall and shut the door.

'Well, I never,' she said aloud. She walked through to her kitchen and sat down in the old wheelback chair by the range. 'Fancy that.' It must be serious, for Mrs Standing to come and confide in her like that. Mind you, there was nothing that Ivy didn't know already, hadn't several times discussed with Doris and Ellen and decided that things had come to a pretty pass. But for Mrs Standing to come and tell her direct, and then ask for her help ... 'Well, fancy that,' she said again.

So Mr Richard was going to be High Sheriff of the county, was he? That was one thing Ivy had not known, though it did not surprise her. The Standings were always High Sheriffs, sooner or later. It was expected. Unless, of course, as Susan had said straight out, there was some whiff of scandal that could put a stop to it.

'If you ask me, Mrs Standing,' Ivy had said, 'there's a lot more than a whiff already!'

Susan had agreed with her, and then explained what she had in mind. 'You're the person to get it going, Ivy,' she'd said. Ivy could not remember Mrs Standing calling her by her christian name before, and felt warmed. It was a simple enough plan. Ivy would see to it that words were dropped in the right places, attitudes surreptitiously hardened. She had influence, Susan suggested, and could guide village opinion without anyone realising it.

Ivy had suddenly heard her mother's voice, right there, when Susan Standing was sitting opposite her in the frigid front room. Mother never spoke when people were there. At least, not until now. Rough music! she'd said in Ivy's head. Rough music, that's what Dad used to call it. Mind you, Ivy, she added, there'll be no banging saucepan lids and tin cans. It's still the same, though, when there's somebody to be put right. It's a job for the village.

As a result of her mother's intervention, Ivy had lost the first part of Susan Standing's sentence, but was alarmed at the rest of it. '. . . suggest you get together with Peggy Turner. The two of you together should find it child's play.' Susan had refused a cup of coffee, but accepted a glass of Ivy's renowned elderflower wine. She had proposed a toast in a tense, almost tearful voice. 'Here's to success, then, Ivy!' she'd said, and Ivy raised her glass in an enthusiastic response.

Now, when she'd cooled down, she thought again of Susan's words. Get together with Peggy Turner? Some chance of that! But Susan had been quite firm, and clearly expected Ivy to do what she'd suggested. Years of schooling in knowing her place, in respecting authority and not arguing, struggled with Ivy's persistent dislike of Peggy Turner. This would need some working out. She walked into the hall, took her grey cardigan off the chair and, locking the door carefully behind her, set off up to Macmillan Gardens to see if Doris was at home.

* * *

'I think we're halfway there already,' said Doris. 'Folk are not fools. What's more, they don't like being treated like fools. Silly girl seems to think she can carry on with the squire in front of our eyes, and still play the virtuous mother and wife all round the village. Parents' Association, Church Council, Derby and Joan committee, playgroup—you name it, Ivy, and she's in it.'

'For the moment,' said Ivy enigmatically. 'Now listen, Doris,' she said. 'Here's what we're going to do.'

Doris Ashbourne was torn. 'Mrs Bishop's not all bad,' she said. 'She was very nice when Joey had that fit. And the kids are nice. You don't get nice kids from really bad parents.'

'Don't be silly, Doris,' said Ivy sternly. 'Nobody's all bad. That's not the point. Mrs Standing has asked for our help, and I for one am willing to give it.' Should she tell Doris about having to enlist Peggy Turner into the plan? Oh, well. Sometimes Doris had something useful to say.

'Mrs S. said I should ask her at the shop to help.' Ivy didn't look at Doris, but stared out of the window at the colourful gardens.

Doris laughed. 'Dear me, Ivy,' she said. 'That won't suit! Still, could be a way of getting over that stupid feud. And don't tell me Beasleys never forget.' She saw Ivy's face, and quickly changed her tune. 'Don't you see, Ivy,' she said, 'you'll be one up on her. Mrs Standing

380

came to you, didn't she? Came to you first. That'll put Peggy Turner in her rightful place, and with you being pleasant, she'll not be able to refuse.' The idea of Ivy being pleasant to Peggy Turner caused Doris to choke back another burst of laughter, so she headed for the kitchen. 'Now then,' she called, 'do you want tea or coffee, Ivy? This could be a long job.'

*   *   *

A few days later, it began. Annie Bishop was hurt and puzzled when she rang Sophie Brooks at the vicarage to offer her help with open gardens Sunday and was told everything had been organised, thank you, and there just wasn't anything for Annie to do. Sophie had been polite, but had put down the phone before Annie could make her suggestion for improving the information sheets.

Must have been having an off day, Annie thought. But when she met Richard as usual by the spinney, she'd mentioned it to him and found him not particularly sympathetic. In fact, he'd seemed abstracted, not really with her. For the first time, she'd had to take the initiative, had found him less than wholly worshipping.

Now she stood in the shop and stared at Peggy Turner. 'But it's my turn,' she said. 'Mrs Price asked me to give the vote of thanks weeks ago. I've been mugging up on the speaker's

381

subject so that I could make my contribution a bit more relevant than usual.'

Peggy looked away, fiddled about with the cover for the cheese, and said, 'Well, I'm just passing on the message. WI committee decision, I think. They've asked Mrs Ross. She used to do weaving herself, apparently.'

Annie was about to say that she'd been at the committee meeting, and no such decision had been made there. It must have been later. But who had decided? Just then, Ivy Beasley walked into the shop, and without acknowledging her, pushed in front and asked Peggy Turner for a small brown loaf.

'Excuse me,' said Annie crossly. 'I hadn't finished, Miss Beasley!'

Ivy turned with a surprised look on her face. 'Oh, sorry,' she said, 'didn't see you there.' But she didn't look in the least sorry, and didn't move away until Peggy had wrapped her loaf and taken the money. 'Good morning, Peggy,' she said, and although she seemed to choke on the last word, she smiled crookedly and left the shop.

*   *   *

'Could I have volunteers for helping with the children's painting exhibition?' said Sarah Barnett to the gathering of parents. Annie's hand shot up, but Sarah seemed not to see it. 'Do I see you offering, Mrs Dodwell?' she said, smiling at a young mother sitting by the door. 'Thank you so much. Now, anyone else?'

Annie waved her hand backwards and forwards, and finally said, 'I'd be glad to help. I've got some ideas how it could be staged.'

She might as well have been absent. Sarah pounced on Sandra's tentatively raised arm, and thanked her enthusiastically. 'That's fine,' she said. 'Mrs Dodwell and Mrs Goodison. The two of you should manage that very well. We'll have a get-together after school tomorrow.'

When Annie opened her kitchen door and shepherded the children inside, she was near to tears. It couldn't be a coincidence. What was going on? Oh, well, give it a day or two and things were bound to settle down. Probably Andrew stirring it up. But he never went out . . . At least, not until today, when he'd suddenly rung the office, announced he'd be back the next day, and spent hours going through his wardrobe sorting out his clothes. He'd then set off for Tresham looking quite reasonable, saying he'd be back for tea and should he bring a cake or anything? He hadn't seemed to notice that she didn't answer.

The children were subdued, feeling that their mother was upset. When the door opened and Andrew walked in, smiling and producing doughnuts from a large paper bag, they rushed to greet him.

'You've had your hair cut, Dad!' said Bruce. 'Can I have my hair cut like that, Mum? Can I,

383

Mum?'

Annie felt the ground shifting under her feet. It was all getting out of control, and she couldn't work it out. 'Don't be stupid, Bruce,' she said sharply. 'Well, since you're here,' she added, glancing angrily at Andrew, 'you can give the children their tea. I've got things to do upstairs.'

Andrew immediately began pouring out mugs of milk and set out his doughnuts on a large plate. 'Fine,' he said. 'Off you go.'

But there was nothing for Annie to do, and she sat on her bed staring at the telephone. With luck, Susan would be out, meeting Poppy from school. She dialled.

'Hello? Hello? Who is that?' Annie bit her lip, and carefully replaced the receiver. So she was there, after all. The sun streamed in through the bedroom windows, bright with their flowery curtains, and shone on Annie's blonde head, now buried in her pillow. It was just as well she could not see Susan Standing's quiet smile as she put down the telephone and went to find Richard in his study.

CHAPTER FIFTY-TWO

A very few days later, Richard Standing swivelled his desk chair round and stared out of the long window, across the rainswept park to the distant trees, but was blind to the soft, muted greys, blues and greens of the wet landscape. He was now an unhappy man. That letter, announcing his proposed appointment as High Sheriff of the county, had changed everything. In spite of his initial reaction that all could go on as before, after a few days and more than a few acrimonious conversations with Susan, he saw quite clearly that it could not.

Scandal was a destroyer for anyone in his position. It might already be too late, but, as Susan had said, with the village behind him he should be able to pull it off. Keep it out of the papers at all costs. Just leave it to me, she'd said.

But could Susan fix it for him, as she had so often done in the past? He was in deeper this time. Something small and blue, moving slowly across his view, caught his eye. Oh God, it was Annie, dawdling along with Tinker, hoping he might be looking out. Little Annie . . . He knew then that he did love her, but not enough. There were so many things more important to him than Annie. Tradition, the estate, his inheritance and his obligation to it, his father's trust, still strong from the other side of the grave, all weighed heavily against his desire for a lovely young woman.

'She belongs to Andrew,' said Susan's quiet voice. She had come up silently behind him and put her hands on his shoulders. Richard turned in his chair and buried his face in Susan's smooth, cool linen skirt.

'He'll take her back,' Susan continued, 'but you have to put an end to it, Richard. Only you can do that.' She disengaged herself and walked to the window, watching until Annie was out of sight. 'I thought you'd like to know,' she said, 'that Annie Bishop has resigned from all the committees and groups she had joined. Letters of regret have been sent to her, but none will try to persuade her to carry on.'

'Oh my God, poor little soul!' said Richard, standing up violently and glaring at Susan. 'There's nobody to touch you, is there? God forbid I should ever be on the receiving end of your wrath.' And then, finally, it occurred to him. 'But I am, aren't I? This is punishment for me as well as Annie, isn't it?'

Susan stared back at him, her face expressionless. 'I love you, Richard,' she said, and quickly turning away from him she left the room.

*   *   *

A continuous stream of cars along the main street held up Annie Bishop at the crossing by the school. None of them stopped for her, until she finally stepped out into the road, dragging Tinker behind her, forcing a black, dark-windowed Laguna to screech to a halt. Anonymous, totally anonymous, she thought, trying in vain to see the driver's face. That's how I'd like to be right now. And a million miles away from Round Ringford.

She still could not believe it. The rain had cleared and she'd looked forward with the usual excitement to meeting Richard in the spinney. With her new short haircut, she'd felt free, light as air, as she ran through the trees, expecting to wait a little while for him. He was always late, but he always came. This time, he had arrived before her, and was sitting on the edge of the tree hide platform, his long legs dangling over the edge. As soon as she saw his face she knew there was something wrong.

They'd sat inside the hide, on the rug spread out to cover knots and splinters of wood in the floor, their backs to the rough walls, their arms around each other. After Richard had told her that their affair had to stop, and why, she'd burst into a storm of tears and he had held her tight until it was over.

'But what about me?' she'd said, wiping her face with his handkerchief, and putting it in her pocket. 'What shall I do? Andrew must hate me, the whole village hates me. There's only you, and you don't love me any more.'

Richard had pushed her away from him, until she was at arm's length and her face in focus. 'Annie dear,' he said, 'I don't think I ever really loved you, not properly, not in the way that lasts for ever. And no, don't cry again, because I think the same is true for you. Andrew is your real love, isn't he? That's how marriage is. Unless we're actually beaten up, or there's real cruelty. I loved Susan when I married her, and I've never really stopped. That's a different kind of love. Maybe you're too young, but I think you'll find that's how it is with Andrew.'

Annie had jumped up and stared down at him. She could see a bald patch in his dark hair that she'd never noticed before. 'How bloody dare you?' she said. 'How dare you tell me about love? You know nothing about me and Andrew! I would have been quite happy to leave him for you, if only you'd had the courage to do the same.' But even as she'd said it, she knew it wasn't true. Still, why should he get off lightly? My God, I'll make him suffer. Annie's face had been granite, and she had ripped off the little enamelled brooch from her shirt. She'd thrown it at him and hit him in the face, the pin ripping his skin and drawing a bead of red blood.

'I'll see everyone knows just what a shit you are, Richard Standing!' she had yelled as she went down the wooden ladder to the leafy floor of the wood. 'Just wait! High Sherriff, huh? You'll be lucky!'

Now she stood outside the school, looking fixedly at the ground so that she shouldn't have to meet the waiting mothers' eyes. Ten minutes to go before the children came out. Tinker pulled at his lead, straining to get at the Jenkins terrier as it trotted by, anchored to a length of blue binder twine which Jean had made into a loop for her hand. Oh no, thought Annie, now I have to face Jean Jenkins. So far, they'd barely nodded at each other from across the street, and Annie had not dared to approach her. Several times, tired and bored with cleaning the rambling old vicarage, she'd been on the point of ringing her to see if she could possibly return to work, but the whole idea of Jean in the same house with Andrew had seemed so horrific that she'd instantly set it aside.

Jean had stopped to chat to Sandra, and now she looked across at Annie. All the misery of the afternoon was in Annie's face, and, unaware of the cause, Jean's kind heart was touched. She walked the few paces to where Annie stood, and said, 'Hello, Mrs Bishop.' Annie attempted a smile, but it went wrong and tears began to fall again. 'Oh dear!' said Jean, alarmed. 'Um, perhaps you'd better be off home. I could bring the children back for you. Should be out in five minutes.' Unable to speak, Annie nodded, turned and half-ran down Bates's End towards the vicarage.

*   *   *

'We all make mistakes,' said Jean consolingly. She'd brought the Bishop children home, and now sat in the big kitchen, pouring out tea for Annie, who had still not spoken. 'Here,' continued Jean, 'get that inside you. You'll feel better. And don't worry about the kids. They're upstairs in the playroom with the door shut. Up to no good, no doubt, but out of earshot.'

Jean said nothing more, but the silence that followed was comfortable. The kettle hissed on the Aga, Tinker snored in his basket, and outside the open door the garden was full of cooing pigeons and squabbling sparrows.

'I do love it here,' said Annie finally. 'At least, I did. It seemed like a dream come true.'

Jean nodded. Her own dreams were still nightmares most of the time.

'But it's all gone sour, Jean. I expect you know most of it. The whole village must know by now.'

'Yes,' said Jean quietly. 'Villages are like that.'

'What would you do?' said Annie. 'What would you do, if you were me?'

Jean shook her head. 'Don't know, Mrs Bishop,' she said. 'I can't imagine what it's like to be you, no more than you can know what it's like to be me.' She refilled Annie's cup. 'But I do know this,' she said. 'A new start has to be made. Something has to be got out of it all. Otherwise it's a terrible waste.'

Annie knew Jean was talking about Eddie now, but she began to see the point. 'You think we could do it, Jean?' she said. 'Make a new start, I mean?'

'No question of it,' said Jean. 'Takes guts,

but I reckon you and Mr Bishop could do it. You got lovely kids, you know. That's what's important, in the long run.' She got up and went to the sink, rinsed out the pot and cups and dried her hands on a tea towel. 'I must go now,' she said, 'but if you need any help, just ask.'

Annie looked up at her, her face blotched and ugly. 'Thanks, Jean,' she said. 'Thanks a lot.'

As Jean walked to the door, she stooped to pick up a large white handkerchief initialled in one corner with a blue 'R'. She held it out to Annie. 'I've got another one like this at home,' she said. 'Found it under your sofa, long time ago. I'll put it on the bonfire, and you'd better do the same with this one. You'll not be needing them no more.'

*   *   *

The evening sun over the valley was spectacular. Beats all, thought Andrew, as he drove home slowly through the winding lanes. It was such a relief that few cars and lorries came this way now. The new road had been completed a couple of weeks ago, and the effect was immediate. Colin Osman had at last relaxed, put away his file marked 'Bypass' and concentrated on the one labelled 'Dog Show'.

The sunlight was like a blessing, Andrew said to himself, a healing benison across the water meadows and the village. He felt himself relaxing, casting off the tension and pressures of the day. They'd been pleased to see him back at the office, and his mother had called to ask him if he would be staying over, not wanting him to push himself too far too soon. He'd refused her offer, kindly but firmly, and left on the dot of half past five. In his first-class seat he'd kept his briefcase shut, resisted the temptation to read the papers on a new and interesting case, and instead opened a fat paperback.

Now, as he turned the corner into Ringford's main street, Tom Price stood on the pavement, talking to Colin Osman. They looked round, as always, to see who was driving into the village, and recognising Andrew, waved pleasantly. 'Nice to see him about again,' said Tom Price. 'Suffered enough, I reckon.'

Andrew drove on, turned the corner into Bates's End, and crawled over the bridge to his own drive. The garden where he'd spent so many unhappy hours of depression and self-pity had forgiven him with a riot of roses and yellow daisies, drifts of larkspur and great multicoloured clumps of lupins. I think I'll have that old buddleia down when autumn comes, he thought. Maybe plant a flowering cherry for the spring.

Total silence in the house greeted him. His heart sank, but with an effort he ignored it, remembered Susan's parting words, 'Trust me,

Andrew,' and went through to get himself a drink. Probably out for a walk. With the children, he hoped. He went into his study, where the low sunlight streamed in, lighting up the mellow panelling, the old leather of his armchair. He turned to his desk, and saw a piece of paper placed right where he couldn't possibly miss it. It had been screwed up, and then smoothed out again. He picked it up, and his head swam. 'Oh, Annie,' he groaned, 'now what?'

It was the agents' information sheet, describing a charming Victorian family house, six bedrooms, two bathrooms, in a favoured position in Highgate. It was their house, and it was Annie's olive branch.

            *   *   *

'Dad's home!' yelled Bruce, as he ran ahead of the others up the vicarage drive. It had been a long walk, across the fields and along the old railway line. Annie had packed up an impromptu picnic, pushed it into the haversack that she and Andrew had bought for a camping holiday in France in the early days of their marriage. It had brought back memories, lovely memories that triggered tears again.

The children had grumbled at first, unwilling to miss their television programmes, and tired after school, but Annie had jollied them along, and they'd all laughed as they sat in a line on the old blue brick railway bridge crossing a track between two fields. They had watched a lazy line of cows wandering slowly home for milking, and Bruce had dropped pieces of bread down on to the broad backs passing beneath, until Annie had stopped him. She'd discovered an appetite, and found that tomato sandwiches had never tasted so good. The children had been pleased in the end, excited by this change of mood in their mother, and Faith had been quick to console Honor when she tripped on the rail-track cinders, grazing her knee.

The sun was sinking and the air cooling as they trudged up the drive, chattering quietly like birds settling down to roost. Annie, though, was apprehensive. Her heart beat faster when she saw Andrew's car, and she fumbled with the side gate latch. 'Round the back, children,' she said, 'don't want those dusty shoes through the hall.'

Would he have seen the house particulars? And what would he say? Annie had a desperate feeling that maybe it was too late, maybe she'd sacrificed everything for a bit of fun and excitement. But then, honest with herself, she knew it had been more than that. She had loved Richard, in a way, but it was all dependent on his absolute adoration, on the need for romantic concealment and secrecy. She'd felt so mature, so sophisticated, with her lover up at the big house.

'Dad!' called Bruce, rushing into the kitchen. Andrew sat at the table, the Highgate agent's details in front of him. The rest of the family trooped in, Annie hanging back, kicking off her shoes and filling Tinker's water bowl from the yard tap.

'Remember this house, old son?' Andrew said, pulling Bruce to his side and ruffling his hair. Bruce shook his head, but Faith leaned over and looked at the smudged photograph.

'It's our old house in London,' she said casually. 'Looks smaller than I remember. What've you got that for, Dad?'

Annie came into the kitchen, avoiding Andrew's eyes, and leaned with her back to the sink. 'We were thinking of moving back,' she said in a quiet voice. The horrified chorus from the children filled the kitchen, and Andrew stood up.

'Well, that's plain enough,' he said. 'Now then, you lot,' he added, 'off upstairs and run the bath. First to be ready for bed gets a reward. And that means you too, Faith. Early night for once, there's a love. You can help Honor, and then read for as long as you like.'

There was something in her father's face that made Faith comply without protest. He really needed them out of the way. Well, she could arrange that. Anything to improve matters between Mum and Dad, she thought, shepherding the rest up the stairs.

Andrew shut the kitchen door, and the room

was quiet and warm. Annie still stood by the sink, staring now at Andrew, frowning, her face full of unhappiness. He looked at her, willing her to speak. She only had to say something, just a word, to get things going. It had to be her, she had to be the first, but Annie still stood speechless, her frown deepening. It won't be any good if she cries, thought Andrew desperately. She has to want more than comfort and sympathy.

Then Annie turned, and for one horrible moment Andrew thought she was going back into the garden, shutting him out again, but with her face to the window over the sink, she spoke. 'Could you give me a hand with this haversack?' she said in a small, breaking voice. 'I never could get it off myself. Always needed your help. Do you remember, Andrew?'

He was across the kitchen in an instant, and had his arms around her, haversack and all. 'It's going to be all right, Annie,' he said, kissing her wet cheeks. 'You'll see, we'll be fine, all of us, together.' He gently pushed her away from him and helped her shrug off the haversack. The flap was not fastened properly, and remains of sandwiches and apple cores fell out on the floor. Tinker pounced on them, and Annie scooped up a half-eaten chicken drumstick just before he reached it. She brushed away the remaining crumbs and stood up. Taking the Highgate particulars from the table, she screwed up the paper into a small ball and threw it with the rest into the bin.

'So we'll not need that, then, Andrew?' she said.

'I think not,' he said. 'Home is where the heart is, as some poet once said. Clever chap, that. Come on, my love, let's see what the brood are up to.'

CHAPTER FIFTY-THREE

'If you ask me,' said Ivy Beasley, 'a dog show's more trouble than it's worth.'

She sat with Ellen in Doris's sitting-room, looking down Macmillan Gardens, where the Jenkins twins were leaning on their gate talking to William Roberts. Summer had gone, the children had been back at school for several weeks, and the chestnut on the green had already begun to drop its yellow leaves on to the seat below. There'd been an early frost, and Mr Ross had advised Doris to bring in her geraniums for the winter. 'Done it,' she'd said smugly. 'Safely in the back bedroom, Mr Ross.' Now she lifted the teapot and refilled Ivy's cup.

'You always say that, Ivy, to any new idea of Mr Osman's. You said it about the auction . . . and the old folks' party . . .' She paused, and Ivy jumped in.

'Yes,' she said, 'and I was right. If it hadn't been for that party, old Fred would still be with us.'

Ellen shook her head. "Is time 'ad come, Ivy,' she said. 'And Doris is right. I reckon a dog show could be a good laugh.'

'Nasty dirty things,' said Ivy, shuddering. 'You'll see. There'll be turds all over the field, sticking to our shoes. We'll be walking it all over the house. Well, here's one who won't.' She sipped her tea fiercely.

'Not goin', then, Ivy?' said Ellen. 'Well, I don't know about you, Doris, but I wouldn't miss it for anythin'. Wish I 'ad a dog meself. Dog With The Waggiest Tail, that's what I'd put 'im in.'

'D'you reckon Mr Ross will allow that little dog of his to enter?' said Doris. 'It gets shampooed just about every day. And they pick it up and carry it when the paths get muddy.'

'It's a pedigree,' said Ellen wisely. 'You got to look arter them pedigrees. Not as strong as yer mongrels.'

Ivy sat silently eating shortbread. Maybe she'd been a bit hasty. It could be an interesting afternoon. The whole village seemed keen, and there were posters everywhere. 'Of course,' she said lightly, 'that Colin Osman never does things by halves. He'll probably have them— what d'you call them?—poop scoops?'

'Sure to,' said Doris quickly, sensing Ivy was relenting. 'We'll just have to keep our eyes peeled. Should be a bit of fun, Ivy. I'll call for you around half past one. At least we can walk down in peace, now that new road's finished.'

398

She knew her old friend well. Make the arrangements, and then Ivy would feel she'd been persuaded against her better judgement. But she'd come, and then they'd all enjoy it together.

*   *   *

The Glebe Field was full of people and dogs. After a worryingly wet morning, the sky had cleared around midday, and Colin and his helpers had given last-minute checks to the two roped-off rings, the entry forms, free gifts from dogfood manufacturers, rows of shining red, yellow and blue rosettes. Foxy Jenkins had brought in the judges, friends of his from Waltonby, breeders of bull terriers. He had also presented a silver cup for the winner of the Rescue and Welfare class. This was for dogs rescued from bad homes, skeleton dogs found wandering around motorways, dogs cowed and nervous from continual beatings. It was to be known as the Eddie Jenkins Memorial Cup.

The afternoon had gone like clockwork, and Colin was relaxed and expansive. He had been a little disappointed that the Standings could not be there. 'Off on a cruise around the Med, I'm afraid,' Richard had said. 'Only time we could fit it in before I get my Sherriff's star!' Colin had laughed with him, and wished them both a happy trip. And now, on the day, there was such a lot to do, it didn't really matter. The

399

number of entries had exceeded Colin's expectations, and Pat Osman and Peggy Turner had kept up a constant supply of tea and buns for the crowd. Every last crumb had been eaten, and everyone gathered around the big ring for the final class, the one competing for Eddie's cup.

'Well, that's another job well done,' said Peggy to Pat, as they folded up the white sheets which had done duty as tablecloths on the trestle table. 'Come on, let's go over and have a proper look at this one. We've earned it!'

Bill Turner stood by the ring and made a space for Peggy as she joined him. 'Well done, gel,' he said. 'Feeling all right?' Peggy nodded, and put her hand in his.

The parading dogs were brought into line in the centre, their owners looking anxiously at the judge as she paced up and down, smiling kindly and taking her time. Finally she retreated to the edge of the ring, and beckoned to the last in line.

Bruce Bishop stepped forward, dragging an unwilling Tinker behind him. Bruce's grin stretched from ear to ear. Jean Jenkins, presenting him with the small silver cup, bent down to kiss his glowing cheek, and had trouble swallowing the lump in her throat. His parents, standing at the edge of the ring, arms linked, exchanged a look of unashamed, unbounded pride.

40

5183M   400